Diego Koegler was born in the state of Pennsylvania, but has lived across several different places as a child. Diego enjoys writing books more than anything, but when he is not writing books he is playing old school Japanese video games on his super old PlayStation to relax. He also reads manga, watches anime, goes outside and climbs trees, as well as watches videos about obscure Japanese games that he will never play in his life.

Diego Leao Koegler

The Journey

Austin Macauley Publishers

LONDON * CAMBRIDGE * NEW YORK * SHARJAH

Copyright © Diego Leao Koegler 2025

All rights reserved. No part of this publication may be reproduced, distributed, or transmitted in any form or by any means, including photocopying, recording, or other electronic or mechanical methods, without the prior written permission of the publisher, except in the case of brief quotations embodied in critical reviews and certain other non-commercial uses permitted by copyright law. For permission requests, write to the publisher.

Any person who commits any unauthorized act in relation to this publication may be liable to criminal prosecution and civil claims for damages.

This is a work of fiction. Names, characters, businesses, places, events, locales, and incidents are either the products of the author's imagination or used in a fictitious manner. Any resemblance to actual persons, living or dead, or actual events is purely coincidental.

Ordering Information
Quantity sales: Special discounts are available on quantity purchases by corporations, associations, and others. For details, contact the publisher at the address below.

Publisher's Cataloging-in-Publication data
Koegler, Diego Leao
The Journey

ISBN 9798895431979 (Paperback)
ISBN 9798895431993 (ePub e-book)

Library of Congress Control Number: 2025902414

www.austinmacauley.com/us

First Published 2025
Austin Macauley Publishers LLC
40 Wall Street, 33rd Floor, Suite 3302
New York, NY 10005
USA

mail-usa@austinmacauley.com
+1 (646) 5125767

1

A young man was sitting down next to the train window. It had been four hours since he last departed from his house. He was going somewhere new, somewhere exciting—at least that's what he told himself. In reality, he was going to some backcountry dump out in the middle of nowhere. The young man despised traveling far from his house. He didn't want to leave, but he had no other option.

The young man had long and luxurious blonde hair. He had a slim yet round face and was quite thin. His blue eyes stuck out like a sore thumb, along with the 4 different piercings he had on his face.

After what felt like an eternity, the train finally stopped. The young man looked out, and he saw what kind of a dump this place really was. The town was called "Wilmhelm", named after the founder, William Helms. It looked like something you would see on a road trip—a town you stopped in to get a hotel or to get a quick bite to eat. Nothing more, nothing less. Everyone looked basically the same, except for the only three black people the young man saw at the train station. The town looked bleak, and there was a strange sort of aura surrounding it. Already, when the young man stepped off the train, he felt something was wrong—something sinister and evil lurking at the center of the town.

The young man wondered why on God's green earth his uncle would ever send him to a place like this. He knew his visit had... certain circumstances, but nevertheless, it was more like torture than anything else. Oh well.

The young man grabbed his stuff and headed out of the station. His ride was supposed to be there already. Yet, he saw nobody waiting for him, so the young man just stared about into the distance while he waited. As he waited, he looked around at the people. He noticed just how... off-putting the people looked. They had their heads down and seemed to only look at their phones or at the ground. They covered themselves head to toe in thick clothing, despite the air being nice and warm.

Finally, the young man heard his name being called. He looked up from the ground and saw a nice young woman waiting for him in a car. She had on a dark blue tank top and had sleek, long black hair. She had very thick and wide glasses—almost as if they were goggles.

"Hello," said the woman in an upbeat tone. She extended her hand toward him. "My name is Andrea. I'll be in charge of taking care of you. Nice to meet you, Jack."

Jack nodded his head and gave her a warm smile. He put his luggage in the trunk, and both of them rode off. Most men Jack's age would kill to be living with a girl as beautiful as Andrea. Jack didn't deny it—Andrea was beautiful—but Jack didn't really pay too much attention to looks, even if they were as beautiful or had as big of breasts as Andrea did.

"So, how was the train ride here?" asked Andrea.

"Not too shabby, kind of boring," replied Jack.

"That's a bummer. Did you bring anything to entertain you?"

"Nah, just my headphones and some comics. That's about it. I got done reading all of it halfway through the trip. The other half, I just listened to some music."

"NICE! What kind of music do you listen to?"

"I like heavy metal. Bands like Disturbed, Decipher Down and Lamb of God. That kind of stuff. What about you?"

"That's a little too hardcore for me. I like Pink Floyd and Creedence Clearwater."

"Eww."

"W-what. What do you mean, eww?"

"They're too mainstream."

Andrea chuckled. "OK then, hipster."

Silence filled the car for some time. Jack looked out of the car as they rode to Andrea's house. The town looked bland and bleak—super casual and normal. Nothing too noteworthy. Jack saw some high school students along the path, and then he remembered that he was going to have to go to school here. Despite the semester being more than halfway through. He would have to attend some foreign school for a few months, and then leave as if nothing happened—all until he was allowed back home again. What a pain.

As they were riding, Jack spoke up.

"I couldn't help but notice that there seemed something odd about this town."

Andrea looked confused. "Really? Like what?"

"Well, for starters, everyone here looked like they were freezing when you're about the only person I've met that's wearing clothes appropriate for the weather. Second of all, everyone looks like they've been drained. Although with a backcountry dumb like this, I don't blame them."

Andrea smiled. "Well, there you go. You have your answer."

Jack shook his head. "No, no, no. There's something off about this place. I have this feeling about this place—a sinister feeling. It's been eating me up from inside ever since I arrived. Even as we speak, I don't feel good. Something is not right. Whatever it is, I have a bad feeling about it."

Andrea chuckled.

"It's nothing, really. I'm telling you, everything will be fine. You just need to get accustomed to life here. Especially coming from such a big city like you. I think you'll be fine."

Jack chuckled, but only to ease Andrea up. He didn't believe her.

After a few more minutes, they finally pulled up into a small villa. It was situated not too far from two other smaller villas. They were surrounded by a small swamp just behind the house.

"Don't worry; there aren't any animals inside that swamp. Just pesky mosquitoes."

Jack nodded his head as he unpacked and entered the house. It smelled of strong scented candles. He noticed that the house was extremely well organized. Someone was clearly showing up for some guests.

The living room was moderate, but it had a nice couch and an even nicer TV. Then there was the kitchen, surrounded by flowers, and more scented candles. There were at least a dozen different cabinets and an absolutely colossal-sized fridge on the wall.

Jack went to his room upstairs. It was completely empty. It wasn't anything too big, and that's just how Jack liked it—not too big, not too small. There was a window overlooking the street and the car outside. Andreas' room was adjacent to his. Down the hallway, near the stairs, there was one last room. It was also empty, and Jack wondered why Andrea had so many rooms if she lived alone.

"I'm going to head to the grocery store to pick up a few things," said Andrea.

Jack nodded his head.

"If you're hungry, I have plenty of food in the refrigerator and in the freezer. Make yourself at home. After all, this is your new home."

Andrea chuckled as she went to her car and drove off. Jack watched from afar. He rubbed his eyes. Despite it being only 4 in the afternoon, Jack was feeling tired. It was most likely from the train ride, but he thought otherwise. Jack wasn't necessarily super hungry, so he instead decided to unpack everything.

After a while, Andrea finally came home. She and Jack had dinner together as they could hear the rain pouring from outside.

"Does it rain often?" asked Jack.

Andrea shook her head.

"No, but every now and then it rains pretty hard. We don't really have a season for rain. It just comes and goes."

"Sounds kind of weird."

"It is. This town is a little abnormal, but that's part of its charm."

After a while, Andrea excused herself from the dinner table and went upstairs, leaving Jack all alone. Jack's suspicions were right. He knew there was something off about this damn place. Ever since he got here, he felt unwell and queasy.

The next day, Jack and Andrea had breakfast early. Today was going to be a long day. They were going to the local high school (basically the only one) to register Jack for the remainder of the school year. Then, they were going to buy uniforms and school apparel. Jack was supposed to bring them, but he forgot and instead decided to bring comics.

As they were making their way toward the school, Jack looked outside to see the students. They all looked so miserable and down as if the school was some sort of prison or something. Even as they were heading toward school, none of the students were socializing. Most of them were either on their phone or just kept their heads down. They were probably tired, thought Jack, but then he remembered what kind of town this really was and his mind changed. He still couldn't forget about what Andrea muttered last night.

How long had she been living here, and what was she talking about? Was this town ever normal? What about its history? That would all have to wait as

Jack and Andrea left the car. Immediately, Jack felt people looking at Andrea. He could only imagine how she felt. She wasn't wearing anything very revealing. She was just a very pretty woman with very big bobs. Most teenage boys would not hesitate to stare if given the opportunity. Even some of the girls were impressed and couldn't help but stare.

"Hello, Jack. My name is Principal Kroger. A pleasure to meet you."

"The pleasure is all mine, sir." Both shook each other's hands in a very firm handshake—too firm. It made Jack feel uncomfortable.

The principal was a massive man—and not by muscles. His shirt was holding on for dear life, trying not to rip from the principal's belly. The vice principal was nearby. She was short, small, and petite—an appetizer compared to the principal. His nose hair straightened out every time the principal even so much as moved, and his giant hands were nearly 1/16th the size of his small desk.

"So, you are the new transfer student. Welcome to Hemsworth High. Here, we hope you can find your academic success and make new friends." There was an uneasy pause, and the principal leaned in. His whole demeanor changed, and he said, "As long as you don't make a ruckus like you did at your previous school."

Jack could feel Andrea feel uneasy, and Jack nodded his head. "I promise." The principal regained his upbeat composure and smiled.

"Wonderful. Now take a look at this syllabus here. As you can see…"

After what felt like forever, Jack left the school. As he was leaving, he saw a woman enter. Now, Jack paid no attention to girls normally, but he would make an exception. And this lady was an exception, all right. Jack didn't understand why, but the instant he saw her, his whole body changed. His mind raced, and he wanted to have babies with her, start a family and move out to the middle of nowhere. He could literally feel his breath going away.

She had short black hair and bright black eyes. Her skin looked as if it could belong to a goddess herself. Her facial features were so pretty; her lips were extremely soft, and her nose was super cute. She looked thin—thinner than Jack. Yet, despite her thinness, she had very large boobs—bigger than Andrea's. He was certain she was being looked at by the other boys. But Jack would avenge to be different, all for this girl. He looked at her, and she didn't even so much as breath in his direction.

"Find her interesting?" asked Andrea. Jack didn't respond. He was too busy thinking about her. He hoped and prayed that she also thought about him the same way he was to her.

Jack and Andrea went around town looking for clothes and supplies, and in mid-afternoon, the day was finally over. Jack will start his new journey tomorrow. He would go to school, and everything would be okay. Everything would become normal. At least that's what he hoped, but in a town as eerie as Hemsworth, Jack knew that was impossible.

2

"Jack… Jack… Jack, wake up!"

Andrea practically dragged Jack out of bed. His alarm clock went off minutes ago, and he missed breakfast. He quickly hurried to make his breakfast and eat it as soon as possible, but once he saw the clock, he knew that he was going to be late. So, he decided not to even bother.

"I'm going to work," said Andrea as she was putting on her shoes. "I'm taking the car. There's an old motorcycle in the garage. If that doesn't work, then take the bike. If the bike is broken, then just walk."

Jack nodded as she headed out of the door. He got dressed and looked to see if the motorcycle was working. It looked like something out of a movie. It was all customized, with spray paint of death at the fuel tank saying, "Your ass belongs to me."

He turned it on, and miraculously, it worked. Jack's questioning of Andrea only increased. She was the last person he would think of to customize and ride a motorcycle. Furthermore, she never once mentioned it.

As Jack was riding to school, he saw someone else in school uniform leaving the house. Jack decided to pull over.

"Need a ride?"

The boy nodded his head. "Yes, please, and thank you."

For the first time, Jack saw a student that didn't look lifeless. In fact, quite the opposite. He looked like he was full of energy and vigor. His emo brownish hair color flowed in the wind, and his darkish skin only added effect to the hair. He hopped on the back, and Jack sped away.

"Thanks, man."

Jack nodded his head. "Of course. What's your name?"

"My name is Yuri. Nice to meet you."

"The pleasure is mine. My name is Jack."

"Are you new here? I've never seen you before?"

"Yeah, I just moved in two days ago if you can believe it. So far... it's alright. The town bugs me out. There's something not quite right abou—"

Out of nowhere, a flying rock hit Jack right in his helmet. Jack skirted across the street with his motorcycle, and his school uniform was torn to shreds. Yuri stumbled backward and ended up hitting the concrete harder than Jack. He felt his skin ripping apart. Thankfully, no broken bones.

Yuri shrieked out in pain as he realized that the flesh protecting his knee, elbow and thighs was gone. Jack got lucky. Way too lucky. He felt sorry for Yuri as he helped him up.

"Are you OK?"

"Of course not. DO I LOOK OK TO YOU?"

Crap, thought Jack as he looked at Andreas' motorcycle. The whole side of the motorcycle was scraped. It seemed that Jack was the only one who was OK.

As Jack helped Yuri up, he noticed something from the corner of his eye. A tall man in a black hat was looking at both of them. Of course, he could have been looking at the crash, but Jack had a feeling and a sense for these kinds of things. He felt a sinister intention coming from the man. After all, from looking at the road, Jack saw no hazardous rubble.

The man started walking away, Jack wanted to go after him but realized that Yuri could hardly walk. Jack gritted his teeth.

"I'm sorry," muttered Jack as he ran toward the man, who had disappeared in an alley. Jack chased him, and thanks to his leanness, Jack was quite a fast runner.

"STOP," yelled Jack as he tackled the man. But as soon as he laid a finger on the man, Jack's whole world shifted. Everything went black, and he felt nothing.

Yuri gritted his teeth as he started to cry. He was only 17 years old, yet the pain was too much for him. This was probably the worst injury he ever felt in his life. He saw the blood gushing out of his body, and he cried out in agony.

People started taking photos, muttering and looking at the crash. Yet, nobody dared even bother poor Yuri.

Yuri thought of Jack and realized he had run off into the alleyway. He didn't see the man, but that was the least of his worries. Every step he took, he felt more blood oozing out. His elbow hurt the most. He couldn't even move his finger. Yuri, pushing himself along the wall with his shoulder and limping with his good foot, went into the alleyway. He saw that the man was slowly standing up, but Jack was nowhere to be seen.

"He was just here," muttered Yuri as he looked around. The pain started to get to his head, and now he was having trouble just standing up. He started to feel tired, and the adrenaline was wearing off.

"Excuse me," said Yuri as he touched the man. Yet, as soon as he touched the man, everything went black, and Yuri felt nothing.

Jack woke up, only to find himself in a weird world. Yuri was asleep next to him. He would wake up soon enough. What surprised Jack the most was that Yuri looked fresh and new. All of his injuries were gone! To make matters better, Jack and Yuri's clothes were back to how they were that morning. As perplexed as Jack was, he was more perplexed by the world around him.

He was surrounded by a yellow sky, with weird monkey creatures flying in the air. Their wings were massive, at least a meter wide, and they howled and screamed as if they were under attack. Below them was a black sea, with creatures that are indescribable, and so hideous that not even the human imagination could fathom what swims in that water. In front of Jack was a massive drawbridge that led to an even bigger castle. The castle looked older than normal as if it were constructed even before the Crusades.

"What in tarnation?" muttered Yuri. Jack spun around, and finally, he was awake. Both men stared in horror and awe at what was happening in front of them. All they did was touch the man and… boom. Here they were.

"Where are we? This place looks trippy," muttered Yuri as he approached the castle. Jack stayed behind. He had a bad feeling about all of this.

"Wait," said Jack as he caught up to Yuri. "Don't you think going inside there is dangerous?"

"It beats being out here and listening to… whatever those monkeys are, scream and howl. C'mon, hopefully, we can get some answers as to where we are."

Before Jack could even think, Yuri left him in the dust. Jack waited for a while, cursed under his breath, and walked with Yuri inside.

They entered the castle, and the inside looked like something out of a horror movie. There were bodies covered on the walls, and the stairs leading upstairs were stained with blood.

"Oh my God," cried Yuri as he flinched. Jack vomited for what felt like ages. The smell was the worst part. He could smell piss and shit littered all over the floor. He was even certain he was stepping on some.

Then they heard something coming. They looked to their left, only to find a hideous creature running at them full speed and force. It was small but jacked, as if it were a professional bodybuilder. It had crooked, jagged teeth, and its skin was pale. It ran toward Jack and jumped up on him. It ripped his nose away, and Jack shrieked out in pain. Yuri kicked the monster away. He helped Jack up, and they scrambled. As they were running down the hallway, larger and more hideous monsters appeared. They ran back, but even more monsters were coming toward them. They were trapped.

Jack had an uneasy sensation—a sensation which only one can get when they know that their time is near. He felt it: this was the end. He felt Yuri tremble alongside him. The monsters growled, hissed and cursed at them in some unspeakable dialect.

"Oh God, man, this is it, man! We're doomed!" cried Yuri as he cried once more. Jack didn't say a word. He was paralyzed with fear. If anything, he hoped to God it would be quick and easy.

"I… I don't want to die. I'm a virgin. I never even got to hold a nice pair of big boobs."

Despite all the chaos and their inevitable deaths, Jack couldn't help but crack a smile. "Is that really what you're worrying about?"

The monster in front of Jack lunged himself at him. Jack just stood there and took the punishment. The creature was massive, and he felt the weight of the creature crush his ribcage. He gritted his teeth, and the monster clawed and ravaged his neck. Yuri was attacked from behind by another creature, and he was being eaten alive.

Jack had never felt such pain before. He hoped it would all be over soon. Yet, as he had a little bit of willpower and blood left, he realized that he would not go down like this. He hadn't even said goodbye properly to anybody. He was not going to be forgotten. He refused to die in some place he didn't know. He refused to be treated like this before his death. If he were to die, he refused to die like this.

Jack, with what little strength he had left, pushed the creature off him. He quickly stood up but was tackled by another creature. This time, the creature was much, much, much smaller—as if it were a little iguana. Yet it packed a bite worse than any other. Jack felt his shinbone snap in half. Never mind, he was going to die.

Jack was never a religious man, but he became one when he believed that God sent him help. This help came in the form of a woman dressed in all black. She wore a set of armor that was all black and looked like it came straight from the Third Crusade. She had a sword that was huge and looked heavy, yet she swung it as a pro baseball player swings a bat. She struck the monster with her blade, and the creature was no more. She slaughtered the entire hallway full of those hideous creatures. She moved and swung her sword so elegantly and with classy style.

Once they were all killed, she grabbed both Jack and Yuri. She quickly ran out of the castle, and soon Jack's senses were gone—and so was his vision.

He and Yuri woke up in that same alleyway where they touched the man—except only this time, the man was gone, and there was a woman standing above them. She had long, silky, smooth dark hair, very pale skin and very pink lips. She looked like she could lift an entire car with the way her body was built. She was still wearing the suit of armor from the castle.

Jack noticed that Yuri still had the injuries from the motorcycle crash, but none from the castle. Jack also noticed that all of his wounds were gone.

"W-what the hell?" gasped Yuri as he stood up too quickly. He fell back down again. The women looked down on both boys, as if they were insignificant and that the mere thought of talking to them disgusted every fiber of her being. Something about her intrigued Jack—not in a sexual way, as a teenager is interested in a pretty girl, but instead an intrigue when you find a piece of a missing puzzle.

She cursed under her breath as she looked around. The man in the trench coat was gone.

"Who are you?" asked Jack. The women barely glanced at him, and then looked around some more. After cursing more under her breath, she talked to him.

"Listen, and listen well. I am only going to say this once, so you better pay attention. I don't like repeating myself."

She looked at both of them to make sure they were paying attention. Jack was, but his glare seemed as if he was more interested in her than what she had to say. The same applied to Yuri.

"My name is Samantha. I am a member of S.H.O.T.

-Special
-Hunter
-Organization
-Team.

"It's my job to find people running amok in this town—more specifically, people who we can't put a trace on."

Jack looked confused. "What do you mean?"

The mere question seemed to anger every fiber of Samantha's being. He could see her eyebrows fleur and her ears twitch.

"Someone who can't be charged, because there is no evidence—yet that person still did the crime. Me and my team are responsible for getting those people and putting an end to their crimes… permanently."

Yuri's eyebrows raised. "You mean like… kill them?"

"Of course, I mean killing them, you fucking retard!"

Yuri flinched back. Samantha didn't let up.

"I was doing so well, and then you two idiots had to step in. That man in the trench coat—I had been stalking him for WEEKS and WEEKS. Oh, today was going to be my special day. I would have gotten a promotion, and gone out with my boyfriend, and everything would have been so dandy. But YOU TWO had to get in the way."

Jack winced. Despite being a woman, she scared Jack more than any man he had ever encountered.

"What do you mean?" asked Yuri. Again, Samantha looked as if she was ready to explode and release a barrage of pure hate and anger.

"The motorcycle. I knew that Howard was hiding here somewhere, yet I just didn't know how to lure him out. So I figured that causing a commotion would draw a crowd out. And sure enough, it did. That is until you decide to catch up to him and enter his twisted mind. You and your friend."

"BITCH ARE YOU CRAZY?" Yuri stood up, and despite the pain, punched Samantha in the face.

"You nearly killed us, you fu—"

Samantha spun around faster than Yuri could react, and roundhouse-kicked him so hard, that his head hit the wall, and he was out cold. Even as he was unconscious, Samantha did not stop kicking him. It was only when Jack stepped in and separated her from Yuri before Yuri would have permanent brain damage.

"You said we entered his twisted mind," Jack started. "How is that even possible?"

Samantha sighed. She looked calmer now, that she released her anger on poor Yuri.

"Some people are born with it; some develop over time. What matters is that you, Yuri, and the rest of my team were gifted. We don't know where this gift comes from, but we believe that we were chosen by God himself."

Jack said nothing.

"You see, S.H.O.T. believes in punishment. What better punishment is there than punishing those who have escaped the law? They may be let free due to a lack of evidence or because they have money, but their crimes still ruin lives. We believe in punishing them. That man in the trench coat murdered countless poor women before coming here. He thought he could come here and escape a life filled with murder. He ruined countless families. He was never convicted, because nobody knew that he murdered them."

"So how do you know?"

Samantha smiled.

"We have our ways."

Jack scoffed and rolled his eyes.

"Yeah, and for all we know, that could be an innocent man, and all you're doing is killing him. Then, YOU would be the one ruining lives. Have you ever thought about that?"

"What are you, five? Of course, I have. Look at his mind. You entered it. Does that really look like something a sane person would think of?"

"What are your… ways?"

"One girl was able to escape him. She lived back in New York. She was able to escape him, and she was a dear friend of mine. She told me all about it. At that time she didn't know about my special abilities—nobody did—but I told her that all would be well. She didn't want to testify in court because she was scared he would come after her. A logical reason. So I decided to enter his mind. When I did, it was a madhouse. I barely escaped with my life. It was 100 times worse than what it was when you entered it."

"Why?"

"Anger. Emotions cause the mind to fluctuate in a… unique manner, let's just say. If a person is angry, then more monsters lurk within the mind. If a person is sad, less monsters, but wherever they are hiding, the place becomes more twisted and distorted, making it nearly impossible for whoever to enter, escape. So on and so on. Now, if a person is happy. Their guard is down. This makes it the PERFECT time for someone to enter and kill them. It was bad today, but that's only because that man was suspicious and paranoid. I spent months tracking him down and found him at this dump. Yet now he's escaped, and if I were to enter his mind again, it wouldn't look pretty. I need to wait a little bit longer."

Samantha became angry again. "I was SO close, and then you had to come along and FUCK it all up. ARE YOU HAPPY?"

As she walked away, Jack spoke up.

"Shut up, bitch."

The air became cold, and the wind died down. A bloodlust unlike any other emitted from Samantha. She eerily stared back; rage and hunger for blood filled her eyes. Her hair started to twist and turn, and her mouth snarled as if a wolf were about to fight another wolf. Her arms tightened up, and the feeling of hopelessness and despair filled the alleyway. Even Yuri, who was unconscious, started to shiver.

Yet Jack felt nothing. A strong resolve swept over him. He would not let anybody disrespect him like that, no matter who they were. If it meant his death, then so be it. But he would not live in this world letting other people look down upon him.

"What… did you… say to me?"

"You heard me."

Samantha lunged at Jack at such a fast-paced speed. She kneed him in his stomach. Jack heaved, and saliva flew from his mouth. She slammed his head against the wall, making a dent. She then flipped him over her and twisted his wrist.

Jack got some dirt from the floor, as they were in a very dirty alleyway, and threw it in her face. She let go of his wrist and shut her eyes hard. Jack jumped up and hit her as hard as he could on her head. Despite his thin frame, Jack was no slouch at punching. He packed quite a punch. Before moving to Hemsworth, he used to practice kickboxing and was even an amateur underground champion competing in the 65-kilo weight division.

She fell to the floor. She wasn't knocked out, but she wasn't going to be getting back up anytime soon. Yuri was still out cold. Jack now felt his stomach start to return to normal. The pain stung him like a million tiny bees were stinging all at the same time.

Jack shook his head and regained his composure. What a day it had been, and it wasn't even 9 in the morning yet. He remembered what Samantha had said about being 'gifted by God.' Was it true? Jack only started believing in God when she showed up to save him and Yuri. Perhaps she was telling the truth. Yet, there was a superstition about Jack that made him not believe—just like how he believed something was wrong in the town when people were telling him that it was 'perfectly fine'.

Nevertheless, he would think about that later, as Samantha got up. Yet she didn't attack him. In fact, she just walked away. Jack could have gone after her and almost did if it weren't for the fact that Yuri was just now regaining consciousness. He didn't want to repeat what he did before by leaving him behind to go after someone. He saw how that ended up.

"Let me help you up," said Jack as he helped Yuri to his feet. He sat down in the alleyway. Both men didn't say a single word to each other. They just regained their composure and thought about the events that transpired in front of them.

After a while, Yuri spoke up.

"We should probably be heading to school."

Jack looked confused. "Like how you are now?"

Yuri waved his hand. "It's nothing, really. Plus, isn't it your first day? You're already late. I would hate for you to not show up."

Yuri stood up. Jack tried to help him, but Yuri just smacked his hand away. Jack had the feeling that he was still upset from ditching him when he fell off the bike. It was only natural he would feel this way. He could tell. His face tightened, and he had a very serious tone to him—almost as if he was on a mission and nothing would stop him.

"Hey… I'm sorry about ditching you. I really am."

Yuri said nothing.

"I know it must suck, especially when you're injured and all. You seem like a really cool dude, and I would like to get to know you more, man. How about this? To make it up to you, I'll buy you lunch. Whatever place you wanna go to."

Yuri cracked a smile. He nodded his head. "Sure, man."

Jack also smiled, partially because he was able to actually have someone to talk to in this dump. He had a suspicion, like always, that the kids at the school weren't all that good. Yet he had his hopes high—something he would later regret.

3

"Hello, everyone, this is your new classmate, Jack O'Hara."

Everyone looked but didn't say a thing. That's kind of how it was when he and Yuri got to the gate. They let them pass since they were students but eyeballed them so hard, that Jack swore Yuri was going to break under pressure. The blood and the ripped uniform—almost halfway through the morning. Talk about some first impressions. It was even worse asking around the school like a madman for directions. He kept being guided to the wrong classroom, or the wrong hallway, and the students looked at him as if he was some sort of extraterrestrial alien.

Still, if one good thing came out of this, it was that Jack was able to catch a glimpse of that girl from yesterday. He saw her heading out of the bathroom. She didn't see him, but he saw all of her. Just looking at her made him feel queasy. He could only imagine talking to her. It would be impossible. She was wearing an extremely short skirt. Normally, Jack wouldn't look as he considered it perverted, but just for today since he had a rough morning, he would make an excuse.

Jack stared at the classroom. He smiled and said hello. Nobody said a word. The teacher directed him to his seat—right smack dab in the middle of everyone. As he sat down, he felt students looking at him, and some gossip already being spread around.

"Oh my goodness, he's so fine. But his piercings are a total no. Eww."

"What happened to him? Is he OK? Why is he covered in dirt, and his clothes are torn?"

"Late on the first day? Wow, talk about a good student."

"He looks like he'll kill you if you look at him the wrong way. Or worse…"

That one was Jack's favorite.

Yet, as Jack was in the classroom listening to the lecture, he couldn't help but notice something—as if someone was staring at him. He shifted his glance and noticed it was a girl. This girl was not the kind of girl Jack liked. She looked like a total hipster. Her beanie almost covered her face, and she had these massive bangs almost covering her eyes. Her Chuck Norris was a few sizes too big, and her flannel jacket was torn, dirty and didn't look like it fit the girl.

Jack glanced away, as he was more focused on listening to the lecture. Yet, he almost couldn't listen because he could just feel her staring at him. He almost said something, but did not because he didn't want to be rude. Furthermore, he didn't want to start a ruckus, as he already made quite the headlines on his first day for obvious reasons.

Once class ended, the teacher left, and Jack remained seated. This school was different from the other schools he attended. Instead of YOU going somewhere else, you stay in your class. The teacher comes to YOU instead.

As Jack waited, he felt the stares become longer and longer, until one student asked, "What happened to your clothes?"

Jack only responded with, "You should see the other guy." The reception was mixed—mostly negative. Now they all thought he was some sort of madman.

Finally, Jack was saved as the teacher entered. Yet, as soon as the teacher walked in the door and said good morning, he wished he was still in that world.

Samantha locked eyes on Jack for a split second—no more, no less. She glanced away and resumed the day as if today were the most ordinary of ordinary days. She handed out paperwork and acted as if nothing happened. Even when she gave Jack his paper, she didn't say a single word, nor did her demeanor or composition change. It almost infuriated him—her being so tranquil as if they didn't fight in the back alleyway.

Finally, lunch arrived. Jack searched every corner of the school to find her, yet couldn't—almost as if she disappeared into thin air. But that was impossible.

"This place is nice," muttered Jack, his mouth full of food. Yuri took up his offer and ate at his favorite sandwich restaurant. It was right near the school too—less than five minutes walking.

"How was class?" asked Jack. Yuri chuckled.

"Safe to say I probably had a better day than you. I got bombarded with questions about what happened to me. I just told them that they should ask the other guy what happened."

"I'm guessing they didn't respond well?"

"They normally don't, so it's nothing new to me. Besides, if I cared, I would have changed a long time ago. How about you?"

"What do you think?"

"I think you also made quite an impression."

"I wonder what makes you say that?"

Yuri chuckled. "Don't worry about it. It only gets better from here on out. Don't pay attention to what most of these kids say or do anyway. This is their only time to shine since their lives outside of school are miserable."

Jack nodded his head. "Why do you say that?"

Yuri took a massive bite of his sandwich and gobbled it up before he spoke.

"Most of the time when they get home, they have a horrible home life. It's either spent studying, daydreaming about how to get out of this dump or going out and hanging out with friends. The only issue is, with a town this small, your friend circle is pretty small. If your friend circle sucks… you CAN get out, but good luck trying to find a new one."

Jack raised an eyebrow. "Is it really that bad?"

That question actually made Yuri laugh. "There's a reason the kids at our school are miserable. Did you hear how much gossip already started floating about you?"

Jack nearly choked on his food. "Wait… YOU KNOW?"

"Literally EVERYONE knows. Even the damn janitor, who shows up like once a week."

Jack looked disgusted and lost his appetite. Yuri laughed once more and patted Jack on the back.

"Don't worry. Like I said, it only gets better."

Both sat in silence for a while, listening to the cars pass by and people talking on the street. Then, Jack spoke up.

"Did you see her?"

Yuri looked up, confused. "Who?"

"Samantha!"

Yuri didn't say a single word for a long time.

"Um… you know… the girl that we saw in the alleyway?"

"What are you talking about?"

Jack got frustrated. "You know, the girl that saved us from that castle."

Yuri looked up to the sky as if they magically had the answers he was looking for. If this were a cartoon, a lightbulb would appear over his head.

"OH YEAH. Sorry about that, I got hit pretty hard."

Jack waved his hand as if a moment ago he wasn't frustrated. "It's all good."

Yuri leaned in. "She was at the school?"

"Yeah, and get this—she was my biology teacher. We locked eyes for a split second, and then she just acted like everything was OK."

Yuri leaned back in his chair, sipping his iced tea.

"Wait a minute... she was a teacher? I have never seen her in my life."

"I tried to talk to her when she left, but she just vanished into thin air."

"That's impossible."

"Yeah, well, so is pretty much everything that happened this morning."

Yuri didn't say a single word. Both men looked down as if they were out of answers. And then, Jack saw her. He looked to his left, out the window, to see Samantha looking directly at both of them. Yuri and Jack locked eyes and did not move. Her eyes were fierce and strong. She gave them a look that told both of them that she knew they were talking about her. Then a bus passed by, blocking both men's vision. When the bus was gone, so was she.

"Talk about some lady," muttered Jack.

Yuri shivered. "She gives me the chills."

Jack couldn't help but scoff.

As both men were heading back, Jack saw her again—the woman of his dreams. She walked right past him and, just like last time, didn't even acknowledge her. Yet Jack couldn't help but stare, as if she had entranced him in some sort of spell that made his knees weak and his stomach turned. Yuri caught a glimpse of Jack, and his face turned pale.

"Woah, man, you don't want to go down that rabbit hole."

Jack looked like he had seen a ghost. He started to sweat bullets.

"W-what... why?"

"Calm down, man... it's just that she's not a girl you want to get involved with. If you're looking for girls with big boobs, our school has a few. BUT DO NOT go down that rabbit hole."

Jack nodded his head as if he understood. In reality, he threw out everything that Yuri told him. He didn't care. The lust had taken him over. He was paralyzed with it.

"Hold on, I have to use the bathroom. Go ahead without me, I don't want you to be late."

Yuri looked back. "I can wait, it's okay, re—"

"NO… I mean, I'll be fine. I'll catch you in a bit."

Jack ran off without Yuri saying a word. Jack sprinted until he was finally able to catch up to that girl. He didn't know what to say, as he almost never did this kind of thing before. Yet she was so pretty that he believed he would be able to say the right thing.

"Excuse me," said Jack as he tapped the girl on the shoulder. She turned around and looked at him.

She spun around quickly. She was in a cold sweat, and her eyes had heavy black circles underneath them. She was pale and shaking.

"What?" she said harshly.

Jack caught a glimpse of her arm. Albeit briefly, he saw that there were red marks around her bicep. There were very small holes, and her skinny arms looked veiny. She caught him looking and pulled it away.

"What do you want?" said the girl once more.

Jack was now starting to understand what Yuri said. Still, he had hope and wanted to see if something could happen. After all, she was very pretty.

"I'm Jack. Nice to meet you…"

She didn't say a word. Jack cleared his throat.

"What are you doing out of school?"

"I-I'm going to go and get lunch."

"At this time? Lunch is almost over."

She gritted her teeth. "LEAVE ME ALONE!"

She spit on his shoes, and she ran away.

Jack stood there, baffled by the events that transpired before his eyes. In the distance, he heard laughter. He looked back to see Yuri.

"I told you," was all that he said.

Jack stuttered for a response but did not have any. Yuri smiled, put his arms around Jack's shoulders, and both men walked back to school together.

As Jack was heading out of school, he looked up to see Samantha waiting for him with Andrea's bike. She had a quirky smile. Jack decided not to even say anything, as the day had been so confusing and was getting even more confusing as it went along.

"I fixed up your bike," said Samantha as she gave Jack the keys.

Jack just nodded his head and started the bike. He didn't say anything else to her. Samantha, on the other hand, was not quite done with him.

"Are you free right now? I want to talk to you about what happened earlier today."

Jack looked at her nonchalantly and looked away. Now she was calm? He was starting to think she had some sort of bipolar syndrome. Jack hesitated for a while and nodded his head. She smiled and hopped on the back of his bike.

"My house is a few blocks from your house," said Andrea.

Jack's eyes widened. How on earth did she know where he lived? Then he calmed down a little bit and realized that this was not out of the ordinary for a woman of her caliber. He sped off, a little too fast, and Samantha nearly fell off. She gave him a smack on the shoulder.

As they sped along the highway, Samantha spoke up.

"So, I have a proposition for you. Would you like to hear it?"

Jack said nothing.

"It's about earlier today. Like I said, you have a gift, and I'm sure you have many questions as well about what happened. I can assure you that everything will be answered, as long as you promise me something."

Jack gave her a glance.

"You won't tell anybody. Not even your mother, Andrea, or anybody else. This stays between you, me, Yuri and the rest of the S.H.O.T members. Am I understood?"

Jack just chuckled. Even if he told the whole world, it's not like they would believe him. If anything, they would think he was crazy and some sort of drug addict.

Samantha sighed and continued.

"Members of S.H.O.T have been... disappearing. (Let's just call it that.) We could use more members to not only help investigate what's been going on, but furthermore, we could also use more manpower. You and Yuri have potential. I can see it. With the right kind of training, both of you boys can be some serious threats. I know you're here only for a little while, but it sounds nice. What do you say?"

Jack didn't utter a single word. He just kept on riding. The ride to Samantha's house was filled with silence by the both of them.

Once they arrived, Samantha hopped off and gave him a piece of paper.

"This is my number. I won't force you into doing anything, but I really believe you should join. Also, talk to Yuri about this. I would like to get him to join as well. I'll see you tomorrow for class. I hope you studied."

And with that, she was gone.

Jack's mind raced as he rode back home. This trip here was supposed to be relaxing. Instead, he was thrown into a world in which he never wished to be a part—both figuratively and metaphorically. He wondered if Yuri thought as much, or if he was okay with it all.

At dinner, Jack didn't utter a word. His mind had been racing. What if he was killed? What kind of training WOULD he have to go through? Also, why was that girl acting so strange?

Andrea tried to ask him if everything was OK, but all Jack could do was nod. He was too focused to be talking—so focused he even forgot to call Yuri and tell him about Samantha's proposition.

Jack lay down in bed, looking up at his ceiling. He thought so hard he thought he was going to puke. What a day this was turning out to be. Jack tried to sleep it off, but it would have been easier for a kitten to beat a tiger than for Jack to have slept. He spent the whole night thinking.

Finally, he came to a conclusion. It was 4 in the morning. Jack decided that, for the heck of it, he would join Samantha. After all, why not kill some time while he was in this dump? He told—and lied to—himself, saying that it would be to help out those innocents that were killed. Yet, in reality, he was far from telling the truth. The real reason he joined was because he wanted to have some excitement—the thrill of almost dying, just like in the castle. It reminded him of a roller coaster: when you fall down and go at such high speeds, you think it's all over. Then it goes back up, and everything is OK. With whatever training Samantha would give him, surely everything would be OK, right? Of course!

Jack got a quick power nap before he was able to go to school again. He called Yuri and asked him about what he thought. Yuri was intrigued, but cautious about the whole ordeal. He still had many questions about everything, but Jack assured him that all would be well and he wouldn't have to worry about anything. Yet an eerie feeling—one that Jack tried so hard to suppress—told him that everything WOULDN'T be well and that something bad would happen. He had a strange feeling.

School went as normal, but Jack couldn't help but think about S.H.O.T. He was, hopefully, going to be a part of that organization and be a badass—stopping crime and having the time of his life. He was thrilled about it. Yuri seemed more or less excited. He was more fearful about what would happen if something went wrong. Jack told him off and said he was worrying too much. Yet, deep down, he knew Yuri had a point.

Once the day was over, Samantha told both of them to go to her house. Once they arrived, they were shocked. Her house was TINY—as if a dwarf could live there. It was quite interesting since Samantha was quite a strong and large woman.

"Oh, hello," said Samantha as she greeted them. She was wearing a bright pink dress, and her hair was neatly done. Jack was convinced she was bipolar. Her entire front yard was covered with neatly decorated plants and statues of cute little animals. There was a nice wooden chair on her front porch. As both men passed by, they looked at the chair. There was some cannabis. Jack considered Samantha the last person he ever thought would smoke, but then he wondered... Was she calm BECAUSE she smoked, or because she was crazy?

He would have to think about that later, as he entered the house and was met with a smell of such strong incense it made his nose shrivel up. Yuri almost collapsed to the floor. The house smelled of cinnamon, weed, roses, and honey—a... unique combination.

"Welcome to my humble abode," said Samantha as she opened her arms. The house looked like it was out of a movie. There were bright lights everywhere. Plants and flowers filled the downstairs, and the kitchen was huge. Again, Jack's confusion only increased as there was no way the Samantha he knew would ever have a house like this. He thought she lived in some sort of dungeon or chamber, waiting each day with rage and chaos.

"Would you guys like some coffee, or some tea?"

Yuri nodded his head, and Jack politely declined. With her smile, she raced off into the kitchen. Jack sat down on her nice leather couch. Yuri looked around the place as if he were in some sort of amusement park.

"It looks very nice," said Yuri. Samantha gave him a warm smile.

"Thank you. I like it too. It took me quite some time to decorate."

"How long?"

"Almost as long as your training."

Both men looked at her. Her smile slowly started to fade away, and that luxurious aroma also faded away. Samantha cleared her throat.

"I guess there's no beating around the bush then. Both of you, starting today, will undergo intense training by my friend and former member of S.H.O.T., David George."

Jack interrupted. "Former?"

"That is correct, but don't worry. He's still relatively young AND in amazing shape. He only retired because he wanted to live a normal life and open up a flower ship. It's all good.

"Now, I would train both of you, but unfortunately, I need to track down that man in the trench coat once more. In the meantime, you'll undergo a series of tests to strengthen your skills—training to strengthen your speed and agility, and combat training. Any questions?"

"How long will this take?" asked Yuri.

"However long it needs to be, don't worry, I am confident in you two. It shouldn't take too long, I decorated this house almost as long as I finished MY training. You two should be fine. Stay put; let me go get David."

"W-wait," started Jack. "We're starting now?"

Samantha looked at him with a gaze that was filled with rage and hate—the same one he saw when he called her a bitch. She gritted her teeth, and Yuri took a step back.

"Members of S.H.O.T are ALWAYS supposed to be prepared! If you're not willing to sacrifice your lives, I'll sacrifice them for you. UNDERSTAND?"

Both men nodded. She quickly rushed upstairs.

"Crazy woman," muttered Yuri.

After a solid minute of both men's anticipation rising and rising—which was not helped by the silence—David came down by himself.

He was a MASSIVE man. His biceps were bigger than Jack's thighs. His shoulders nearly ripped apart his shirt, and his chest was bigger than Andrea's. His hair was extremely short, and from an angle, it looked like he was bald. His legs were the equivalent of a tree trunk. It was pure muscle. He nearly took up the entire hallway with his size. Yet, despite his massive appearance, his face was soft, and his baby blue eyes were even softer.

When he spoke, his voice boomed across the hallway and filled up the entire house. Yet there was a serenity to it that also made it… tranquil.

"Nice to meet both of you."

David pointed at Jack.

"I'm guessing you're Jack. And…"

David's gaze shifted, and he looked at Yuri.

"Would I be correct in thinking you're Yuri?"

Both men nodded.

David's smile lit up the room.

"Perfect. I imagine Samantha introduced me already, but if not, my name is David. The pleasure is all mine. I will be your teacher for the next few years."

"FEW YEARS?" exclaimed Jack. He jumped up. Yuri said nothing but looked uncomfortable.

"Of course. What, do you think being a hunter is easy? It took me forever to get to where I am now."

Jack was speechless. Yuri was uncomfortably silent, and David just looked at both of them with his soft, yet hard eyes. It wasn't until both men started to look sick, that David cracked a smile.

"Got ya. Hahaha. Just kidding. It won't take any more than a week at most. Relax—under my belt, I'll make both of you flourish into hunters that Samantha wished she could be. Are you boys ready?"

Both men nodded, although hesitantly. David smiled once more.

"Perfect. Now, play rock paper scissors against each other."

Jack and Yuri looked at each other with confusion on their faces. What a strange night. They played. Jack threw out a rock; Yuri threw out the paper.

"Perfect," exclaimed David. He pointed his index finger sharply at Jack. "Jack, you're with me. Yuri, just stay put for now. If you want, feel free to get anything you like from the kitchen, or turn on some T.V. If Samantha says anything… just tell her that I said it was OK. I'll deal with her later. Don't worry."

David walked to the bathroom, and Jack followed. The bathroom was small and tight. The walls would have been a nightmare for anybody claustrophobic and were small enough that David had to squeeze himself to go to the toilet.

"Don't worry, I know this looks weird, but trust me—it's OK."

David flushed the toilet, and the room started to disappear. The walls became bigger, and there was more space. The floor started to go down as if they were on some sort of elevator. After a while, they reached a training room.

There was a massive area in the middle of the room that looked like it was used for combat training. There was a mat, and some dummies to hit. Outside of the massive area, weight machines and treadmills were scattered about. The room was cool but not too cold—warm but not hot. Just the right temperature.

There was also a set of swords on display located near the walls. The room was dark with blue lights scattered all over.

"So, what do you think?" asked David as he went to go and start up the treadmill. Jack looked around. It was certainly flashy, but he didn't want to say that to David.

"It looks… very nice."

"I know, right? I helped build it. Although I think it's a little bit flashy. The whole idea of the blue lights was Samantha's idea. I don't like it too much, but don't tell her I said that. Hehe."

The training was tougher than anything Jack had been through. First, David made Jack run as fast as he could. Once he was done, he made him run as far as he could. Water was given, but without him stopping.

After a short rest, Jack was made to see how well his strength was. Jack was a little bit impressed with himself. Despite his thin frame, he was able to pick up quite a heavy amount of weight for someone his size. Then came the part he least liked—the weapon training. After hours and hours, Jack was forced to try to kill a dummy with all sorts of weapons. David didn't even instruct him on how to properly use the weapon. He just said to 'feel it and see what you can do with it.'

Afterward came combat training. Jack did a series of drills and even got to spar with David. He never said it, but David was extremely impressed with how agile and flexible Jack was. His kickboxing skills were way better than David had hoped. Even after being fatigued, Jack still seemed to be flashy, but practical.

As all of this was going on, David kept on writing down notes in his notebook, studying and analyzing Jack as if he were a guinea pig, and David was conducting a new drug. Finally, the training stopped. Jack fell down in exhaustion. He threw up and nearly collapsed. After a while, David spoke up.

"OK then, Jack, I think I got everything I need. Thank you very much."

Panting and nearly passing out, Jack spoke up.

"W-what were… you writing?"

"Oh, just some notes on your skills and physical capabilities. Would you like to hear them?"

Jack nodded.

"So, from what I've been able to see, you're clearly a very fast runner. Your top speed was 27 miles an hour. Most athletes can't even do that. As well, you're able to run that fast for a very... very long time. Longer than most people can. Quite impressive stuff, man.

"As far as your strength, you're pretty strong for someone your weight class... but I've seen better. You're a little lacking in strength. Don't worry, though—I'll whip you up into a supersoldier in no time. I will say, you do have very powerful legs. When doing the squat, I was impressed with how much weight you were able to go down and up with. Nice stuff!

"What really impressed me more than anything was your combat skills. I don't know where you learned to kick like that, but you're the best kickboxer I have ever seen. No doubt about it. Your grappling is weak, though, and definitely needs work. Your striking is excellent. I don't think I could improve much of it if I'm being honest. But I'll try!

"As far as weapon training... with everything you used, you seem to be a natural when it comes to the sword. You seem to already have a... good GRASP with the HANDLE. Hahaha. Get it?"

Jack didn't laugh. David looked awkward and cleared his throat.

"OK, you can go home now. Be ready for tomorrow. We got a BIG day ahead of ourselves!"

David flushed the toilet once more, and the room returned to normal. Jack walked out of the bathroom only to find Yuri sleeping on the couch. He watched as David politely and gently woke him up, as a parent does when they need to wake up a child for school. Jack walked out of the house, covered in sweat and some of his own puke. Despite all of the horrible feelings that he felt during the workout, now that it was over, Jack felt... really good. He smiled and started to find this training thing intriguing.

Jack did not go to school the next day. He was way too tired and exhausted to even get up from the bed, let alone train some more. Yet that did not stop Yuri from going over to his house and knocking on his door to get him.

Jack got ready, and both made their way to Samantha's house.

"Is that your mom?" asked Yuri. Jack shook his head.

"Just my caretaker for now. But anyway, did David also take notes for you?"

Yuri nodded his head. "He said my strengths included my stamina AND my physical strength. Everything else I need to work on."

Jack smiled. As they were walking, Yuri spoke up once more.

"Why did you decide to move here—to this town?"

Jack looked at Yuri slowly. A sense of danger and alertness filled Jack.

"Why do you ask?"

Yuri shrugged. "Just curious. I mean, it's not like this town is the best in the world. Plus, I don't think you would have moved here if you knew what was in store. Also, there are only a few months left for school. Would you really move here to finish it up when you could have easily done it in whatever city you lived in?"

Jack took a sigh. He hoped it wouldn't have to come to this. The whole reason he was caught up in this was because of what he did back in his hometown. He looked up and realized that they were standing in front of Samantha's house. Jack turned to Yuri. He spoke in a calm manner, hoping to make Yuri forget so he wouldn't have to explain.

"I'll tell you once we're done with training."

"For today?"

Jack shook his head. "For good. It's kind of a long story, but forget about that for now. Anyway, let's head in."

4

After what felt like years of training—when in reality it was just a few weeks—both boys had finally finished their training.

The training was worse than death. Both men were pushed to their physical and mental limits by David. He made sure they would not forget him AND the training he would put upon them. Hours of running, only followed by hours of combat training, took a toll on them. Yet, despite all of this, they saw noticeable results.

Jack saw his body had transformed. He was still lean, yet he definitely noticed the muscularity that had formed. Yuri became a monster—just as big as David, if not bigger. Jack could swing a sword like a pro with his eyes closed, and Yuri became skilled in all manner of martial arts. Jack's grappling drastically improved, and Yuri was not amazing with one weapon like Jack was but was good with all of them. Finally, the day had come for their last test.

They stared at one another with happy eyes. It will all be over today. David said that there would be a test at the end to see who would pass, and who wouldn't. Both men sat down on the couch, talking and eagerly waiting for David. They had not seen Samantha in a long time. She was still busy trying to find the man in the trench coat. He was still in the city but hiding deep.

Finally, David instructed both of them to head into the bathroom. They went into the training room, where David talked to both of them. He cleared his throat, and his voice was louder, and much firmer than it had ever been.

"Gentlemen, I just want to say that it has been all my honor to train both of you. You two started out as chumps, and look what happened in just the span of a few weeks. With hard work, dedication and someone screaming in your ear, you two were able to transform into men you never thought you would be able to become. Give yourselves a round of applause, because as much as I have helped you, you have helped yourself more. Good job!"

Yuri could not contain his smile, and Jack chuckled. The excitement was getting to him. Whatever test would come, he would be prepared. No hesitation. Yuri was beyond prepared; he had been waiting for this moment since day 1 of training.

David smiled. "I see both of you are ready for your final test. Good. Now then, for your next challenge—and your last one—I want you two to fight each other."

The happiness in each other died down, and both men looked confused and perplexed. They each looked at each other in disgust, and then back at David. The air shifted, and the sense of anticipation was substituted with fear. Fight each other?

"Let me clarify. I want you two to fight each other until the other one dies. I don't care how that happens. Just fight each other until one dies. Understood?"

"W-wait," said Jack as he stood up. David shut him down.

"Oh, sorry. I am afraid questions are going to be answered AFTER the test. I can't talk anymore. With your skills and knowledge, grab whatever weapon of your choice and make your way to the center of the room. Or don't. Hehehehe."

David walked away into the shadows. Both men looked at each other. Yuri was unwilling—he would not hurt his friend Jack. Yet, as he looked at Jack, he realized a terrible truth. Jack was different. He wouldn't hurt him, but if it meant graduation, then Jack would hurt Yuri. This almost made Yuri laugh. At first, it was Jack who was against the idea, now it was Yuri. It was interesting to see how the tables had turned.

Jack pretended like he was in disbelief. In a sense, he was, and he didn't really want to hurt Yuri… yet, if it meant graduation, he would do anything. He was NOT going to move to some dumb town to join some sort of secret organization, only to NOT join because he valued his friendship too much.

Jack looked at Yuri, and Yuri shook his head.

"There's got to be some other way," said Yuri, but David was gone. He was just talking to a dark wall.

Yuri looked behind and saw Jack already grabbing a sword. Yuri felt anger and betrayal. He thought Jack was his friend. Was he really going to kill him for some underground organization?

"Jack," said Yuri. Yuri's tone changed. No longer was he fearful, but instead, he was focused. He tried one last time to convince Jack to lower the weapon, but Jack had made his decision. What disgusted Yuri even more was that he saw a hint of a smile on his face. Yet, Yuri wouldn't lower himself to Jack's standard. Even if he were to die, he considered at one point Jack a friend. He wouldn't ever hurt his friend. Never. Even if it meant his death. Yuri looked at Jack; both their eyes locked. Yuri stood there, defensively.

Jack sprinted at such high speeds at Yuri—sword in hand and ready to kill. Yuri protected himself. This was it—here was his reward for being such a good person.

"STOP!" yelled David.

Both men felt their bones shiver to the core. Jack dropped his sword and clutched his chest. Tears started to fall from his eyes. He had never heard a scream so powerful and frightening in his life. Yuri was standing up but was shaken as well.

David stepped out of the shadow. His demeanor had changed. His face was angry, and he looked furious. When he spoke, you had better listen—or else you would face the consequences. Jack looked at him like a child looked at his father when they were about to get beaten. Fear filled his mind and his body.

"Yuri, congratulations—you passed. Jack… you fail."

Jack slowly stood up.

"W-w-what?"

"I SAID IT CLEARLY!"

Jack fell back down to the floor. David shifted his attention toward Yuri, and his demeanor changed back to normal.

"Good job. To commemorate, let's go and get some burgers—free of charge. Also, your ceremony will be held tonight. Don't be late."

David flushed the toilet, and the room changed. Yuri walked out, but Davis stayed behind. He flushed the toilet, and the room changed again.

Now, there was a mix of rage, confusion, fear and horror all lurking within the room. David looked at Jack so menacingly, even a predator would have shit themselves if they saw David in the wild. And poor Jack was the prey. He lay down on the floor, helpless to move due to him being paralyzed with fear from head to toe.

David shook his head. "You disgust me."

He walked toward Jack's sword and put it away.

Jack spoke up. "B-but why… what happened?"

"DID I NOT SAY YOU FAILED? WHAT THE FUCK IS WRONG WITH YOU? ARE YOU TOUCHED IN THE HEAD? ARE YOU?"

Jack started to cry. David rolled his eyes.

"Holy shit, are you crying?"

Jack curled up into a ball. David started to laugh.

"I knew it. I knew you didn't have what it took to make it into S.H.O.T. Look at you, crying like a little bitch. Do you want to know why you failed, dipshit? Hmm? It's because you attacked your friend!"

Jack slowly got out of his ball. Betrayal hit his face like a wave hitting a rock. "B-but I thought you said I was supposed to kill him? You LIED TO ME?"

David ran toward Jack. He didn't hit him but instead towered over him like a massive skyscraper.

"WHO ARE YOU RAISING YOUR VOICE TO? WHOOOOOOO? You fucking no-good piece of shit. You damn loser. No wonder you don't have any friends. Your only friend was willing to die for you because you were willing to kill him. You disgusting trash. I HATE YOU! The reason I said that was because I wanted to see if you really were willing to kill your own teammate. We are part of S.H.O.T. The T stands for teamwork. I wanted to see if you would actually attack your teammate. Unfortunately, you did.

"I was messing with your mind. When you go inside a target's mind, your own mind starts to shift, and you start to hallucinate if you stay there too long. Furthermore, you can't tell what's real and what isn't. What hurts and doesn't hurt? It's a dangerous job, but it's less dangerous when you have teammates. You were supposed to see through my lie. Do you honestly think I would ask you two to hurt each other?

"It seems like you could use a lesson in teamwork, idiot. Didn't anybody ever tell you there's no 'I' in the team?"

Jack would later regret what he would have to say, but he said it anyway with a slimy smirk.

"No, but there is an 'I' in incredible."

David kicked Jack's mouth so hard that both his back teeth flew out. Blood gushed out of his mouth. Davis yelled so hard that spit flew all over Jack's mouth.

"WHO THE FUCK DO YOU THINK YOU ARE? I CAN KILL YOU IN 50 DIFFERENT WAYS IN LESS THAN A SECOND. DON'T GET SO CONFIDENT WITH ME, YOU LIMY LIMP DICK SAD SACK OF HORSE SHIT!

"You're done. You're so fucking done. Get out. GET OUT! Good job effing this all up, idiot. Yuri will pass. You're not allowed at his graduation ceremony. You're not allowed at this house, except if Samantha needs a request. Also, forget ever talking to Yuri. If I were him, I would be done with you. Get out of my sight."

The toilet was flushed, and David threw Jack out of the house. What made matters even worse, it had started to pour. Jack got up and yelled at the house.

"FINE! I don't need any of you. I have my own training. I have my own skills. I don't need ANYBODY. Least of all some idiot like you! COCKSUCKER!"

There was no response. Jack cursed some more under his breath and made his way home. As he was walking home, he couldn't help but break down, and cry until he physically couldn't.

The next few days were the same. Jack would wake up, and try to commit suicide. He found a gun in Andrea's closet, furthering his suspicion of her, and played Russian Roulette. Unfortunately, he was unsuccessful. He would then go to eat breakfast, change his clothes and go to school. At school, he would fantasize about dying a horrible death that he was deserving of. What's worse, he saw Yuri walking around super happy. He tried talking to Yuri one time, but Yuri ignored him as if he was never there. Jack stopped trying afterward. He also saw that girl he liked with another guy. One way skinnier and uglier than a rat. This only fueled his depression. Samantha mysteriously stopped going to school, and Yuri intentionally avoided Jack as much as he could. He didn't have any friends at school, but he would hang out with David and the rest of the S.H.O.T members that Jack never knew about. He had friends and was happy.

The highlight of his day was training. He would train almost every day after school. Running, lifting, weapons training—whatever it was, he would do it. He started to notice that each day, he would become more and more powerful. Yet, it hardly mattered if his brains were on the floor.

At night, he would cry himself to sleep. He would wake up in the night, and just to feel good, he would shoot some heroin in his veins. That was the best part. He didn't need anybody. All he needed was his training, his drugs and himself. Me, myself, and I. Then, he would come down from his high and fall back asleep. He would wake up a few hours later and rinse and repeat. A lovely schedule indeed.

One day, though, as Jack was walking to school, he was approached. He looked back to see who had tapped his shoulder. It was that hipster girl. Oh great, thought Jack as she smiled nervously. Ever since he had shown up to school, she would not stop staring at him. At first, Jack thought there was something wrong with him as she never looked away. Then, realizing, he thought there was something wrong with her. Why did she stare so often? Was she crazy?

Jack also noticed that she stalked him a little bit. She maintained her distance well enough, but Jack felt somebody follow him home every day. He thought it was David or Samantha, but never thought about this crazy girl. That was until he caught her slipping one day, and he noticed her. She turned as red as a tomato and awkwardly walked away as if nothing happened.

"Yes," said Jack. His tone was pretty rude.

She jumped up. "Oh… m… I wanted to give you this."

She handed him a small piece of paper. He looked back up, and she was running for her life. He scoffed. What a strange girl.

He didn't even bother opening up the paper. In class, the staring got so bad that Jack actually said something. Nothing too bad, but just said 'hi' to demonstrate that he was not blind. Yet, she blushed when he said that.

When he got home, he finally opened up the piece of paper. It was her number with a million different hearts on it.

He rolled his eyes and threw it in the garbage. He thought nothing of it. Yet, when he went for a run, he saw two couples walking down the street. The guy looked like he won more than the lottery, as if God had blessed him. Jack started to think but then realized that his girlfriend was pretty. He would never date that girl. But then again, he also remembered thinking that he didn't care about how a girl looked.

He caught himself thinking about that girl all day long, and even at dinner, had trouble talking to Samantha. He cursed himself and went to the trash to pick it up.

He dialed the number and called it.

"Hello," said the girl.

"Hey, this is Jack from your classroom. You gave me your phone number earlier."

There was silence. Jack almost hung up the phone, disappointed that something like this would happen, and decided to go and shoot some heroin before he heard her say, "Oh hi, yes. Sorry about that. Hi Jack! How are you doing?"

Her voice became incredibly high-pitched. Was she OK?

"I-I'm doing good. I never caught your name."

"It's Audrey."

"I see... that's not a bad name."

She giggled. Jack cursed under his breath. Why did he say something like that? It just came out of his mouth without him even thinking. Almost as if... God was telling him what to say. Jack's tone even changed.

"So, what are you doing now?" asked Audrey. Jack sat down in his chair.

"Oh... just chilling. Nothing too major. What about you?"

"Oh, I was just reading a book."

"Oh sorry, did I interrupt?"

"NO... I mean, of course not. Not at all. I'm actually happy to be talking to someone like you!"

"Like me?"

"Well... um you know. Someone new like you. I love new faces. Sorry if that came out weird, it's just that I'm so excited and—"

"Why are you so excited?"

"Oh... well, because I met this really cool guy at school and he's SO hot. Like... I could kiss him and mess around with him and go out with him, and I think he's into me!"

A wave of depression hit Jack. He was actually starting to like to talk to this girl, and now he realized she liked someone else. Audry senses the silence from the other line of the phone.

"BUT I don't think he's into me, so it's OK really. It's OK. But enough about me, um... what do you like to do?"

Before long, Jack found himself conversing with the girl until the next day. He had no idea why this was happening, but by the time he was talking to her, he knew more about her than he did about Yuri.

Her favorite flavor of ice cream was mint chocolate chip, she loved to read old-school novels and watch foreign TV shows. Audrey especially loved to listen to bands such as Pink Floyd and Nirvana—something Jack despised, but he didn't mind. She almost never worked out, but she did love to play video games like The Witcher and Final Fantasy. Her favorite drink was a lemon smoothie, and she was both a cat AND dog person.

She disliked racist people and hated rude and obnoxious people. She seemed to have a general distaste for hurtful and mean people. As well, she despised drugs since she told Jack that most of her family died from an overdose. This made Jack cringe, as he hoped she never found out about his heroin use. She also disliked the beach—something he found quite interesting considering that most girls her age would kill to spend a nice day at the beach.

They talked for so long that both fell asleep on the phone. Jack fell asleep with a smile, something he hadn't done in what felt like ages. Audry fell asleep with the phone snuggled up next to her as if she were holding Jack himself.

It only got better. The next day, both met up at the entrance to the school. Jack changed his seat and started sitting next to Audry. He didn't pay attention to anything in class, as he was too focused on talking to her. Furthermore, Jack noticed a change in her clothes. She started wearing tight outfits. She still looked like a hipster, but instead of her clothes being 10 times bigger than her, they were 10 times smaller. This made Jack notice just how frail and skinny she was. She wasn't abnormally skinny, but she looked like she could use a nice sandwich and a salad.

"Do you want to head over to the sandwich shop near school?" asked Jack. Audry nodded her head. She had a massive smile. Both of them made their way there.

Jack started to think she had lice. She would always play with her hair whenever she was around him. She also looked at him as if he had some sort of answer as to cure her lice. He merely looked away, as he didn't want to disappoint her. The walk there was great. They could not be separated. Even when the teacher moved them away from each other in class, they couldn't stop looking and laughing at each other.

As they were eating their sandwich, Audry spoke up.

"Can I ask you a question."

"Anything?"

"What happened between you and your friend? I always saw you two together, and now you barely even look at him. What happened?"

Jack hesitated for a moment. Too long, in fact, and Audry started to form an answer in her mind. Jack saw it.

"Well… let's just say that we had a difference of opinion."

"What was it?"

Jack didn't say anything. Audry looked disappointed in herself and looked away.

"I'm sorry for asking."

"No, no, it's quite alright, really. Don't worry about it."

As they were eating, Jack noticed from the corner of his eye Yuri passing by. Yuri didn't dare look at Jack; yet, his gaze was fixated on Audry. Jack felt a wave of emotions rush over him. All of it was unclear, yet he knew one thing: Audry was his and his alone. She made him feel a way he hadn't felt in a long time. He was not going to let Yuri ruin it for him.

Yuri entered the sandwich shop, ordered his favorite sandwich and sat next to them. The tension in the air was so thick, you could cut it with a scissor. Yuri kept on eyeing Audry, and Jack kept on eyeing Yuri. Audry noticed the tension palpably rising, and figured that in the next few seconds, if something did not happen to distract both men, there would be a fight. And she had a feeling it would be ugly.

Her suspicions were right. Yuri smiled and leaned in on Audry.

"What's your name, sweetheart?"

Despite being nearly triple the size of Jack, Jack was not afraid of Yuri. If anything, Jack was able and willing to kick his ass in front of everyone. Jack eyed Yuri so hard that Yuri backed off.

"Leave her alone," said Jack. He put his sandwich down. Yuri glanced at Jack. His face was as angry and as hateful as David when he first yelled at Jack, and as menacing as Samantha when Jack called her a bitch.

Yuri growled. Audry looked at both of them. She started to feel uncomfortable. She just wished this whole thing would blow over. This only reinforced her notion that men were much more complicated and much more stupid than girls were.

"Or what?" said Yuri. Jack's eyes widened. An uncontrollable rage devoured him, and he was mere seconds away from letting all hell loose. He would have probably murdered Yuri if it weren't for Audry stepping in.

"Let's calm down now. I think both of you should talk about what's wrong. You two used to be good friends. What—"

"Stay out of this!" snapped Jack. Audry was taken aback. All the time she knew him, he never talked to her like that. She wasn't angry or upset... just shocked. Now her curiosity was rising. What really happened between those two?

"That's not how you talk to a lady," replied Yuri. "This is why every girl at school always shits on you, you—"

Yuri was cut short as Jack yelled on top of his lungs and jumped across the table. He grabbed Yuri's neck and tackled him to the ground. Audry stepped back and saw both men trying not to hurt each other, but genuinely kill one another. Yuri gouged Jack's left eye, and Jack shattered Yuri's collarbone.

Yuri kicked Jack off him, but that did little to nothing as Jack lunged back at him with such speed that even Audrey couldn't have noticed it. Jack kicked Yuri in his shin so hard it broke. Yuri screamed and fell to the ground. Jack got on top of him and grabbed his arm. He put it in an armbar and broke it.

Yuri, now filled with pain and rage, decided he had enough. He grabbed Jack by his hair and slammed him against a chair. Yuri then got up and grabbed Jack, lifting him up in the air. In the air, he threw him down as hard as he possibly and physically could on the concrete. Jack heard several bones shatter. Jack had trouble moving. Yuri smiled.

"You bastard! You were always a no-good piece of shit."

Jack spun around on the floor and kicked Yuri upward, breaking his jaw. Jack then smoothly got up and grabbed Yuri's hand. He twisted it so hard that if Yuri were not human, his hand would have snapped off. Yuri gritted his teeth as he spun around and tried elbowing Jack. Jack dodged it and proceeded to nearly murder Yuri as he grabbed a chair and slammed it against the back of Yuri's head. Yuri fell down to the floor, and Jack continued to beat him. Over and over, until Audrey, from the top of her lungs, yelled out, "STOP!"

Jack spun around quickly. Audrey was in tears. Her face was full of worry and fear. She shook her head.

"What's wrong with you, Jack?"

The adrenaline and rage came to such a screeching halt, that Jack nearly collapsed. Seeing Audrey like this... it made him want to cry. He tried to approach her, but she just took a step back. With tears flooding her face, she turned away and ran.

Jack stood there, standing. Despite being the victor, he felt like he lost badly. He looked to see Yuri on the floor. His face was nearly unrecognizable, and his body was in shambles. Jack called an ambulance and walked away.

He tried calling Audrey several times, but she didn't pick up. He even went to her house to see if she was there, but she wasn't. Her mom said she hadn't seen her since this morning.

Jack walked home, but as he did, he was approached by David and Samantha. *Great,* thought Jack as he saw both of them. They looked as if they had finally found a murderer or a ghost who had been stalking them forever. Now, they were about to get justice.

"You ass," said David, pointing his finger at Jack. "Yuri can't even talk now. Nor can he move. Are you happy?"

Jack said nothing. This was not what he needed right now.

"I thought we told you to stay away," said Samantha. Jack saw something. She was hiding a sword. David had brass knuckles. All Jack had was his wits, guts and a badly injured body. He thought about running away, but if he did, he would only be furthering the inevitable.

"Listen… Yuri came to me. I was just eating at a sandwich place."

"Oh, we know," said David. "In fact, we saw everything. We told Yuri to go there and talk to Audrey. We wanted to test you just one more time. To see if you had changed ever since you started talking to this girl. I actually hoped you had… unfortunately, I was wrong. You're still too rash, and you're too much of a wildcard. Sorry, Jack, but you're permanently banned from ever joining S.H.O.T.

"Not only that, but do you want to know what we do to people who nearly kill other members of S.H.O.T?"

Jack sighed. Samantha pulled her sword out, and David started walking toward him. "Just my luck," said Jack as he cursed under his breath. Seeing no way out, Jack took a deep breath and prayed to God. He quickly ran toward David and Samantha.

Jack jumped over Samantha and landed behind her. Before David or Samantha could react, Jack kicked Samantha in the face as hard as his leg could. She spun around and fell to the floor. What he didn't see was David sucker-punching him in the jaw. Jack quickly regained his balance, and nearly dodged all of David's barrage of haymakers. Unfortunately, he didn't see David kicking him in the leg so hard that it nearly broke. Jack backflipped away and dodged one of Samantha's attacks. He ducked under her sword but hit David in the stomach.

He got even lower and kicked Samantha in her shin. She cursed and pulled the sword down lower. Jack rolled out of the way, but he still felt his left shoulder being sliced. He quickly looked up, and his face was met by David's knee. His face hit the concrete. No time to rest, thought Jack as he rolled out of the way from what would be a fatal blow from Samantha's sword. Jack's heart quickly raced. Now he knew that they weren't there to hurt him. They were there to kill him.

I gotta get out of here, thought Jack. Yet he would be reminded that was impossible, as David quickly kicked him in his cracked ribs. Jack cried out in pain. He grabbed David's leg and kicked his other one, causing him to fall on the floor. Samantha swung her sword and Jack jumped out of the way. Still holding David's leg, Samantha chopped off David's leg.

"Oh, crap," said Samantha as David screamed out in pain. Jack threw the leg at Samantha's head. It hit her, and Jack kicked her straight in her mouth. Her teeth flew out, and she hit her head on the concrete.

Jack quickly went over to David and put pressure on his leg. He didn't know why he was doing this, but he didn't want him to die. He felt as if he was responsible for this whole mess. Whatever chaos that God would put down upon Jack later would be OK in Jack's book. He realized that he deserved it for everything. But for now, he would actually try not to be a fuck up.

He took off his shirt and wrapped it around David's leg. David cursed out and screamed in pain. He called Jack many different names. None of them were good. Jack didn't care though; he didn't want David to die. Partially because if he did, only God knew how many members of S.H.O.T would be hunting him. But also because now Jack understood. Now Jack realized, everything was his fault. The reason for Yuri being in the hospital, the reason for him not being able to join S.H.O.T., the reason for David having his leg chopped off, and for Samantha losing nearly all her teeth. All of it was his fault. What's worse, he felt as if he would lose Audrey forever. She made him feel so good, and happy. More than heroin did. Jack, even though David probably hated him, still acknowledged and liked David. After all, it was David that changed his life and made him into a weapon. Jack could never repay him. No matter how hard he tried.

After a while, the bleeding stopped, and with it, the screaming. Jack quickly called an ambulance and waited for it to come. It got both David and Samantha into the back. As they were about to head off, one of the paramedics asked if he knew what happened. Jack nodded his head and told him that a horrible monster had come and ruined both their lives.

5

Audrey watched the whole fight from her bedroom window. Her perception of Jack shifted. Where did he learn to fight and move like that? Was he always this ruthless? Audrey started to cry. She cursed herself for liking a man such as Jack. She thought he was hot, cool and overall a good person. Now, she realized that he was batshit crazy. He was violent, and he showed no mercy. Yet, even after cursing herself, she still felt something toward him. What was it?

She put her face on her pillow and screamed and cried out. She had seen so much violence today, all from Jack. What if she started to date him? Would this be an everyday occurrence? Would he get as violent and as ruthless on her? She thought about dating him, but now, she thought about running away. What a crazy bastard.

Yet, she hesitated. If he was really that crazy, would he have helped that poor man who had his leg cut off? Would he have called an ambulance and waited patiently for it to come? A madman would have killed both of them and left them there to rot. She was no expert in combat; heck, she had never been in a fight before, but Audrey saw the way Jack fought. He looked like he wanted to hurt them, yes, but not kill them. Those two, whoever they were, looked as if they were trying to kill him.

Ever since she got introduced to Jack, her life was getting crazy. Would it be like this if she were to date him? So many questions ran through her mind. She was so happy and carefree with Jack. She felt like the whole world would be OK as long as she was with him. She didn't want that feeling to go away. She knew who he was… and she loved him.

Yet, she still felt resentment toward him. She still thought he was crazy and batshit. Why, oh why, God, why did she love him? What was it about him that made her go crazy? Both in a good and bad way. What did he have that nobody else did? It made her head hurt thinking about all of this. She laid down on her bed and cried some more.

Audrey heard a knock on her door, and her mother came in with a happy face that quickly shifted into sadness.

"Oh, Audrey, what's wrong?"

Hearing that made her cry only more. She sobbed, and her mother rushed to her side and put her face on her large boobs.

"W-what happened, Audrey? Why are you crying?"

Through tears and snot, Audry was able to speak.

"I-I-it's... a b-boy."

"Ohhh... men can be so complicated can't they."

Audrey chuckled a little but quickly went back to sobbing.

"What boy is it? Is it someone I know? Wait... is it the one you told me to tell that you weren't home if he knocked on the door?"

Audrey nodded her head. "Y-Y-Yes. His n-name is J-Jack."

"I see."

There was silence. Audrey's mom was thinking hard. From the impression she got from Jack, he was indeed attractive. He seemed quiet, but what really got to her was that he was covered in injuries. He looked like he had been in one hell of a brawl. And shortly after he left, she heard an ambulance. She thought he was nice but troubled. She had lived in this town for 40 years, yet she never saw him before. Was he new? He could be struggling to fit in. That's always a possibility.

"What do you like about him?"

Audrey started crying some more. Her mom held her close.

"I-I-I... I don't know. I just... I..."

She couldn't even talk. She was too busy crying. Audrey's mom sighed. She went through a similar phase when she was Audrey's age. She just chalked it up to Audrey being a teenage girl, but then she thought differently.

Audrey had several boyfriends in the past. Even though she was quiet, she always seemed to have a boyfriend. Some she dated just to say, and others she dated because she genuinely liked them. Yet, never once did she cry as much about a boy, or think or care or even associate as much with a boy in such a short little time, as she did with Jack. Whoever this Jack kid was, he was special. That's for sure, because she never saw her daughter cry over a boy like this. Even when she was Audrey's age, she never cried over a boy like this. It seemed as if she was getting a divorce from a man she had been married to for over 50 years.

She REALLY seemed to care for this Jack kid. Whoever he was.

"Do you know where he lives?"

Audrey shook her head. "H-h-he lives down the street. A few blocks away from us. H-his house… is t-that small villa i-in… front o-o-of t-t-he swa… mp."

Audrey's mom stayed with her until she fell asleep. Then, she grabbed her coat and headed out. It was now pouring outside, and the temperature had dropped.

Jack sat down on his bed. He could barely breathe. He was afraid that if he were to go to bed, he would never wake up. He did a little bit of heroin to ease the pain, but it wasn't much. He thanked the Lord that they were alright. He wasn't trying to kill them. He just wanted to get away from them. Look how that turned out.

His rib felt like it had exploded, his face was numb, and he couldn't feel anything. His legs practically gave up walking. Yet, despite all the injuries, his mind raced. All he could think about was Audrey. He read in a book somewhere that if you think deeply enough about someone, they think about you the same time you're thinking about them. Was that true? Was Audrey thinking about him?

His questions would have to wait, as he heard a knock on the door. Andrea had gone out of town for the week. Something about visiting her family. Jack didn't believe her, as he was extremely suspicious of her after everything he saw about her.

Jack struggled to walk downstairs and opened the door. He saw a woman who looked like Audrey. Except she was on the heavier side and had very big boobs.

"Hello," said the woman. Her voice was soft and kind, yet firm and demanding. He had a feeling about who she was.

"Are you Audrey's mom?" asked Jack. Literally, every word stung like a million bees. He figured he would let her do the talking.

She nodded her head. "Why yes, I am Audrey's mom. My name is Sara. Nice to meet you."

Jack just nodded his head and smiled. He saw that rubbed her the wrong way (for some reason).

Sara cleared her throat.

"Listen, I just want to say that it seems that my daughter really likes you, and she seems to like you more than anyone else from what I've seen."

Jack's eyes widened. She… likes him?

Her demeanor quickly changed. She became firmer, and serious.

"Now, I don't know what goes on with you or your life. But I just want you to know that my daughter is interested in you. More than any other boy I've seen. If you so much as hurt her, I will hunt you down and castrate you like a dog. Make no mistake. I am willing to go to jail for my baby. And that means killing. I am willing to make you suffer if you ever do anything bad to her. Understand me, young man?

"I don't care who you are. My daughter seems to like you enough that she's making the biggest fuss of her life about it. That's enough reason for me. But let me be clear. If she comes home and is crying because you did something to her, know that God's wrath, no, my wrath will fall down upon you. I don't care if you're some… extremely skilled or badass fighter who can take down multiple trained people at the same time. I don't care if you're strong enough to break bones, or fast enough to outrun animals. I will do ANYTHING to protect my daughter. If that means coming after you, then so be it.

"I will stop at nothing. You hear me? You may be special, but the love that I have for my daughter goes beyond any training you may do, or have done. Understood, young man?"

Jack nodded his head. If it ever came down to it, he thought he would wipe the floor with her. No competition. Yet, after she gave him that speech, he thought it was the other way around. He heard about how some animals' mothers would go to extreme lengths to protect their cubs. Yet, that was only in the wild; that couldn't apply to us humans, right?

"Good. Now, if you'll excuse me, I need somewhere to be."

She walked away. Jack closed the door. He laughed. Not because he thought it was funny, but because he realized that if Audrey ever told a bad story to Sara, his ass would get castrated by her. He shivered. Sometimes, women scared him more than any nightmares.

6

David woke up in a hospital bed. He was stationed in between Yuri and Samantha. Samantha was still out cold. Yuri was barely awake. He just mumbled and groaned.

David felt his left leg, yet he knew it was gone. He felt as though he was moving it, but in reality, he was just imagining things. His head hurt like hell, and his body was practically giving up on him. Worst of all, he was beaten by his own student—one who, before fighting, had already been in a fight and got whooped up pretty badly. And yet, he was still able to beat him and Samantha. Some S.H.O.T. members he was.

This made David angry. He normally has a cool and calm temper, but this was too much. That damn Jack. Still, knowing how Jack was, he shouldn't have been surprised. He hoped he would have changed by now. His hope dwindled once he saw his fight with Yuri, and dwindled even more once he fought him. Yet, seeing that act of kindness done by him actually still burned the flame of hope deep inside of him. Not by much, but enough.

Jack made his way toward the hospital. There was practically only one in the whole town. It looked OK. Decent enough. It seemed here that people really didn't need to go to the hospital all that often. Injuries and murderers were almost second to none. Furthermore, with how small the town was, Jack was surprised if this place ever got full.

Jack got in and asked to see David and Samantha. After a while, the nurse let him see them.

"You have a visitor," said the nurse. Both Yuri and Daniel looked up, and Jack walked into the room.

"Could we have a moment?" muttered Yuri. The nurse nodded, and it was all 4 of them alone.

There was a horrific awkward silence for an uncomfortably long time. They all stared at each other and didn't say a word. Yet, each one's eyes spoke a million different things: betrayal, sorrow, guilt, anger, hatred and much more. Jack didn't look too much better than them. He also looked as if he had been through a warzone.

Finally, after a while, Yuri spoke up.

"How are you doing?"

Jack nodded his head. There was a hint of a smile on his face.

"You know… good enough. My ribs hurt like heck, but besides that, it's all good. What about you?"

"Take… a good look."

Jack winced his eyes. It horrified him to even think that he was the one that did this. All of this to the three of them.

"What do you want?" asked David.

Jack took a deep breath. He knew David wasn't going to react well to this, but it was at least worth a shot. He hoped Yuri would react better. After all, Daniel did not have a leg thanks to him, AND his cool and charismatic demeanor had completely evaporated away.

"Look… I just want to say I'm sorry. For everything. I know it was my fault that you guys are in the situation you're in now. I don't expect forgiveness, but I can't go on living like this. I—"

"SHUT THE FUCK UP! SHUT UP!" roared David. Even Yuri was taken aback, and Samantha woke up. Jack stood helplessly as he stared at David.

"Oh fuck no. I'm not having this shit. You hear me? You can kiss your apology goodbye. I'm not hearing one word of it. Know this, you dipshit. Once I'm feeling better and healthier, I'm gonna hunt your ass until the end of the world. Then, I'm going to kill you and revive you. And kill you and revive you until I die. Then, when we're in the afterlife, I will NOT stop until I find your soul, and tear it apart!

"I don't give a shit if you changed. Good for you, now you're some saint or angel. I don't care! I DON'T HAVE A FUCKING LEG THANKS TO YOU! YOU HEAR ME? YOU'RE DEAD TO ME! YOU SHOULD HAVE DIED THE MOMENT YOU WERE BORN! CURSE YOUR MOTHER AND YOUR FATHER FOREVER FOR GIVING BIRTH TO A WORTHLESS SAD SACK OF SHIT LIKE YOU! I HATE YOU! I'M GONNA FUCKING KILL YOU!"

Jack stood motionless. He never had his feelings hurt this badly before, not even by his own uncle. Yet, it felt as though his heart was breaking. Those words hurt more than any punch that David had ever thrown at him.

Jack said nothing. He dared not show his tears in front of him.

"I see… okay then. That's all right."

Jack was about to walk out the door when Samantha stood up. She was weak and still in her clothes in which she fought Jack.

Jack turned around. She was barely able to stand, yet she limped over to him and gave him a key. She leaned in and whispered in his ear.

"You want forgiveness? Then do this. Kill that man in the trench coat. You're more than ready for what lies ahead. He's still a little paranoid, so his mind is more messed up than when you entered it, but knowing your skills and abilities, you'll wipe the floor with him.

"You need to find out where he is in the castle (Most likely the throne room). Killing him is not as easy as killing a simple human. You'll see. But I believe in you. I've given you a key that opens a special chest in my house. It had an outfit specifically equipped for you and a special sword. It was supposed to be your graduation present. I guess you'll need it now.

"He's located in an abandoned warehouse near the east riverbank. Get him, and only come back to us when the deed is done. If not, then I never ever want to see you again. Now get out of my sights."

She pushed him away and limped back to her bed. She passed out once more. Before leaving, Jack looked at Yuri. Yuri gave him a nod, and mouthed the words, "kick ass." That was all Jack needed as he stepped out of the hospital.

He reached Samantha's house. The house reeked of weed. But that didn't bother him in the slightest. He spent hours looking for a chest and finally found it beneath her bed. It was labeled "Jack."

Opening the thing nearly gave Jack goosebumps. He felt a rush of cold air and saw his outfit. He took it out and put it on. It was a white robe with a large hood. He had a sheath that was next to his belt, which was filled with medicine, tools and throwing knives. Furthermore, there was a red sash. On the red sash was a note. It stated that the red sash was only given to members of S.H.O.T. who were the best of the best when it came to speed and hand-to-hand combat. Jack smiled reading this. There were two leather boots for combat. Each one had a hidden sheath next to the straps to tighten the shoe. He also had two matching metal gauntlets. Perfect for giving a massive punch, and as he swung his sword, realized that gauntlets gave his wrist more mobility, making his sword swings much easier.

His sword was thin but very sturdy. It had a metal handle, and the rest was pitch black.

Finally, he was ready. Jack put up his hood and exited the house. He had one thing and one thing on his mind only: completing the mission. Even if it meant his death, he would kill the man in the black trench coat. He had several questions about that 'other world.' All of them would have to wait. As for right now, he was heading to the east river bank.

Once he arrived, he noticed a series of warehouses. They all looked abandoned, yet only one could be housing that wretched man.

He spent hours searching but found nothing. It wasn't until later on that he was able to find where that man was hiding. It was a small warehouse located right in the middle of two larger ones. Jack opened up the door and found the man. Simply staring at him made Jack's bones chill.

The man in the trench coat looked like he had been waiting for Jack. He had an eerie smile on his face, and his skin was pale. Jack saw a good look at his face. It was all twisted and disgruntled. Now Jack was starting to wonder if he had subconsciously entered that other world.

"You're by yourself?" asked the man in the trench coat. He extended his hand. "This is going to be easy."

Jack was certainly going into a trap, but he didn't care. He needed to prove his worth to everyone. He needed to show them that he was meant for S.H.O.T. He carefully approached the man, sword in hand. *I could just kill him now,* thought Jack as he imagined himself cutting the man's head off. Then he looked around. There could be cameras, and he could be imprisoned. Even if he was wearing a hood, he didn't want to take any chances. He had been too brash before. Now he had to be calm and cool.

Jack touched the man's hand, and soon he felt black and saw nothing. Afterward, he woke up in that world again, staring at the castle. Although this time, it was different.

The sky was bloodred, and the water was pitch black. The castle was twisted and distorted as if it had been sculpted by a 5-year-old. The floor was dark green, and there were pieces of several different organs scattered throughout the courtyard.

Jack gripped his sword tightly and made his way inside. There were no monkeys; there were no animals in that horrid water. The air was stiff and dense. It reminded Jack of when he first entered Hemsworth. Jack felt his breathing get tighter and tighter. He started to lose it. He heard soft grunts from inside the castle. He felt his mind wander, and visions hit him like a brick wall. Visions of him dying, and visions of him losing. Now he understood what David was telling him.

"Fuck… I'm losing it," mumbled Jack as he entered the castle. The castle looked even more horrible than it did before. No words could describe the imagery. The castle would haunt Jack even until his final breath. Jack was losing his mind. He wasn't ready to become a S.H.O.T. member. David was right. He was just some kid who needed help. Yet, deep down, he wanted to prove himself. Something about proving other people wrong always made Jack feel good. It was a pleasure he enjoyed more than anything else. Seeing their faces when he did something mere seconds after they said he wouldn't be able to do it.

Jack had a particular instance he remembered. He was being picked on by a bully in 5th grade. The bully kept on bullying and harassing him every day after school. It got so bad that Jack nearly committed suicide. His parents suspected something, but they never got involved in it. Partially because Jack refused to say anything. Then, finally, one day, Jack had enough. Something inside of him snapped. No more would he tolerate this fat bully's beating and humiliation in front of everyone. So he told him that if he were to ever pick on him one more time, he would make the bully regret it. All the bully did was laugh, and he told Jack in his face, "You won't be able to do anything, you tiny bitch." The bully tried to mess with Jack after school that day. Jack brought a knife with him, castrated the bully and fed him his own balls. The bully moved towns and was never seen again.

Remembering that memory made Jack smile. He knew that everything was going to be alright. He knew who he was… and he would never change for anybody.

The castle almost killed Jack. It was no easy feat. He fought waves and waves of countless and endless monsters. Some of them were not so challenging, and all it took was either a kick or a single sword swing. Some other monsters were so barbaric, so horrid, so brutal, that it took all of Jack's sheer willpower to kill just one.

What's worse was that the monsters were smart. When Jack tried to attack one, they would recognize his attack patterns, and escape into the darkness that crept around the castle. They would then communicate with the other monsters, and it would only make it more difficult for Jack. Still, he never gave up, and his training proved to be effective. Unfortunately, it came at a cost. Jack didn't even know how far or deep he was into the castle, and he had lost one hand, half of a foot, chunks of his body, and his nose and left ear.

Jack could have never imagined that the castle was this big. Every hallway he entered was bigger and filled with more monsters than the last one. What's worse, every time he entered the room, it felt like he was staring right into the abyss. The rooms were monstrous and seemed as if they had no exit. Jack couldn't leave one, and it took him 4 hours to finally leave one.

His perception of time had completely changed. He didn't have a mirror to look at, but he felt as if he had aged 100 years. His eyes had grown heavy, his body numb, and his mind was fried. He was hallucinating hard. He couldn't differentiate between a monster and a statue. From a distance, it looked as if he was a madman, running and screaming at the top of his lungs. He swung his sword violently no matter where he went. In his mind, monsters were swarming him everywhere, when in reality, all the screaming he did only attracted more of them.

He genuinely felt like he already lost. Even as he ventured further and further, he only seemed to grow more and more insane. Now, Jack was staring into a black wall. He had lost his mind, unfortunately, and already accepted his defeat. He was barely standing, as if he were on heroin. He wished he was, as he could use a break right about now.

Jack fell down to the ground. The place around him looked like a bleak and empty hallway. As Jack's eyes were closing, he heard a horrific and sinister laugh. He felt something colder than the floor approaching him. Jack looked up, to see in the distance something pure white. It illuminated the room. It looked as if he was being saved, but Jack felt that wasn't right. He knew that whatever that was, was going to kill him. In this castle, you always had to be on your toes.

Jack scrambled to get up and tightened his grip around his sword. He breathed heavily. His clothes were completely torn. The white parts of his clothes were not either dark white, or red from all the blood. Jack tried to speak, but no words came out of his mouth. His eyes were rolling back, and he could barely hold on. That white... thing approached him. It reeked of death, and Jack sensed the bloodlust.

The creature merely smiled. His teeth were bloodshot red. His fangs stabbed his lower cheek. Jack knew what this was. It was the man in the trench coat. Looking straight at him. Jack looked back and saw death awaiting him.

"Y-you," was all Jack managed to say before his vision changed. Now he was in a massive throne room, looking at the white man sitting in a chair.

Jack swung his sword in the air. It hit nothing, and he collapsed on the floor. The white man chuckled, and he spoke. He sounded like there were hundreds of people talking at the same time.

"Not what you were expecting. Am I right?"

Jack's mind nearly exploded. He screamed out in pain. He felt it. Death was grabbing him and tugging him away. He gritted his teeth and nearly cried. He gasped for air as the man in white spoke some more.

"Did you really think one single, unqualified, limp-dick member of S.H.O.T. could take me down? You're dumber than I thought. You really didn't think it was going to be this hard, did you? How do you feel? You look unwell. Can I get you a glass of water?"

Suddenly, a cup formed in the man's hand. He threw it on Jack's face. Jack felt his face melt, and he screamed out in more pain. The man laughed, and Jack's face opened up into a million different holes. He could take it no longer. *Death, take me away,* thought Jack as he laughed hysterically.

Yuri, Samantha and David had all been released from the hospital. It had been a week since Jack had departed, and nobody had heard from him ever since. Yuri hoped to God that Jack was still alive and that he was just at home resting and recovering. Samantha and David said nothing... they knew what they threw him into. It was their last-ditch effort to kill him. They prayed they would succeed.

Yuri spoke up. "Hey... you guys want to head over to Jack's house?"

Samantha shook her head. David gave Yuri a look that indicated he would rather do anything else. He was royally pissed right now. For the entire week, he was there, he had around 20 hours of rest. His leg was replaced with a metal one, and he was afraid he would never be able to live life normally. Thanks to his contributions to S.H.O.T., Samantha promised him that he would get a new and better one. David said nothing. He hoped that Jack was dead. Samantha as well, but something deep down made her feel bad. Whatever it was, she made sure she repressed it well so as to not show it to David. He was a walking landmine right now. Everyone stayed clear of him.

They all said their goodbyes and went their separate ways. Yuri immediately headed over to Jack's house. For the entire week he was in the hospital, all he could think about was him. He felt it completely idiotic to send him in alone. No matter how good he was. Samantha told him horror stories of how some teams never make it out alive. Let alone one man. Yet this was Jack they were talking about. He hoped he would be fine.

Furthermore, Yuri felt bad. He felt as if he was the one that started all of this. He felt like it was his fault. If he hadn't gotten so upset at Jack and hadn't interfered with his happy life, all of this would be in the past, and who knows? Maybe David and Samantha would have given him another chance.

As he was walking to Jack's house, he saw Audrey walking in his direction. He put his head down and said nothing. He felt her stare intensely at him as he walked by. She said nothing as well. From the corner of his eyes, she saw her holding a card and flowers. Did... Jack gave those to her, thought Yuri as he looked up. Finally, he made his way to Jack's house. He knocked on his door, and after a while, Andrea opened it up. She was covered head to toe in designer fashion. She had a bunch of makeup on.

"Oh, hello," said Andrea. She extended her hand. Yuri politely accepted.

"Sorry to interrupt, but is Jack here?"

Her eyes widened. "Oh my God... I forgot."

Yuri looked confused. She screamed and rushed inside the house. He was nowhere to be found. She came back out in tears. She fell down to the floor but quickly got back up. She rushed to her car and turned it on. Before Yuri could say anything, she raced out of the driveway. Even with rolled-up windows, Yuri could hear her freak out and call his cell. Yuri looked back inside to see that the door was still open.

He felt bad about doing this, but he was a little bit curious about Jack. They were friends, after all, so it would only be natural to learn more about him... right? Yuri took a step in. It felt so wrong, yet so right. Jack was a mystery, and while Jack knew a lot of things about Yuri, Yuri certainly knew almost nothing about him. That would all change as Yuri entered Jack's room.

The first thing he saw was a pile of heroin on his desk. Yuri's eyes nearly rolled back. Drugs. He should have figured. Dammit. What was Jack thinking? Yuri looked around some more. The room was a total and utter mess. It smelled of dirty clothes, and his bed was in shambles. As Yuri investigated his dirty and smelly room, he saw Jack's diary. His mind raced. The angel on his right was yelling at him to not do it, but the devil on his left sinisterly told Yuri to open it.

Yuri looked at the book as if he was looking at some sort of... holy object. He liked Jack a lot, despite their differences. Yuri believed that he himself the issue. He wanted to know more about Jack. Every time he tried prying Jack about his past, all Jack would do was change the subject. Not anymore, not this time. He would finally have his answers. He reached for the diary. Even touching it felt weird. The leather prickled and poked at his skin. His breath was shortening. What in the world was going on? This was just a diary. There was no need to freak out about it.

Yuri closed his eyes. *Dammit,* he thought as he put the diary back down. He could feel the devil shrivel away, and the angel jumped up and down in gleeful joy. As much as he wanted to know more about Jack, he knew that this was the wrong thing to do. Sometimes, it was better not to know too much. There was a reason he was hiding so much from him.

Yuri looked around the house some more, but he couldn't find him. His stomach tightened and turned. His worst fears were getting clearer and clearer. *This can't be happening,* thought Yuri as he ran out of the house. He wanted to go and ask Audrey, but he knew that would be bad. He thought and thought, and then remembered what Samantha said. He quickly raced over to the east riverbank, hoping that he wouldn't be too late.

Jack laughed so hard that the white man was taken aback. Who was this crazy man?

Then, out of nowhere... Jack stood up. The white man gasped. "WHAT!" was all he could say. Jack got up, laughing hysterically and manically. His mind was lost, and his pain had seemingly gone away. The insanity that had taken hold of him had made him almost immune to pain. The white man screamed at him, but all Jack did was laugh back.

He grabbed his sword from the ground and swung it at the white man. His agility and his timing had diminished. No longer was he being precise and accurate. Now he was a madman. He was using pure strength powered by his insanity. He felt no pain as the white man attacked him, stabbing him in his ribs. Jack just smiled as he headbutted the white man. His precision was replaced by power, and his timing had been replaced by speed. It was as if he had transformed into a different man altogether.

"HOLY SHIT!" yelled the white man as he saw Jack avoid all of his attacks. Jack chopped the white man's hands off. The white man screamed out in pain. Jack gritted his teeth as he leaned in and bit his nose off. This angered the white man so much that he shoved his whole arm down Jack's throat, getting a feeling for his intestine. That was his mistake.

Jack bit down on the white man's arm. So hard, in fact, that he chopped his arm off. The white man staggered back and yelled out loud. Jack smiled as he pulled the arm from his mouth. He could feel his insides move and shift, yet he felt no pain. His mind had been altered. Jack said nothing. He only chuckled and stared at the man with such intensity, that even the white man felt scared.

"Damn…" the white man shifted reality one more time. It had zero effect on Jack. Now they were in a hallway full of monsters. The white man tried to escape, but that was futile. In what seemed like a flash, Jack slaughtered all of the monsters and chopped off the white man's leg. The white man fell down and screamed out in pain. Jack grabbed his leg and shoved it down the white man's mouth.

"Do you like that?" was all Jack said as he clenched down on his teeth. Seeing that man suffer made Jack… feel like he was on cocaine. His jaw locked, and he felt a rush that he hoped would never die.

Saliva and blood gushed out of the man's mouth as his leg was being pushed in further and further by Jack, until the point where it could no longer be pushed. To fix this, Jack cut open the white man's stomach and fondled to grab the leg. He ripped it out and beat down the white man as he bled on the floor. This happened, all while Jack sinisterly looked at the white man's lifeless body.

"CURSE YOU!" was all Jack yelled. Now, his insanity was being filled with rage and hatred. He would kill that white man 100 times over if it meant he could feel even a small portion of the pain he made Jack feel.

After a while, the leg was broken. The white man's head was non-existent. Instead, there was only a puddle of blood with bits and pieces of bone, brain and flesh. Jack sat down on the cold floor and finally shut his eyes. He embraced the darkness, and soon everything went black. He felt nothing, no more.

After a solid minute, Jack woke up to find himself in that abandoned warehouse. The man in the trench coat was missing. Jack looked down to find that his injuries were gone. He felt healthy, and well again. Even his clothes were OK. What in the world was going on?

Jack felt hungry and thirsty. He walked outside. He felt like a vampire. The sun was burning him up alive. He hissed as his eyes adjusted to the outside world. How long had he been out? It was almost nighttime when he went to that warehouse. Now it looked like it was mid-afternoon. Either way, Jack made his way back into town. Except he felt… off. Almost as if losing his mind was actually transferring over into this world. Almost as if… he was starting to go crazy. He shook his head. What a silly thought.

Samantha went outside to attend to her garden. She was smoking a joint, as it helped numb her pain. As she was flowering, she bent over, only to see Jack walking toward her. She dropped the joint as her mouth was hanging loose. Seeing this only put a smile on his face, but he quickly became angry. He now knew why she asked him to go.

With a reaction like hers… she figured he would never come back. Damn bitch. It made him want to spit in her face. Yet, it also made him happy. Again… he loved it when he proved people wrong.

"Hey," mumbled Jack. Samantha didn't even hear him. She was too dumbfounded to see that he was standing right in front of her.

"Y-y-y-y-y-y-you…"

Jack cracked a smile. *Shows her,* he thought as he nodded his head.

"The deed is done. Sorry I ruined your plans, but you're not getting rid of me that easily."

With that, Jack walked away. He felt Samantha still looking at him, her mind racing and boggling at how he was even alive.

Even though he was walking, and still a-OK… Jack felt as if a part of him did indeed die with the man in the trench coat. He felt as if a piece of his mind was missing. Still… he pushed that thought off to the side. All he wanted to do was lay in bed and sleep.

"You called me," said David. He was lying down on Samantha's couch. He had been taking a much-needed nap that was interrupted by Samantha. She was pacing herself back and forth across the living room. The weed was kicking in hard. She looked like she was half asleep with how shut her eyes were.

"Yes, I did. Jack is alive. I saw him today. He killed that man... all by himself."

David muttered something under his breath. As much as he refused to believe, he knew this was going to happen. He could only hope for the best. Knowing someone like Jack, he wouldn't go down without a fight. What surprised him, even more, was that he went into that fight completely injured from his fight with Yuri, and Samantha. Jack almost shivered, thinking about how dangerous Jack was becoming. If he were to join S.H.O.T., he would be an insane asset... but also a total wildcard. It went either way.

"Well then... what do we do now?"

Samantha was pacing herself back and forth more and more. She grabbed some cookies from the closet and ate them as she thought about their next course of action. She looked at David, and both of them had the same thought. Seeing Jack like this, made David change his mind. As MUCH as he hated Jack, he knew that it would be foolish to pass a golden opportunity like this up. Samantha thought the same thing. The only issue was how they were going to be able to contain him. It looked as if he was calming down, especially with that girl keeping him in check. David wondered...

"I think we should talk to Natalia and see how she feels," said David as he got up. Samantha looked at him with crazed eyes.

"I think we need to convince her first."

"No, we need to tell her as it is."

Samantha was taken a step back. "How should you know? When was the last time you talked to her? Last time I checked, you barely even talked to her when you left."

David sighed. He was starting to get agitated. Ironically, for someone supposed to be chill and high, Samantha was being a real pain.

"OK, well, why don't you talk to her?"

"How do I know if she wants to listen to me? How do I know if she wants to accept a new member?"

"Didn't you literally ask me to train them?"

"Well... yeah..."

David's eyes closed. "Are you seriously telling me you asked me to train two prospects... without telling the head chairmen?"

Samantha said nothing. David's eyes widened as he laughed hysterically.

"Holy shit. You need to stop smoking ASAP. Were you high when you called me?"

"Listen… I thought it would be a good idea. You're such a good trainer, and I wanted to surprise her. I haven't been doing anything good lately, so I thought bringing in two new prospects would help solidify me in S.H.O.T. And for your information, I only ate half a brownie."

David rolled his eyes. "Goodness… listen, let's just… go and talk to her. See what's up."

Samantha nodded her head. She looked like she was paranoid. David walked out of the house. Samantha screamed at him.

"WHERE ARE YOU GOING?"

David nearly flipped out as he spun around. He almost fell. The new leg was going to take some time to get used to.

"Holy crap, relax. I'm going to go home. We'll finish this conversation later."

As he walked away, he spun back around and pointed his finger at Samantha.

"You know, for someone who smokes so much weed, you sure get antsy and paranoid. What the hell is wrong with you?"

"I AM WORRIED!"

"Would you just calm down for a second? I knew it. You're crazier than Jack. You're actually bipolar. I never should have gotten you hooked. I'm taking your weed away."

David walked back into the house. Samantha's eyes widened. It was as if she was seeing the devil come inside and take her baby away. She screamed as she grabbed the weed and ran outside for her dear life. David cursed under his breath and followed her.

He couldn't catch up to her. His leg was slowing him down. Samantha screamed so loud that all the neighbors could hear them. They all looked out the window and saw the both of them run down the street. Some stared, some judged and most of them took photos and posted them on social media.

"Dammit, look at the mess you're making. Just calm down, lady."

"SOMEONE! SOMEONE HELP ME! HE'S TRYING TO RAPE ME!"

David's eyebrow raised. Dammit, would she just keep her mouth shut?

"Calm down, you fucking cr—"

David fell down and hit his nose on the concrete. Blood gushed out. He mumbled and gritted his teeth. He heard Samantha's scream be cut short as she got hit by a car. He heard a loud honk. David cursed and ran toward Samantha.

"Oh my God," said Sara as she got out of her car. Samantha was face-down on the concrete. Sara nearly shrieked as she looked down. She helped Samantha get up. In the passenger seat, David could see Audrey. He rolled his eyes. Talk about a coincidence.

He looked around. Everyone was taking photos; some people got out of their house to see what was going on. David panicked. He almost never did, but now things were getting out of hand.

"What's going on?" said Yuri as he approached David.

David thought to himself, *how in the FUCK is he here? Don't tell me…*

"I thought you went home," said David.

"I heard someone screaming and I wanted to help. Is that…"

"Listen, it's better if you just head home. I have—"

"Samantha." David recognized that voice from anywhere. It was Jack. David was nearly losing it. All he wanted was peace, quiet and a nice bed for him to sleep.

"You have absolutely got to be kidding me."

Yuri's eyes widened. He ran toward Jack and gave him a massive hug. They embraced each other.

"I… I thought you were dead!" said Yuri as tears nearly overcame his eyes.

"What do you mean?" asked Jack.

"I… I went to the east riverbank to look at the warehouses. I couldn't find you at all. I thought you had died. YOUR ALIVE!"

"I missed you, Yuri. I'm so sorry for everything. It's okay if you hate me."

Yuri slapped Jack in the face. He violently pointed a finger at him and leaned in so close Jack could smell his breath. His eyes narrowed in on Jack.

"Don't you ever say that again? You my friend. We sometimes fight and argue, but that's what friends do. I love you, man."

He gave him a hug, and Jack embraced him.

Samantha woke up, and Sara was so relieved she looked like she won the lottery.

"Oh my God, are you okay, ma'am?"

Samantha groaned and shook her hair. She looked around. "What happened?" was all she managed to say before collapsing back into the ground.

Sara shrieked, and Audrey got out of the car. She looked at David, then at Samantha. She tried to calm her mom down to no avail.

Then, she saw him, and he saw her. They both made eye contact with each other. The instant they locked in… they knew something. Both of them did. They felt… a strong sensation. Like something was pulling them apart. Audrey quickly turned away. Her face was red. Jack continued to stare at her. Was she angry at him? He wanted to go up to her, but judging by her reaction, he would wait.

Audrey looked back. Seeing Jack with Yuri made her smile. She was happy they were together again. Then she caught herself doing it. Doing that thing she always did whenever she thought about Jack. Caring for him. Why… Yuri was HIS business. Why was she getting so attached to his life? She knew the answer but refused to accept it.

David threw his arms up and walked away.

"Good grief."

7

David was looking directly into Natalia's eyes—the headmaster of S.H.O.T.

Natalia was a short, yet strong woman. She had piercing black eyes and thin, frail brown hair. Her skin, despite her age, looked relatively young, as if she was using some sort of magical formula to look young and pretty all over again. She wore these super dorky glasses, which completely went against her seriousness. In her entire lifetime, she only smiled and laughed once. It was when she became head chairman of S.H.O.T. Her nails were ALWAYS painted black.

When you approached Natalia, it was as if you were approaching your parents when you knew you had done something wrong. Even if you were an excellent hunter, and were the best of the best, she gave off an indescribable feeling that made you put your head down and look in the other direction. Most people couldn't look her in the eye. Hell, not even her husband. Only one person could say they actually could, and that was David.

Partially because he wasn't part of S.H.O.T. anymore, so he wouldn't feel afraid about having to be fired or being in trouble. Another thing was that, when he was a member, he was actually good friends with her. Most people were intimidated by her since she only spoke very few words. Those being:

-Yes.

-No.

-You tell me.

-You're fired.

And her favorite one:

-What do you think?

She always did that one on purpose in order to see if people would crack. You couldn't, as a hunter. Even in business meetings, she would like to test people. David knew she was testing him right now; he just didn't know how. But he knew. It's who she was. When he was a hunter, he was told that Natalia didn't even hold a candle compared to her mother. According to Natalia herself, she only mentioned and referred to her mother one time in her life. It was when the discussion of religion was brought up one afternoon. Natalia overheard the section about Christianity. Someone mentioned Satan, and Natalia said, "I know her. That's my mom."

She never spoke about her mother ever again.

Natalia didn't say anything. She was waiting for David to say something.

David cleared his throat. Just by looking at her, she already knew what he was going to say before he even thought about it.

"So… how is everything?"

A brief silent moment.

"Alright… so I have something you might like. There is a potential candidate for S.H.O.T. His name is Jack O'Hara.

"As far as Jack O'Hara… I have legitimately never seen anybody like him. I know you have very high expectations, but believe me when I say this kid will blow your mind out of the water. He's INSANELY fast and is the best hand-to-hand fighter I have ever seen. He is proficient with a sword and has top-tier stamina. He is built like a tank and can withstand almost anything that comes his way. Unfortunately, he is kind of… crazy. But, I feel like I can fix him.

"I believe Jack should be looked at. He is incredibly gifted and deserves some recognition."

Natalia said nothing for 5 minutes and 13 seconds. She merely looked at David. David almost looked away. He was feeling nervous and uneasy. The way she looked at him, it made him shiver. Finally, after a while, all she said was, "What do you think?"

David left the facility.

S.H.O.T. was located all across the globe (Even in Antarctica, they have a small underground base). They recently set up a base in Wilmhelm not too long ago. It's located right underneath David's flower shop. All you have to do is go to the bathroom and flush the toilet 3 times. After the first flush, wait 4 seconds, then another 4 seconds, and then you'll be taken underground into a facility completely surrounded by computers, a TV screen, training grounds and so much more. Natalia's office is located in the exact middle of everything.

You can't go anywhere without going past Natalia. She was the head chairman of ALL of S.H.O.T. Every single hunter across the world had to report to her (she spoke every language, so there is no need to translate). It was one of the biggest bases that S.H.O.T. has. In fact, this is THE base you go to for when you become a hunter. The other bases are either too small or don't have the capacity to throw as big of a party as they did.

When David left, his mind pondered about Jack. Had he been too hard on him? Perhaps so, but maybe not. What he did think was that whoever that girl was, sure put him on a leash. It was as if Jack was, almost, an entirely new person. He was intrigued.

He went over to her house disguised as an electrician. Earlier, he saw Sara leave the house to go somewhere. *How convenient,* thought David as he knocked on the door. Audrey opened it up.

"Hello, is Sara here?" asked David. He was putting on a very good, albeit kind of fake Italian accent. Audrey shook her head. Confusion gripped her.

"OK then. Mind if I come in? I'm the electrician your mom hired earlier."

"Um… OK."

David walked in. His first impressions were that the house was quite neat. Sara seemed like she really liked to tidy up the place. The kitchen was, however, by far the most impressive thing he ever saw. Some royal family members didn't even have as nice of a kitchen as they did. It kind of shocked him in a way, seeing as how thin Audrey was (her mom, however…).

"Can I get you anything to eat and drink?"

David shook his head. "No thank you. I was told the A.C. is in your room. Do you mind showing me the way?"

Audrey took a step back. "My mom never said anything about this."

"Really… well, that's quite surprising. I assure you it won't take any more than 15 minutes TOP. Don't worry, you'll be able to go back to playing video games and gossiping with your girlfriends."

Audrey was not amused by his jokes. "I don't have a video game."

David walked upstairs. He saw the way Audrey looked at him. She was onto him. Thankfully, she wouldn't recognize him from that Samantha incident since his leg was covered up. He entered her room.

It smelled like fine wine and peaches. What a combination. There was a lot of pink, and the room was just as tidy as downstairs. Her bed was made, and there were bright stickers everywhere telling her that she was a boss and that society sucked. David had a feeling Jack's room was a little bit different.

He locked the door. He peeked around the room to see if there was anything he could find on this girl. So far, she was quite a nice lady. Offering him drinks and all of that. He did like that she was hesitant toward him. If Jack were to try anything funny… (David doubted it, but Jack was still a teenage boy).

Finally, he found the holy grail—her diary. He nearly giggled at the sight of it. This took him back to his teenage years when he would torture his little sister by reading her diary out loud in front of her. She would get upset and kick him as hard as she could in his balls. David quickly stopped after a while.

He scanned through the pages. Nothing too worthy to discuss. Just girl issues. That is, until he reached a few pages before the end. She was talking about Jack. He smiled as he quickly read through the pages. He pretended to make some thumping noises so it seemed as if he was doing something important.

The pages talked about how much she loved Jack, but she couldn't understand why. She described how she wished he had never gone into her life, yet, when he did, it was like her whole world had changed. She also mentioned that she felt like he was up to something—something dangerous. She had never seen someone fight like Jack did. She thought he was crazy, yet that craziness about her turned her on like nothing ever did. Not even porn.

She described in detail how much she wanted to kiss him (not necessarily to have sex, but she did mention on one page that she would love to lose her virginity to him). Yet, more than anything, she wanted to be with him. She felt so happy when she was with him. As if there was such a strong sense of love. Even though they had only just recently met, she knew he was the one. She had no doubt about it.

She thought about forgetting about him for a while, but in the end, she couldn't pull herself to do something like that. She liked him. No… she loved him too much to do it. She wrote that she was quite hesitant to love someone so fast, and she never did that before… but Jack was the exception, not the rule. Her friends, whatever ones that she had, gossiped about boys. Audrey didn't, because she was so head over heels for this boy named Jack who just showed up out of the blue somewhere. She didn't even look at any other boys. She was too focused on Jack. He was better looking, despite his piercings, and had more muscles than the boys at her school. Almost all of them (but not as much as Yuri, which she mentioned several times).

She wished to see him more often and be with him as much as she could. She loved him.

David put down the diary. He kind of chuckled. It seemed that she had become fanatic about Jack. Judging by how Jack behaved, it seemed that she almost put a spell on him. He was like a puppy whenever he was with her—obedient, and he behaved himself. A far cry from the outside. He smiled as he walked out of the door. It seemed like this girl was doing good for both him and Jack. He had nothing to worry about.

As David was walking downstairs, he saw Sara open the door. Crap.

"Sorry, sweetie, I forgot my card. I'll be—"

She looked up to see David. David started sweating underneath his clothes. Her eyes widened.

"WHO ARE YOU?"

Audrey looked at David. "Wait, I thought you were the electrician?"

"ELECTRICIAN!" gasped Sara's mom. Oh crap, thought David as he looked for a way out. The door was so close, yet it was being guarded by a massive mother with gigantic boobs. If he didn't have metal legs, he would have been easily able to push past the two of them and get out of there. Unfortunately, he didn't have the privilege to do that. Maybe this was God punishing him for snooping where he shouldn't have.

He heard Audrey calling the cops. If he didn't get out of there soon enough, it would spell bad news for him. Sara grabbed a Taser from her purse. With a single idea in his mind, David grabbed his leg and threw it at Sara. It hit her straight in the forehead, and she was knocked out. Audrey shrieked as David picked up the leg, put it back on and waddled out of there. Audrey went to go and get her mother. David was running down the street, and Audrey was yelling at him.

For almost an entire week, Jack only lay in his bed. He was so fatigued and tired from that castle. He partially felt as if a part of his mind was gone forever. He did some heroin here or there, but nothing too major. He just needed some rest. Some days, Yuri would come over, and they would watch TV or eat pizza. But for the most part, it was just Jack.

Andrea scolded him for being out for so long. Jack scolded her back for forgetting about him, which increased his suspicions of her even more. She quickly was quiet after that. To make up for being such a bad caretaker, she made him whatever he wanted nearly every night. Jack wasn't complaining, as he ordered some insanely complicated and over-the-top meals that most chefs wouldn't be able to pull off. Andrea cooked it all with a very fake smile. Jack watched her cook and nearly lost her cool with a very real smile.

As he rested, he thought about her. The girl that made him feel better than anything. He caught himself listening to love songs as he lay in bed, staring at his ceiling fan and imagining going out with her—talking and cuddling up with her. Even though they weren't dating, it sure felt like it. It got to the point where Jack would feel sick because he thought about her so much.

Then... Jack decided to do something about it. He didn't want to be with her; he HAD to be with her. As if his life would have been completed. This woman, whoever she was, had completely transformed Jack. Jack had never been so stricken with love before.

Jack went out and bought flowers. He even wrote a special note for her. With this note, he was taking a huge gamble. If it failed, he promised himself and God he would overdose and die. It was all or nothing.

Audrey went out and bought flowers. Ironically, from the same place as Jack—David's shop. Although David wasn't there today. He was over at Samantha's house smoking some weed. She bought him a series of beautiful flowers and wrote a card addressed to him. She poured EVERYTHING out on this card—all of her feelings and everything. If Jack rejected her, she would kill herself. She couldn't bear the heartbreak. She braced herself. Her heart was pounding as she wrote the letter. Then, she heard a knock on the door.

Jack's heart was racing. He felt ill and sick. He almost threw up right then and there. He was sweating, and he was as pale as a piece of paper. He hoped it didn't come down to this. He wished it wouldn't. Yet, this woman was quite fascinating. Jack knew in his heart that he loved her. She was the one. He saw the doorknob turn, and Audrey was there at the door.

8

"Hey," was all Jack managed to say. Even as he said it, it was as if there was something stuck in his throat. Audrey saw the flowers and the card. She turned pink. She also couldn't talk. Her heart was stuck in her throat.

Both of them didn't say anything. They merely looked at each other. Jack gulped. Audrey looked away as if she was embarrassed to even be associated with him. In reality, just looking at him made her heart rise, and she turned red all over.

Jack cleared his throat. It was now or never.

"I got you these flowers, and I wrote you a card. I…"

Audrey took the flower with a shaky hand. As if she was getting a bomb. One made from love. She took the card too. Never did she feel the way she did now. She felt as if she was going to die right there and then. Her heart was beating too fast, she was too warm, and she couldn't speak. Her mind was racing at a zillion miles an hour. All she could do was nod her head and give him a warm smile. She went upstairs to put the flower away. She went to go and get her flower… but stopped.

She nearly collapsed on her bed. She fell down. It was getting too much for her. She gulped. With shaky hands, she opened up the card. Her breathing was heavy. She told herself to relax, but that was the equivalent of telling a homeless crackhead to stop using drugs.

She opened the card, and read it.

Dear Audrey,

I do not know how to explain this to you, but I'll try my best. Whenever I look at you, my heart races and stops at the same time. I feel as though I'll pass out. Whenever I'm alone with you, you make me feel like I am whole again. You make me feel as though I cannot live without you. I need you in my life.

You are so wonderful. I see it in your eyes. Your sparkle of life. You are beautiful both inside and out. You are very smart and are a wonderful and amazing human being. (Sorry if the handwriting is bad. My hands are shaky.) Look at what you did to me. I can't even write a card to you because I am so stricken with love. I love you, Audrey. I know we only just met, but I have to say that you are very special. Never have I been like this. You are the drug that I need in my life. You are the person that I have been searching for my entire life.

You are that one thing. The thing that makes me feel as though all will be well and good. And that nothing bad will happen. God has blessed me with your love. My sweet Audrey. Forgive me for everything that I do. But I PROMISE, and I never go back on my promise, I PROMISE you that I will be the best person to be around. You can think whatever you want of me now, but I can assure you that I will be there by your side.

Even when I'm gone somewhere, just know that I'll be there with you in spirit. Because I am always thinking about you. You, who is more special and beautiful than she could ever imagine. You, who is smarter and more capable than she could ever imagine. You, who could never realize the impact she could make on a person like me. You... who are the love of my life. Audrey, I just want to say that no matter what happens, no matter how things turn out to be, I will love you. I promise I'll be better. I promise I'll try my hardest. I will... because I'll be doing it for you. You give me strength like no other. You wouldn't believe it.
Would you be mine, Audrey?

Audrey collapsed to the floor. "Oh my God," she mumbled as tears overflowed her eyes. She couldn't see. This was it... the man of her dreams loved her! GOD SHOWED FAVOR AND BLESSED HER! HE LOVED HER!

She ran downstairs and jumped on Jack. She hugged him as tight as she could. She sobbed and cried on his shoulders, gripping him as her life depended on it. Jack was beyond confused, but he smiled as he thought he knew what this meant.

She looked up at him.

"Of course, I'll be yours, you crazy bastard!"

She kissed him right then and there as the sunset. Both of them embraced each other. Jack also started to cry. He never imagined such a thing as a "match made in heaven…" that is, until now. God smiled down upon them on his throne. This… this he approved of.

The kissing became intense. Audrey was struggling to breathe as she grabbed Jack's pants and started pulling them down. Jack's heart raced a million miles a second.

"Come inside," was all she said. She slammed the door and shoved him on the couch. She jumped up on him and violently made out with him. She shoved her tongue down his throat and ripped his clothes off. Jack's eyes were wide. This girl was crazy, but he loved her, and he wouldn't trade the world for it.

She grinded on Jack violently. Her breathing grew heavier and heavier. Jack was also struggling to breathe, except it was because of the onslaught that Audrey was throwing at him.

She licked his face and bit on his neck. Jack ripped her shirt open, and she seductively made her way down toward his crotch.

They had sex for HOURS. Even when Jack finished, or when she finished, they didn't stop. The only words that came out of their mouths were "I love you." They automatically knew which position to be in, and what to do. It was as if they shared some psychic connection. They stopped having sex for the night when Sara's mom nearly killed Jack as he violently thrust in Audrey.

"DON'T YOU EVER COME BACK HERE! DO YOU HEAR ME!"

Jack didn't care. He howled and yelled at the top of his lungs. Life couldn't get any better.

They were INSEPARABLE. They went everywhere together. They went out each and every night. And no matter where they went, they couldn't stop having sex. If it was a restaurant, they would sneak into the bathroom and do it for hours. At the movie theaters, and doesn't even get started whenever she goes over to Jack's house. His room practically became a sex dungeon. It was sex, cuddling, watching movies and repeating the process afterward. It went on like that for hours and hours. Even when they were at school, they secretly texted each other during class about new sex positions. They never got tired of each other. They loved each other too much.

Audrey would constantly cook for Jack. Whatever he wanted, she would make for him, no questions asked. Jack cut off all his contacts. Yuri barely even saw him, and David was convinced that he died. Samantha tried going to his house, but all she heard was laughing, grunting and moaning. She felt a little bit jealous. What it was like to be young. She had a boyfriend, but unfortunately, they broke up when she found him cheating. Then, she remembered someone.

David was over at her house, watching TV when Samantha opened the door.

"Hey, David, how are you doing? Whatcha watching?"

"What do you want?" replied David. She was almost never, EVER like this toward him. It was either seriousness, being like a friend, or damn near trying to kill him. She was only this cheery if she needed something. She was as easy to read as a book from kindergarten.

She sat down next to him. She twirled her hair and scooched closer to him. A little too close. Did she change her perfume?

"Oh, you know… it's been quite lonely lately. And I've been SO upset ever since my boyfriend broke up with me."

David looked at her eerily. She started unbuttoning her flannel shirt. His eyebrows raised. Was she… making a move? Never once did she show any interest in him. Actually… There was one time. He remembered it clearly.

It was when he, Samantha and a few of his hunter colleagues all went to go fishing. It was extremely hot. Nearly 50 degrees Celsius. Everyone was dying outside, and David took off his shirt. Then, Samantha started giving him way too much attention and was being very flirtatious with him. David chuckled that day, as he knew what Samantha's type was.

"Um… well, I'm sorry to hear that. I hope you can find another one."

"MMM… I hope so too," she said that looking directly at David's eye. In another world, that would have worked, but this was starting to feel more like a porno than anything else. He wasn't in S.H.O.T. anymore, so he could have relationships. Although he wasn't sure if Samantha wanted a relationship or just a good afternoon.

He used to be attracted to Samantha when they first met. He never did anything because he didn't want to blow his chance. Plus, they were pretty good friends, and he didn't want to ruin that. Yet… she was very pretty. They weren't too far apart in age either. (He was 3 years older.)

David played along for now.

"Do you… have anybody in mind?"

Samantha merely looked at him. David cursed himself in his head. Was that really the right thing to say? Girls confused him 9 out of 10 times.

After a while, Samantha nodded her head. "I actually do."

"Oh... and who might that someone be?"

Samantha smiled and licked her lips.

"I can't say, but they are quite muscular." She grabbed his biceps. "As muscular as you."

Yuri was in S.H.O.T.'s main base. Jack was so busy hanging out with Audrey that he hardly had any time to hang out with him. Furthermore, Samantha didn't want to hang out as she was too busy hanging out with David. He didn't think they were dating, but David did indeed go to her house on several occasions. David didn't seem like Samantha's type. Yuri figured Samantha to be more of a girl who liked skinny stoners. But that was just his thinking. David was the kind of guy that rednecks would be interested in: the semi-handsome, very jacked person who liked to live an honest lifestyle. From what Yuri knew, David didn't do any drugs. Yet he hung around Samantha a lot. So maybe he smoked some weed.

Leaving David all by himself. He didn't mind... at least that's what he told himself. In reality, he did care. He thought he could be a perfect boyfriend. Someone who was loving, trustworthy, honest, reliable and the perfect gentleman. Kindness and caring would be his motto. But his dad always belittled him and told him he acted more like a girl than a man. If only he could see him now. All jacked up, and working a job he could never imagine. Which was another thing about S.H.O.T. he liked. However, one thing he didn't like was that it didn't pay at all. In fact, he worked a regular job most days when he wasn't doing anything for S.H.O.T. Although it did baffle Yuri a little that Natalia was absolutely loaded with cash. He heard rumors that she had her own private island and several dozen garages filled to the brim with exotic cars.

Yuri was happy just having a two-bedroom house and a bathroom with a grandma's car. He didn't care for too much.

As he was training, he looked and caught something from the corner of his eyes. He couldn't believe it. His mouth dropped, and he dropped his axe. He saw her. He ran up to her and tapped her on her shoulder. She turned around and nearly gasped. She was even more shocked to find him here.

Yuri gasped. "Andrea. You're a hunter?"

Andrea nodded her head. She looked like someone had told her that she had cancer. *What was Yuri doing here?* thought Andrea, as she took a step back. Now it all made sense—now Yuri understood why Andrea was never at home. Why she barely looked after Jack and why she had all these really weird things in her house?

"I… what are you doing here?" asked Andrea.

"Same as you. Working. I'm a hunter."

Andrea raised her eyebrows and whistled. "Wow… um, okay. The boy from down the street is a hunter as well. Really wasn't expecting that. How… have you ever gone inside of someone's mind?"

"One time. It was with—"

Yuri stopped. If she didn't know about him, then she didn't know about Jack. Good, he preferred to keep it that way. But also, he didn't want to leave her in the dark or leave Jack in the dark too.

"With who?"

"Nothing. Are you working on any leads right now?"

She nodded her head. "Yeah, I and my pal were assigned to take care of this corrupt politician who purposely sent money to aid a genocide in a foreign Asian country. Everyone knows about it, but he can't be proven guilty. That's where we come in."

"Who's this buddy of yours?"

Andrea pointed to right behind Yuri. "His name is John." Yuri turned around.

John was a lean man. He looked to be 181 centimeters. He had zero fat at all and was ripped to the bone. Yuri could see every muscle fiber moving as John moved his arms and shoulders to stretch. Instead of David looking country, it was John who did. He was a white dude that was extremely tan. He had a cowboy hat on, and some really baggy jeans. His black sleeveless shirt really exposed just how shredded he really was. It was as if someone grabbed a pencil and drew a bunch of lines on his arms and shoulders.

"He's pretty good. One of the best from what I've been told," said Andrea as she put her weapon away.

"Wait a minute," said Yuri as he caught up to her. "You said it's you and him. Shouldn't there be more hunters going in with you to whoever this politician is?"

Andrea shook her head. "From what I've seen, he's pretty okay. A little bit happy, actually, that nobody's accused him. This is PERFECT for entering his mind. In fact, I would go so far as to say I or John could do it alone. But it's better to take two, just to be safe."

"Is he here in Hemsworth?"

She shook her head. "Yeah. He owns a vacation house just on the outskirts. Near the country. Perfect for partying and doing whatever rich people do to have fun. We will strike tonight."

Yuri nodded his head. "I see."

He looked at Andrea. She was beautiful, and her boobs were so big. He did think about dating her but quickly blew that idea away. She was way older than him, and he was just a high school senior. Yet, just being around her gave him visibility. Especially after today, she wouldn't forget him. Yuri wondered for a moment.

"What about if I joined?"

Andrea chuckled. "That's kind of you, but I think we're good for now. After all, this guy is a crooked politician and you've only entered someone's mind one time. Nevertheless, I like the way you think!"

John finished stretching and saw Yuri. His eyes lit up, and he smiled brightly, revealing a golden tooth. He jogged over to Yuri.

"Are you the new guy?"

Yuri shook his head. John had such a thick country accent Yuri hardly understood a word John said. John howled in excitement. "Yeehaw, partner! My name is John. The pleasure is all mine, Yuri!"

"You... know my name?"

"Man, what kind of question is that? Of course, cowboy! It's my job to know. Everyone here is like a brother and a sister to me. You're now a part of my family, and I make sure to take care of my family. Yuri, I gotta head back to training but I would LOVE to get to know you. Are you old enough to drink?"

He shook his head. John howled in excitement once more. "Oh boy, I remember being a little teeny grasshopper like you. But not quite as big. Holy cow, you look like you could eat my grandmother with how big your shoulders are. How much do you bench?"

"My max is 400 pounds."

John jumped up and down and howled as loud as he could. "OOH, boy. No wonder you're a hunter. Goddamn, son. Man, when I was your age, I couldn't even bench 222. Let alone 400. Yowzers. Anywho, got to go. I'll talk to you later, big man!"

Yuri smiled as he saw John go for a run on the treadmill. He liked this guy already. Yuri wrapped up whatever he was doing, and headed on out. As he was leaving, he ignored what Andrea told him. He was going to go to this politician's mind, and he WAS going to help both of them. This was his time to shine, AND his time to impress Andrea.

He waited outside of Andreas' house for a while. Finally, she left. She was wearing a tight blue tank top with a very short black skirt. Her boots were knee-high, and her hair was in a tight ponytail. She was carrying a gigantic sword. It was double her entire body. She strapped it on her back and rode off on her motorcycle. Yuri was in his mom's car, and he followed. She stopped on the way to John's house (who lived just a block or two away from Samantha's house). John was wearing a very tight, dry-fit shirt. He had semi-baggy black combat jeans and country gloves. He looked like he was ready for a war. He had a shotgun and a rifle on his back. On his holsters, he had two pairs of guns: a .50 caliber and a .45 caliber pistol. He had a combat knife strapped to his pants, and one strapped just below his waist belt.

They rode off. Yuri pursued them, but it was quite difficult since whenever there was traffic, they would just weave and curve their way out of it. It was a little bit harder when you had to operate a minivan. After a while, he lost them but was able to find them again when he heard the bike from a mile away. Finally, from a distance, Yuri parked his car and got out. He had arrived. Yuri was no slouch; he also looked like he was prepared for a Viking war. He had a massive white furry jacket on with very large white, furry pants. He had slim white gloves and was holding his massive axe in his right hand. He kept his distance from Andrea and John as they entered the mansion. It was MASSIVE, to say the least.

It was three stories high. It was very modern and neat. There was a massive garage that housed all sorts of cars (not nearly to the extent that Natalia's garage had). Furthermore, on the top, there was a massive swimming pool.

Yuri saw Andrea and John walk inside. He followed behind them. Inside was a MASSIVE party. There was music blasting through every speaker, and at least a few people were passed out from drugs. Booze littered the floor and furniture. Yuri made his way through the crowd that paid him no attention. Everyone was just too busy partying.

"Hot damn," said John. "If I weren't here to kill him, I'd sure as shit be downing some whisky and moving my hips."

"It does seem quite fun," said Andrea as they walked upstairs. Yuri kept a safe distance from them. The upstairs was where the guest rooms were. People inside the rooms were primarily drinking and doing drugs. The politician wasn't there. Finally, they got to the third floor. There was a single door, and Andrea bet all her money that the politician was behind that door. She could hear moans and grunts. Several of them, actually. If they were to be caught now, going inside would have been a real pain in the butt.

Then, out of the corner of his eye, John saw him. Yuri's axe was poking out of a corner.

"Hey, Yuri! What in the world are you doing here?"

Crap, thought Yuri, as he quickly put his axe away. He peeped out to see that Andrea was walking toward him.

"What in the world are you doing here?" she demanded. Yuri stepped back. "I was just… this place seems big. You guys could use some help."

She sighed. "I told you. You're not ready for this mission. I appreciate the concern, but believe me, we'll be more than fine."

Yuri grumbled. All he wanted to do was impress her. Now, it seemed like he lost brownie points with her. Way to go. Then, an idea clicked in his mind. They looked like they needed help going through that door without being seen. Yuri had an idea.

"It looks like you guys really do need help. I'll take it, you're trying to get through that door?" Yuri pointed across the hallway. She nodded her head.

"That's right. We don't want to spook him, or his mind will go on full alert. Are you thinking of something?"

Yuri nodded his head. "I have an idea."

9

Yuri went around the party asking people about the room upstairs. It seemed that there was an orgy going on. The only way to enter was if the host wanted more… entertainment. Lucky for Yuri, he wanted exactly that.

Yuri asked how he could join. The man gathering the people for the orgy looked up and down at Yuri.

"You seem muscular, and have a pretty hairstyle. You're a good candidate. We need more men. You're in luck, kiddo. What's your name?"

"Um, Lenny."

"Well, Lenny, today's your lucky day. Come with me."

Yuri followed Lenny. He looked back at Andrea and John and nodded his head. They followed from a distance. Lenny was taken to a room filled with other boys and girls. They were all blasted out of their minds. Meth, cocaine, ecstasy, acid, weed, whatever you could think of, they were on it. They looked at Yuri as if he was a zombie. They swarmed him, and he pushed them away. After fending them off for a while, the man came in and told them that they could head upstairs. They all did. Yuri looked back to see where Andrea and John were. He had lost sight of them.

The doors opened, and Yuri wished he could forget what he saw. An orgy, a massive one. A breeding party if you will. There were girls having sex with guys. Girls have sex with girls, and guys have sex with guys. And the sex was powerful, violent and out of control. People were hurting each other, ramming into each other, biting into each other. It was insane. The room reeked of piss and shit. He saw the politician in a gangbang with at least 5 different women.

Yuri went to approach him but was quickly grabbed by a beautiful girl. She was completely naked. Yuri had never seen a naked girl before. She jumped on Yuri and licked his face. She pushed him to the ground and started violating him.

He punched her off him, and he scrambled to his feet. John and Andrea were nowhere to be seen. He managed to touch the politician right before he caught a quick glimpse of him. It was just a brief glimpse, but it was all he needed.

Yuri woke up in what appeared to be a sex dungeon. Erotic noises were being spoken aloud. The place was dark, creepy, cold and overall not a place he wanted to be. On the floor, Yuri saw privates from women and men. Who was this guy?

"Are you okay, Yuri?" Yuri spun around. It was Andrea. His heart breathed once more. Thank goodness. John was next to her, also looking a little freaked out.

"Thank God, it's only you," muttered Yuri. His voice was out of breath. This place was too much for him. Now he understood what Andrea meant.

She could tell by the look on his face that he seemed that he already had enough. Unfortunately for him, the mission just started. She put a hand on his massive shoulder and told him, "You ready?"

Yuri shook his head. "I don't think so. But oh well." She nodded her head. John whistled a low tune.

"Well, I'll be damned. This sure ain't a place I would want to have sex anytime soon. And believe me, I've had sex in some horrible places. I once had sex in the back of a temple with this Jewish girl, and then in her daddy's bedroom, and then I once had sex in my old high school! I got expelled that day, but I'll be damned. Everyone was looking and yelling and screaming. I was like, damn, it's just sex."

"Okay, John. That is enough. Let's get moving."

They ventured further into the dungeon, encountering several monsters along the way. John was a natural with a gun. He never missed a single shot and always hit the vital points. Andrea was insanely skilled with a sword. (She was even better than Jack.) Even though her sword was massive, she was still a pro. She cut down waves of enemies as if they were nothing, and she was as agile and flexible as a human can be. She dodged and weaved with quick precision and grace. Yuri was an absolute monster. He swung his axe like a madman. His strength definitely did most of his work for him. Whenever he would hit a monster, the sheer force of his axe would disintegrate the monster. It shocked John.

As they ventured further into the dungeon, something seemed wrong. The walls and hallways started to change. Instead of being regular hallways, they started changing into what looked like a massive strip. There were poles scattered across, and the walls were replaced with red curtains with explicit images and phrases. What's worse, no matter where they went, there was a moaning noise. When monsters lurked, when they fought, and discovered new rooms. The moaning sometimes said phrases such as:

"Oh... I can't do it anymore."

Or "Oh... come closer."

The entire party became increasingly more and more uncomfortable with everything that was happening.

Yuri saw a curtain with a giant outline of a lip. "Guys, I think there's something there," said Yuri as he went to go and investigate. He opened the curtain and entered a room. It was a massive room, with curtains covering the walls. In the center was a massive podium with a gigantic pole. There were couches and seats, and more noise came from the boomboxes scattered around the room. There were no monsters here, though. Yuri turned around to leave, but realized that the curtain was gone. There was no exit, and Andrea and John were gone.

Yuri knew that this wasn't the time for panicking, but he couldn't help himself. He started to freak out. Did people die in other people's minds? He hoped not. He looked around the room, all while the blasted moaning screeched in his ear. He shook his head. Dammit, there was nothing. No way out. And then he heard something else.

"Come here." The voice was extremely sensual and erotic. Yuri slowly peeked behind to see who it was.

"Andrea," muttered Yuri. She was sitting on the couch. Completely naked. She smiled and teased him by playing with herself. All while making direct eye contact. Yuri's face grew red. He looked away. The shame he felt was indescribable, as he couldn't help himself, and he looked back. She was giggling and laughing. All in an exotic manner. Her breasts were bouncing up and down. Hypnotizing him. She licked her nipples and spread her legs open.

"Yuri... I need you. I need you now. Oh... come on." She was fingering herself. Yuri felt a force so strong, so powerful, it made him look. He could not look away. What was worse... he was getting closer. Why... why was he moving in her direction? This was a hallucination just like Andrea described it… but the feeling of his heart pounding a million miles an hour was real. The sensation of him losing his breath and his senses was real. The sensation of his pants getting tighter and tighter was real.

He got close to her. He had nothing to say because he couldn't say anything. His breath was choking him. He gulped and tried to shake his head to have his blood flowing to his head.

"What's wrong?" Andrea suddenly got in a face-down, ass-up position and opened up her vagina. Yuri nearly screeched. Oh my goodness, oh my goodness, oh my goodness. Yuri gulped.

"Oh please, Yuri. I want to fuck you so bad. Your big muscles. I want you to fuck me. Fuck me. Fuck me. Fuck me hard. Fuck me now. Oh, Yuri… oh please."

Her voice had completely seduced him. There was no turning back at this point. May God help him. He practically ripped his pants off as he got closer to her. She smiled. "That's it. Oh my goodness… it's so HUGE. Oh my…"

He was breathless. His body was pale, and his face was bright red. His hands were shaking. Oh my goodness. He blinked very hard. He was about to put it in.

"Yes… right there… right THERE!"

The naked Andrea screamed. Yuri jumped back as his life flashed before his eyes. Andrea swung around with her massive claws. Her claws were green. Yuri had his chest scratched, and he gritted his teeth. It was a very deep wound, and he nearly lost balance. He regained his composure and rolled out of the way as she swung violently. He quickly picked up his axe and swung it around. It missed her as she rolled out of the way. She jumped up on him and tried to eat his face. He kicked her in her boobs and jumped on her. He slammed the blade of his axe on her neck, slicing open her neck. She hissed and screamed out in pain. It was only then did Yuri realized that it was not Andrea. Merely a monster in disguise. He felt ashamed and disgusted. He shook his head as he felt an immense guilt. He nearly died. He almost died… all because he wanted some pussy. Yuri learned a valuable lesson that day.

He tried to escape but did not find a way out. The room only kept getting smaller and smaller by the second. He tried ripping open the curtains on the walls, but that was fruitless. He shook his head. As the room got smaller, he had to crotch, and then he was practically stuck in a box. Oh God, this is not how he wanted this to end.

His bones were being crushed. He yelled as his spine nearly shattered in half. He gritted his teeth as his legs were being broken. He clenched his face as the bones in his hand were being shredded. He felt no greater pain. Not even when Jack gave him a beating. He closed his eyes, said his prayers and accepted the sweet relief of death.

That day wouldn't come until a long time, as the room suddenly grew bigger and bigger again. Yuri gulped for air as if he had been stuck underwater for minutes. He looked back and saw John with the barrel of his gun smoking. In his hand was a monster's head. The monster had horns, erotic lips and eyelashes. Yet had the facial shape of a man's head. What a strange creature.

John chuckled. "Turns out this P.O.S. was playing mind games. He was using some hallucination to create visions of what you 'truly' desire. Kind of interesting. I just wish he wasn't so shitty or else I would have liked to be friends with him."

"How did you escape?" asked Yuri as he barely managed to stand up. John smiled.

"The thing is when he tried to create an illusion of what I 'truly' desired, he just ended up making a hallucination of a pirate ship. I knew it was too good to be true for a pirate ship to be inside this pervert's mind, so I blasted it to smithereens. Then I heard this mofo yelling halfway down the corridor. I ran over there, saw him and filled him with enough holes to make a cheese grater feel jealous. Then I ripped his head off for… a souvenir. That's what he gets for messing with my imagination and my dreams that I've had ever since I was as young as you."

"You wanted to be a pirate when you were a kid?"

"OF COURSE! Now what kind of question is that? Most kids want to be pirates. My brother wanted to be Captain America. Unfortunately, he's dead. He overdosed on heroin. Great guy though."

John helped Yuri up. Yuri screamed as he was unable to get up. He couldn't walk. He slowly sat back down on the ground.

"I… I'm sorry, John. I shouldn't have come. I nearly died, broke almost all my bones, and now I'm a walking liability."

Yuri put his head down in his lap. So much for trying to impress a girl. This was the result of that inspiration. Yuri learned two very valuable lessons that day. John looked at him with an intensity that not even Natalia had. Yuri felt it, and he immediately put on his game face.

John pointed his finger at Yuri. "You didn't come here just because you wanted a challenge, or anything else. There's a reason you came here."

Yuri said nothing. John smiled and nodded his head.

"I knew it. It's that Andrea girl, isn't it?"

Yuri went blank. He had nothing to say. He tried defending himself, but he was only able to stutter instead. John howled in excitement as he sat down next to Yuri.

"Son… I know how you feel. I was the same way when I was your age. There was this girl I liked, her name was Rebecca. She was the most gorgeous girl you have ever seen. I'm talking, her legs were so thick and powerful, every time she walked I would get bricked up."

Yuri chuckled. Somehow the pain was getting better.

"How did you know I was interested?"

John smiled. "Man, you were eyeing her like a rooster eyes a chick. Man, you couldn't stop looking at her boobs. I don't blame you. Lord help me if I ever laid my hands on such a monster. Those two beasts may kill me. But do you like her?"

"What do you mean?"

"I mean do you like her because of the person she is, or do you think she's just pretty and you want to get your dick wet?"

Yuri thought about it for a moment. He hadn't really gotten the chance or opportunity to really talk to Andrea. After all, he had only said the typical 'hello' and 'goodbye' when he was over at Jack's house. He engaged in some small talk, but nothing too grand. John smiled, that was all he needed to see.

John cleared his throat and continued to talk.

"Listen well, cowboy. If you like her, then go and talk to her. If you think she's pretty, tell her she's pretty. Be like, 'Hey, baby, I think you're beautiful and all. Wanna go get a beer? I would love to get to know who you are.' See what I mean?

"Listen, man, you don't want to be like me. Remember Rebecca? Well, I liked her so much, and I stared at her every day when I was in high school… but I did jack shit about it. All I was, was some random dude to her when she was all I could think about man. Man, I failed chemistry because of her, because I couldn't pay attention in class! I was just thinking about her, man. I never said a simple hello. I was too shy.

"Then, one day I was heading home, and my poor heart broke. I saw her kissing some random ass dude next to a tree. Man, I went home and I cried like a little bitch! I was so devastated. That could have been me! Instead, I was the dude that was crying over her because she didn't even know who I was.

"Even if you go and talk to Andrea, at least you'll have an answer. If you shoot your shot and she says no, she says no. At least you can go to bed knowing you tried. Sure, you'll be upset, but hey, man… you tried. Don't be like me. I still think about what could have happened more than a dozen years ago. Even if… even if all fails. You did something. That's more than what most people could say. After all, fortune favors the bold. Promise me something."

Yuri nodded his head.

"Once we get out of here, and we will, I want you to go up to her and tell her how you feel. Do you think she's attractive? Well, then god dammit tell her that, cowboy! She can't read your mind. And so what if she rejects you? At least you told her how you felt. Move on."

Yuri looked up at the ceiling with erotic art. He thought about it. He had never once told a girl how he felt, and he suffered just like John. He knew the names of all the girls he liked in middle and high school. All because he wasn't able to say anything to them. Just looking at them from a distance. A single word or phrase was all it needed for someone to enter into your life and change it.

Yuri nodded his head. "Alright then… cowboy. You have yourself a deal."

John Howlett in excitement again. "Man, I haven't been this happy since I drank an entire bottle of Jack Daniels on New Year's Eve."

Yuri laughed, and the two laughed together.

10

"Where in the world are they?" mumbled Andrea. She was aimlessly searching and wandering around the strip. So far, she hadn't encountered any monsters. That was usually a bad sign. It meant something big was about to go down. Normally, she wouldn't be worried, but her teammates were nowhere to be found. She gulped as she hoped she could find them and get rid of that politician.

Half of her wish came true when she heard a sound behind her. She quickly spun her head, with her sword in hand. Behind her was… Jack.

"J… Jack," muttered Andrea. What was he doing here? Seeing him, she felt a guilt over her. She felt so ashamed for being away. She told herself she was just doing her job being a hunter and trying to find a new target. Yet, deep down, she knew that was a total load of B.S. She should have been at home, taking care of him. She lied to herself saying that Jack was old and responsible enough to be at home by himself. Yet, his uncle paid her to do a job, and she was doing a shitty one at that. What if he were to go back to him and tell him how she was never home? She would never be a caretaker ever again.

"Jack… what are you doing here?"

Jack smiled. Something seemed off about him. He seemed more chill, and more… extravagant. He was wearing something that a modern-day vampire would wear. He looked paler, and his eyes were bloodshot red. There was a general feeling and vibe about Jack that made Andrea grip her sword harder. If this was really Jack.

"I came to see you," said Jack as he walked closer to her. With every step that he took, she took two steps back. His smile creeped her out. He seemed as if he was stepping closer only for evil intentions. As if he might force her to do something that she didn't want to do.

His smile grew even larger. "I miss you. I miss how we would eat dinner together, and how we would talk about things. You made me feel loved."

His voice was sly, and his tone was seductive. Andrea gripped her sword harder. Behind her was a curtain she couldn't even open. She gritted her teeth as he stepped in ever so closer.

He looked deep into her eyes, and Andrea felt all of her senses suddenly vanish. She went numb and cold. She tried to move, but couldn't. Her breathing stopped, and her heart pounded. Her legs were shaking. Jack took off his shirt.

"I miss you. Won't you come back home to me? I promise I'll be good."

He touched her. Her arms felt numb and weak. He smiled as he looked at her. She was losing her consciousness. She was starting to feel wet. His smell… it was so seductive. But she knew that this wasn't Jack. She must resist… yet when he looked at her with his extremely toned body, she couldn't help herself.

He started fondling her boobs. She became even more wet. He leaned in and kissed her. She was sweating bullets. Her eyes rolled to the back of her head. From a distance, it looked like she was on drugs. And like on drugs, everything that Jack did felt soooo good. She moaned as she kissed him. She felt her pants being taken off. She felt Jack's dick rub against her vagina. It made her feel so good. Every touch and sensation was indescribably good.

He started biting down on her neck. She moaned and cried out. Her breath shortened as she couldn't help herself. She went full-on nude. She hoped she could fuck him right then and there on the spot. She hoped she would have the best sex of her life right then and there.

"WHAT THE HELL ARE YOU DOING TO HER?"

Jack turned around. Yuri was looking with a red face at him. Rage and disgust filled his eyes. How dare he do something like that to her? John readied his gun. Immediately, Andrea came back to her senses. She screamed out and hid herself. Jack screeched as he swung his foot around and kicked Andrea as hard as he could in her face. She felt her orbital bone break, but she continued to hide her body.

Yuri charged at Jack. He swung his axe. All of his senses had left him. Now, he was blinded by rage and driven by pure hatred. He spun around and was able to slice off Jack's leg. Jack screamed, and soon he started to shift.

"YOU… YOU BASTARD!" The voice was distorted, vile, sinister and seductive all at the same time. Jack transformed into a massive monster. Soon, the room started to change as well. Andrea quickly put back her clothes when nobody was looking.

The creature was nearly two and a half meters in height. It was riding a silver chariot with flaming horses pulling it. Riding the chariot was a massive one-eyed monster. It had ten different tentacles sprawling out of the chariot. Its teeth were massive, and its tongue was grotesque.

"What in the fuck?" yelled John as he grabbed his gun and shot the beast. Soon, they were no longer in the strip anymore. Now, they were in some sort of weird dungeon. A medieval one. But instead of the room being small, it was the size of a battlefield.

The monster screeched. The horses ran at full speed. John was barely able to get out of the way; Yuri was able to jump over one horse and slice its head off. Andrea was stunned. For a man as massive as him, he sure had speed and quickness when he wanted to.

The other horse came to a halt. It yelled and charged at Yuri even faster. Unfortunately, Yuri was unable to escape and was hit pretty hard. He was trampled and felt even more of his bones break. What's worse, a piece of his ribcage ended up stabbing his left lung. Blood oozed from his mouth as John screamed. He grabbed his pistols and started blasting away. The monster was distracted, and Andrea took this advantage to go ahead and slice off the other horse's head. The monster screamed again and hit her in her stomach, sending her flying and breaking her bones. John gritted his teeth as his guns were seamlessly doing nothing. The monster, however, couldn't move. It was a sitting duck. John smiled; he was waiting for this moment.

He grabbed his two pistols and they seemingly transformed. One end of his .50 extended and opened up revealing a small hole. The other end of his .45 did the same thing. He inserted the two pistoles. The design of the pistols changed, and soon it looked like a small sniper rifle. He got to a faraway position and started firing. The monster screamed.

Andrea got up and quickly rushed over to Yuri's side. She kneeled down on him. "Just stay with me a little bit longer, OK?"

Yuri shook his head. He gave it his all today. He was done for. He had nothing left in the tank.

"Don't say that. You'll be fine, just wait a little bit longer. You'll be fine."

"H… How?" was all Yuri managed to say before the cold started taking over. His eyes were nearly rolling back.

She gulped. "Trust me, you'll be fine. All you need to do is stay awake a little while longer. PLEASE! STAY WITH ME!"

John was relentlessly firing upon the beast. The beast screamed and cried. It wailed its tentacles as far and as powerful as it could. It hit nobody. Finally, after forever, the deed was done. With just one more good bullet, John was able to make the beast scream out in pain. It cried and cried, and soon it fell down and collapsed.

The whole place started to shake. A white light was coming underneath the floors. Andrea smiled as she looked around. She looked back at Yuri… but it was too late. His eyes were already rolled back. He couldn't breathe.

"YURI! YURI! YURI!"

Soon, everything went white. And nobody could feel anything anymore.

11

Andrea woke up just outside the politician's room. Her head was in a daze, and she shook her head. She slowly stood up. Everybody had left. Only the aftermath of the party remained. She looked at John, who was barely standing up. The politician was nowhere to be seen. That means they did their job. Mission accomplished.

Then… she remembered Yuri. She collapsed back on the floor and started to sob. She hated losing team members. Especially on their first time. He had so much potential, so much latent talent. He saw what he was able to do for a short while… and now he was gone. She never should have even mentioned the damn thing to him. She felt a slight responsibility for his death, as if it were her fault. Just like ignoring Jack, she now had this on her shoulders. Some person she was.

"What's up, Yuri?" said John cheerfully. Andrea spun her head back so fast that it nearly broke. Yuri was standing up. He looked fine. Andrea giggled a sigh of relief, but then nearly slapped Yuri when she gave him a hug.

"What… everything went so fast I didn't have time to…"

John smiled. "It's OK, partner. You OK now?"

Yuri chuckled. "But how? I thought I had died?"

"Turns out you didn't. You were just very close," said Andrea as she wiped a tear from her eye.

"I feel… great. Why?"

"I'm guessing you weren't told this, but any injuries you sustain in a person's mind don't transfer over to the real world. However, if you die, you die in real life as well. Game over."

Yuri nearly exploded at that statement. "WHAT? None of you guys thought it was a good idea to tell me that?"

"I thought you already knew, but by seeing our reaction on the battlefield, it seems like you didn't know. Oh well, a job well done nevertheless," said

John as he walked out of the house. Andrea followed, and Yuri stood there for a solid second. He shook his head.

As they were walking out, Andrea started thinking about Yuri. She looked at him. There was a different motive for him coming here. She didn't know him well, but she knew him well enough that he simply wouldn't risk his life for a job. There was some sort of ulterior motive behind his actions. Whether they were good or sinister, she did not know, but she had a feeling he did this for a reason.

She called ahead to John. "John, don't wait up. I'm gonna stay here for a while." She poked Yuri and eyed him. John nodded his head.

"You got it, sweetheart. I'll see you tomorrow." As he was about to leave, he eyed Yuri and mouthed him the words: "Promise."

John hotwired a random car, and he rode off into the distance. Once she felt like they were alone, she slapped Yuri on his arm.

"What was that for?"

She looked at him angrily. Yuri took a deep breath but did not back away. He promised John something. He promised he would tell her. Even if he was rejected, at least he would have an answer.

"You didn't come here just because this was a mission you wanted to go on? There was some other reason, wasn't there? Some other reason for risking your life and putting your neck on the line."

"What do you mean?"

She slapped him again.

"Dammit, you almost died. I won't have that on my resume AND on my conscience. Why did you really come here?"

Yuri looked at her in her eyes. He remembered John saying something about 'fortune favors the bold.' He said, "I... I really decided to come here because I wanted to impress you. I think you're a very pretty woman, and I wanted to get closer. As well, I wanted to show you my skills and impress you. For a first-time hunter, to go on a mission like this, well, I thought you would at least find that 'heroic' or 'brave' at the very least. I want to get to know you more as a person… Would you like to go out sometime?"

Andrea looked at him. Silence for a solid minute. At this minute, Yuri was screaming at himself. This was such a stupid idea, this was so bad. Why did he do something like this? He should have just died in that politician's head.

Now… now she was going to think he was a suck-up, and she would try to use him to her advantage. Furthermore, she would…

"HAHAHAAHAHAH. Oh, Yuri… that's actually sweet of you, but dumb, yet very sweet. Unfortunately… you're too young for me. I try not to make it a habit to go out with guys that are almost half my age. But don't change, Yuri. I actually find it attractive that you almost died just for me."

Yuri nodded. His mind was split into two. On one end, he was happy that she thought it was attractive. On the other hand, he didn't have a chance with her since she was in school by the time he was born. Oh well. Despite all of this… a sense of clarity came over Yuri. At least now he knew, and at least he would never have to worry about her romantically ever again.

Andrea smiled and played with her hair.

"BUT, if you want, I can suck you dry?"

Yuri's eyes widened. "E-Excuse me?"

Andrea smiled. "Calm down, no need to overreact. Yes, you're too young for me to date. BUT I would definitely blow you. Maybe if I'm even in the mood, I'll let you lose your virginity (if you haven't lost it already). What do you say?"

Yuri was breathless. It was just like in the dream. Although there would be no monster coming to kill him. Was she trying to mess with him? Yuri thought so, but at the same time, he would be a fool not to pass on this opportunity. He was so nervous though. A woman as beautiful as her… he had a crush on her for so long that she was literally asking to blow him. It sounded like something out of a comic book.

"Um… OK," said Yuri shyly. As if he was about to ask his mom if he could stay up late.

She smiled. "Great!" She grabbed his hands, and they went back inside to the house.

He didn't even last 2 minutes. He had never had a blowjob before, but he knew that nothing would compare to what she gave him. He felt as though his soul was being sucked out… but in a good way. His eyes and face lit up as she sucked and swallowed. He gasped for air every second. Holy crap.

Once he was finished, she smiled. "I think I'm in the mood."

Yuri looked as she took off her clothes and lay down on the couch. He was instantly bricked up again. To lose his virginity to a woman as beautiful as her… it really was a dream come true.

Yuri didn't last 5 minutes. Still… he knew that if he ever had sex again, it would never be as good as with Andrea. What was even better, even once he was finished, she still insisted on going again. Yuri smiled as he had the best night of his life.

12

Jack and Audrey were laying down in bed. They had just finished having sex and watching a love movie. As they were lying down, Audrey looked at Jack. She smiled, as she was so grateful to have a man like him in her life. She kissed him on the cheek. She said nothing… she just admired his beauty.

Jack did the same. He looked into her eyes. He prayed and worshipped God every day for bringing in a woman like her in his life. He kissed her on the forehead, and they embraced each other. How did he manage to stumble on to a girl like her? If he had never entered Wilmhelm… he would have never met the love of his life. Funny how God works.

Like Jack, she thought the same. If she had never attended the school, hell, if she never was from Wilmhelm, she would have never met the love of her life. She dated guys from different parts of the world who came here on vacation. But nobody ever likes Jack. Then she started thinking.

"Jack… how did you manage to end up in Wilmhelm?"

Jack looked at her. The light in his eyes went away, and Audrey embraced herself for something. She didn't know what, but she embraced herself mentally.

"Why do you ask?"

She shrugged. "Well… if you never came here, I would have never met you, the love of my life."

Jack smiled. "Me neither."

He said no more on the subject matter. Merely looked up at the ceiling. Audrey knew that she shouldn't press on, but they were growing so close to each other. And Jack was so mysterious. She wanted to keep that edge on him… yet she also wanted to know who exactly this hot man was in her bed.

"So… why did you come here?"

Jack didn't look at her. He merely stared up at the ceiling for a while. Audrey regretted asking the question and felt the mood die down. She was about to put on her clothes when Jack replied, "My uncle sent me here."

She lowered her eyebrows in confusion. "Why would he send you to a place like this?"

Again... more silence. This time, Audrey was drawn in by Jack. She leaned in closer as if the secrets of the universe were going to unfold. Jack, still looking up at the ceiling, spoke, "I was arrested for producing and smuggling drugs. I ran a small drug cartel."

Jack wished he could hide this from her forever. He knew that she was extremely anti-drugs, and now here he was, telling her that he used to run a cartel.

She chuckled. It was the chuckle you had when something was so out there, something so false, you just couldn't believe it.

"Yeah, OK. And I'm a princess."

He looked at her, and with the look in his eyes, she knew he was dead serious. An uncomfortable and awkward silence filled the room.

Then Audrey, feeling suspense and mystery, asked again, "What happened?"

"I originally lived in a small house in Pittsburg, PA. It was very small, and I was the only child. My father and mother were still together, but I could see a divorce coming from a mile away. All day and every day they argued. Specifically my mom... she was always upset at my father."

"Why?"

Jack took a deep breath. "He was always balls-to-the-wall high. Cocaine, meth, heroin, whatever... he was on it all day every day. I didn't blame him though. He worked a dead-end, shitty construction job that paid nothing at all. My mom was a school teacher working at some elementary school in the hood.

"I was around 17 when I was first introduced to any substance. Most people start off with weed... I started off with heroin. I was at a party, and people were snorting something. I smiled and went to go and try it, simply out of curiosity. When I snorted it, I became so high I was out of it. People were trying to talk to me, and girls were trying to hit on me. I was completely gone. I was so high I couldn't even walk."

Audrey gulped. She didn't like where this was going.

"So... then what?"

"Then... I was hooked. I started doing heroin almost every day after school. Except I was snorting it. I didn't start injecting it until later down the line, but anyway... I was a drug addict. Then, my friend told me about his friend who knew a guy where you could get some crazy stuff. I wanted to meet him. Later that week, I did buy some more heroin. Then, he asked me if I wanted to try some... other stuff. I said yes. Soon enough, I was hooked.

"I did EVERYTHING. Meth, crack, coke, speed, krokodil, PCP, acid, mushrooms, salvia, ecstasy, you name it, I was on it. I also popped pills like a madman. (Although that was more of my uncle's forte.)

"However, out of all the drugs I did, cocaine and meth were by far my favorite. I soon realized that I was spending all the money I had on buying drugs. So I decided to make some. With the remaining money I had left, I paid a man to fly all the way to South America and get me some coca leaves. After a few weeks, he did. Then, I learned how to make cocaine."

Jack looked at Audrey. Her jaw was wide open, and her face was pale. Her eyes did not leave Jack's gaze, and she was breathing hard. He placed his hand on her hand to comfort her. She smiled just a little bit.

"Then my uncle found out. He tried a line and he said it was the best coke he's ever had. I was actually so proud of myself. It was my first time making coke, and my uncle said it was amazing. He told me I had talent. REAL TALENT. Not the one you see on American Idol, The Voice or some other B.S TV show. So he told me to meet him on Monday after school at his house. I did, and he took me to a crackhouse. There, I cooked and sold cocaine for a few months. I was making bank. Crackheads were coming in left and right to buy this stuff.

"I made so much money I realized, or thought, that I didn't need school. So I dropped out and started making drugs full-time. I first started out with cocaine, but later found ways to make meth and even krokodil. A quarter of the money I made went to buying the supplies and hiring guys to get me what I needed."

Audrey spoke up. Her lips dry, and her throat stale.

"W-what about your parents?"

"My mom died of a heart attack shortly after I got hooked on heroin. My dad stuck around until I started cooking cocaine. Then he packed his bags and left somewhere. I think he was actually jealous. Jealous that I was making more than him... at least that's what I thought. I think in reality, he was going through it. His wife had just died, and his son wasn't even there to support him. (Because he was too busy being high as balls.) Plus, the drugs had taken a mean toll on him. Once he left, I went to live with my uncle."

"T-then what... happened?"

"I was OUT OF CONTROL. I mean, I was on meth all day, every day, all I did was drugs. It was drugs, drugs, drugs, drugs. My day started out by doing drugs. I would wake up and bake first thing in the morning. Then, I would snort a line of coke and cook some cocaine. At around 9 in the morning, the customers would line up. My uncle would take care of them. I would be in the back making meth and krokodil. Then, at around midday, I would 'take a break.' By 'take a break,' what I really meant was I would get higher than I would ever get the day before. I would smoke crack, then smoke some PCP, then smoke some meth, and finally top that off with some salvia. Then I would go back to work and cook some more. I would finish by around 7 or 8 at night. My uncle would like to go to parties, so I would accompany him. At these parties, I would get HAMMERED. I would drink an entire bottle of whisky and accompany that with some crack or some meth. This went on up until a little bit after my 18th birthday. On my 18th birthday, I had to be escorted to the hospital since my heart stopped. I snorted 5 kilos of cocaine."

Audrey placed her hand on her mouth. Tears were rolling down her face. Jack tried to fight the urge to cry, but he couldn't help himself. He closed his eyes and frowned. He wished he could forget those memories. They embraced each other.

Jack continued as he wiped the tears from his eyes.

"I... I was such a mess. My life was out of control. I hardly drank water or ate any real food. I had kidney stones, and I was 183 inches at 44 kilos. It was bad."

"Oh my God." Audrey threw herself at Jack. She was sobbing. Jack embraced her as he clutched his eyes and full-on wailed. The pain. The pain of those days. Somehow he was alive... somehow. He didn't know how, but he was. By God's grace, he was. He wished he would have stopped. Yet, if he did, he would have never met the beautiful love of his life.

Jack wiped the tears from his eyes. He continued on.

"Me and my uncle were making so much money, we didn't know what to do with it. We had people that worked for us who would go out and sell our products. We had shops that would launder our money and smuggle the drugs.

We had people who would go and fly our shipments out across the world. We had made it big… but not in the way we thought. Even with all the money I had, I still lived in a crackhouse because I spent all of it on drugs.

"Things really went to shit a little bit after Christmas. One of our beauty shops had been busted for laundering illegal money and drugs. The guy that was arrested told everyone, and we all went to court. Thankfully, we had enough money to bail ourselves out of there. Yet, we had the cop's eyes and ears all over us. At that moment, we knew we had to quiet while we were still ahead. A lot of the guys did… me included.

"I told my uncle I was leaving. He said I was making the biggest mistake of my life. And that I didn't know better. I told him I was done. I didn't want to be in jail. I had enough money to get me through for a few months. I decided to take that chance. I used my uncle's phone to contact a caretaker. Her name was Andrea—the one I'm living with now. From what I heard, she used to live in Pittsburg. She moved out to Wilmhelm because of… some sort of job. I'm not sure. Anyway, I used my uncle's phone and contact to pay her.

"After a while… before I was about to leave… my uncle sort of came to his senses. He was recently thrown in jail and had to use the rest of his money to get out. He told me that I was doing the right thing… sort of. He said that, although I was doing the right thing, we could make one more batch—for old time's sake. I shook my head and told him I was sorry. He nodded his head and I never saw him again. Before I left, I learned he died from an overdose of cocaine.

"Now… here I am."

Audrey had no words. She merely hugged and kissed Jack. She buried her head deep in his shoulder. She was so happy he was here. She never knew. Now… she wished she never knew. She still loved Jack no matter what, and loved him for who he was. But now, every time she looked at him… she looked at him differently.

"Do you… still do any drugs?"

Jacked looked at her straight in her eyes. He held his hand tightly and had a big smile. He kissed her on the forehead.

"Of course not."

She smiled. Oh, thank goodness, her love was OK for now. His old life really was gone. She smiled as she kissed him, and the two proceeded to have sex. Once they were done, they went to bed.

"Jack," Audrey muttered. Jack grumbled as he felt someone poking him. He muttered something as he slowly opened his eyes. The first thing he saw was Audrey's crying eyes. Her face was red, and snot was running down her nose. The worst part about her was that she looked angrier and more frustrated than anything.

Jack immediately put himself upright. He leaned against the wall. She was standing up and was only wearing her oversized shirt. She gritted her teeth. Her eyebrows furled, and she hissed and screamed at him. She was hiding something behind her back.

"What… what in the world is this?"

She showed Jack what she was hiding—needles and a bag of heroin. Crap thought Jack as his gaze shifted from the bag to her face. The more he looked at her, the more she seemed to grow frustrated.

"Listen… I—"

"WHAT IS THIS?"

"Look would you… listen, it's not what it looks like."

Audrey opened her mouth. She was stunned, puzzled and perplexed all at the same time. She took a step back. Her eyes were bulging out of her face.

"I'm sorry. It's… not what it looks like? Because what it looks like is that your FUCKING USING HEROIN AGAIN!"

Her tears were trickling all over her shirt. Jack sighed; he wished it hadn't come to this. Jack put on his pants and stood up.

"Just… please give me the bag."

He stepped closer to her. She cowered away like an animal that was about to be eaten.

"No."

Jack sighed again.

"Look… I can—"

"Explain this bullshit to me right now!"

She threw the bag at him. He caught it. She was showing him her teeth as if she was a wild animal. Tears fell down her face. Her face and eyes were bloodshot red. She was hyperventilating, and Jack swore that if he got any closer, she would scratch him with her talons.

"OK. But first, I need you to calm down." Jack's tone was calm and cool. He appeared unfazed on the outside. Yet, on the inside, he was freaking out. He prayed to God that this day wouldn't come, and he dreaded thinking about if it did. Now here it was, and his girlfriend was a ticking time bomb. One wrong word, one wrong explanation, and she would explode. Jack hoped he wouldn't have to clean up the mess or see such a disaster.

He knew what she was like when she got angry. He saw it once when he picked on her (playfully). He pulled her hair and teased her about it being too long. She spun around and nearly hit him. He saw her face—the same face a wolf makes when it's about to attack, or when a lion makes when it's about to defend its pride and territory. She had that same face today… only much, much, much worse.

She didn't seem to calm down at all. She only seemed to grow more distraught as Jack got close to her. His eye contact never left her. Her hissing and growling only heightened as he was mere centimeters away from her.

"Audrey…" His tone was so gentle and so smooth. His eyes were soft and beautiful. He leaned in closer.

"Don't fucking touch me!" She pushed him away as hard as she could. He only went an inch or two back.

Jack, frustrated, knew he had to explain things before she would lose it. He took a deep breath and sighed.

"OK… look. I was going through a… brief phase of depression a little bit after my fight with Yuri. I felt like things weren't OK. Furthermore… I was just depressed in general. I just wanted to feel good. I had back luck with another girl, and—"

"ANOTHER GIRL?"

"It was before I met you. It was when I first moved here, and—"

"YOU WERE SEEING ANOTHER GIRL?"

"Look, would you just please calm down? I'm trying to—"

"You… you're a bastard! You're a filthy junkie. You maniac, I can't believe you—"

"BITCH, WOULD YOU SHUT THE FUCK UP ALREADY!"

The tension in the air died. So too did Audrey's face. It quickly contorted into a horrified and fearful face. She looked at Jack as if he was some sort of monster. Jack soon realized that he was the ticking time bomb, not her. He cursed himself in his mind as he saw the tears rolling down her face. *Crap,* he thought as he realized what he had done. She shook her head and quivered her lips. She hid her face away from him.

"Audrey, I'm sorry."

She started to cry. Cry hard. She sobbed as she hid her body away from him. Jack tried to suppress his depression at that time… but he knew it was fruitless. He bowed his head down as he walked over to her and embraced her.

She muffled to let go. He didn't. He embraced her and kissed her.

"Let… let me go."

Jack felt his tears roll down his eyes.

"Audrey… I'm so sorry."

"Let me go!"

"Please forgive me. I'm… I'm such a bad person."

Audrey stopped resisting. She looked up. This was the first time she ever saw Jack cry like this. Usually, he was either too stoic or too much of a 'man' to ever cry. This was the first time he really opened himself up to her. It pained her heart to see just how sad he was calling her that.

"It's OK." She embraced him, and both of them fell to the floor. This time, Jack was the one crying into her shoulder. She patted his head as he wailed and sobbed. As he cried and flailed, she saw the bag of heroin on the floor. Then she looked at Jack. She shook her head as she kissed him on his blonde hair. What kind of mess did she get herself into?

After a while, Jack calmed down. Audrey did a little bit too. Jack stood up and wiped the tears away from his eyes. Audrey stood up and kissed him. She hugged him… but later pushed him away.

"I love you, Jack. More than you can imagine." She looked deep into his eyes—no, his soul. She smiled.

"I really do, but it pains my heart to see you like this. I don't want to see you doing any more drugs. You don't have to explain anything to me. I just want you to promise me something."

"Anything!"

"I want you to promise me you'll stop. I want you to promise me that you love me so much, that you're willing to stop doing heroin, cocaine or whatever it is you do. I don't care. I just want you to stop. What if you overdose and die? I can't have that in my life. Please… will you promise me?"

Jack, without even thinking about anything, nodded his head. "Of course. I would give up anything for you… ANYTHING!"

She smiled. She grabbed the bag of heroin and flushed it down the toilet. She looked around the room and saw only an eightball of cocaine. Nothing more, nothing less. She flushed it down the toilet. She spun around at him.

"It's done. It's over." She held up her pinky. Her face leaned against his chest.

"Pinky promise me you'll never do any drugs ever!"

Jack nodded as he pinky promised her. She smiled as she pushed him on the bed, and they made love once more.

David was lying down on Samantha's bed. He was smoking a cigarette. Normally, he didn't smoke cigarettes, but today he would make an occasion. Actually, the entire week marked a "special occasion." He started… 'dating' Samantha. Although dating would be a very loose term. They just hooked up often—usually when Samantha was not working on a case, or when David was away from the flower shop. It normally started with a smoke session, followed by a very intense make-out session. That usually led to clothes being ripped and torn. After that, the rest was history.

David was lying on her bed, smoking. They just finished having sex, and Samantha was ready to go to S.H.O.T. headquarters. She had been called by Natalia to attend an 'important meeting'.

"I'll be back," said Samantha as she walked out. She was extremely well-dressed, wearing a very fancy business suit and she clearly had her hair done, and copious amounts of makeup.

David nodded his head. He was high as a kite.

"OK… um, before you come back, could you get me a bite to eat?"

"Hmm?"

"Like… cheeseburger and bacon. Hehehehe. Like… a burger. Did you know burgers are actually German? I knew a German guy once. I went on this mission all the way to Shanghai, China, where I was stationed in a desert. In this desert, I met a guy, and we quickly hit it off. Then, an enemy attacked and—"

She ignored everything he said as she walked out of the house. She quickly drove over, went into the bathroom and flushed the toilet three times. She went downstairs and went to go and see Natalia. As she entered her room, she felt the air completely change. Natalia was looking at her… very, very intensely. She gulped as she sat down. For a moment, there was silence. Nobody moved, and nobody said anything. As they sat in silence, Samantha couldn't bring herself to look at Natalia. The pressure was too intense. Finally, her hero had come to her rescue, but it wasn't who she expected.

"You called me," said Jack as he entered the room. He looked at Natalia and Samantha. He seemed more perplexed than anything. Samantha nearly gulped down her heart as she jumped out of her chair, then she quickly sat back down. The nape of her neck was burning from how much Natalia was looking at her.

Jack sat down on a chair next to Samantha. "Is everything OK? You called me here?"

Samantha was taken aback. "Me? I don't even—"

"You called me saying that you wanted me to come here? You even gave me instructions to flush the toilet and everything."

Samantha rubbed her eyes. She feared she was getting a little high from the second hand smoke from where David was. She shook her head. "No. I—"

"I called you here," said Natalia. Instantly, at the same time, Jack and Samantha shifted their attention to her.

She cleared her throat.

"I didn't want to use my real name, so I used Samantha's contact and name. Anyway, that's not important. I want to tell you, Jack, that David came to me and wanted me to analyze you as a potential hunter. I did exactly that. Congratulations. Now you're an official hunter. I expect you to be here every day and do what you're told. That's all. Good day."

Samantha nearly screamed. She stood up but immediately sat back down with the glare that Natalia gave her. Jack looked confused. He stood up. "What if I don't want to be a hunter?"

"Too bad. I have analyzed you. You are a good fit. Bye-bye."

Jack stood up and pointed his finger at her. Samantha nearly collapsed at the mere sight.

"Now listen here, lady. I don't care who you are, but—"

Jack fell down to the floor, grasping his heart. He screamed out as loud as he could. A sudden and powerful rush of pain came over him so violently, that he thought he might die. Samantha looked in horror as Natalia merely looked down on Jack on the floor. She shook her head as Jack's pain only intensified. Now Samantha was sure that he would die. She closed her eyes.

Then… Jack felt the pain slowly go away. He was in a cold sweat. His eyes were wide open. Saliva was oozing from his mouth. He couldn't speak. He grumbled and mumbled as he tried to get up from the floor. He gritted his teeth as he sat back down on the chair. He looked at Natalia… and she had an evil smile.

"You're a hunter. Now quit bitching and take a card."

She opened up her collection of Tarot cards and placed them flipped backward. Jack looked down on them and then looked up at Natalia. His breath was fading, but his heart was semi-beating back to normal—as if he had finished a super intense workout. He cleared his throat and picked a card. His eyesight never left Natalia. Samantha bit down on her nails. The tension was so thick, that she could feel herself literally suffocating. Jack picked up a card and flipped it over.

It was blank. Completely blank. Natalia chuckled.

"That's all I need to know about you. Now get out."

Jack eerily stood up, even as he was about to leave, his eyesight never left hers. Samantha walked away, not waiting for Jack.

Jack walked out of her office. As he went to go up, he saw Samantha was panicking.

"Are you OK?" asked Jack as he tapped her on her shoulder. She hissed at him and smacked his hand away. He growled and snarled at him. As if she were a rabid animal. Jack took a step back. First Audrey, now this.

"Good Lord, woman, calm down. What's wrong?"

"What's wrong… what's wrong? You! You are my problem, you no-good son of a bitch!"

Jack put his hands up in the air.

"Well, sorry for offending you in some way, princess, but I have no idea what I did wrong. If you want to hate me for it, then that's on your consciousness."

Samantha scoffed.

"Are you SERIOUS? Do you hear yourself now? What's wrong with you? Do you know who that lady is?"

"Some woman."

She scoffed again.

"You should have never been a hunter. That's Natalia—head chairman of all of S.H.O.T. You… you just barged in there, pointed your finger at her and kept eyeing her like she was a piece of meat. Do you have no respect? Do you have no dignity?"

Jack sighed. "Is all you ever do bitch and moan? Last time I checked, we are now officially teammates. That means we have to be cool toward each other. Which means you can't freak out like this. If you do… I might have to knock your ass out one more time and send you to the hospital."

Both were silent. Samantha furrowed her eyebrows and her nostrils flared. She spun around, and her hair hit Jack in the face. "Whatever," was all she said as she went up, and walked out of the bathroom. Jack shook his head. Women really confused him.

Samantha stormed out of there and immediately headed back home. That Jack kid was really starting to get on his nerves. As she was leaving, Yuri was heading in. He had a big smile on his face.

"Hey, Saman—" Samantha quickly pushed him out of the way, ignoring him and mumbling something about weed under her breath. He looked at Jack, who looked at Yuri and shook his head. He scoffed and walked away. Yuri followed up behind Jack.

"Is everything alright?"

Jack shook his head. "Not really."

"Why? What's the matter?"

Jack stopped walking and looked at Yuri. "Apparently, I'm now an official member of S.H.O.T."

Yuri nearly jumped up and down as his face gleamed even more. "Man… that's awesome. I'm so proud of you, man. Congrats!"

Jack chuckled. "Thanks, but I'm actually not feeling it. I don't want to be a hunter."

"Really… why?"

"Well… I guess that It's just something I'm not particularly fond of, you know? I don't really like the idea of going out and risking my life. Am I doing good? Yeah, of course! But… I mean it's cool and all. Yet, I just don't really see it. Know what I mean?"

Yuri shook his head slightly.

"A little bit. Just give it a shot. You are very talented, and an organization that helps out other people and punishes those who need to be punished. They would very much be pleased to have a man of your caliber joining them. Plus, you're doing good no matter what."

Jack nodded his head. Perhaps. Although what really was bothering him was Audrey. He knew he wasn't allowed to tell anyone. What if one day he went out on a mission and never came back? He shivered at the heartache that would cause the poor girl. Yet, he was doing good at the same time. If he was a believer as he said he would, then he knew that doing these missions would be to help other people. But it also says, "Vengeance shall be mine."

Jack pondered. "I'll see. I mean… can I really say no?"

"I don't think so."

Jack scoffed. "So what was the whole point of this conversation if it doesn't mean anything? I don't have a say; I'm supposed to do this whether I like it or not."

Yuri couldn't help but laugh.

"That is true, my friend. However, think about this convo when times get tough. When you feel like not going to work, remember—you're helping other people out. You could be avenging several people if you took down a corrupt businessman or politician. Since you're a Christian, doesn't it say to help others? Wouldn't you like it if someone helped you get justice in a similar situation?"

Jack faced Yuri.

"It also says, 'Vengeance shall be mine' in the Bible."

Yuri smiled. "If you say so. Think about this."

He patted Jack on the back and went to the shop, leaving Jack there to ponder.

"FUCK!" screamed Samantha. She was furious. She had never been so angry in her life. She needed a way to relieve herself and calm down. Weed wasn't gonna do it, so she knew a better alternative.

She was having hardcore sex with David. Balls to the walls, nonstop hardcore pounding. She kind of liked it like this. She was sweating bullets, and David was hammering her. She gritted her teeth and started to finger herself. David was horrible at giving head, so she decided to do the next best thing.

Both were panting and sweating. The bed looked like it had been thrown into an ocean with how wet it was. One thing that really turned her on was dirty talk. It pleasured her in a masochistic way.

"Talk to me," yelled Samantha. David knew exactly what she was talking about.

He talked dirty to her. REAL dirty. She smiled as she moaned. She climaxed. Finally, she felt better. She helped David climax by giving him a very special handjob. Once they were done, they sat down and collected their thoughts. They looked like they got down with a super intense workout.

She took a shower and put on her clothes. The feeling of pleasure only lasted for a little while. Now she was back to being miserable and angry. She decided to go and train. Hopefully, that would calm her down.

But she was wrong. Not even training could make her relieve her stress. She wished Jack was dead. She regretted ever trying to cause a scene with him. This was what she got. This was her divine punishment by God.

As she was nearly done with her training session, Yuri came up behind her. This time, he didn't have a smile. She knew he was there, but she ignored him. Hoping he would go away. Yuri said nothing. He merely looked at her.

After an uncomfortable time feeling someone stare at her, she quickly spun back and pointed her sword at Yuri.

"What?" she said rudely. Yuri paid no attention to her tone.

His tone was the exact opposite. It was empathetic, calm, and kind.

"What's wrong?"

She lowered her sword. "Your friend, that's my issue."

"He's your friend too, you know."

Samantha nearly laughed at that comment. She smiled as she shook her head at Yuri. Then, she saw that he was serious, and her smile faded.

"No. Definitely not."

"But you're teammates."

She pointed at everyone around them. "These hunters are also my teammates, but you don't see me socializing with them."

"I also don't see you getting frustrated by anything they do. What's the deal between you and Jack? If anything, shouldn't you—"

"Look, just keep your mouth shut, brat. I don't need some kid like you telling me what I can and can't do."

"Woah. I never said that. I just asked—"

"Oh, and for the record, I just want to let you know that I don't think you should be a hunter. You're too much of a liability, and I heard you nearly died on your first mission. So great job with that, you—"

Samantha didn't finish her sentence as Yuri punched her square in the jaw. He could have easily broken it but held back. She staggered backward and yelled. She charged at him, and soon there was a brawl.

Yuri dogged sideways and kneed her in her stomach. She elbowed him in his face and broke his nose. She then tackled him and put him in a chokehold. He was able to escape by simply pulling her legs apart, and he hit his head on her nose. She gritted her teeth as he was now on top and landing elbows and hammers on her face. She broke a few of her bones. She headbutted Yuri in his broken nose, and he actually cried. She scrambled up and kicked him in his neck, breaking it. He spat out blood and hit his head on the floor. She went over and started kicking his unconscious body on the floor. That is, until she felt a hand grab her on her shoulder.

She looked back and soon saw black as Jack knocked her out cold.

He smiled. He knew that this was going to happen, in some way or another. He shook his head as he saw Natalia eerily peek out of her office. She looked pissed off... and that genuinely scared Jack as he took a step back from the whole fiasco. Great, he thought as she walked out of her office and made a straight B-line to them.

All 3 were in her office. She looked at all of them. Each one she looked at, she made direct eye contact and shook her head in absolute disgust. Jack bowed his head. She was royally pissed from last time, and today she seemed like a ticking time bomb. And this time... she was much worse. Ten times more than Audrey.

After a while, Natalia stood up and walked around the office. She merely did circle loops. Everyone watched as she said nothing. Merely she just walked around the office. After a while, she sat back down. Again, there was more silence. Nobody said a word.

Then David opened the door. He looked at all three sitting down.

"You called me, ma'am," said David as he grabbed a chair and sat down. She nodded her head. David didn't even bother paying attention to any of them. Although he did give Jack a side eye as he grabbed his chair. After David sat down, there was still a very uncomfortable silence. Even David, despite him being out of the force, felt uneasy, and he could only imagine how everyone else felt. Then Natalia spoke up.

"I'm going to say this only once, so listen up, all of you. You are all teammates, and you need to behave as such. What good will fighting each other do, when all of you are fighting for your lives wherever you go inside someone's mind? What good will distrust and dislike do against one another, when each one of you will have to trust one another and rely on one another inside someone's mind? I will have no more.

"Yuri and Samantha. I am extremely disappointed in you two. Especially you, Samantha. You're older and supposed to be a bigger woman. Yet you still insulted the poor boy with a barrage of insults and belittled him. I could belittle you every day, you whiny bitch. Yet I keep my tongue.

"As for you, Yuri. I am disappointed in your ability to control yourselves. The instant someone says something negative about you, you lose your cool and throw things at them. That is unacceptable. What if, inside someone's mind, you lose your cool? What then? You could die a very unfortunate fate."

She shifted her eyes at Jack. He bowed his head. She gritted her teeth. "Look up at me when I'm talking to you… fuckface!"

Jack looked up, but his eyebrows were furrowed, and his eyes locked in with hers. Natalia smiled.

"Just as I imagined. I say one negative thing to you, and you're starting to lose your cool. My God. Jack, you got involved in a business that's not your own. I'm told you're a religious man and seek God. Now, to that, I say this. In the Bible, it states, 'Only a foolish man gets in the way of two dogs fighting.' Perhaps next time you'll learn to mind your business. Even if it is two friends fighting and you want to defend your friend. Your friend got themselves in that position. They should learn to deal with the punishments."

There was an awful sense of dread and distaste in the air. Jack felt sick, Samantha felt guilty, and Yuri dared not look at the headmaster. He was too ashamed and just wanted to go home and curl himself in bed. Natalia cleared her throat and began talking again.

"Now… I am disappointed, yes, but I am also worried that if all three of you continue down this path, you'll all end up screwed. Especially you, Jack."

Jack looked at her square in the eyes. Natalia couldn't help but crack a smile.

"You… I know about you. You are miserable, no-good son of a bitch. You junkie. Soon you're going to end up on the streets, sucking biker dick for 20 bucks so you can buy some meth. Isn't that right? Good Lord, I don't know how your idiot girlfriend can keep up with you. Holy shit, I feel miserable for her—for having to put up with an excuse of a man, no, a fucking human being. She must be as desperate as ever."

Jack stood up so fast, that his chair flew backward. The air filled with rage and tension. He growled at her and nearly jumped across her desk. Natalia stood up, and Jack realized the mistake he had made. When she stood up, Yuri passed out and Samantha threw up. There was an energy to her—an unmistakable energy of pure and unsaturated power. A power so powerful, so great, it appeared as if she came to some other planet. As if, with a single touch, she could turn Jack into a vegetated state. Jack winced back and quivered as if he were a sick puppy. Natalia howled at him.

"You intolerable piece of shit. You wanna fuck with me? Do you want to try something? I dare you. Go ahead, loser. Yeah, you piece of shit. Look at you now. Looks like you can chew off more than you can bite. I knew it. You're pathetic. You should have never been a hunter. How DARE you try and step up to me! Do you know who I am? Don't you ever fuck with me ever again, you limy, limp-dick, no-good, sad sack of dog shit. I'll kill you faster than you can blink. I'll end your whole fucking life. I'll butcher that pretty girlfriend of yours and make you eat her! I'll be the one to kill your dreams by putting you in a coma until you die. I'll make you into a vegetable the way you're gonna be lying in a hospital. Wanna do something? Better do it now. Because I SWEAR if you ever try this again, you're done. You're so fucking done! I will rip you a new asshole and shit down it until your so fucked your gonna be dead. Understand me, you piece of shit? Go ahead. See what happens. I'm just itching for you to do something. GO AHEAD, FUCKFACE!

"I hate you. You're a disgrace. You should have never been born, you understand me? Die! Go home and die. You're worthless and pathetic. You screw everything up. May God kill you now because you're no good and useless. You understand me, motherfucker? How about you go and die now? Die. Get out of here and go commit suicide in a hole, you piece of filth. You are so disgusting. Raising your voice at me, how… HOW DARE YOU! I can't stand to look at you."

Natalia grabbed her chair and sat back down. She cleared her throat. The air died down now. Yuri woke up, and he heard the whole thing. Jack just stood there. His head bowed down. His hands… soft. His body was numb and frail. Natalia threw a piece of paper at him.

"Sit down, you fucking retard!"

Jack grabbed his chair and sat down. His head was still bowed. Samantha looked at him. He wasn't shedding any tears. His body looked numb and lifeless, as if he were a very flexible mannequin.

Even David felt sorry for him. He wanted to say something to Natalia, but he didn't. He didn't want to face her wrath.

"Anyway… what I was saying was that you need to get along better. All of you. I…"

She trailed off and looked at Jack. Natalia never once in her life left bad. Today marked the one and only day she did. She looked at Jack's bowed head. She felt a wave of remorse and guilt. The clarity of her actions hit her, and she felt as if she was like her mother. Goosebumps rolled across her arms. What had she done?

"Jack… I'm terribly sorry. I really am."

Jack squeaked.

"It's OK…"

She nearly collapsed from shock. What did he say? There was no way. Was he… accepting her apology? She couldn't help but chuckle. She was going to say something again, but she couldn't get what he said out of her mind. She was baffled, puzzled and dazed. WHAT? She leaned back in her chair and looked at Jack. His blonde hair covered his face. She became very serious as she looked at him. She tried to get back to saying what she was saying previously, but she couldn't. All her attention was focused on Jack. Then she realized something. Never once in her entire life did she ever put this much emotion and attention into a hunter. Whoever this kid was… wherever he came from… made her change herself in a matter of minutes. She looked closely at him. Underneath the blonde hair… she saw a smile.

Son of a bitch… this was his plan all along, she thought as she couldn't help but chuckle. In another world, she would have gotten mad, but what he did, nobody had ever done in her life… ever. She rubbed her forehead and leaned back in her chair. She appeared more nonchalantly and surprised than ever. She spoke up.

"You… son of a bitch."

Jack said nothing. Everyone else merely looked at her. She shook her head and laughed some more.

"Well, Jack… I'll be damned. Judging by your smile, I think that you think you won. But how do you know I won't do anything?"

Jack looked up, his smile still intact.

"If you want to do something... then go right ahead. I'm right here. Although be warned... I'll give you only one chance."

David, Yuri and Samantha all collectively opened their mouths. Natalia was baffled. She chuckled some more. Her eyes nearly popped out of her mouth. He was playing an extremely dangerous game. Perhaps more dangerous than he thought. If he wasn't careful...

"How... what makes you so positive I won't kill you right here and right now?"

Jack smiled some more.

"Knowing your skills and capabilities, you could have killed me the second I walked into this room. Yet you didn't. You can kill me at any second you want, and yet you didn't. You've never been amused and shocked ever like this in your life. Nor have you ever shown so much emotion. I think you're a little bit intrigued."

Damn, thought Natalia as she smiled.

This smile... it was genuine. A real and first genuine smile that she had. That of happiness and wonder. Jack smiled back. His smile was genuine with a hint of fear. Then, an awful smell filled the room. It was so bad that Natalia dismissed everybody.

"Before all of you leave, I do want to talk to all of you. Meet me at David's flower shop at 10 tomorrow night. I hope to see you there!"

As they all left, Natalia looked at Jack and saw his pants. He had shit himself. She burst out laughing and cackled for minutes—another thing she had never done. She showed more emotion today than she did in her entire life. Never had she met a man like Jack before. She was intrigued by him, to say the least.

Outside, Jack puked as hard as he could. Never in his life had he been so nervous. He was sweating bullets, and his heart was racing. He prayed to God he would never have another gamble like that ever again.

As he was walking back home, he saw Andrea from the distance. He went to go and say hi but saw that she was talking to someone. He looked like he was wearing a cowboy hat. Jack waited until the guy left. He was riding a motorcycle and rode past Jack. As he rode past Jack, he made eye contact with him. Jack saw what he looked like, and he recognized the guy from S.H.O.T. headquarters.

As he watched the man ride off into the distance, he heard the sounds of someone sobbing. He looked back and saw Andrea with her head in her hands. He jogged toward her.

"Hey," said Jack as he put his arm around her. The smell of shit was still lurking in his pants. Andrea pushed him away. Her eyes were red, and she looked tired.

"W-what is… that AWFUL smell?"

"Um… it's kind of a long story. But anyway, what's wrong?"

Andrea quivered her lips and put her head down. After a while, she shook her head.

"I'm getting fired."

"Oh no… that's terrible. I'm so sorry."

She continued to cry some more. Jack thought about giving her a hug but decided that he should just leave her alone. After a while, she calmed down and was able to speak clearly.

"Can I ask why you're getting fired?"

"Yes. I… Jack, please for the LOVE of all things, don't tell anybody this. OK?"

Jack nodded his head and made an imaginary X over his heart. "You have my word."

She smiled. "I knew I could count on you. Anyway, I… I slept with my co-worker, and now I'm getting fired."

"Oh, yikes. That's always complicated."

Jack tried to chuckle to lighten up the mood, but that did the opposite of what he was hoping for.

"It's NOT funny."

"I know I'm sorry. I mean… who is this co-worker you hooked up with?"

"I don't even know how to tell you this."

"Well… just lay it on me. I had quite a day, to be honest."

She sniffed the air again. "Good God, what is that awful smell?"

"I shit my pants."

"WHAT? What are you, five years old? Come on, dude."

Jack chuckled. Andrea got even more mad at him, but Jack couldn't help himself.

"I know, I know. Again, I had a long day. Anyway, you can tell me if you want to. If not, that's OK. If you need anything, I'm here for you."

Andrea smiled.

"Thanks, Jack. No, I do… It's just that this person I hooked up with is someone you know."

Jack's smile slowly started to fade away as he knew who she was talking about. At first, he shook his head in disbelief, but as he saw her facial expression remain the same, he knew she was being serious.

"You hooked up with Yuri?"

"Yes. I know, I'm sorry, I shouldn't have. But he was so sweet, and it was kind of in the moment. I regret it now, but he seemed so nice, and I wanted to—"

Jack didn't pay attention to the rest as his mind shifted elsewhere. He thought about it for a moment. She said she was getting fired from her job. The only job Jack knew Yuri worked at was…

Jack interrupted her for a second. He knew he shouldn't disclose this with anybody that he didn't absolutely know was a hunter, but he was positive of his theory.

"Are you a hunter?"

Andrea took a step back. She gasped and was paralyzed.

"From your reaction, I'm guessing you are. I'm also guessing that the guy that passed us on his bike is also one as well?"

Andrea was flummoxed. She chuckled.

"You, out of all people… wow. I'm shocked. I'm guessing you met Samantha and David?"

Jack took a step back. He was almost as shocked as Andrea.

"How do you know them?"

"They're co-workers. I went on one mission with David while he was still in the force. I trained with Samantha only one time. I stopped because she was a lunatic and a sex freak. Just like you."

Jack raised his eyebrows and smiled. "What do you mean that she's 'just like me?' I don't—"

"Jack… I hear you from all the way downstairs, moaning and grunting several times a day. I imagine her mom is not too happy. If anything happens, don't go putting it on me, OK?"

Jack smiled. "OK then."

There was a moment of awkward silence, that was filled with the smell from Jack's pants. Jack spoke up once he realized that the smell was getting bad.

"So… when are you getting fired?"

Andrea sighed. "I'm not sure. I was told to meet Natalia tomorrow at 10 to discuss this whole… situation. Has Yuri said anything of this to anybody? I don't know how this got out. Oh man, what a bummer…"

Jack patted her on her shoulder. "Cheer up. Did you have a good time?"

She nodded. "He was a virgin, but he seemed to know what he was doing for the most part. We went at it that night."

"Well… there you have it. No regrets, right?"

She chuckled. "Is that your code of life? Aren't you a Christian?"

"It is neither good to be too righteous, nor too wise. Do you know who said that?"

"King Solomon."

Jack smiled. "Very good. You know your stuff?"

Andrea shook her head. "Not really. I read a lot when I was younger as my parents forced me. Then, when I found out I had the ability to go into other people's minds, I thought it was a gift from God. I don't know what happened, but I just lost faith over time. Know what I mean?"

"I understand. It happens. I look at it like this… God calls people to his faith. If people are religious, it's because he wants them to be. He has chosen them. Some people try their hardest to become religious, and it just doesn't work. Some people aren't at all, and then out of the blue… they suddenly believe in Christ. He calls them to be a part of his flock. Know what I mean?"

"I actually do."

Jack smiled. Andrea cleared her throat.

"Why did you become religious?"

"Would you believe me if I said it was because of Samantha?"

Andrea laughed out loud. Jack laughed along with her, and they both cackled at the night sky.

"Can I ask what happened?"

"Course! I went to some mysterious mind world by this serial killer, me and Yuri, and we were trapped. We thought we were going to get eaten by monsters, but Samantha came in and saved us, and we got the hell out of there. At that moment, I felt as though she was sent by God. I don't know why, but I felt as though God saved me through her. Ever since that day, I... I have been a believer of the Lord."

She smiled. "Do you still think that way of her now?"

Jack shook his head. "Absolutely not." The two continued to laugh into the night sky.

They both entered the house. Jack went to go and take a shower, and Andrea went to go and clear her face. Once he was done, the two continued chatting and talking. Andrea liked the chat so much that she broke out some alcohol. The two had copious amounts of whisky to drink (along with vodka, wine and rum).

Jack was absolutely hammered. His cheeks were red, and his face looked like it was in a permanent smile. Andrea couldn't stop laughing. She giggles at everything that Jack said.

When she looked at Jack, he became more and more handsome, and she became more and more sexually aroused by looking at him. She was not a fan of his piercings, but with the influence of alcohol, they suddenly looked better on him. Same with his hair and his very defined muscles. They all looked hotter and more attractive to him. She smiled as she saw that now, he looked like a hot supermodel.

"And so... I was saying that was TOTALLY not true and itz cane frex... eeeeee."

Jack was so plastered he could hardly even say a sentence without even dozing off. Andrea laughed at his jokes anyway. He was so hot. As he was talking, she started to think. Now that she was getting fired from S.H.O.T., she would be free. As well, she lived with Jack. He unfortunately had a girlfriend, but she thought about his quote from King Solomon.

She cut Jack off.

"Hey, JACK! How do...feel about girlfrendz?"

"WHAT?"

"Um... girlfrinzsa."

There was silence. *Crap,* thought Andrea as she thought she was messing her plan up. In reality, Jack understood batshit what she was saying.

"WHAT? Hmmm. You mean Audrey? Oh yeah, she's my girlfriend. What about herrrrr?"

Andrea shrugged her shoulders.

"I mean… what if you cheated on her?"

Jack burst out laughing.

Andrea chuckled along with him, although she was starting to get nervous. She hoped Jack didn't catch on to what she was trying to do.

"Listen… I LOVE my girlfriend, okay? She's like… the BeAstest and bestest and… um…she's awesome. I think that my exhamanshan hsonchanganag I don't even know whatsssss I'm saying I'm SOOOOOOOOOOOO drunk llolololo kkkkk. It's best and the exmenshermen."

What in the world is he talking about? thought Andrea as Jack passed out on the couch. His face was planted on her coffee table. His body went numb and he slept in a very awkward sitting-down position. She shook her head. This was God telling her to back off. She knew she didn't have a chance with him anyway. Besides, he was too young and she was starting to feel like a pedophile. Still… at least she tried.

"Absolutely not," said Samantha. She was sitting outside watering her plants when Yuri came by all of a sudden. He knew that tensions between teammates were rising, and he wanted all of them to chill out and relax. After all, they were going to be working together. Yuri proposed that they all take a little vacation and go on a road trip. It would be perfect for bonding. Samantha was not a big fan.

"Oh come on… please?"

"NO! Why don't you just leave? I'm busy watering my plants."

Yuri was growing frustrated with her. She seemed to be getting more and more agitated by the day. It frustrated Yuri that he had to deal with her and that she was more experienced and a higher-up than him. If anything, she was too immature and too rash to be in the position where she is now. At least that's what Yuri thought. He grabbed her can of water and threw it away. Samantha stood up quickly and mean-mugged him.

"Do you want a repeat of last time… dick?"

Yuri smiled in her face. "This is exactly what I mean. You need to chill. You and everyone else against each other. Why don't we go on a road trip? It will be nice. It's a good time for bonding."

"NO!"

"For all that is holy and good, why not? What harm comes from fixing a broken relationship?"

Samantha chuckled and scoffed. She let out a laugh that made Yuri sick.

"Um... first of all, there was never any bond to begin with. We are simply just teammates. Thats that. Second of all, if there WAS a broken bond (which there isn't), I wouldn't care. I'm doing my job first and foremost. If they want to tag along, then fine. I don't mind. But I don't want them to interfere with my job."

"What if I told you that actually having good bonds with people can make your work life a thousand times better?"

"Explain."

"If you know that person well... they're more likely to fight harder for you since they know you on a deeper level. Plus, they might actually help you in case you're stuck in certain situations. Like how you saved us from that guy's mind. If you were stuck in a sticky situation... YOU could be saved by someone."

Samantha said nothing. Yuri nodded his head and smiled.

"Yeah, that's what I thought. Plus, I asked Natalia about this. She actually agrees with my philosophy."

Samantha sighed deeply.

"Who else is coming along?"

"So, it will be you, me and Jack of course. I asked David and he was originally against it. After some... convincing (let's just call it that), he decided to join us. Also, I don't know if you heard, but Andrea is being fired. I also thought it would be a good idea to get her along since she'll be free. Plus, she looks like she could use the company. Furthermore, John has shown interest in joining us since he is my partner after all and we did go on a mission. Overall, that's 6 people."

Samantha shook her head. She could just say no and refuse. However, if she did, her two other companions that she talked to would be leaving as well. Leaving her all by herself. She already despised going to her job as it was. She only put up with it because David was waiting for her at home with her weed.

Samantha sighed deeply once again. "OK then... when do we leave?"

"Tomorrow. Pack your bags. We'll be leaving for quite some time."

"WHAT! You're just telling me this now?"

Before she could yell and question Yuri further, he walked away. She wanted to go chase after him but realized it would only be a waste of effort. She cursed herself and went to go and smoke some weed.

13

"Rise and shine," said Andrea. She woke Jack up. It was 5 in the morning and still quite dark outside. Jack barely managed to get out of bed by the time Andrea was all done and ready to leave. She made Jack breakfast to get him to hurry up. It did the opposite of what she was wanting, as Jack took his sweet time eating his eggs and pancakes. This only seemed to infuriate Andrea as she yelled at him to hurry along. Jack rolled his eyes and groaned. If it was going to be like this the entire road trip, he hoped to God he could overdose and die.

He quickly got ready. He threw on a pair of extremely oversized jeans and a very tight long-sleeve shirt. He walked out of his bedroom with his backpack filled with the essentials: toothbrush, animal crackers and water. He was planning on bringing a few kilos of heroin and cocaine, but he remembered his promise to Audrey. That was the worst thing about this trip: Audrey.

He was going to miss her so much. Before he left, he asked her if they could just go WILD in bed. She agreed, of course, and they spent the entire afternoon at his house trying and experimenting with new things. That day, Jack learned that doing things upside down never really works.

"Where are they?" muttered Andrea as she looked at her watch. It was pretty cold outside, despite it nearly being summer. She was wearing a long-sleeved shirt just like Jack, but instead of wearing pants (like she should have done), she was wearing a very long black skirt.

"Who are we waiting for?"

Andrea sighed. "David was supposed to pick us up in his minivan. But I don't see him anywhere. Dammit, he was supposed to be here."

Jack shrugged his shoulders. "I mean… It's not like we're gonna be late anywhere. It's just a road trip going on. And besides… where are we going?"

Andrea turned her head toward Jack. She looked frustrated. "It's still good to leave at the scheduled time. Maybe if he didn't smoke so much weed, he would be here on time instead of being high. Jack… never do drugs. Drugs are bad for you. He only does weed, and he can't even be here on time. Imagine if he did something heavier like heroin, or God forbid, cocaine."

Jack nodded his head. He kept his mouth shut.

"We're going to Philadelphia," said Andrea. "Hopefully, we can actually see and do some cool stuff there. I'm hoping to go to a baseball game. Is the season still going?"

Jack shrugged. "Beats me. I stopped watching baseball a long time ago. It's too boring."

"Well… yeah, that's true. But it's American. Isn't it so fun to sit around and eat a hot dog, and watch America's past time?"

Jack chuckled. "You sound like an immigrant."

Jack looked at Andrea. She took offense to that. She dropped her jaw and looked at Jack as if he was a serial killer who murdered her entire family. Her eyes were nearly building out of her head.

"Well, excuse me, but I'll have you know that my parents WERE immigrants. My mother came all the way from Germany, and my father is from Scotland! So yes, I do sound like an immigrant because my family is FILLED WITH THEM!"

There was an awkward silence. Andrea put her head down and shook her head.

"I'm sorry… I don't know what got over me. I didn't sleep well last night and… I'm going through some women's issues."

"I see… It's alright, really. No need to worry."

"No… I feel bad. I sound like Samantha."

This caused both of them to laugh. They chuckled as Andrea told a story about how one time when she went on a mission with Samantha, Samantha came into S.H.O.T.'s headquarters higher than a kite. When she went inside a serial killer's mind, she was tripping balls and curled up into a ball, and Andrea had to finish the mission by herself.

"Lesson learned, Jack… don't do drugs. Understand me?"

Jack nodded his head. Again, he kept his mouth shut.

After a few more minutes, Jack saw in the distance a black van rolling up. Soon, David pulled up to the driveway. Inside, Jack could already make out Yuri and Samantha. But no John. Jack got inside, and he knew why David took so long. It smelled like an entire plantation inside. Jack caught a peek of

David's eyes... and he looked like he could barely see. His eyes were bloodshot red, and he appeared to be pondering the secrets of the universe.

They rode off into the morning. David told Andrea that John was going on ahead, as he woke up earlier than expected and didn't want to wait up for anybody. *That seemed reasonable enough,* thought Jack, as he sat all the way in the back next to Yuri. Yuri was looking out the window. He seemed to have the same synopsis as David. Samantha, on the other hand, looked fine and normal. A little bit agitated, but that was to be expected.

Jack tried talking to Yuri, but Yuri took forever to respond to a simple question, that Jack didn't even bother. This suddenly shocked Jack as he pondered to himself if he was really like that when he was on drugs. Perhaps maybe on heroin, but what was he like when he was on meth or coke? He never was really conscious, as he normally said and did what was on his mind when he was high on those substances.

There was tension in the car that made everyone feel uncomfortable. It was now 7 in the morning, and everyone seemed to calm down. Yet, Jack wished they were still high. He felt the stares and intensity that were being emitted by David. He still wasn't too happy about his leg, and he had mixed feelings about what Jack did to Natalia. Samantha was also furious with Jack, and the air only grew heavy as time passed. To add insult to injury, Yuri and Andrea couldn't stop looking at each other, only making the situation uncomfortable.

For another hour, the car became so unbearable that Yuri nearly passed out. He put his head on his pillow. He was not enjoying the ride so far. At any given moment, anybody in the car could have said something, and a nuclear bomb would have gone off. It was brutal.

Jack cleared his throat.

"Do you think you could put on some music?" Even the words coming out of his mouth felt destructive. Everybody was walking on a thin line, and anything they said or did could have made them break that very thin line. If that line was broken, then all hell would have broken loose.

David shook his head. "The radio is busted."

Bullshit, thought Jack, as he could see that the volume was just turned off. Who did David think he was? Jack was about to say something when Yuri grabbed him by his arm. Jack looked at him, and with a petrified face, Yuri shook his head and mouthed to Jack, "Leave it."

Jack smirked. Hell no.

He grabbed something from his backpack. Something he brought along from Pittsburg.

"The radio may be busted, but I bought a CD."

David glanced back. Jack was holding a CD from the metal band Korn. David quickly grabbed the CD with intensity, Jack was taken aback. He mumbled under his breath.

"Try that next time and see what happens."

David heard this, and he spoke up.

"Wanna say that again?"

Jack shot back.

"Wanna lose another leg, asshole?"

David swerved the van to the side of the road, nearly flipping the car over. He quickly halted to a stop and opened the door.

"GET OUT!"

Jack was now starting to grow increasingly frustrated with this man's antics. His face became red, and veins in his neck became clearly visible.

"WHY DON'T YOU MAKE ME? But be careful, you might lose another leg!"

"Both of you, please let's stop," said Andrea as she showed her hands. Samantha spit at her skirt.

"Shut up, whore. You're no better. You got fired because you couldn't keep your vagina in your pants. You think you're any better?"

"Excuse me, but what the fuck did you just call me?"

"You heard me, cunt!"

"EVERYBODY ENOUGH!"

Yuri grabbed a gun from his backpack and fired it. Everyone nearly shrieked, and suddenly, the tension that was rising came to a halt and died. Everyone looked at him.

"Look at us... Natalia was right. I mean... we can't even drive 3 hours without nearly pulling a car over to try and kill each other. What's wrong with you people? What's done is done; just forget about it. We're here for a reason, and that's to try and mend broken wounds. That means learning to forgive and forget. If I hear one more bitching and arguing, so help me God I will kill you. (May the Lord above forgive me.) If you need even more motivation, know that we are stuck together for a while, so we better make the most of that time.

You know that saying, 'When life gives you lemons?' C'mon, guys. We can do better!"

Everyone was silent. *He was right,* thought David as he looked at Jack. After all, Jack had the right to defend himself. He was trying to kill him, after all. Then he thought about Yuri. He had literally fought the man and beat him to a bloody pulp, and now they were best buddies, not even a month later. Here David was, still holding a grudge. He sighed as he started the car back up again. They drove off.

The car ride was silent for a while until David decided to pop the CD in. It was from Korn's album *Follow the Leader.* He put on a song, and it quickly filled up the car.

Jack saw something he thought he would never see. He saw David tapping his fingers along to the rhythm of the song, and mouthing the lyrics from the song *Freak on a Leash.*

Jack spoke up. "You… like Korn, David?"

David nodded his head. "Yeah. I used to listen to them back when they were popular. Now I don't, but it's nice to hear them again."

Jack took a while to process that information. He didn't believe it. DAVID? A Korn fan? From what he was aware of, he never thought David listened to music. Jack smiled and chuckled.

"Nice. I like their stuff too. I kind of stopped listening to them after this album, but they have some good hits here and there. I like Korn for sure, but I also really like this band called Evanescence. Ever heard of them?"

"Yeah, they're pretty good. One of my former hunter buddies was into them."

"Was?"

"He died during a mission."

Jack was silent. "I'm sorry to hear that."

David waved his hand. "Ah, don't be. I mean… he was just a colleague. He knew what he was getting himself into."

Jack wanted to argue and say that despite the risks, they were still teammates. But he didn't want to pry any further. He just kept silent and listened to the music. Still… it baffled him to think that a man like David listened to a band like Korn.

Yuri turned to Jack.

"There's another one you might like, called 'Hed P.E.' Ever heard of them?"

Jack shook his head. "Never."

"They like… if Disturbed and Linkin Park had a baby. That's Hed."

"Hm. I might have to check them out. That sounds interesting."

David pitched up from all the way from the driver's seat.

"Hed P.E. is awesome. I didn't know you listened to them, Yuri."

Now Jack had lost it. What in the world was David on? Did he really listen to those bands, or was he just making stuff up? Judging by his conversation with Yuri about all things Hed P.E., Jack assumed that David actually did listen to them. He scoffed. What in the world?

All three men continued to talk about music for a while. The mood clearly lightened between them. As for the two women in the car, it was a different story. Andrea was just happy that there was a conversation growing between those two. She felt a clear sense of hostility coming from Samantha. *Damn bitch,* thought Andrea as she eyed her, and put her head to the window. How dare she call her a whore? She had no idea who she was messing with. But then… she thought about what she said.

Maybe Samantha was right. Maybe she really WAS a whore. After all, she banged Jack's best friend and even tried to make Jack cheat on Audrey. What's worse, she's almost double their age. She closed her eyes. She needed to change ASAP. What had she done? Her mother had always scolded her about being a 'proper' woman and the need to possess virtues that would attract any man to her. It was quite ironic, considering her mother had been divorced more times than she could count. Even when she was an adult, Andrea's mother did not stop howling at her about not flashing her boobs so much in public. She couldn't help it. They were just too big.

Samantha scoffed. Who did Andrea think she was eyeing like that? She would have what was coming to her. She would show her. It took Samantha forever to get to the spot where she is now. She started off when she was 17 years old, and now nearly in her late 30s, she was able to get to the spot she felt COMFORTABLE in. She still wished she was a higher-up and wished that she was respected more. Way more than Andrea, that is. She heard all her male colleagues, and even her female colleagues, talk about her. It sickens her stomach. She wasn't even a proper hunter. She hadn't been in the force for more than a decade, and she was getting praise and respect like she never heard before. Almost as much as Natalia. Samantha grew jealous as the days passed, as she wished she could be like Natalia.

All the guys talked about her breasts, and all the girls talked about her beauty. None of them even thought about her skills as a hunter. She was weak, and Samantha could fold her in less than a second. Why? Why did she have so much attention when she barely put in the work and effort? Nearly dying on every mission. Everyone worried about her then, but when Samantha was in the hospital, nobody even showed up to visit her. Even some of David's friends went to go and see him, and he quit. Was it because she wasn't beautiful? Was it because she wasn't as attractive or had as good of a personality as Andrea did? Was it her temper that her father always scolded her about?

She looked down. Samantha was a 26AA bra size. Nothing to boast about. She looked at Andrea, and hatred grew deep within her heart. Andrea looked like an E-cup. How come she was gifted by God's grace? Furthermore, her breasts appeared fuller and nicer. Samantha never looked in the shower when looking at her breasts. They appeared almost uneven, and her nipples looked misplaced. Samantha shook her head. She shouldn't be thinking about those things. She should be more focused on her mission and on her training. So what if Andrea was prettier in every way? At least she was a better fighter and a more accomplished hunter. That's all that matters.

At least… on paper. In retrospect, Samantha thought way too much about Natalia when Natalia barely even knew who Samantha was. (Except for that one time with the weed incident.)

She had better hair, and clothes, and was prettier. Samantha cursed under her breath, and David gave her a cold look.

Don't look at me like that, thought Samantha as the music continued to play. He was no better than Andrea. He had sex with Samantha every day, and when they did have sex, they banged like they were a couple of wild rabbits. Then, a creepy and horrific thought appeared in Samantha's mind. Was Andrea better at sex than she was? There was only one way to find out.

"Let's take a break here," said David as he opened the car door. They were at a pit stop in what seemed like the middle of nowhere. Woods and forest critters surrounded the small little gas station. Everybody got out and stretched. The car reeked of weed, animal crackers and smelly farts (thanks to Jack and Andrea. Something was up with their breakfast).

Jack clapped his hands. "OK. If anybody needs to use the bathroom, I think now is the proper time to do so. I feel as if we still have a few ways to go."

"Agree," responded Yuri as he made his way toward the restroom. David stood outside and started smoking some more weed. Andrea eyed Samantha as she walked inside to buy some chips. Samantha grumbled, and she went to go and talk to David.

"What do you think about Andrea?"

David shrugged. "She seems alright to me."

"What do you mean, alright?"

David eyed her.

"Is everything alright? You were acting funny in the car, and now this. Don't tell me you're still upset about the bickering and bantering earlier this morning?"

Samantha took a deep breath. She had to learn to control her anger if she wanted people to start liking her just as much as they did with Andrea.

"Well… I mean, I was just curious. She is quite a pretty girl, don't you think?"

"Yeah. A little bit."

Samantha smiled. "What do you like so much about her?"

She knew what he was going to say from a mile away, yet she asked just so she could confirm her suspicions.

"I think she has… a very nice personality."

Samantha flipped. She couldn't help herself.

"THAT IS BULLSHIT! You just like her because of her boobs, don't you, you pervert."

David chuckled. "Well, actually I was being sincere. I didn't even think about her boobs. Yet, here you are making such a big fuss about it. Maybe you're a pervert."

Samantha grew quiet. David's smile only got bigger.

"ALSO, you're much bigger and stronger than her. It seems like you're trying to contemplate something."

"Just for the record, my boobs have nothing to do with me being strong and liking to work out. It's good for—"

"For your job, yeah, I've heard that before. It's nice being jacked and all. (I mean, look at me.) But when it's all you focus on, it starts to ruin your personality."

"Are you saying I should stop?"

"I'm just gonna keep it a buck and say you need to find other stuff to do. Gardening is great and all, and so is going to the gym. Yet... it seems like that's all you do. (And smoke weed and have sex all day every day.) Maybe try doing some other stuff?"

Samantha took offense to that.

"I'll have you know that's plenty of stuff that I do!"

"Some people may not agree. Let's say I'm having a conversation with you and we're talking about... I don't know, the ocean. If you don't have anything good to say about the ocean, then I can barely even interact with you."

"Knowing about the ocean is pointless."

"I talked to Andrea for 45 minutes the other day just about the geography of the ocean floor."

That made Samantha quiet. She felt like crying, screaming and murdering Andrea. She grumbled and went back inside the van. David shook his head. He felt bad for Samantha.

So many people talked smack about her. She did have issues, yes, but at the end of the day, she was only a human who was prone to emotion and making mistakes, just like everyone else on earth. Yet, she seemed to get the worst end of the stick. He never forgot when she showed up high to a mission and couldn't continue because she was blasted off the walls. For YEARS, people didn't stop talking about it. They weren't lovers or anything, just people who made love in the afternoon. Yet, David felt a certain obligation to go and help her.

He opened the car door, and he saw Samantha crying. She looked at him and hissed at him.

"GO AWAY!"

He sighed. Why did it have to be like this? Suddenly, seeing her like this made him feel a certain way. He didn't know what it was. Perhaps it was because they had been friends for so long, or because they had so much sex, but seeing her like this broke his heart. He remembered seeing her knocked out. He nearly lost it toward Jack when he saw Samantha in the hospital. At that moment in the car, a strong feeling was pulling him toward her. He didn't know what it was, but he didn't care. He felt as though she needed someone to help her out of her hole... and he was the one to help her.

He got close to her. He grabbed her by the shoulders and stared deeply into her eyes. Samantha started to be freaked out.

"W-what are you doing?" Tears were falling down her eyes. He smiled and spoke deep from his heart. All the feelings about her he tried to repress were suddenly flooding back into one moment. He could barely handle it, so he wondered how Samantha was going to handle it. Yet, if he didn't do anything, she could be like this forever. And he would rather die than see her like that.

"Samantha... It's OK. I know things have been hard for you for so long, and that's just part of life. Sometimes, these things happen. But I just want you to know that I'll be here for you."

She stopped crying and looked deep into his eyes.

"We've been friends for some time, and you know you can always count on me. I will be here for you always. I'll help you out in struggles and times of need. You're crying now, but just know that the pain you feel is nothing compared to the joy that is about to come. Samantha, listen to my words. You do need to change a little bit, yes. (Especially your temper.) Yet, I will love you just the way you are now. I can't bear to see you like this anymore. I care for you deeply, and it hurts my heart to see you suffering.

"You want to know why so many guys like Andrea and not you, but... have you ever thought that there may be a guy that likes you? Yet, you just don't know about it because you're so focused on other people when you need to focus on yourself."

She looked into his eyes, and she saw what he was talking about. She saw who that other man was.

"Y-you... like me?"

He leaned in and kissed her. In a split second, millions of different emotions ran through her head, all of them made her want to cry. Yet, she didn't stop kissing him. She remembered the first time she met David. He partnered up with her to go on a deadly mission in Tibet.

She remembered the plane ride there, and how he wouldn't shut up about how annoying the new actor for Spiderman was. She remembered him saying that he was too much like a pretty boy and too cool for school. The absolute opposite of Spiderman. Only he could say something like that. Then, they went out at night to kill the murderer who had fled. It took them nearly forever to kill him. Almost an entire month. They nearly died. And Samantha remembered passing out and thinking she was going to die. Thankfully, she had David. David protected her through thick and thin. Through every monster that appears at every corner. He was there defending her. Even during their first mission, David felt obligated to protect this poor and helpless hunter. He didn't know why… until today. He loved her. He didn't know why, as they were quite opposite in personalities. But as the old saying goes, 'Opposites attract.'

David even remembered feeling almost betrayed when Samantha got a boyfriend. David looked up and down at him and nearly folded him like a chair. He stopped talking to Samantha for a while, and really only worked on his business idea. He then quit being a hunter to go full-time with the whole flower ship. Samantha never forgot when he left. She felt betrayed and cold. She felt sad. Her friend was about to leave. She didn't even have sex that night with her boyfriend. She was too sad at losing David. And now here he was, kissing her with such intensity and passion that Samantha had never felt in her life.

She used to be attracted to David at one point. She thought his body was cute. Yet, she never did anything because she was too shy. She focused more on trying to be a better hunter, only because she wanted to cloud her shyness away with hard work and training. In reality, she did care and liked David. Yet, she made the big mistake of waiting for him to make a move. Now here he was, finally doing what she wanted him to do for so long.

"Goodness, how many animal crackers does this place have?"

Jack was looking around at all the snacks inside the gas station. There seemed to be a massive amount of animal crackers, but hardly any other snacks. Jack didn't mind, as he loved animal crackers almost more than any other snack. He bought 70 bags and practically spent all his money on animal crackers.

"Um… are you sure you want to buy that many?" Yuri was looking at the sheer quantity of animal crackers. In fact, there were so many that even the cashier looked uneasy and appeared to be sweating from all the bags he had to scan. Jack nodded his head.

"Of course. We need snacks for the ride. Why not get some animal crackers?"

"What about healthy snacks? Like… bananas and apples and some yogurt?"

Jack looked at him, his face contorted and perplexed.

"Are you kidding me? Yogurt, on a 3-hour car trip?"

"We can just buy a small container and eat the whole thing on the way there."

"What if I don't want yogurt?"

"Well, yogurt is better for you than eating damn near an entire gas station's worth of animal crackers!"

"Animal crackers are yummy."

"That doesn't mean that they are healthy. Look at how skinny you are. Maybe if you wanted to gain some muscle or hell, just some mass in general, you should start eating healthier and more whole foods."

Jack snickered.

"First of all… I'm not skinny. I'm pretty cut, to be honest. Look here." Jack lifted up his shirt. It seemed as if someone got a pencil and drew a bunch of lines and muscles. Yuri nodded his head.

"Quite impressive. Yet, how about your arms?"

Jack winced and chuckled at the same time.

"You know, they're not bad. Yeah… they're definitely not as big as yours, but it ain't too bad either."

"How many inches?"

"Let's find out, Yuri."

Yuri grabbed a measuring tape from his backpack and Jack flexed his arm. Yuri put the tape around it and snickered.

"Well then, it looks like it's 14.5 inches. Could be better."

Yuri grabbed the tape and measured his arm. His smile greatly increased, and even Jack was surprised by just how big Yuri's arm was.

"Look at that. 18 inches. I'll be damned, even I didn't think it would be that big."

Jack suddenly crafted a bold idea. If he couldn't beat Yuri in muscle mass, he could surely beat him in definition.

"Now lift up your shirt."

Yuri nodded. Jack was initially shocked at Yuri's stomach. Despite his size, he still had a clear and well-defined stomach. Nowhere near as impressive as Jack's, of course, but it was still nice in its own way. Even more impressive considering just how big Yuri was.

"Not so bad myself," said Yuri as he saw the cashier put all the animal crackers in the bag. Jack nodded his head.

"Yeah, well, I preferred to be toned. Plus, too much muscle will weigh me down in combat. You're more of a brute kind of guy. I prefer stamina and speed."

Yuri couldn't help but laugh.

"You know that you can still add more muscle AND have speed and stamina. In fact, why don't you try training your legs more? Since you like to run so much, it can help you run and spring farther and faster. Adding some upper body muscle would also benefit you in battle since you would be much stronger."

Jack frowned. Everything he was saying, Yuri was telling him to do better. Now, Jack doesn't really care about being a hunter. Yet, he did care about his performance. Could what Yuri was saying really be true, or was he just messing with him? Jack chuckled. Yuri would never do that.

Jack grabbed the animal crackers and threw them in his backpack. He went to go and buy some fruit and a sandwich, trying to eat some more whole foods. Yuri had a face of approval as he purchased his burrito.

Andrea came out of the bathroom. There was definitely something clearly wrong with the breakfast that she and Jack ate in the morning. Yet Jack seemed fine now. So why was she so gassy?

She looked around to see what she could buy. As she was looking, she looked back at Yuri and looked away. *Dammit,* thought Andrea as her mind started to race. She should have never had sex with him. Now she was going to get fired, and things were super awkward in the car. The last time they talked was when they had sex.

Yuri looked back at her. When he saw Natalia, a sense of disappointment and depression hit Yuri like a heavyweight boxer hitting his opponent. Did she just have sex with him because she was in the mood, or because she had feelings for him? Women always confuse him. He tried to talk to a girl one time in school to ask her out because he thought she was interested in him. When he tried to talk to her, she accepted his date. Yet, she never showed up for the date. That really frustrated Yuri, and after that day, he was so traumatized that he never talked to a woman ever again in an explicit or flirtatious way. So was Andrea different, or was she just like that girl at school?

His thoughts would be interrupted as he saw a familiar face enter. Yuri's eyes widened as he saw who it was. It was Jack's old crush from when he first moved here. She looked absolutely miserable.

She was already skinny, but now it appeared that she lost a few dozen kilos. All bones practically. Her face was pale, and there were heavy bangs under her eyes. Her clothes were tattered and torn. Her lips were very dry, and she was struggling to walk. She reeked. It looked and smelled as if she hadn't showered in a week. Worst of all... her left arm. It was... it was destroyed.

Yuri quickly walked up to her.

"Is everything OK?"

She looked at him. Her eyes were totally gone, and her mind was in a daze. She looked dead. Yet, somehow she was barely hanging on.

She muttered something.

"I... bathroom. Get me to the bathroom."

Yuri quickly rushed her to the bathroom. Jack and Andrea saw the poor girl. The cashier was begging to get his money. Andrea quickly went with Yuri, and Jack stayed behind to pay.

"Here. We're in the bathroom."

They were in a family restroom. Yuri let go of the girl and she ended up falling to the ground. Yuri went to go and help her, but she slapped his hand out of the way and she got up herself. She smiled. Some of her teeth were missing.

"Thanks," she muttered as she grabbed some heroin and crystal meth from her pocket. Andrea quickly slapped it out of her hands. The girl screeched and jumped onto Andrea. She tried to claw her eyes out, but Andrea quickly restrained her. It was as if she was a wild animal that had just been caught. She was making such a tangent, and genuinely losing her mind at the thought of Yuri flushing down her drugs.

"NOOOOOOO! WHAT THE FUCK ARE YOU DOING?"

"Putting an end to your misery," said Yuri as he flushed the toilet. She screeched and elbowed Andrea. She lunged at Yuri, but he pimped, smacked her away, and she fell on the floor. She hissed at Yuri.

"Damn you... DAMN YOU! Look at what you've done to me! You ruined everything!"

Yuri and Andrea merely looked at her as she stuck her hand in the toilet, trying to get her drugs back. It was fruitless.

"Don't you go to Wilmhelm High? What are you doing here?"

She ignored Yuri as she continued to scrape the bottom of the toilet with her broken nails. Yuri asked her again one more time.

"What are you doing here? Don't you live far away?"

She creepily turned her head toward him. Her face was in a contorted frown and bulging eyes. She seemed like she came out of a horror movie the way she looked and smelled… and how she hissed nearly every word.

"I CAME HERE TO GET AWAY FROM WILMHELM! My boyfriend and I were going on vacation, and we just needed to take a… quick pit stop."

"Didn't you go to Jack and I's high school?"

"Yeah, but I dropped out."

"Why?"

"Wouldn't you like to know, nigger?"

Andrea kicked the girl in her face as hard as she could. She hit her head on the toilet and spat out a few of her teeth. Andrea picked her up by her shirt and started hitting her. Yuri pulled Andrea away for a second.

"What the hell is wrong with you?"

Andrea nearly spit on the poor girl. "That junkie deserves what she gets for calling you such a slur."

Yuri shook his head. "Let me deal with that. I appreciate your integrity and kindness, but right now that poor girl needs help instead of being treated like garbage. Just… please."

Yuri helped the poor girl up.

"What's your name?"

It took her a while for her to respond, but she said, "The name is Helena."

"Nice to meet you, Helena. Now… can I have a chat with you and your boyfriend?"

Outside, Jack was waiting for all three of them when he noticed someone inside a black car. The car was turned on, but the person inside was slumped. Jack went to investigate. The van had been locked, and he heard some strange noises coming from inside. Since he had nothing better to do, he decided to investigate. He got closer and saw that the man was asleep. Although he was in a word position. He was hunched over, and his head was hitting the steering wheel. *Strange,* thought Jack as he got closer to the car.

Jack dropped off all of the groceries. The man was dead, and there were kilos and kilos of meth, heroin and cocaine all in the backseat. *Holy cow,* thought Jack. This obviously wasn't his first time seeing all of this, but it was his first time seeing a dead person. Jack opened the car door to investigate even further.

"Holy…Oh my God." Jack leaned over and puked. The sheer smell of the body was enough to make any man go mad. Jack nearly cried.

"What in the world?" Jack looked back to see Helena screaming and crying. She pushed Jack away from the car and looked inside. She screamed even louder as she collapsed on the floor and cried. Jack soon realized that the man inside the car was probably her boyfriend. Jack recognized the girl.

"Hey, aren't you—"

"SHUT UP!" She clawed at his arm and blood oozed from his forearm. It actually hurt. He stepped away from the wild and feral animal that was in front of her. Looking at the way she looked, and how she acted, reminded Jack of some sort of animal that was stricken with some sort of unknown and horrible syndrome. An animal that was ready to pounce and attack at any given moment.

Helena scrambled inside the car and grabbed all of the drugs. She shoved them down her shirt and her pants.

Yuri walked outside and became furious seeing her doing such an action. "What do you think you're doing?"

He walked over to Helena, but she clawed at him the same way she clawed at Jack. Yuri stepped back, avoiding the damage. She started grabbing more and more of the drugs. Jack and Yuri looked at each other uncomfortably. Jack shivered. Was he… ever like that?

"Hey, calm down," said Jack. He tried touching her but realized that it wouldn't be such a good idea. She would probably just attack him again. Andrea had enough, and she grabbed Helena.

Helena tried to claw Andrea's eyes out, but Andrea simply kneed her and slammed her head into the car window, shattering the glass and making Helena fall over. Blood oozed onto the concrete like how cement oozed out of a truck.

"What the hell is your problem?" asked Jack furiously as he put his hands on Andrea. She quickly yanked her hand back. "Don't fucking touch me!"

"Damn it, woman! What is your problem? All day today you've been acting up. What's the matter? Can't you see that she needs help?"

Jack slammed the car door and helped Helena up. Helena pushed him away and tried to go back to the drugs, Jack pulled her away as she screamed and hissed. Jack held her firmly as Yuri went and took out all of the drugs from her clothes.

"HELP! RAPE, RAPE! HELP ME!"

Jack and Yuri shivered as people started coming out of the gas station. Now people were looking at them, and nearby cars were taking photos and pulling over to see what was going on.

"Dammit," muttered Jack. "Can't you just be quiet for a second!" His voice was powerful, and firm. It nearly made Helena shut up.

"Hey, what's going on?" A father stepped out of his car, and his wife and two children were looking. *Oh no,* thought Andrea, as the father took a look at the car and at Helena. She screamed out for help. *Great,* thought Jack, as his eyes widened when he saw all of the narcotics and the dead boyfriend in the car. He nearly shrieked as he went back to his car and called the police.

Andrea ran over and grabbed his phone. She threw it away. He pushed her, and she roundhouse-kicked him. The wife from the car screamed as she stepped out. This time with a loaded gun. She cocked the revolver back and shot it at Andrea. Andrea nearly dogged it as it grazed her shoulder. She gritted her teeth. The worst part about all of this was that it hit a fuel pump. Oil quickly splattered out, and soon chaos ensued. The people inside came outside to see the commotion occurring.

Jack and Yuri were quickly distracted, and Helena took this time to escape their grasp. She screamed for help as she ran inside the gas station.

"HELP ME! THESE MEN ARE TRYING TO RAPE AND KILL ME!"

Jack tried to remain calm, but it was quite difficult when the passing cars pulled over to see what was happening. Soon, Andrea, Yuri and Jack were met with nearly two dozen people yelling and cursing at them. To add fuel to the fire, they heard police sirens.

"We need to get out of here ASAP," said Jack as he tried to run away. Yuri grabbed his hand.

"No. We need to help Helena."

"Man, she's a junkie. I'm sorry, but we can't help someone who doesn't want to be helped."

Yuri looked at Jack. His face was disgusted, and he almost spit on the floor. He shook his head at Jack, and Jack felt a wave of guilt crash inside his heart.

"Don't you have any sympathy? Wouldn't you like it if someone were to help you?"

Jack remained speechless as Yuri went away and tried to get Helena. The mob swarmed him. They attacked him and started beating him. *Lord, forgive me for what I'm about to do,* thought Yuri, as he started fighting back. He hit an old lady and shattered a man's collarbone. He grabbed Helena as she screamed again and called for help. Soon, people were attacking and grabbing Helena in all of the confusion.

Andrea was paralyzed with confusion and fear. She quickly spun her head and saw the mother reloading the gun. She was about to fire it at Yuri, who was being nearly beaten to death. Jack tried to help him, but he had his own battles to face as nearly a dozen people swarmed him and tried to attack him.

Andrea lunged at the gun as it went off. She was able to push it slightly to the right. Unfortunately, it would be a grave mistake. It quickly hit the oil that was splashing out of the fuel pump.

Fire was seen, and people started to panic. Yuri grabbed Helena, and he made a break for the van. The police had finally arrived.

"EVERYBODY FREEZE!" The police officers emerged from their vehicle with their weapons showing. Andrea put her hand up in the air as fast as she could. Yuri ignored them as he opened the van, only to find David and Samantha going at it.

"Holy shit, I leave you two alone for 4 fucking seconds and—"

The gas station exploded.

Jack was not sure what happened much after that, as he was too busy trying to grab his severed arm. Blood was dripping and oozing out of his left shoulder. His arm was gone. Burning to bits. Jack looked around. There were several people burning, dying and bleeding. The cars were exploding, which only added more confusion to the chaos. The van nearly flipped over. And a naked David had to push it upward. The police cars exploded, killing the two cops. The gas station had become a fragment of itself as there were bodies piled up on top of one another. The air was hot, and he could hardly see.

He looked around to see where his friends were. Helena's upper half was all the way across the gas station, and Yuri's leg was nowhere to be seen. He was unconscious on the floor... or maybe even dead. Samantha walked outside to see the aftermath. Andrea was on the floor. She looked like she had been in a war. Her hair was bloody, and her body was bruised and scraped. The screams of the children only added to the sheer horror that Jack was witnessing. All of this... for one girl who wasn't even alive.

Jack screamed as more of the gas station blew up, sending him flying out onto the open highway. He stood up, but it was too late. He was hit by a car going nearly 100. It sent him flying into the fire. Jack screamed once more as he felt the blood coming from his shoulder becoming more and more painful by the second. His lower leg started to burn, and he quickly ran out. He looked like a horror monster. He was on fire, and his limbs were missing. Truly something horrific.

David grabbed a fire extinguisher in the van. (Yes, there was one.) And put Jack out of his misery. Jack fell to the floor. He passed out.

"We need to leave now," said Samantha as she heard more sirens. They grabbed everyone and quickly drove off. David looked in his rearview mirror at the absolute insanity that had happened.

"Oh my God," said Samantha as she put her hand over her mouth. She was trying to stop the blood from oozing out from Yuri's leg, but it was nearly impossible. He was losing too much blood too fast. Jack was starting to spasm as well.

David tried driving faster, but they were still quite some distance from the nearest gas station.

Yuri was losing it. He started fading in and out from life and death. Samantha saw his eyes roll back and forth several times. Oh no, not this. This was supposed to be a fun road trip, dammit. Why was all of this happening? It seemed like no matter where they went, trouble was sure to follow them.

"Oh my God," muttered Samantha as she was trying her absolute hardest to cauterize and pressure the wound. Andrea was out cold, and Jack was also on the brink of death. Just nearly hanging on because he had a beautiful girlfriend at home that was waiting for him. He couldn't possibly imagine dying without his love. No, he wouldn't. He would stay strong… but he didn't know if he had anything else left in his tank. He was tired, and everything was starting to feel cold. He could feel it, he could feel death standing above him. With an eerie smile just WAITING for him to give up so he could take him. In fact, even Samantha felt it. Death was in the car, just waiting for all of them.

Death smiled as Yuri gasped out for the last time in his life. The loss of blood was too much. He could no longer take it. As his eyes rolled back, he could see a warm light. He felt warmth, and he could smell honey and bread. It smelled so good, and he felt a wonderful and amazing comfortable feeling. A feeling of pure joy and happiness. One he had never felt before. He felt his body… flying. Flying up. He could see… Helena in the distance. She was wearing a beautiful and pretty white dress. She was waiting for him. Yuri felt a little bit sad, he was leaving his best friend. He didn't want to go actually, he wanted to stay with his best friend. But… Helena told him that it would be alright, and that soon they would all see each other again sooner or later. He wouldn't have to suffer anymore. Yuri smiled.

"YURI! YURI, STAY WITH ME!" Samantha was trying her hardest, but it didn't help. She yelled at Yuri, but it was fruitless. Yuri's soul had already left his body. He was with Helena now, and the warmth they felt was wonderful. Soon, there was a figure next to them. Holding them both with love and care. He kissed them both on the cheek and told them how well and wonderful they had done. Soon, Death smiled as he also went up. His job here was done… for now. He would be back later.

Samantha pressed her head against Yuri's chest. He was no more.

Yuri was dead.

Samantha sat down, she appeared dead. Her face and her body went pale.

"Samantha, is everything OK?" asked David. He was driving as fast as he possibly could. Samantha looked at Jack. He was still alive, but she figured that he wouldn't be for much longer. She looked back at Yuri, and she couldn't help herself. She cursed, screamed and cried. David didn't need to look back to figure out that Yuri was no more. He smelled death. He bowed his head down and shook his head. Dammit… why Yuri? He was the best man out of everyone. Why him? Why, God?

Samantha gripped Yuri's body tightly and cried into his shoulder. The stench of death, fear and sadness filled the car as David rode on.

They had all made it to the hospital. Jack was barely hanging on and was in the ICU. Andrea was in a room having emergency surgery done on her. Several pieces of car shrapnel had entered her stomach and legs. Samantha and David sat in the waiting room, slowly taking in everything that had happened.

They both sat in silence as they heard people talking and cell phones going off. David looked up to find the TV news coverage of a gas station that had killed 14 people. Jack, Andrea and Yuri were now all wanted criminals. Once they were done with Andrea's surgery, they would send her to jail. Once Jack's recovery had finished, they would send him off to prison. David and Samantha would be questioned as to how they were in contact with those three, now two, fugitives. Yuri's body was still in the van.

David bowed his head down. He hadn't felt this depressed since… well, almost never, actually. This was the first time he was feeling a strong and horrifying sense of dread, and a sudden urge to end it all. Samantha didn't feel quite so strong, but she did feel as though things were hopeless. They called John, and he was quickly on his way over.

As they waited, a doctor came out to greet them. Both quickly stood up.

The doctor had a sad and disappointed look on his face. David was frightened merely looking at the doctor. Samantha quickly left the room. She had a feeling about what he would say, and he didn't want to hear it.

"Doctor... is everything OK?"

The doctor merely looked at David. He gave a very weak and fake smile.

"I'm sorry, but my team and I tried my best. Unfortunately, the wounds that your friend Andrea sustained were too much. She passed away midway through the surgery. I'm sorry."

David's heart nearly ripped in half. He felt a cold breeze pass by him, and he could feel death leaving the hospital. As he left, Death whispered in Davd's ear, "I'll be back. Don't you worry."

David closed his eyes and nodded his head. He held down all his emotions at the bottom of his heart for now.

"I see. Well then... what about Jack?"

"Jack is in critical condition. To be quite frank, I am unaware if he will make it or not. He had sustained too many injuries, and his body's vitals are rapidly decreasing. We are trying our hardest, but it's too early to say if he'll pull through or not. Right now, he's in a coma."

"A WHAT?"

"I understand this is difficult, sir. I'll give you some time alone."

The doctor walked away as David sat down. He closed his eyes and started to cry. Not this again. He shook his head as his lips quivered. He had never cried so horribly like this before. He took a step outside and started to cry more and more. Why... why was all of this happening? This was supposed to be a fun trip, dammit. And now two of his friends were dead, and one was in a coma and might not survive.

He sat down on a curb and started smoking some weed. It didn't help one bit. In fact, it made it worse. He sat by himself, having no idea where Samantha possibly was. He didn't care, though. In fact, he was starting to care about nothing. Everything was going to end, so why even care? David had thought about ending it with Samantha since nothing mattered anymore, right?

John pulled up on his motorcycle. He quickly rushed over to David.

"Hey, man... what's going on?"

David looked up. He had never once seen John sad, or worried in his life. Another rare thing to happen on this road trip.

"Nothing too good. Yuri and Andrea are dead. Jack's in a coma, and he's also a wanted fugitive."

John sat down abruptly. "I see." He sat next to David. He also was quiet and didn't say anything for a while. He soaked up all the knowledge that was given to him.

"Well… I'll be damned. What happened?"

"A gas station exploded."

"WHAT? How on God's green earth—"

"It's a long story. Yuri was trying to help some poor junk, and in turn, things went south real quickly. It's a real mess, let me tell you. I have no idea where Samantha is and… and…"

David started to cry again. He put his head down and sobbed as John hugged him, like a mother hugging her child when he was sad or depressed.

14

Jack woke up. The room was a complete blur. He saw nobody at all, and he was cold. His head was pounding like there was a hammer inside. He went to move his left arm… but realized that there was nothing there. He looked down and saw in horror that his arm was gone.

"Oh my goodness," muttered Jack as his mind raced. He felt ill and sick. He felt like he just wanted to stay in bed all day long. The room was dark, but he could see something in the corner of his eyes. Jack's head hurt so much that he dared not move it, but he could see something staring at him from the corner of the room. Something dark, and sinister. It looked at Jack and had an evil smile. It quickly arose and made itself apparent.

As it moved closer to Jack, Jack could feel the stench of death and the cold, cold air that went with it. There was a sense of impending doom and dread as it moved and appeared closer to Jack. Jack's eyes widened, and his mouth dropped open. He realized what this vile and horrible thing was. It was Death. Staring right into the depths of his heart AND his soul.

"Hello," said Death. Even its voice was foul and horrifying. Jack nearly screamed, but he couldn't. Almost as if Death was preventing him from screaming. Its giant white smile and its horrifying grin made Jack become so fearful and so horrifying, that he was suddenly now filled with energy to run and get out of there.

Jack started to hyperventilate. He couldn't believe it. It was actually Death, staring into his soul and his eyes. Jack felt his heart rush and race at a million miles an hour. He was sweating bullets, and his lips suddenly became dry. His mind was a mess, and his body shook in cold misery. Death howled in excitement.

"Calm down, boy. I'm not here for you… at least not yet. I've come here to give you a message."

Jack was freaking out. This… evil thing was speaking to him.

Death laughed once more. This time, even louder. Nobody in the hospital could hear him, as he heard nurses and doctors talking outside without a care in the world.

"Don't worry, boy, I'm not evil. I won't hurt you, but then again, I'm not good either. I'm just here to do my job. God calls upon me whenever someone's time is near."

Death pointed his finger at Jack.

"You, my boy, have luck. God himself has cast His smile upon you. It seems you're quite lucky. Several times you were supposed to die, and yet, here you are.

"When you overdosed on cocaine all those years ago in Pittsburgh, I was supposed to take you. Yet, God had different plans. He gave life to you once more and told me to wait. Today, you were supposed to die. I was there in the van, just itching to take your soul. Yet, once again, God has shown his mercy and compassion upon you. He told me to take Yuri instead. That poor man was too good for this world anyway. Andrea, on the other hand… well, let's just say that God will be talking to her firmly.

"Anyway, my dear boy, that's not what I'm here to talk about. In reality, I'm here to give you a message. God wants me to tell you that your time is near. Enjoy the moments with all the people you can. With your beloved, with your friends… anybody you can think of. Don't worry when that time is, because only God knows. I don't even know.

"You, my friend, truly have been blessed by God. Not only should you have died several times, but as well, you have that 'gift.' The one that can enter other people's minds. I don't think you thought too much of it now, but know that God gave you that gift for a reason. A gift like that is special and should be treasured. Yet, I don't think you thought too much of it. In fact, you don't even want to be a hunter. Don't worry, though, It's all part of God's plan. It's your divine destiny to be a hunter. Everything in your life that has happened was by God's sovereign will. Even if you nearly overdosed and ran a small drug empire… yeah, that was God's will. Yuri dies, and the gas station explodes. Yeah… that was God's will. I don't know why he does those things, but then again, it's not my job to. I simply only take people's souls when God tells me it's time.

"It's not your time yet, but soon it will be. Be prepared, and use your gifts wisely. Your skills and attributes were not given to you by accident. Go forth and do what you're told. Remember me, Jack, I'll see you again. This time… for the last."

Death cackled as it suddenly vanished away.

Jack threw up a little bit. *Holy cow,* thought Jack as he rubbed his eyes. A nurse came in and was shocked to see Jack.

She quickly rushed over to him and helped him out. Soon, doctors were coming in to examine him. They were bombarding him with questions and analyzing him. He shouldn't have been up so early, and he shouldn't have been as healthy as he was. It was… as if God had shown him mercy.

All the while this was happening, Jack couldn't get out of his mind what Death had told him.

'I'll see you again. This time… for the last.'

Only God knew when that was. Jack might as well spend as much time with his friends as he could.

Jack was sitting on his bed when he heard a knock on his door. Without even skipping a beat, Yuri entered through the door. Jack perched up. Yuri!

"Yuri… what are you doing here?"

Jack smiled as he hugged Yuri.

Yuri smiled back. He looked as healthy as he had ever been.

"Well… I actually came here to talk to you," said Yuri as he sat down next to Jack. Jack smiled. Yuri smiled alongside Jack. His smile was so comforting, and so filled with warmth.

"To tell you the truth, Jack… I came here to talk to you about your behavior."

Jack's smile slowly started to fade away. "Excuse me?"

"Let me explain. Jack, you're a wonderful person. More than you could ever think of. Yet, sometimes you need to be nicer! That girl, she needed help. Yet, you just wanted to abandon her and ignore her. How would you feel if you were in need of help, and people decided to ignore you? You wouldn't like it?"

Jack shook his head. "No, but she was ignoring our help."

"Only because she wasn't in the right mindset. With a little bit of help from some friends and doctors, she could become normal again. After all, you were like her for a point. Don't you remember?"

Jack was taken aback. "How do you know that?"

Yuri smiled. "Don't worry about it. Anyway, when you were like that, you needed help. It wasn't until a series of events showed you that you needed to quit that lifestyle. Unfortunately, that poor girl didn't have the chance to have those events. She needed people to help her. You could have been one of those people, but you instead chose to ignore her. I was the one who tried to help her, and because of it I'm now dead."

"W-what? You're talking to me right now."

Jack touched Yuri. "See, my hand-"

"Listen closely, Jack." Yuri grabbed Jack's hand firmly. Even his touch was filled with care and love.

"Be a better person. If not for the people that you can save, then for me. Please, Jack, I would love to see you become a better person. Change, my friend. Change into the man that I know you can become. Change into the man that God made you out to be. Please, my friend?"

Jack nodded his head, thinking nothing of what Yuri was telling him.

"Why, yes, of course, but—"

"Good."

Yuri stood up and hugged Jack once more. He smiled as he walked out of his room. Before he walked out, he looked back at Jack and said, "I miss you, but I know we'll see each other again soon."

Then Yuri left, and Jack became very tired and closed his eyes.

Jack woke up once more. This time, with handcuffs attached to his right hand. He looked around, David, Samantha and John were all staring at him. Jack felt a wave of confusion as he looked up. The room was much brighter than before, a stark contrast to the dark room he was just in. Plus, three of his friends were there. Where was Andrea and Yuri?

"Jack, oh thank goodness, you're awake," said Samantha as she hugged him. Jack could feel his left arm move, yet he knew that it was gone and that he couldn't grab anything. It was miserable.

David walked over to him. His face, despite seeing Jack being okay, was still one of great worry. The same with John.

"How are you feeling?" asked John. Jack nodded his head.

"A little bit… eerie. Dispute that, I'm all sunshine and rainbows."

A quiet dread fell over into the room. Samantha spoke up.

"Jack… this is gonna suck, but Yuri and Andrea are dead. You're also being taken to prison for your involvement in the gas station incident."

Jack felt like his body shattered into a million pieces. What was she talking about? He just saw Yuri a moment ago, and… was he really wanted? He hardly even did anything.

"W-what?" said Jack as he stood up.

"I just saw Yuri a moment ago, and I had nothing to do with anything at the gas station. I—"

"Wait, you saw Yuri?" John got closer to Jack. "Well, dammit, son, where is he?"

"He came in here a moment ago. I swear I—"

"Jack," said Samantha. Tears were strolling down her eyes. She looked depressed and had aged about two years in the span of an afternoon.

"Yuri is dead. I saw him die. So is Andrea."

Impossible, thought Jack as he looked at the door. Just moments ago Yuri was there, talking to him. Now they were saying he was dead… impossible.

Jack tried to argue, but it was fruitless. No matter what he said, they just didn't believe him. He bowed his head… still refusing to believe the truth. Perhaps… he was imagining things. If he did talk to Yuri… was that really Yuri then, or his ghost, or was it just a dream? Yet, he still remembered what Yuri told him. About changing who he was. If he remembered that, then he could also remember what Death told him. He… really wasn't imagining things. Yet… how could they not see it, but he can? It made no sense.

"Anyway," continued Samantha. "The police are here. They were just waiting for you to wake up. I'm sorry, Jack, but you'll be taken to court, and you'll be tried there. I hired a lawyer, but I don't think you'll win this one."

She leaned in and gave him a kiss on the forehead. "I'm sorry about this, Jack… this was all supposed to be a good time, and instead…"

She couldn't bear to finish her sentence. She cried as she walked away. David followed behind her, leaving only John and Jack.

John sat down on a chair next to Jack.

"Well, I'll be damned. Quite a day today?"

Jack said nothing. John coughed.

"Sorry about that, just making some light joke for the moment."

"It's quite alright… John, was it?"

"That's right!"

Jack smiled. "Sorry, I don't think we've been properly introduced. I'm guessing you're also a hunter simply by your association with Samantha and David?"

"Sure am. Was born and raised in Wilmhelm. A damn small town, but it has its charms, wouldn't you say?"

Jack chuckled and shook his head. "Yeah, no way. It's too small for me, and there's this weird vibe with the people and everyone else around the surrounding area. I don't like it, and it freaks me out. I wish I could get out, but I already found myself stuck in a job that I can't quite leave."

"Heh. I feel you a little bit. It is weird, but I guess that's part of its charm. It's like that town you stop at when you're on a road trip and you just want a bite to eat, or you just want to rest somewhere. Doesn't that sound like the perfect place to put a top-secret organization right smack underground?"

Jack nodded his head with a smile.

"Yeah, in that sense, I guess you could say that S.H.O.T. headquarters would be a good place to be in a town like that, yeah. Haha. So... how do you know David?"

"Oh... we used to be best buds, to be honest. That is before he got fired."

Jack perched up a little bit. His curiosity was heightened. "I'm sorry... fired? He told me he quit."

John did the same as Jack. "Quit, man. Natalia fired him on the SPOT when she caught him... actually, never mind."

"No... what is it?"

John shook his head and waved his hand.

"I... I don't know if I can say. Not too many people knew what happened. Only me, a few other hunters, and Natalia and David, of course. It was... a bad situation that David was in, let's just say that. Once he got fired, we kind of stopped talking since he was angry at Natalia and decided to open up a flower shop. The flowers there ain't so bad, actually."

Jack was shocked. There was so much information happening all at the same time. He didn't know how to process it.

"Wait. You're telling me that David was fired, and not even Samantha knows about this?"

"Nope. Like I said, it was a bad situation. It was even a scandal, really. Shit hit the fan real quick, and Natalia had him go immediately. She did her best to cover it up and threatened me and my buddies if we ever told anybody. She also threatened David if he ever said that he was fired.

"He was well-liked in the hunter organization. Most hunters would have complained to Natalia if David was fired, and I don't think she was trying to deal with all of that. They would have complained partially because they liked him so much, but also because he almost never did anything wrong. I think… Nah… I can't say. I don't know too much of the details. All I know is that we best keep it a secret and don't go and tell Natalia about this, or she'll have my head. Understood, compadre?"

Jack nodded his head. John smiled.

"Bueno."

Jack looked ahead. His eyes blank and his mind racing. Perfect, just perfect—more information today that he didn't need to hear.

There was a knock on the door, and the cops came in. They gave John a look, and he quickly walked out of there. Before he left the room, he gave Jack an earnest smile and a nod, practically saying, 'Good luck, kiddo. You got this!'

Jack smiled as he was interrogated by the cops.

"Oh, what are we going to do?" Samantha was leaning next to the van outside. She was holding David's hand, and tears were streaming down her eyes. She looked inside to see Yuri's body. It was making the car smell, and the stench was too bad for a nearly 4-hour drive back to Wilmhelm. Yet, she didn't just want to leave it anywhere. She wanted to give it a proper burial. A proper sending away. She thought about what Yuri would want. Where would he like to be buried?

"Maybe… we can bear the stench and ride back to Wilmhelm. Perhaps we even bury him there?" said David.

Samantha shook her head.

"I don't know. I don't even think he would want to be buried there."

"What makes you say that?"

Samantha took a deep breath and shrugged.

"I don't know, it's just… It's been such a hard day, and I can't even think straight."

She leaned into David's arms, and he held her close. He peeled inside the glass to find Yuri's lifeless body staring right into his eyes. He had a smile, something David had never seen on a dead body before. In a way, it almost creeped David out. He put his head down, still feeling the cold stare of Yuri's dead body.

David spoke up as he kissed Samantha's head. "Did you speak to the doctor about Andrea's body?"

Samantha nodded her head. "Yeah. He said that he's gonna keep it in a mortuary until we can find a funeral director."

David chuckled. "Do you want to do that?"

Samantha shook her head. "No. We can't collect the body. Only the family can. And to be quite honest, I don't think her mother or her damned father would want to come and collect her body. From the brief time that I've ever talked to her, she mentioned that her family doesn't think too highly of her (especially her mother). I don't think they would want to come and collect her body."

David was silent for a moment. Despite his looking away from Yuri's body, his gaze always shifted back to his lifeless and soulless eyes. It was as if it was trying to trap David into staring into its impending gaze forever and ever. It wasn't until Samantha pulled him aside that he was able to break his gaze.

"Are you OK?"

David nodded his head. "Yeah, I'm just…"

He was at a loss for words. What would he say? OK? Because he sure as shit wasn't, and to make matters even more complicated, they had no way of getting Andrea's body back. Furthermore, Jack was being escorted away into the back of a police car.

"Oh David… What are we possibly ever going to do?"

David took a deep breath. He had a plan brewing inside his mind for Andrea. As for Jack… well, he would leave that up to God. Although he did have an ace up his sleeve. A very tricky one that could cause him lots of pain and suffering, but he still had an ace up his sleeve.

David looked to the entrance to see John leaving. David quickly rushed over to John and greeted him. He whispered something in his ear, and John's eyes widened.

"Man, do you know what would happen if they caught me?"

David put his hands on John's shoulders.

"I know, that's why I'm asking you. Please, I need your help. You're the only one that I know can do it right now."

John shook his head as he walked away. "Why not… Samantha?"

"She's… not in the best spot mentally right now. I can't because I'm going to try to get Jack out of the mess he's in right now and—"

"How are you possibly going to do that? Man, he's going to prison!"

David gave John a very stern, and confident look. John's eyes widened as he shook his head. He nearly laughed as he was finally understanding David's ace card.

"Listen, David, do you know what will happen if your 'master plan' backfires? Hell, even I wouldn't want to—"

"I fully understand the risks involved. And I'm willing to take it. I am NOT going to let Jack suffer right now. Now after everything that has happened. Please, don't forget that I'm also putting a lot of stress on myself for this. If you could just please do a little bit—just a little bit on your end—I would forever be grateful to you."

John opened his mouth, he was about to say something when he stopped. He took off his cowboy hat and wiped his hair with his hand. This plan… it was making him sweat. If he was caught, then it would be game over.

Still, David was also risking damn near his entire career and life to get Jack out of prison. Surely, if he was going to do that, then John could do a simple, yet big favor. John closed his eyes. The last time he was in a sticky situation like this was when he was 15 years old. He was busted for trying to break into a movie theater. The cops at the time were willing to take him to jail, but they told him that if he did them a 'small' favor, then he would be let go, and they would turn a blind eye. John immediately accepted as he was so scared of what his super strict parents would do to him if they ever found him in jail. John never forgot that feeling as he accepted their little 'small favor' and they forced him to suck their dicks.

John nodded his head, Hoping that something as bad as that wouldn't happen. "OK then, partner. I'll help you out."

David smiled as he hugged John.

"Thank you so much, John. You're truly an angel, my friend."

"Not yet I am. I still need to uphold my end. Remember to do yours, and please… be careful."

David nodded his head. John smiled as he waved goodbye to both of them and rode off into the sunset.

David walked back to Samantha and kissed her on her forehead.

"OK. First thing first, we take Yuri's body back to Wilmhelm. We tell his family and let them decide what to do with the body. They will hate us for sure, but at least they'll have the peace of deciding what to do. As for us… you'll stay home and just relax for now. I have some stuff I need to attend."

"Like what?"

David shook his head as he started the van. "Don't worry about it. Just relax for now. The worst is over now."

He wished he was telling her the truth.

15

It was nearly midnight, and John was standing outside the hospital. David had asked him to steal Andrea's body. John initially denied it because if he got caught, then he might as well be in the same prison cell as Jack.

He was sure that there were so few people inside that he could easily sneak into the morgue. He circled around, avoiding the spotlight from the guards, and he made his way inside through the back. He had no idea where the morgue was, nor did he have any ideas, but a favor was a favor, and he would scour the place as much as he could until he found Andrea's body. He was nearly caught several times. David thought he was the right man for this job, but he wasn't. During all his years of training, he was horrible at stealth. Still, for sneaking around a hospital late at night, he felt as though he was doing pretty well.

John snooped around until he found the stairs that led to the basement. He quickly rushed downstairs to find the morgue. It was freezing cold, and John could see his very own breath. The stench was horrendous, too. John searched the bodies to find which one was Andreas. As he searched, all the bodies that he saw looked horrifying. Some had their stomachs exposed, others had limbs missing, and one body was practically just a torso with a right arm. Yet, even after searching for quite a while, he couldn't find out where Andrea's body was.

His thought process would be interrupted as somebody approached. John quickly hid in an empty storage area but quickly regretted it as it was freezing cold. He would have to suffer, though, as a doctor entered, humming a very similar tune.

The doctor looked through some old paperwork as he examined patient #8. A poor woman who had half of her body ripped to bits and pieces when she was near an explosion at a gas station. Her family was on the way to pick her up.

As the doctor examined the woman, John quickly got out of the storage area and snuck around. The doctor heard him and exclaimed out loud, "WHO'S THERE?"

No answers. John could feel his heartbeat in his chest. Great, oh great, if he was caught, he was done for. His parents might just come back from the dead to whip him like they used to when he was younger. The doctor examined the silence a little bit more and then went back to examining patient #8. That was close, thought John as he started sneaking his way toward the exit. He was so close, just a few more steps. However, what really surprised him was that Andrea's body was nowhere to be seen. David had told him that he was certain it was here, yet he looked all over the place, and it was missing. Something was off.

John would also have to think about that later as he stumbled over something, causing him to trip and make a huge ruckus. The doctor quickly spun around and pointed his finger at John.

"HEY! What do you think you're doing here?"

Crap, thought John as he quickly stood up.

"Where is Andrea?"

The doctor looked shocked. "Excuse me?"

"Andrea. The lady who was transferred here after the gas station incident. Isn't she here?"

The doctor shook his head. "That's confidential information. You're not supposed to be here. Stay here while I—"

John rushed him. He grabbed the doctor's throat and slammed it against the table, John quickly put the doctor in a triangle hold, and soon the doctor was fast asleep.

"Sorry about that. I just can't let you go telling this to anybody."

John grabbed the doctor's clothes and put them on. He quickly hid the doctor's body and rushed upstairs, acting nonchalantly as if nothing happened. As he was walking, he was getting weird and uncanny stares. He bowed his head down. They were catching on. Dammit, he had to get out of here fast, or else things would go sideways.

John was quickly stopped by security personnel.

"Excuse me, doctor," said the officer. He was massive and looked like he could fold David in half with his pinky.

"Um... sir. What could I help you with?"

"There is an emergency in room 212. The doctor upstairs is missing, and the nurses need medical personnel immediately."

John quickly followed behind the massive man. *Oh great,* thought John as he headed up the stairs. He quickly entered the room to find a patient giving birth. The midwife was next to her, comforting her. The nurses were panicking as they were frantically running around the room like chickens without a head.

"Um… sir. You have mistaken me. I'm not an obstetrician. I'm—"

"Doctor, thank goodness you're here," said a nurse as she pulled John away. John's heart sank. He had never ever delivered a child before. Sure, he got a few girls pregnant, but they usually get abortions and cut off all contact with John. Nothing more than that. John panicked as he did not know the first thing to do.

He looked at the women giving birth. His heart stopped. He recognized this woman. She looked up from her pain, and her eyes were filled with rage. She gritted her teeth and clutched her hands together.

This was the same woman he had a drunken one-night stand with all those months ago. Could this child be…

"YOU!" she yelled as she screamed out in pain. John could barely see the head of the baby coming out. He started to sweat as she yelled and cursed at him for ignoring her.

"Um… nurses. Quick, give her more painkillers. She's becoming delusional from all of the pain."

John started to sweat. This is NOT happening right now. The nurses were helping her out and examining the baby. The woman was screaming too much, and no matter how hard she pushed, it just seemed like the baby wouldn't come out.

The nurse shook her head and grabbed John by his shoulder.

"Sorry, doctor, but we need to do a C-section."

"A WHAT?"

The nurse quickly grabbed a cart full of surgical knives. John panicked as the knives looked more like instruments of horror than anything else. He gulped down and panicked. No, no way, this was some sort of dream. He would wake up and—

"DOCTOR, PLEASE HELP UP!"

Oh NO! John grabbed the knife. As the old saying goes, 'Fake it till you make it.' But if he did one wrong thing, it was game over.

John got closer to the woman's stomach. Her angry and frustrated face never once left John's eyesight. John gulped. It was already hard as is doing what he was, but with an angry lady looking at hi,, John only prayed above that the baby wasn't his. *OK... just think,* thought John as he examined the woman's stomach and genitals. His mother tried explaining to him one time how C-sections work. She explained it to him since John was born via C-section. (He weighed almost 5 kilos when he was born.) Yet, he ignored her since he was too busy daydreaming about girls. Now here he was. He sure wished that he had paid attention to his mom.

The nurses were screaming at him, and one even went out to get another doctor. John took a deep breath and tried his best. If he failed... oh well.

John held the knife firmly. He made a slow and deep cut on the woman's abdomen and uterus area. She screamed some more as the painkillers were starting to wear off. John could see the head and the general body of the baby. He grabbed the baby's head.

"DOCTOR, WHAT ARE YOU DOING? YOU NEED TO MAKE A BIGGER HOLE?"

"Oh yes... I knew that."

John cut the wound open some more, but he made too big of a cut. Now the poor woman was bleeding out. John gritted his teeth as the nurses looked at him. He recognized that look. They figured him out. Still, they had a childbirth that was right in front of them that needed to be taken care of.

John grabbed the baby by the head... and ripped it out of the mother's stomach. The woman screamed so loud she shattered her vocal cords, and the nurses and everyone else were screaming. The baby was shrieking, and John was holding the baby with two hands by its head.

"Oh... congratulations. It's a baby boy. With a fine set of lungs, too."

John quickly cut the umbilical cord and handed it over to the nurse to clean it up. As he was handing it over, the blood made his hand slippery, and he accidentally dropped the baby.

Oh no, thought John as chaos ensued even more. The nurse grabbed it from him and pushed him away. The women cried tears of joy and sadness, all while angrily looking at John. John looked at the baby... and had a sigh of relief. The kid looked nothing like him, thank goodness.

The chaos wouldn't end there as the doctor from earlier, along with some security guards, burst in the door.

"THERE! That's the man that knocked me out."

Uh oh, thought John as he made a run for it. He ran toward the window and jumped out. It was not as badass as it was in the movies. He felt his face being cut into small bits and pieces, and he landed in a strange way and broke his leg. Thankfully, there was a hospital to treat his wounds nearby.

John quickly stood up and started to limp away. He hopped on his motorcycle and started riding away. The police started following him and ordered him to pull over. He refused, and he sped up. The police continued to warn and warn him… but John denied all of their attempts to plead with him to pull over. John continued to speed down the highway, nearly hitting a bunch of cars along the way. The police had enough and opened fire.

John swerved as many cars as he could, and started going so fast that his motorcycle started shaking. If he even hit a rock, his life would be going in a different direction. Soon enough, a bright and massive light was flying over John: a police helicopter with a sniper.

The sniper fired a bullet at John, hitting his shoulder. John practically used up all of his willpower to not make the bike swerve off the road. He yelled at the top of his lungs as he grabbed his gun and pointed it upward. He concentrated… and fired a shot.

A single bullet hit the pilot square in the forehead. The helicopter crashed in the streets, causing a massive explosion. Killing 4 policemen and severely injuring two. A couple of passenger cars blew up as well.

"HOLY CRAP!" yelled John as he continued to speed away. He looked back, and the explosion kept getting farther and farther away. Soon, he was in the clear… at least, on paper, he was. John had to pull aside and puke. What had he done? He killed innocent and random people. What was he doing? He just meant to hurt the sniper, not kill the pilot and crash the whole damn helicopter.

John raced away back to Wilmhelm. To add insult to injury, he couldn't even find Andrea's body—something he promised David he would do. John shook his head as he sped along the highway.

David gulped. He was nervous—extremely nervous. He was driving to Natalia's house. He was the only person who knew where she lived… and that was smack dab next to Jack's house.

Natalia had told David to never, ever show his face near her ever again. Only when she called him was he allowed to come. Besides that, never again was he allowed to ever come near her. Then... she fired him. David would never forget the day that she did.

He was actually being promoted. He had just traveled halfway across the world in some poor African country to kill a mad warlord who was trafficking human cargo to fund his genocidal racial campaign. Nobody dared take up that assignment, as it was too risky. Everyone refused... except for David, of course. To be honest, David didn't think he would make it out alive. He actually hoped he would die. He was going through a rough depression, as the girl he liked so much didn't even care at all for him. Worst of all, his father had passed away. He later became a depressed alcoholic, and soon life was meaningless to him. He hoped he could die on this mission.

Instead, he found purpose when he traveled abroad. Natalia, with all of her connections, had exchanged a meeting for him to meet with the crazed warlord. When David landed in the country, his eyes would never make him forget what he saw that day.

Hundreds, if not thousands, of civilians were all brutalized and massacred. Boys, girls, men, children, rebel soldiers—it didn't matter. All of them met their fate the same way. The bodies were burned, and the heads were used as displays to cover up a field that was once used for religious purposes. David shed a tear seeing what he saw. The worst was yet to come.

When he got to the city, he saw just how much poverty there was. Boys and girls begging for food. Women and men dying from malnutrition. Violence plagued the streets. David saw a dog eat a baby girl because it was hungry. The soldiers were raped and killed, and nobody batted an eye. The buildings looked hundreds of years old, and blood and dirt littered the streets.

When David entered the mansion of the drug lord, he became sick to his bones. Little boys were dressed in revealing clothing, offering pleasure, and food and drinks. David declined, and his heart sank more and more. There were special rooms where little girls were taken to be impregnated so that the future generation of soldiers could be born.

David never forgot the face of the warlord when he entered the bastard's room. There were perverted photos and pictures of himself with young boys and girls. Men and women—it didn't matter. He raped and killed them all. The ones he liked, he kept their heads as a trophy.

David remembered sitting down with the man. He was so egotistical, and truly believed what he was doing would better the world. David remembered entering his mind and becoming scared for the rest of his life of what he saw there. He quickly killed the man, and David regretted it. He wished he could make the man suffer. He quickly left the country, although this time with a new resolve. He now had a purpose and an order he lived by. He swore he would protect and help all those as much as he could with his powers. He did this because he didn't want to see a world where men like that warlord ruled over the earth. He would rather die trying to fight for good than live trying to fit into evil.

David remembered at the promotion celebration, Natalia pulled him aside and told him that he had done a great job.

"David, I am quite proud of you. It seems not only have you ended up making a new resolve for yourself, but you also took on a mission nobody else would. And you succeeded… all by yourself.

"I have to admit that I actually am impressed. (I will never say those words ever again, so cherish them while you can.) You did something incredible, and fantastic. All the hunters here owe you a great thank you for your commitment to S.H.O.T., and your abilities have been shown today. Thank you, David, for everything."

David smiled. "Thank you. I try my hardest and—"

"Which is why I am asking you to tell everyone that you are retiring."

David was taken aback. He looked puzzled. "Excuse me?"

Natalia broke his finger and reached into his pocket. She pulled out 4 massive blood diamonds.

"WHAT IN THE FUCK IS THIS?"

David cringed as he grabbed his finger. "Listen, it—"

"No. I know what this is. Say nothing if I'm right, and if I'm wrong, tell me something so I can scream in your face about how fucking miserable you are. Listen up! These are blood diamonds you stole from that damned country. Blood diamonds you stole from that crazed warlord. You stole these because you wanted to sell them so you could make some money. Maybe… oh, I don't know, open up a flower shop or something like that. Something nice and pretty. Benefit from slaves who risked their lives for their families so they could afford to share half a can of beans for dinner.

"You stole them as if they were regular one-dollar bills. Correct me if I'm wrong, but you knew these were blood diamonds and not just any regular diamonds. And yet, you still took them knowing that countless died for these… all so you could get some money in your bank account. Am I right?"

David said nothing. Her words hurt more than any injury. He looked ashamed.

"Oh, what's wrong? Do you hurt? You got the look of a puppy dog. Well, too FUCKING BAD! You deserve all misfortune on what's coming to you. I thought you made a vow to protect others and help others out. Now you're here stealing blood diamonds. What if you decide to kill a pimp, and vow to protect women for the rest of your life? What, you're gonna buy hookers for the rest of your life?"

"Look," muttered David. "That's diff—"

Natalia slapped David with the blood diamond.

"SHUT… UP! You're fired. Tell everyone you quit. Be glad I'm doing this instead of telling everyone what you really did. Think of it as my last favor to you. EVER! I never ever want to see you here again. Only when I call you. Your soul may be free, but your ass belongs to me. Open up whatever damn flower shop you want, I'm not buying from that shit. Nor will I ever come and see you. I swear to God, if you ever so happen to meet me in person on PURPOSE, then you will face my wrath. And believe me, David O'Connor, death is a preferable alternative to that. Get out!"

David told everyone he was quitting. As he made his retirement speech, tears were rolling down his eyes. Everyone smiled, as they realized what a moment this meant. What they didn't know was that David wasn't crying from giving the speech.

Soon, later that night, David would try to commit suicide by putting his pistol in his mouth and firing the gun. Unfortunately, he survived, and he used the blood diamonds to buy the flower shop. The rest of the money he had, he gave to poor countries in Africa to support their fight against poverty and discrimination.

David would spend the rest of his life miserable, developing a split personality. One he would show other people, to show them that he was happy and charismatic and that everything was OK. The other he would have to himself, curing himself forever doing such an action. He never forgot what Natalia had told him.

And now here he was, driving to her house. He parked his car outside of her house. It was pouring rain outside. He looked over at Jack's house. He shook his head. He would get Jack back… even if it cost him his life. As he walked toward Natalia's house, he felt a cold breeze. A chilly and gut-wrenching feeling took over him, and he could feel death's presence.

There was only one single light visible from Natalia's house, and that was the downstairs living room. David took a deep breath, as if he was plunging into the abyss, and he rang the doorbell. All the seconds that followed up felt like an eternity. His heart raced, and his head pounded. Oh no… here it comes. His breath was failing him, and he became lightheaded. He was about to pass out.

The door slowly opened. David embraced himself… but there was nobody there. David was breathing heavily. Was… Natalia not home?

David peeked his head inside. There was nobody there, yet he could smell food and wine.

"Hello," croaked David. He waited patiently and silently, yet there was still no answer. David's heart pounded even more as he took a step inside, closing the door behind him. As he entered the house, David started to feel… worried. Something was definitely wrong. Where was she? He could hear her outside just a second ago. Now, she was gone. Worst of all, David had a feeling that something was lurking in the house. Watching him. David started to sweat. Calm down, man, he told himself, but as he continued to walk around in the living room, he felt as though there was something behind him. There was, and it was Death, yet David couldn't see the massive grin on Death's face as it loomed over David.

David nearly dropped to the floor as he tried walking further. He dared not even yell out Natalia's name. He was too scared.

"What are you doing here?" said a voice from behind. David quickly spun around. His body was sweating uncontrollably, and his eyes nearly jumped out of his eye sockets. There was someone hiding in the shadows. David recognized the voice. It… sounded like Natalia. Yet, it was also too harsh to sound like her.

"I-I-I…I'm…" David couldn't even talk. He clenched his heart and put his hands on the wall to try to balance himself. Was… this what Natalia meant when she said a fate 'worse than death'?

Saliva was coming out of his mouth. He couldn't stop himself, and his nose was running. His eyes became bloodshot red, and soon they were starting to become dry and painful. The voice spoke up once more.

"Did you remember what I said? All those years ago? I told you to never ever come here again. Or ever show your face around here again. What…are you doing here?"

"N-Natalia, please, I…" David clutched his chest one more time. He was having a heart attack. No, it couldn't end like this. He needed to get Jack out of prison. No matter what it took. He needed to help him… even if it meant his death.

With everything he could muster, David spoke up.

"J-Jack's… in prison. Please… I know you have contacts and money. Please help him out. He's innocent… please help him."

There was an eerie silence. The figure in the shadow did not speak. The more David looked at it, the more he became uneasy and his stomach turned. Good God, was that really Natalia? Was this really her house? David felt his heart exploding inside of him. His ears started to bleed, and his nose spit out blood. He cried tears of blood, and his fingernails started to come off. What in God's green earth was happening?

There was still more silence. "P-please, Natalia… please…" David practically gasped for breath. His body went pale, and he physically couldn't sweat anymore. He started to become cold. His tongue was purple, and it was trying to suffocate him by reaching into his throat. David gurgled as his mind slowly started to phase in and out of this life. Dammit, he couldn't let it end like this. Not like this, not here, not now. Jack needed him.

"N-Natalia?" David looked up once more. The figure in the shadow was gone. David slowly got up. The lights turned off. And now, there was nobody there. Death had left… but David still felt something wrong. *Oh my God,* thought David as goosebumps ran along his entire body. He was… in some sort of haunted house. He wished he could get out. He ran for the door, but he couldn't open it. His mind raced as he started to cry. Get me out of here, get me out of here. David slowly started to lose his mind.

He gasped and nearly coughed. He quickly shifted his head toward the staircase. Oh fuck, oh fuck, there's something on top of there. David was paralyzed with fear. He dared not move as his mind was going a million miles an hour. The figure moved closer and closer to David. Soon, it was at the bottom of the staircase. Yet… there was nothing there. It was pitch dark, and David could hardly see. Still, he felt as if there was something right in front of him. David put his hands out… and only felt the air.

David hurled over and puked. He was losing it. This is what Natalia meant, a fate worse than death. He needed to get out of here. This was…

David fell down to his knees. He grasped his head. Oh God, he just wanted to leave. Fuck it. Forget Jack, he needed to leave or else he would die. No, even worse. Something much worse would happen to him. He had a feeling that death would be a preferable alternative.

David tried moving his hands… but they failed. He collapsed to the ground. He was still panting and breathing rapidly and uncontrollably. He couldn't move… he was too scared.

David closed his eyes. Oh please, oh please, God, just make it stop. Make all of this go away. He just wanted to help his friend.

David's eyes opened as Natalia grabbed him by his hair. He could see her face clearly now. She gritted her teeth, David had never seen her this angry in her entire life before. She had rage and hatred in her eyes. David felt true fear for the first time in his entire life that day in her house.

"YOU! WHAT… ARE… YOU… DOING IN MY HOUSE?"

David gulped. Oh my God, this was it. David started to cry just like Jack did. David tried closing his eyes, but his vision never left Natalia's gaze. She leaned in closer, and David could smell death on her breath. David wanted to speak… but couldn't. He was too shaken and too scared. He pissed his pants and shit in his underwear.

"What did I tell you? Do you remember, you ass?"

David nodded his head. Saliva was uncontrollably running down his chin and out of his mouth. He was huffing and puffing. The more he looked at Natalia, the more he wished for the sweet release of death.

"Listen please… just… I-I-I, J…"

"WHAT ARE YOU TRYING TO SAY?"

She threw David's head on the floor, shattering his nose and breaking his orbital bone. It actually helped David. The adrenaline kicked in, and the fear started to slowly dim away.

David stood up. His hands were in a defensive position.

"Please… I need your help. Jack's been taken to prison and he's innocent. You have money, and you have resources. Please, can't you help him out?"

Natalia said nothing. She only spit and kicked David's face. Only causes greater injury. David fell to the floor. Tears rolled down his eyes. He imagined that he looked so pathetic right about now. He held his face in his hands. Natalia paced around the area for a few seconds.

"I know. I saw on the TV. They took him already?"

David nodded his head. Natalia mumbled something under her breath and kicked David in the ribs.

She sighed. "OK... I'll see what I can do. Do you know where they took him?"

David shook his head. She kicked him again. This time breaking his ribs.

"Fine... I'll have a look. If everything goes well, he should be here by this time in a few days. I'll contact you about the updates. Now, get out of here before I kill you."

David nodded his head as he slowly got out of the house. Natalia practically pushed him out, and his face planted on the concrete. He laid down there for a minute. More than half of his head was covered in cuts and blood. He slowly picked himself up and started walking away. As he was heading out, he saw John's motorcycle pull up next to him.

"John," mumbled David. John looked surprised seeing David.

"David. What in the world happened to you?"

David waved his hands. "It's... anyway... how are you doing?"

John shook his head as he lit up a joint.

"No bueno, my friend. Andrea's body was missing. And now I'm wanted."

"Wait... what happened?"

John shook his head. "Bad things, my friend. Anyway... news on Jack?"

David shrugged. "Natalia said she'll deal with it. Shell call me whenever she gets any news or updates. In the meanwhile, all we can do is sit around and pray for all of this to blow over."

David sat down on the curb. John sat down next to him, and the both of them smoked together.

"What a day it has been," mumbled John. He smiled as he looked at David. David wasn't smiling.

"Sorry, just trying to make light of the situation."

David shook his head. "No, no, you're OK. It's just that... you're right. A lot has happened. I'm taking it all in right now. It's been quite a headache. And now you're wanted. I guess you can't leave or show your face outside of Wilmhelm anymore."

John chuckled. "Well, lucky me, I guess. It's not like I really go out anyway. I like it here."

"I'm glad you do."

The two sat in silence for a moment, and then David asked a question.

"John… about those blood diamonds. Do you think I did the wrong thing?"

John looked at him. "What blood diamonds?"

David smiled. "You don't need to play dumb with me. I know you overheard my conversation with Natalia. I saw it on your face when I gave my retirement speech. It's OK. I'm just glad you didn't tell anyone."

John gave him a fake smile. Thankfully, the people that John did tell kept it a secret. A damn good secret.

"Well, David… If I'm being completely honest, I feel like that was the wrong thing to do, man."

David bowed his head down. Ashamed and disappointed. Feelings of suicide were coming back stronger than ever.

John patted him on his back.

"But… judging by the way you are now, I can see that you've regretted your decisions. You regretted taking those things for yourself. Perhaps… maybe it was actually good that you did take those diamonds."

David looked at him, his face uncanny. "What are you talking about?"

"David… are you a religious man?"

David shook his head. "Never."

John smiled.

"My mother and my father were one, but they were insane and it scared me away. I did everything I could to get away from that lifestyle. It wasn't until later that I started developing a passion and a love for God himself. Anyway, I always felt guilty about not getting closer to God when I was younger, and for most of my adult and teenage life, I was ashamed and I carried that guilt with me."

"John… what exactly are you trying to say to me?"

John took a puff. "Perhaps… perhaps what I'm trying to say is that I can still see that you carry that burden of those diamonds with you, EVEN till this day. Perhaps if you… perhaps if you were to ask for forgiveness, then maybe, just maybe, you won't have to carry that burden with you. And you'll be free of your past. Maybe you've suffered so much because you just couldn't get the image of those diamonds out of your mind. Perhaps… perhaps you were meant to take those diamonds, so there would be a moment in your life where you could find your purpose, and even draw close to God, even."

David nodded his head. "I see. But... I'm not religious though. I don't believe in God."

John nodded his head. "True... but as they say, there's a first time for everything. Just give it a shot, man."

"What if God rejects me?"

"Listen, I'm no expert on the Bible. Yet, from what I know and from my one understanding, God will never deny you if you try to go to him. Even if you're a horrible man. Try to repent and you'll see the changes. You know, there's this one story in the Bible where a man who's so holy and so good, does nothing bad, he goes and prays to God. He thanks God for making him so perfect and wonderful and never doing anything bad. Then, there's another man who's a poor, poor sinner. He knows he's a sinner, and he still doesn't believe in God. (Sounds like someone I know.) So he goes and prays. He's so ashamed that he doesn't even pray properly, but with his head bowed, he beats his chest. He asks God for forgiveness because he's a poor, poor sinner.

"You would think that God would be more favorable to the man with the holiness and the man that has done nothing bad. Yet, God took more favor on the nonbeliever who was a sinner, because at the end of the day, the man KNEW he was wrong, and he asked for forgiveness. The holy man exalted himself too much. Perhaps... perhaps if you were just to give it a shot, then maybe you can live the life that you want. A life is free of everything that shackles you down. Just... give it a shot, man."

David nodded his head. "I see. And then what?"

John shrugged. "Only one way to find out."

They continued to sit around and smoke weed in silence. Now, it was John that popped the question.

"David... do you think things happen for a reason?"

David nodded his head. "Yeah."

"Well... maybe the incident with the diamonds was supposed to happen. Maybe we're supposed to have this conversation."

David looked confused. "You're too high. You're making no sense."

"Dammit, David, I'm being serious! Listen, things happen for a reason. Once you come to understand that aspect, then you can live a good life."

David was starting to grow frustrated with John's philosophical talk.

"OK then... what if horrible incidents are supposed to happen? Then what?"

"Then you learn from them. Just like maybe you were supposed to take those diamonds and get fired. Then, you learned from your mistake and now you decided to never do something like that again."

"OK, fine then. What if I knew what I did was wrong, even though it was 'supposed to happen.' Perfect, but what if I do the same thing again? What if I go to another foreign country and steal jewels that people, innocent people, have died for?"

"Then you would be a damn fool. Doing something bad, but not knowing it's bad, is one thing. Doing something bad, because you know it's bad, now that's being a straight-up clown."

David looked at John, extremely agitated. He wanted to punch the man in the face.

"What the fuck are you telling me all this for?"

Now John was starting to grow frustrated. He smoked the last bit of weed and threw it away. He got up and went to his motorcycle.

"Maybe I'm telling you this because I'm trying to help you? I see you're still suffering from those diamonds, even after all these years. I'm just trying to help you feel better, and trying to find some solutions to your damn problem because you're my friend!"

David gritted his teeth and yelled at John.

"FUCK YOU! You think you know better than me? Is that it?"

"Damn it, I never said anything like that! Oh, you miserable son of a bitch. No wonder nobody wants to stick around you anymore. I have no idea why that whore of yours, Samantha, even bothers to put up with—"

David threw a rock at John's head. It was a very hard and heavy rock. John didn't see it coming. It hit John right in the temple of his head. He fell off his bike and hit his head on the concrete floor. David huffed and puffed. He needed to control his rage. It was getting to him too quickly.

John wasn't getting up. Soon, fear and worries started to rise in David's mind. Oh no.

"John," said David as he walked over to John's bike. John was slumped on the floor, as if he were on heroin, or was some sort of ragdoll. Blood was oozing out of his head. Oh no.

"J-John!"

David picked him up. Blood was rushing out of his head fast. He was about to call an ambulance, but then he realized that he was a wanted man. Great. Jack's house was probably locked, but there was one house that he knew could help him out.

He quickly rushed inside Natalia's house. She yelled at him and nearly stabbed him when she saw John's body.

"YOU DIDN'T CALL AN AMBULANCE?"

"No time to explain. He needs help ASAP! You're trained, right?"

Natalia pushed David out of the way as she started to fix and help John. David stood back and watched as John started to lose more and more blood. This... couldn't be happening right now. No, not his friend. If John died because of him, he would never... EVER be able to forgive himself. Despite not being a religious man, David decided to pray.

He couldn't watch. He sat near the living room, hearing Natalia struggle as John was hanging on for dear life. How bowed his head in disappointment, what had he done?

A few hours had passed, and John was lying on the couch with some bandages around his head. He was OK. He was going to make it! Thank the Lord. David had a sigh of relief. His hands were shaking from all the emotion. It was 2 in the morning, and he was super tired. Still, he wouldn't leave unless he saw John wake up and talk to him.

Natalia came downstairs. She was in her pajamas. She looked disgusted as she looked at David.

"You're still here?"

David nodded his head. "Yes. I want to make sure my friend is OK."

Natalia menacingly looked at David. David looked away but still felt her cold and eerie presence. He gulped as he left the house. He couldn't stay anywhere near that woman anymore. He quickly went over to Samantha's house to see how she was doing. She was fast asleep. David kissed her on the head as he went back to his house. He ate a quick bite and passed out for 14 hours.

16

Jack was sitting in his holding cell. He was given a new prosthetic arm. It was nowhere near as good as the ones he saw on TV or in video games, but it would suffice for now. It still felt so weird and abnormal not having an arm. Jack swore up and down he could feel and move his left arm, yet it wasn't there— Only his prosthetic one. Even his fake arm was horrible. He could barely pick anything up and mostly restored to using his right arm.

Jack sat down on his bed. His mind raced. Soon, he would go to court, and after that, prison. Already… he hadn't even graduated high school. Worst of all, could the court bring up his original record of his involvement with narcotics? He doubted it, since he was able to pay himself off court practically. Still, there was a chance that the judge could see that and become more in favor of sending Jack to prison. How many years would he do? Where would he go? What would he do? So many questions, and so little time. Jack bowed his head down. Dammit… it wasn't supposed to be like this.

As Jack was self-loathing, a police officer approached him.

"Jack… you have a visitor."

Jack looked up. Hope reached his soul. Could it be David? John? Samantha? Anybody would be wonderful right about now.

Jack stood up as the police officer opened his cell.

"You have 20 minutes to talk to her. Kissing and hugging are permitted, as well as holding hands. You must make sure to show each other holding hands on top of the table, in full view. You will be permitted to take anything or give anything. Understood?"

Jack nodded his head. A girl? Could it be Samantha? As Jack walked over to the visitor's room, his heart dropped. Of course. How could he possibly forget about the one girl who he KNEW would track him until the ends of the earth? The one girl he knew would quite literally go through hell and back to see him, one that would drive 4 hours just to talk to him for 20 minutes and then drive back.

Jack looked at Audrey, and his heart exploded. His mind raced. Was she upset? Worried? Angry? Happy to see he was OK—or a little bit of all the above? (Jack thought of the latter.) He sat down. No words came out of his mouth. She was pretty and was wearing a flannel jacket and a large beanie that Jack gave to her when they went out one night. It was similar to the same clothes she was wearing when he first met her.

Audrey smiled. Her voice sounded rough, and she looked very, very tired.

"Hello, Jack. It's… nice to see you."

Jack smiled. Hearing her voice, it was like an angel was speaking to him. He immediately cried. Finally, some good news.

They held each other's hand.

"Audrey… it's so nice to see you too! How… are you doing?"

She nodded her head. "OK."

She looked like, at any given moment, at any given thing that Jack said, she would burst, and a wave of uncontrollable tears would stream down her face. Jack was careful with what he said. She looked at his prosthetic arm.

"Is that…"

Jack nodded his head. "Yeah. I lost it in the explosion. But don't worry, I think I know someone who can get me a better arm. I—"

"Jack… please stop."

Her voice was now harsher, and tears were now falling down her face. She looked sad, disappointed, and nervous all at the same time. Something was wrong, Jack could feel it in his heart. He gulped down. He realized a horrible feeling in his stomach. She came here to see him, yes, but she also came here to tell him something.

"Jack… did you cause that explosion?"

"ME? Of course not. I'm innocent."

"Then why are you in JAIL?"

Jack shivered. He could see the officers all looking at him. He leaned in the glass.

"Please, just calm down. Listen, some bad things happened. I… I don't know how to tell you this, but Yuri and Andrea are dead."

She dropped the phone. She screamed so loudly that he could hear her from the other side. She started to bawl and cry. She quickly grabbed the phone and yelled into it, looking horrifyingly angry at Jack.

"What did you do?"

Jack was taken aback.

"Me? I didn't do anything. I promise you I—"

Audrey shook her head. Jack was losing his breath. What was this woman… what was she thinking? He knew she was emotional, but right now was not the time to do this. He would have to deal with her later.

"Listen… please just listen, Audrey. Do you love me?"

She nodded her head.

"Then you know I'm innocent."

She nodded her head again. The tears rolling down her cheeks grew ever so stronger—like a waterfall practically.

"I know that… but I still don't understand why it says you are labeled a criminal. Everyone at school talks bad about you, and they look at me like I'm a monster."

Jack rolled his eyes. "Look, they talked badly about me the day I got there. Don't worry, and who cares if they look at you weirdly? They do that already, don't they?"

She said nothing. Jack pretended to cough.

"Um… sorry. Anyway, what I'm trying to say is that this will all be over soon. I have a feeling. Don't worry. Every little thing is gonna be alright. So don't you worry… about a thing. Listen, when this is all over, I'll come over, and we can be with each other. How does that sound?"

She shook her head.

"I'm sorry, Jack… but I'm breaking up with you."

Jack's smile faded away. She was… what? No, not Audrey. And especially not right here and not right now.

"W-why?"

She started to cry some more. She greeted her teeth and closed her eyes. She couldn't bring herself to speak. She had to calm down before she could say anything. All the while, Jack started to cry as well. Please, this couldn't be. The love of his life… was ending their relationship?

"Jack… I love you. I love you more than you can ever imagine. That's why we can't be together. You… nearly dying from that… drug overdose. Now you're going to prison, and you're labeled a criminal. Ever since I met you, my life has gone to shit. I haven't slept properly ever since I met you. My life is spinning and going out of control. My mother now hates me because I hang out with you. My father hates me because I spend too much time out of the house. Can't you see that you only make my life miserable?

"I can't be with someone who I am always worrying about. Oh, Jack... I love you so much. I really do, and you'll never understand just how much I love you. But I can't continue this relationship. Too many things have happened for us to continue. Your life... it's not suitable to mine. I just can't anymore. I worry too much, and I always fear for you. I don't want to do that when I'm dating somebody. I don't want to stay up at night thinking if the next day is the last day I'm gonna see my boyfriend. I don't want to think that they might overdose again and this time, never wake up.

"I'm sorry, Jack. I know the spot you're in right now. But I can't keep doing this. We're done. I love you, Jack. Don't you worry? I'll never forget about you, and I'll never date anybody ever again. You'll always be my cherished treasure. Jack... I love you so much. More than you could ever imagine. I love you, my dear. I wish we could spend an eternity forever because I want to be with you forever... but it can't be like this."

Jack spit in the glass. He yelled into the microphone.

"FUCK YOU, BITCH! You stupid cunt, you stupid whore! I should have never dated you, you ugly, sad sack of shit. Your mom's fat and should die in a hole. Your dad sucks, and I hope I can kill him! You... you bitch! I hope you die in a miserable car crash and rot in hell. Stupid piece of shit. You stupid hoe!

"I can't believe this... I always knew you were too soft! I always knew you were too emotional. I should have never dated you! THIS IS ALL YOUR FAULT! I was happy with the life that I was living. You ruined EVERYTHING! I hope I never see you again, I hope I never ever have to deal with your misery again! You hear me, bitch? I FUCKING HATE YOU!"

Audrey dropped the phone and ran out of the room, her hand in her face and tears rolling down her eyes. Jack nearly jumped over the glass, but the cops had to secure him. He yelled all sorts of horrible and nasty insults at her as she cried and ran away. The police officers beat Jack and threw him back in his jail cell.

Jack was so furious he yelled into the wall and broke his hand by punching it so hard. Audrey ran into her car. The tears couldn't stop. She couldn't even drive because she was crying so much and could hardly see. She just sat in her car for hours and hours, crying. She knew she did the right thing, as she loved Jack so much that she couldn't see him suffering anymore. If he suffered, she suffered 10 times more. She knew that he would never understand, but that's alright. All she needed him to know was that she loved him more than anything! Still, what a fiasco. She buried her head in her lap and bawled her eyes out until the sunset.

Jack sat in his jail cell. He had calmed down… a little bit. If he ever got his hands on her… no. He shouldn't be thinking such evil and vile thoughts. Once he got out, he was planning on getting so hammered. He would snort all the cocaine in the world, drink all the booze, smoke all the weed, all the meth and shoot all the heroin. She wasn't there to stop him. And since they weren't dating, he decided to go to a brothel and have sex until his balls turned blue.

Until then, he would just be staring at a wall and contemplating. May God forgive him. After all, he was just a poor sinner.

Audrey was driving home. It was pitch dark outside. Her mind never left Jack. She promised him that she would never, ever date again, nor would ever see another man. She loved Jack too much for that. If need be, she would kill herself if that's what made Jack happy.

Despite all of this, she still felt sad. She couldn't hold him anymore, nor could she be with him. If he was willing to turn his life around, then she would be happy and embrace him with open arms. That is… if he changed. And… if he accepted her. The way he yelled at her, Audrey imagined that he would never ever go back to her ever again. She wanted to cry, but physically couldn't. She cried so much that there were no more tears to shed. What a day it had been.

She drove home and refused to eat dinner. As she walked upstairs, her parents discussed.

Sarah spoke up.

"I think she broke up with that boyfriend of hers."

The dad nodded his head. "Here's hoping. I always thought he was trouble."

"Hmm. Why?"

"I could see it on Audrey's face. She came home from his house one night and was in shambles. I was ready to go over there and kill the bastard myself. He couldn't take me on."

Sarah chuckled. "I'm sure, but from what I've heard, Jack's quite the fighter."

"JACK? What would he know about fighting?"

"Perhaps more than you, but I agree, Audrey has been feeling down ever since she started meeting that wretched man. I'm glad she was able to end it. Although she doesn't look too happy now. Oh… teenagers."

"Were we ever like that?"

Sarah nodded her head. "I'm sure. According to my mom, I was quite a pain when it came to relationships. Your mom said the same thing about you."

The father chuckles as the two of them continue to eat their dinner.

"What are we going to say?" Samantha was standing right outside Yuri's house. David was sweating. He didn't want to be the one to break the news that their son tragically died in an explosion, but if it came down to it, he would.

"I… I don't know," said David as he rang the doorbell again. Samantha was nervous. She already wasn't liked in the neighborhood for her… wild antics. This would only ruin her reputation even more than it already was.

The door opened, and there was Yuri's dad. He was a typical middle-aged American father, although he did have quite a massive and combed beard.

"Hello," said Yuri's father. Every time he spoke, his beer belly jiggled. David smiled as Samantha stepped forward. David's eyes widened. He hoped she didn't say anything outlandish.

"You Yuri's father, correct?"

Yuri's father nodded. "Yes, my name is Jeff. Nice to meet the both of you." He shook out his hand. His smile, his face, his demeanor—all so similar to Yuri. David had to turn away as he couldn't control his tears anymore.

"Is everything OK? What's this about Yuri? I haven't seen him in a while, and he was on the news a day ago. What's happened to him?"

Samantha took a deep breath. Here goes nothing.

"Sir… I'm sorry to inform you that your son tragically died in the gas station explosion. I tried to take care of him—I really did—but we couldn't get him to a hospital on time. He lost too much blood. He died… in my hands. I'm sorry, sir…"

Samantha trailed off as she started to cry. Jeff merely looked down at the ground. His sweet, sweet son was now gone. Not even 18 years old. He closed his eyes and nodded his head.

David went to the van and grabbed the body. It was already decomposing. He gave it to Jeff. Jeff broke out into tears as he held his son. From a distance, Samantha could see Yuri's two younger sisters and his mother all coming to see what the commotion was. She dared not stay any longer.

"If you have any questions," said Samantha. "I live down the street."

Jeff nodded his head as he closely gripped his son's dead body. The mother shrieked as she saw what was going on. The sisters were too young to be figuring out what was happening, but they could recognize that their father was holding their brother and that something was off.

Samantha and David walked away and walked over to Samantha's house. They sat on the couch and said nothing for a while. They were soaking in the moment. After a while, Samantha spoke up.

"Did you find Andrea's body?"

David shook his head. "John found nothing. I can't ask him anything right now because he's resting. As for Jack… Natalia hasn't said anything to me yet."

Samantha nodded her head. She leaned in closer to David.

"Will you make love to me tonight?"

David shook his head. "No, not tonight. I'm sorry."

He got up and walked outside. He wasn't in the mood, and with the way he was feeling, he wasn't going to be having sex for a while—at least not until things settled down.

As David was walking away from Samantha's house and going back to his place, a very nice old lady passed by him. She stopped and stared at him.

"Excuse me," she said. David turned around. Despite her old age, she had a very strong voice and a very muscular body.

"By any chance, are you David O'Connor? Friends with Andrea?"

David took a step back. What was this lady talking about? How did she know Andrea?

"Um… yes?"

The old lady chuckled. She was laughing at David's face. He seemed so shocked.

"I see. My name is Rebecca. I'm Andrea's mom. Nice to meet you."

She stuck out her hand, and David shook it. David never once ever heard Andrea mention her mother or her father. Hell, she never even mentioned her entire family. From what he was seeing, the mom didn't seem all that bad. If Rebecca was here, then that must mean that she heard the news about Andrea. This also means that there is a possibility that she was the one who picked up the body at the hospital before John arrived.

"Nice to meet you, Rebecca," said David. His eyesight met hers.

"May… I ask what you're doing here?"

Rebecca shook her head. "Not at all. I'm here to see my daughter. I heard that she was on the news in a terrible explosion. I went to go and pick up her body from the morgue. I already cremated it earlier this morning."

David nodded his head. That cleared that up. Now, another thing was bothering him—her expression. She didn't look the least bit concerned that her daughter had been killed a few days ago. Moreover, what shocked David was that she almost looked… relieved. As if she was happy to get rid of such a nuisance like Andrea. David didn't want to ask any questions, so he decided to play it safe and see where it went.

"Well… I'm sorry for your loss, ma'am."

Rebecca waved her hands. She said nothing more. David grew suspicious of her as she smiled and walked away. Her demeanor resembled something normal—as if she was talking to a random stranger on a very random day, instead of talking to her dead daughter's friend.

David watched as she walked away. It was very late at night now, and David needed some rest. He wanted to leave, but his eyes were ever so fixated on Rebecca. Why on earth was she acting so nonchalantly about her daughter's death? Something didn't sit quite right with David. He tried to say that maybe the mother didn't care so much, but he figured it was more than that. He figured that there must be something more. What it was, he didn't know, but he decided to do a little bit of investigation. He followed her home—back to Jack's house.

John woke up, his head was hurting like a motherfucker. Natalia was waiting for him. She stood up and rushed over to his side.

"John, are you OK?" She had been waiting for so long that she even lost some weight. She didn't eat anything, nor did she sleep. She was so worried about John that she didn't leave his side even once. She didn't watch TV, or entertain herself with anything. She was too afraid that if she was distracted, something might happen to John. She didn't want to take that chance.

John looked up at Natalia.

"Do I… know you?"

Oh no. Natalia took a step back. Dammit, David, what did you do?

John looked around the room. "Where on earth am I?"

He tried to stand up but had to lean on something to stop his headache. Natalia couldn't believe it. He got hit hard… real hard.

John sat back down for a moment and looked at Natalia. The way he looked at her—it was as if he was a small animal and she was some sort of alien.

"Who are you?"

Natalia regained her composure. She would have time to panic later.

"My name is Natalia. I am… your S.H.O.T. supervisor and coordinator."

"My what?"

"Do you… know anything about being a hunter?"

"A hunter… like hunting animals and killing them?"

Fuck. Natalia was trying to think of some questions. How much did he forget?

"John, I'm afraid you have amnesia. You're supposed to know me and a bunch of other people, but unfortunately, you seem to have forgotten."

John leaned in. "Wait a minute… I'm supposed to know you? What's going on here?"

"Just try to stay calm for now. Tell me a little bit about yourself."

John was quiet for a moment, and Natalia was almost certain he was going to refuse, but knowing who he was deep down she was sure he would comply.

"Well… my name is John. John Everdeen. I was born and raised in Wilmhelm, PA. My mother is Elyssa Everdeen, and my father is John Everdeen the senior. I'm… 32, I think?"

Natalia clenched her hands. Dammit, this was worse than she thought. He couldn't even remember his damn age.

"I know that I went to high school here and that I almost never left here… but… that's about it."

Natalia took a deep breath. "Can you remember the names of your friends?"

John looked up to the ceiling as if he were coming up with an insane mathematical formula or equation. After a while, he shook his head.

"Nope. Damn… I don't even know where I work! Holy shit! I forgot everything."

Natalia stood up. Good, at least he knew that he was forgetting things. Only sometimes did people know that they had amnesia. It all depended on the individual's mind and behavior. Thank goodness that John knew.

"Good, John. This is good. My name is Natalia. You're supposed to know me."

"Well... yeah, I think you told me earlier. Dammit... who are my friends again?"

"A nice group of people. Their names are David, Samantha and Jack."

John looked at her funny. "That's it?"

Natalia nodded her head. "Those are the only friends you have right now."

John nodded his head. He looked at her suspiciously. "Well then... if you say so, Natalia. Now, do you know how I became like this?"

Natalia thought to David. What had happened between the two of them? She didn't even have time to ask him any questions, as she was too busy trying to bandage up John's cracked head.

Natalia shook her head. "No, not necessarily, but I do know someone who does."

Natalia grabbed her phone and called David.

"Hello?"

"David... this is Natalia."

There was a silent moment across the line.

"Is Jack OK?"

Natalia shook her head. "Now's not the time for that. I need you to come here ASAP!"

"Well... I'm actually kind of busy right now, and—"

Natalia looked out her window. She saw David spying on some lady entering Jack's house. It looked like Andrea's mother. Natalia only ever saw her one time, and that was in a random supermarket in Pittsburg many years ago—before Natalia even knew who on earth Andrea was.

"I can see you outside. Come here right now, or else I swear to God, something so horrible and so horrifying will happen to you, that you'll wish you would die! Your friend needs you right now. So stop it!"

She hung up the phone and saw David nervously chuckling and went inside Natalia's house. He opened the door and saw John sitting on the couch. David rushed over to him.

"John, you're OK! Thank goodness. How are you feeling?"

John nodded his head, giving a lukewarm smile.

"I've felt better before. Natalia says you know what happened to me?"

David looked confused as he peeked at Natalia giving him a sinister face. She nodded her head.

"That's right, John. Now David, to fill you in, John here has amnesia. He doesn't know anything about ANYONE. He wants to know what happened, and since you were with him last, I decided to call you since you MUST know how John got to be like this... right?"

David nervously smiled. *Damn bitch!* It's like she wants to ruin David's life. David mumbled as he looked at John. What would he possibly say? It was his own fault? Well... it was, but David was afraid of what would happen if he said that. He had a strong gut feeling that Natalia probably knew, but she was only making David say it because she got some twisted desire from torturing David.

David started. "Well, John... you fell off your motorcycle and hit your head pretty hard."

He wasn't lying, thought Natalia. She saw the whole interaction occur. She was just itching to make David say to his friend that he got so blinded by rage that he made him forget nearly everything. Yet, she knew that David wasn't going to say anything else. She couldn't leave it at just that. So she asked a question.

"David... how did he fall off his bike?"

David quickly spun around. That hag, she was getting on his nerves! David nearly furled his eyebrows at her but stopped once he saw her facial expression. It scared the bejesus out of John, who had no clue as to what was happening. David was scared shitless. She knew what happened; he could see it. She was playing him like a damn fiddle. David started to panic. He didn't want to tell John the truth, but he didn't want to face Natalia's wrath. If his entrance to her house was any indicator that she acted like that when she was upset, he dared not do anything to anger her.

"Well... I... am not sure. I didn't see it quite clearly."

Bastard! He did see it, but not as clearly as he could have since the headlights were nearly blinding David. He wasn't lying, but he wasn't telling the truth either. *Oh, that slimy son of a bitch,* thought Natalia as she clenched her fist even harder. John could feel the tension in the air between the two of them. He slowly stood up.

"Um… actually, you know what? I think it's fine. Maybe we could—"

"SIT DOWN NOW!" Natalia yelled so hard that John's and David's poor bones shook. Even David sat down. John nearly screamed as he curled himself up into a small ball. Natalia walked over to John and David, her eyes filled with hatred and chaos—a true evil mastermind. Despite her being a headmaster, David always figured that she could turn into a supervillain. Even when he was a respectable member of S.H.O.T., she always scared him shitless, just by doing anything.

Natalia glanced at David with such ferocious hatred. She was gonna get him. She had enough of him. When she was done with him, she was going to tell everyone over at S.H.O.T. Then, she would tarnish his legacy even more by dragging his name in the dirt and telling lies and stories about how evil he was! Who did he think he was, to fuck with her? What kind of balls did this motherfucker have? He was either stupidly brave or just bravely stupid.

David looked at Natalia. She was crazy. Yet, he remained firm in his action. This was no longer about John anymore, or his legacy, but more so about sticking it up to Natalia. In all honesty, David was astounded by what Jack did to her weeks ago. He made a HUGE gamble and practically won. Now, he was planning on doing the same thing. He just hoped that it wouldn't end with something horrible or miserable happening to him.

Natalia shot a look at John. "John, this man here—"

"Did nothing at all. In fact, John, this stupid woman right here is the reason you're in this mess in the first place!"

Natalia took a step back. She clenched her hands. Oh, this little worm, what was he planning on doing?

John looked confused. David continued.

"I was there with you, man. The whole reason you're in this mess is because of her. In actuality, you were fine a moment ago, but she forced you to go on a dangerous journey, and because of it, you now lost your memory. Oh, you also wanted to. That's her fault too. EVERYTHING IS HER FAULT! Don't listen to a single word she has to say!"

David had a sly grin as he turned around and stared at Natalia. *Take that,* he said quietly in his head. John looked confused and distraught as he stared into Natalia's eyes.

"Is this true?"

She shook her head.

"Of course not. This snake here likes to lie and manipulate. He's the worst of the worst. If you don't believe me, then ask him what he did in Africa!"

David snapped. "You damn bi—"

"SAY IT! I swear to anything that is holy, say what you're about to say. You're done, your so fucking done. That's it, you're done! You AND your little pride and arrogance. Who do you think you are, messing with me? You're gonna get what's coming to you!"

Just then, David gulped. He saw it and felt it. Right above Natalia was Death, awaiting his moment to strike. Someone here was not going to come out alive from this house. John could feel it too. The feeling was unmistakable—something there was going to come and take his life away.

Just before all hell broke loose, there was a knock on the door. Natalia looked back, and she quickly looked at David and John before she went to open the door.

"Who is it?" she asked.

"It's your neighbor."

Natalia felt puzzled. She only had one neighbor to her left, and that was Andrea. Yet, Andrea was dead. So who could it be?

Natalia opened the door only to find Andrea's mother. Natalia shook her hand.

"Hello, nice to meet you. My name is Natalia."

Rebecca nodded her head. "Yes, my daughter told me all about you."

"I see. What are you doing here so late?"

"Well... I heard some very loud noises, and I just wanted to see if everything was alright. Is everything OK?"

Natalia gave a fake smile and nodded her head. "Why, yes. Everything is quite alright. My apologies. I was cooking a cake for my friend's birthday, and I must have made quite a noise when I dropped some of my tools. Hahaha."

"OOOH. A cake! I love cake. Do you mind if I take a peek? When I was in college, I used to bake a lot. Although not cake, but more so cookies."

Natalia shook her head. "Apologies, but it's not ready now, and the kitchen is a mess. Plus, I don't like guests in my house. Sorry."

Rebecca felt offended, but she understood and smiled.

"OK then. Well, if you need anything, just feel free to come and get me next door. Bye-bye!"

Natalia didn't give any smiles as she closed the door. She quickly spun around... and saw that both David and John had escaped. WHAT? How was this possible? She gritted her teeth as she tried searching the house for them. Then, she heard John's motorcycle start up outside. She quickly rushed outside and saw the two men leaving. She yelled at the top of her lungs. She had never been this angry in her entire life. When she got her hands on David... he would pray for death to come. She quickly got in her car and followed behind them. Thankfully, they weren't going too fast. And they were going uphill to get away from her. Good... she had a plan.

David looked back. She was quickly gaining speed on them. They were driving up a mountain, and to their left was a massive dirt wall with rocks and grass, leading only upward into the mountain. To their right was a small railing—that was the only thing protecting them from inevitable death. Below them was a small portion of Wilmhelm. If they fell, they would be done for.

"I-I can't, man," said John as he looked in his rearview mirrors. "If I go any faster, I won't be able to turn, and we'll fall off."

"Trust me, John, death is a better alternative to what she had planned for us!"

"Who is that crazy woman?"

"She's a headmaster for an organization called S.H.O.T. I used to be part of it, until... things happened. I'm just glad I got away from her. But now, she's crawling up our asses, man. We gotta hurry."

"I'm going as fast as I can without driving us to our deaths!"

David looked back, panicking as Natalia was driving faster and faster. *Damn woman,* he thought. Her eyes were wide open. Her teeth were grinding against themselves, and her jaw was clenched. He could see her veins nearly popping out from her head. She looked like a madwoman, coming straight from depths unknown to men for obvious reasons. She was out to kill them. David started to panic. If she ever got her hands on him, he would never ever be able to walk again, have sex or do anything. He would most likely be in a vegetative state for the rest of his life. If that were the case, then death would be better.

Natalia screamed at the top of her lungs. The more she looked at David, the more she grew furious. Her heart nearly exploded as she was now drooling. Her eyes were bulging out, and her face was tomato red. Her hair was nearly sticking out as she shrieked as loud as she could. She drove even faster and rammed her car into John's motorcycle.

"OH CRAP!" yelled John as the bike went off the rails and fell down the mountain. So too did Natalia's car, as she was not able to slow it down on time. Both vehicles fell, and they crashed into the street below.

It was such a massive height from which they fell, that Natalia's car exploded on impact, killing her. John and David were turned into jelly on the sidewalk. John's bike exploded as well. Nobody survived, and they all died. Death watched on from above, with his sinister grin. His work here was finished. He grabbed his scythe and vanished, only appears much later.

The people went out and screamed and yelled. They had never seen anything like this before—such disaster and such chaos. The flames went up in such disarray and power, that a few people who were nearby also caught on fire. They screamed as the firefighters put them out of their misery. Kids screamed, and parents turned their heads. From the fire, Natalia's corpse could be seen, burning into a crisp. Her face was still angry and the same as it was only mere seconds ago. She truly was a vile woman who was in charge of being given power. Nobody deserves to have suffered under her rule. God would see to it that she would be judged—her and David, along with John. They were all waiting patiently for the fateful day of judgment to come.

From her bedroom window, Audrey saw the explosion. She clasped her hand over her mouth and ran to go and see what had happened. She cried out in horror as she saw what had happened. What evil had occurred here? Next to her, Samantha also watched in horror. She tried calling David, but there was no response. She fell to her knees as a sinister feeling arose in her stomach. Could… David somehow be involved? She thought it impossible. David had nothing to do with this. But the more she thought, and the more she looked at Natalia's body slowly burning away into ash, she started to realize that her worst fears could be a reality. She screamed some more and cried.

Audrey saw Samantha on the floor, crying and begging for David. Audrey soon started to cry, as she imagined if Jack was in the crash. She couldn't bear the thought. She went on her knees and gave Samantha a hug. It was the least she could do. She closed her eyes and embraced her. They felt the warmth of the flames hit their faces. They gripped each other tightly. May God have mercy on all 3.

Days later, the chaos that ensued would be broadcast live on TV, and Jack saw it all from his jail cell.

17

A few days had passed since Jack was put in jail. He had lost about 3 kilos from his lack of appetite. All he could think about was Audrey, and getting out of here. How could she do this to him? Did she know the position he was in right now? He couldn't believe it. She drove all of this way to tell him that she was breaking up with him. Jack shook his head as he buried his face in his legs. What a day.

A police officer knocked his baton on the cell door.

"Jack... you're free to go."

Jack looked up. What was he talking about? He still had to go to court? Now he was being let go free—no charges? What on earth?

Jack stood up as the police officer opened his cell door.

"W-wait... what's going on?"

The police officer looked annoyed with his question. "Like I said, you're being let go."

Jack was confused as he got out of his cell. Of course, he was not complaining by any means. Jack went and got all of his stuff. Once he was done, the officers told him to wait a second. Then... Jack was a free man.

When Jack walked outside the station, there was a man in a black suit waiting for him. He had a very nice fedora and a very precisely knitted suit. His black sunglasses only added to his strange and fashionable aura. He was a very, very, very tall man—at least 7 feet tall. But by all things, he was a slim man. The suit had to be specially made so it would appear fitting on the man, and not oversized. He extended his hand toward Jack.

"Hello, Jack. My name is Dr. Benjamin. Natalia sent me. Don't worry, I know about everything. I used to be a hunter myself."

Jack nodded his head. The sun was out and it was bright. It was blinding Jack's vision as he had to constantly shield himself with his hand.

"Come, I'll drive you home."

They both stepped into a very nice and vintage Jaguar. It was an older model—a Mark 1. It was customized to be as black as possible without arousing any suspicion. In the middle of the night, this car could practically vanish. It looked like it came straight out of a James Bond movie.

Inside, Dr. Benjamin took off his sunglasses, and Jack could get a better look at his face. The man was blind. Not only that, but he had a very small but very noticeable third-degree burn mark on his right cheek. His hair was thinning and it was very dark gray.

"I see you looking into my eyes. Don't worry, son, I can drive perfectly."

What? thought Jack as this man started to interest him. How on earth did he know he was looking? The man was blind, for crying out loud. Benjamin started the car and the two drove off.

Dr. Benjamin spoke up.

"I'm afraid I have some bad news, Jack. Natalia, David and John are dead. They died in a car crash when their vehicles drove off a mountain in Wilmhelm."

Jack gulped. He wanted to cry. Good God, not this again! First Yuri, then Andrea, now with Audrey breaking up—combined with the deaths of people he loved (maybe not so much Natalia)—Jack couldn't help himself. He shed a tear and didn't stop. Dr. Benjamin wasn't bothered as he stayed quiet and listened to Jack bawl his eyes out.

This was all too much for him. He needed a break. He wanted to feel good just for a little bit. He wanted to forget about everything and everyone—to either die or just go away somewhere and be by himself.

Dr. Benjamin patted his hand on Jack's back. "There, there son. I know how you feel. I also lost some comrades of mine many years ago when I was a hunter. I'm sorry for your loss. If there's anything I can do for you, please, feel free to let me know."

Jack paid no attention to him as he screamed at the top of his lungs. Oh why, oh why, God, was this happening? Why was he going through all of this? He repented and tried to be a better version of himself. And now this was the price he had to pay. He couldn't take it anymore. He had enough.

Once Jack was done, there was more silence in the car. Jack looked at Dr. Benjamin. The man radiated and oozed a sort of aura that was indescribable and unpredictable. It was captivating, and it even made Jack forget about his worries and issues.

"Dr. Benjamin, how are you driving when you're blind?"

Dr. Benjamin smiled.

"I have very good hearing, let's just say that. Plus, I have a technique of mine that allows me to actually be able to see and feel the road for any oncoming vehicles."

"And that technique is…?"

"One day you'll learn. For now, let's just forget about it."

Jack nodded his head. He looked at the man some more. He knew that Jack was looking at him. How, though? Also, this man was a hunter. Yet, why didn't Jack hear anything about him?

"If you were a hunter, how come I've never heard anything about you?"

Benjamin smiled. "I left early. Just like David, I retired when I was still relatively young. I wanted to be a lawyer, and I felt that being a hunter was too taxing on my mind. So I left and went to law school. The rest is history."

"What kind of lawyer are you?"

"I work with narcotics."

The instant he said that, he turned his head away from the road and looked at Jack. Even with his blind eyes, he could stare deeply into Jack's soul. He looked at him and smiled. He said nothing more. Jack felt uneasy. He knew that look, and he probably knew more about Jack than he let on. Still, Jack didn't care. He didn't care about anything at this point. He just wanted to die.

After a while of a god-awful silence, they reached Wilmhelm. Dr. Benjamin left Jack off at Andrea's house. Before he drove off, he gave Jack a piece of paper.

"In case you ever find yourself in any trouble—either legal or not—give me a call. I live an hour away from here. Keep in touch… and don't do anything stupid."

Jack nodded his head, and Dr. Benjamin drove off. Jack looked at Andrea's house. Just looking at it gave him chills. He couldn't go inside. No… not yet. Even though Jack smelled, and was kind of hungry, he didn't want to eat or take a shower. He had too many things on his mind. He wanted to forget everything and have fun and kick back—something he hadn't done in quite a while. Jack knew exactly where to start.

As Jack was walking, he passed by Samantha's house. He dared not even say hi to her. She was probably struggling harder with David's loss than he was. He hoped she wasn't next, or else Jack would have to resort to suicide.

Later, Jack passed by Audrey's house. It was empty, and the family probably went out somewhere. Jack cried. That damn bitch! How dare she. Jack became so frustrated and so angry, yet so sad at the same time. Dammit... he loved her. He loved her so much, he was willing to risk it all just for her. And now she left him... she left him when he needed her the most. Oh well, whatever. *I don't need her anyway,* thought Jack as he threw a rock at her bedroom window, shattering it on impact. He cried as he ran toward the liquor store.

Jack stole nearly all the alcohol they had. He went in through the back window and grabbed as many beverages as he could—whiskey, beer, wine, rum, gin. Jack grabbed it all. He was never good at stealth, but sneaking into a liquor store when the clerk was clearly tired was like taking candy from a baby. Jack left without a shadow of a trace and went to an empty hallway, where he proceeded to get absolutely hammered.

In an attempt to take his own life, Jack proceeded to get a fucked up as humanly possible. He drank 3 whole bottles of Jack Daniel's. He passed out and woke up to drink as much wine as humanly possible—he drank four whole bottles by himself. Now he was incapable of walking. That was OK. He didn't need to walk to drink all the beer he gathered—Jack consumed nearly 100 ounces. He passed out again for a few hours. He woke up in the dead of the night.

He limped to the nearest drug dealer he knew. He bought everything and spent all of the little money that he had: cocaine, ecstasy, marijuana, mushrooms, PCP, heroin, meth, salvia, DMT, GHB, bath salts and horse tranquilizer. Jack was BEYOND fucked up. He couldn't walk and was practically a zombie. In less than four hours, his flesh was already rotting, and his nose was bleeding beyond control. He lost so much blood he passed out again. The police tried to arrest him for public indecency, but he attacked them when they tried to arrest him. He killed four police officers and mutilated three more. He ran away and wreaked havoc on the town. He was a zombie and walked like one. He limped with one hand not even being able to function. The other one used to masturbate as he exposed himself.

Jack started eating his hand. He bit his fingers off and ate them. Later, he sold his fake arm so he could buy some more PCP—which is what he exactly did. As he was balls-to-the-wall high and uncontrollable, he remembered her. Oh... how she ruined his life. He would make her PAY. How dare she break up with him! WHO DID SHE THINK SHE WAS? HE WOULD MAKE HER

PAY! HER AND HER WHOLE FAMILY! Absolutely drugged out of his mind, Jack raced over to Audrey's house.

Audrey was sitting at the dinner table with her family, eating a nice Caesar salad with soup.

Sara spoke up. "So, Audrey, how is school going?"

Audrey nodded her head. She had a very big and bright smile. "Oh, it's going good. I got an A on that math test I told you about!"

Her dad rejoiced with joy. "That is amazing, Audrey! I knew you could do it! All that studying paid off!"

Audrey nodded her head. Her warm smile filled the table. Everyone smiled as the dinner was superb!

Sara gave Audrey a sly look and finished eating her food when she spoke up.

"So, Audrey… do you like any boys?"

Audrey rolled her eyes.

"Um… no. I'm not into any guys. Besides, if I WAS into someone, I doubt they would be interested in me."

"Oh, so there is someone then?"

"W-what? I never said that."

"You said if there 'WAS' someone. I think you're hiding something there."

"M-mom!"

"It's OK. You don't have to tell me if you don't want to. I trust your intuition when it comes to men… although you have made some bad decisions in the past."

Audrey looked up from her soup. She looked at her dad, and he nodded her head. She already knew who they were talking about. She quickly became agitated and furious.

"You're talking about Jack, aren't you?"

Sara raised her eyebrows. She was shocked. Her face changed, and soon she quickly became frustrated.

"EXCUSE ME, miss, but don't you raise your voice at me like that! First of all, I know what's best for you, and I know that… that Jack boy was no good. You nearly cried every day. You said it was because you didn't know, then it was because you loved him. Now you cry because you miss him. See, he's no good and I don't want you getting back to him. You better—"

"SHUT UP!"

The table went silent. Audrey was now crying. She showed her teeth and yelled at her mom.

"You don't know ANYTHING about Jack. Jack is wonderful and amazing. He's a better person than you'll ever be! I miss him because I don't want to see him suffer. That's why I ended it. I am planning on getting back to him when he gets better. Yeah, he has some issues, but don't we all? You better not talk bad about him, you don't know anything about him! You better shut up!"

Audrey cried as she ran upstairs. Her dad was about to go when Sara grabbed him by the wrist.

"Leave her. I'll go talk to her later."

Just then, there was a knock on the door. Sara's mom sighed and rubbed her head as she opened the door. She screamed and jumped back when she saw Jack.

Part of Jack's hair was missing; the other half of his hair looked burned, as if he were in some sort of serious fire. His face was a mess. His nose was all messed up, and he had cuts from scratching his face too much. His eyes were pitch black, and a piece of his ear was missing.

His left arm was nowhere to be seen, and his right arm had cuts and holes scattered all across. His penis was erect and showing. His legs were ripped and torn. His body was very red, and there were bruises all across his body. He smelled HORRIBLE, and he was almost unable to speak.

"Uuuhhh," said Jack as he reached his hand out to Sara. He grabbed her breast and started groping her. She shrieked as she slapped Jack's hand away. The father, seeing an opportunity, went and attacked Jack. He punched Jack in the face and started kicking him on the floor. Despite being drugged out of his mind, Jack was still a capable fighter. Best of all, he couldn't feel any pain, so the kicks and the punches did absolutely nothing.

Jack grabbed the dad's foot and twisted it until it broke. The dad yelled as Jack kicked him in the balls and bit his nose off. He ate the nose and jammed both his index and thumb into the dad's eyes, gouging out both his eyes and blinding him permanently. Jack then bit the poor dad's ear off as he yelled and moaned. The dad fell on the floor and wailed like a baby.

Sara grabbed a knife and threw it at Jack. It struck Jack in his stomach. To no avail, Jack charged at her. He limped very fast, and it was like something out of a horror scene. Sara was paralyzed with fear as Jack pushed her to the ground.

She yelled and screamed, but it was fruitless. Jack grabbed her shirt and ate it. He then ripped off her bra and started motorboating her and sucking away. Sara started to cry. Jack hissed in her ear.

"STerrprrsndywufbjahv sargfuwlikhbfzuyapijmdwnfhbuyr."

"J-Jack… Jack, STOP!"

Jack looked up. It was Audrey. Jack couldn't recognize her, though. The drugs were practically eating his brains away. Jack mumbled as he stood up and walked toward Audrey, his hand extended. He muttered something inaudible, and Audrey shook her head, still crying. She pushed Jack away.

"DON'T FUCKING TOUCH ME!"

Jack took a step back. Her words were able to put some sense into Jack. He looked around and saw the mother crying, and the father screaming. He was… finally starting to calm down. He looked at Audrey, and she shook her head.

"I… am… done! Look at what you have done to my life… to my house… to ME! I hate you, you son of a bitch! GO AWAY, AND GET AWAY! I NEVER, EVER WANT TO SEE YOU EVER AGAIN! DO YOU HEAR ME? I HATE YOU. I WISH YOU WERE NEVER BORN!"

Jack sobered up that instant. His eyes returned to normal, and his vision became clear. Jack looked down and realized he was naked. He started to cry.

"Audrey… I'm so, so—"

She punched him as hard as she could. It did nothing, but Jack took it.

"No… I'm done with all of your excuses, with all of your B.S., with all of your drug-filled messes. I'm not going to press charges, but I swear to God, if I ever see you ever again, or if you try talking to me, then I'll call the cops, and I'll personally kill you myself!"

Jack cried as he looked at the chaos and confusion he had caused. He ran out of the house and cried and cried. He went into Andrea's house, where her mother was out buying groceries. He went to his bedroom, and he cried and cried. He went to the kitchen and went to go and slit his throat. He had the knife to his throat and closed his eyes.

"Don't," said a voice.

Jack looked up and saw a massive and super bright light coming down upon him. He closed his eyes, and when he opened them up again… he saw him. The one who led him on his journey.

Jack's eyes opened. The man in front of him smiled. He had tan skin and short, curly hair. His beard was long and well-trimmed. He had a lovable and wonderful smile and such a sweet face.

"Hello," said the voice.

Jack immediately cried upon hearing the voice. It was him... it was Jesus!

Jack cried and cried. Jesus gathered Jack in his arms and wept with him. Jack buried his head in Jesus's shoulder. He wept and wept, and wept so loudly and so greatly Jack thought that he would never stop. Yet, just as Jack was weeping, so too was Jesus.

Jack stopped, and he gathered to his feet. He wiped the tears away from his eyes. Just looking at Jesus made Jack want to cry more. He couldn't understand why, but it just... did.

Jack looked at the wonderful, beautiful and amazing smile that was looking at him. Jesus spoke. His voice was so smooth, and soothing, so calm and so kind. It made Jack want to weep even more.

"My son... I see you're struggling and going through a rough and difficult time right now. I understand that It can be hard, but please don't kill yourself. There is more to life than this."

Jack shed a tear as he turned away. He was ashamed... too ashamed to even look at someone as great and as amazing as Jesus.

"I... I can't. I've done so many horrible things. I ruined Audrey's life... I am a monster. Oh please... please, Jesus... please forgive me for all that I have done. Please forgive my broken soul."

Jesus spun Jack around. Jack faced the light that was coming from Jesus. Jesus smiled as he embraced Jack in his wide and lovable arms.

"My son... Jack. I will ALWAYS forgive you."

Jack cried as he heard these words. Never in his life did he cry so much as he did that day when he met Jesus. Jack buried his head even more into Jesus, and Jesus cried alongside Jack.

Jack wiped the tears away from his life.

"Why... why? Just why? Why had everything gone horribly wrong? Why am I suffering? Don't you love me? If you do, why have you made my life a living hell!"

Jack cried some more. He felt ashamed for even yelling at someone like Jesus. Jesus placed his hand on Jack's shoulder.

"My love for you knows no bounds. Just know this: everything I do… there is a reason for it. I do everything for a reason. Everything that is happening now… I am doing this for a reason. To help you grow and develop as a person. You may not see it, but trust my Father in heaven, who does all things to help you flourish and grow.

"I took Yuri away because he was too kind for this world. I took Andrea from this world because it was her time. My father said so. I took David and John's life away so that this may happen, So that you may grow. You may not see it, but since the day you arrived here in Wilmhelm, my father has been working TIRELESSLY to help you grow and flourish. You have. You just don't know it, but you have grown."

Jack nodded his head. "I-I-I see. But… but…"

Jack cried some more. He was so overwhelmed with emotion—powerful emotions. He couldn't bear looking at Jesus anymore. Jesus, with his infinite love, placed Jack in his arms and hugged him. Jack felt so comfortable, and so sincere when he was with Jesus. It was indescribable.

Jesus smiled. "Do not worry, my son. Everything will turn out OK. Do you trust me?"

Jack nodded his head. "I do."

"No… I mean do you REALLY trust me? If I were to tell you to jump off a mountain, would you do it?"

"Yes. I would."

"Then let me see it, my son."

Soon, they were transported to the top of a mountain. Without even hesitation, and without even looking down, Jack jumped off the mountain. Soon, he was transported back into the white room, with Jesus smiling upon him.

"If you trust me this much, then do you trust me when I say that soon, you will understand why everything is going this way? Do you trust me when I say that I understand how you are feeling, since I too once lived in this world? I too experienced pain and hardship harder than any man has faced. I was persecuted, spit upon, tortured and killed. I know the desires of this earth since the devil tempted me ever since I was able to remember. I know how you feel. My son, I love you! More than you can ever imagine. Now, until the end of the age! My son, do you trust me when I say that I am helping you out right as we speak?"

Jack nodded his head.

"My son, do you trust me when I say that everything will be OK and that things will be better than you could ever possibly imagine?"

Jack nodded his head. Jesus smiled as he embraced Jack once again, and once again Jack cried more and more. He never wanted to leave Jesus. This feeling… it was too powerful. It was… heavenly, and amazing!

Jack smiled as Jesus kissed him on his forehead.

"Now, promise me one thing, my son."

Jack nodded his head. "Anything."

Jesus grabbed a syringe from out of thin air. "You MUST stop this. Do you understand?"

Jack nodded his head. "No more. I promise I will never do any. If I do, then you may strike me down and kill me!"

"Do you know why I am asking you to stop?"

Jack pondered for a little bit. "Is it… because it is bad for me?"

"Yes, but also because I want you to stay sober. I want you to draw closer to me, and I want to be with you. When you are not sober, you are easily more tempted and drawn out by the evil one. Please, stay sober so I can be near to you!"

Jack nodded his head. "I will, my God almighty. I WILL!"

Jesus smiled as he kissed Jack on the forehead and hugged him.

"Then truly I say, my son, rejoice! For soon you shall see the kingdom of heaven!"

Before Jack went, he saw a vision. Behind Jesus, David, John, Yuri, Andrea and Natalia were all smiling and waving at Jack. Jack nearly broke down as he saw them. He cried and smiled as he wept. Jesus kissed him, and soon everything went black.

Jack woke up on the kitchen floor. He remembered everything. He looked at the knife and threw it away as far as he could. He curled up into a ball and started to cry.

18

Jack was in his room when he heard a noise downstairs. He rushed downstairs to investigate. It was Andrea's mom opening the door. She looked surprised when she saw Jack, but she made no noise whatsoever.

"H-hello," said Rebecca as she put down her groceries. Jack was surprised. She didn't seem too concerned with him. Perhaps she knew he was living here? Andrea almost never mentioned her mother, so he couldn't say for certain. Jack walked downstairs and introduced himself to her. He extended his hand.

"My name is Jack. Nice to meet you."

She shook his hands. Rebecca was analyzing Jack and noticed all the scars and holes that were common with heroin addicts. Jack quickly hid his right arm. His face had been healed and he had come down, but he still looked like a mess. He shaved his hair and now had a buzzcut. His face was leaner and thinner. His piercings were now gone.

"My name is Rebecca. I'm Andrea's mom." Jack gave a warm smile as she was putting away the groceries. She took a gander at him.

"Pardon me for asking, but may I ask what happened to your left arm?"

"N-no. Not at all. I lost it in the gas station incident. I was with your daughter."

"Ah. I see. Such a horrible thing, no?"

Jack nodded his head. The images and smell of death were still fresh in his mind. Jack cleared his throat.

"I don't know if Andrea told you this, but for a while, she was my caretaker. I was living with her and now… she's passed away. I'm sorry for your loss."

Andrea's mother waved her hand so nonchalantly, that Jack wondered if the woman ever cared for her daughter at all.

"Don't worry. It's just part of life. Anyway, this is now MY house. Technically it always was. I own this house and a house in Philadelphia. I allowed Andrea to live in this place while she was struggling to find a job. Now that nobody can take care of this house, I might as well take care of it myself. My husband is all the way in Philadelphia."

She stopped putting away her groceries and looked at Jack seductively. She licked her lips and approached him closer.

"How old are you?"

Jack gulped. Like mother, like daughter. She smiled as she approached Jack.

"I'm 18. I will graduate high school soon."

Crap, thought Jack as he thought about high school. He was out for a while, and he doubted Andrea said anything to the school. He had either been kicked out of the system or had some serious makeup work to do. Either way, he was in a world of trouble when he got back. That was for sure. Although right now that didn't matter. The lady in front of him mattered.

She was an oldish woman for sure. She looked to be around in her mid to early 50s. She put her hands on Jack's chest. Despite her age, she was quite pretty indeed. Just like her daughter, she had massive boobs and had long silky brown hair. She had dark green glasses. She was quite toned, despite her age, and had very nice muscles.

Jack closed his eyes and thought about it for a moment. Audrey… Audrey… Audrey… she said it was over… right? So he might as well do it with this GILF. Yet, he knew it was wrong. Despite it being over with Audrey, he felt as though he still had some sort of obligation. Yet… what obligation? He couldn't even be near her without pressing any charges, so why on earth would he ever date her again? Let alone have sex? He might as well enjoy it with this nice and attractive older woman. Still, despite how he felt, he knew that there was a gut feeling, a deep gut feeling inside of him telling him it was wrong. He thought about Jesus and shook his head.

He pushed Rebecca away. "Sorry, but I'm too young." He walked away. In reality, he could have easily done it with her and did not want to do it. Yet, there was an intuition telling him that it was wrong. So wrong to do what he was doing. So he decided to listen to it. As he walked away to go upstairs to his room, he felt good and had a nice big smile as he lay down on his bed and closed his eyes. Right above him, Jesus was smiling.

Jack woke up in the middle of the night with a message from his phone. It was an unknown number. He declined. The number called again. He declined.

A third time and now Jack picked it up and quickly hung up. The number called again.

"Hello," mumbled Jack.

"Oh, awesome. It's me… Terrence. You don't know me, but I'm one of John's friends. Anyway, listen up, you're needed back at S.H.O.T. HQ, ASAP. Think you can make it quick?"

Jack fumbled out of bed and put on his clothes. He quickly ran outside and ran all the way to the toilet. He quickly flushed the toilet and headed downstairs, where the entire HQ was in absolute disarray. People were running around like chickens without their heads on. Hunters were fighting and arguing with each other, and important documents were being thrown around. Files and folders were being burned, and a small fight club had broken. Jack was in shambles as Terrance grabbed him by his arm.

"Come on, I need to show you something, and stay with me, please."

Terrance was an absolute monster. 194 centimeters and 98 kilos of pure muscle mass. He was bigger than David AND Yuri. He had black hair and bright blue eyes. His triceps could easily crush Jack, and his shoulders were almost bigger than his head. He had on a massive blue and black flannel jacket with very, very, very large jeans that were constantly falling. His fingernails were painted black and he had a very small nose ring.

"What's going on?" asked Jack as Terrence led Jack into Natalia's office. In the corner of his eye, Jack saw Dr. Benjamin trying to resolve an argument between what looked like two higher-up S.H.O.T. members, based on the way they were dressed. Benjamin gave him a glance that practically screamed, 'Get me out of here!'

They went into Natalia's office, and Terrence threw away a bunch of important folders and documents from her desk. He then grabbed a piece of paper and showed it to Jack. He handed it to Jack and forced him to read it.

Upon reading it, Jack's eyes practically burst with horror. *Oh my goodness,* he thought as he put the paper down. He sat down on Natalia's chair and rubbed his forehead. He was NOT ready for this, not today, after everything that happened. Terrence looked at Jack and nodded his head.

"That's right. In Natalia's will, it stated that if anything were to happen to her, you would take over as the new head chairman of S.H.O.T."

Jack shook his head. "I mean… I don't even know where to start. Also, why did she choose me? Also, what do I even do? I have so many questions. I mean… I-I-I-this is outlandish."

Terrence shrugged his shoulders. "Sorry to say it, but that's just the way things are now. This whole mess that you see outside is because some people are in favor of this change, and some people aren't."

Jack stood silent for a while. If there was a supposed system in S.H.O.T., then was there someone even higher than Natalia? Jack thought about it, as they would probably know what best to do. Jack looked up at Terrence.

"Who founded S.H.O.T.?"

Terrence chuckled.

"Ha, good luck. It was supposedly founded either in the early or mid-1700s. Anyway, the founder named 'Jared' (nobody knows his real last name) was the first founder of S.H.O.T. Essentially. From what I've been told, he and his friends were basically the first three members. After that, history gets a little blurry, but sooner or later people from all over the world start appearing with the 'gift' that both you and I have. Soon, S.H.O.T. is a nationwide thing, although we tend to stay underground. Even back then, I don't think too many people thought we existed. Heck, I wouldn't if you told me you could go inside people's minds and kill them."

"I see. Is there someone higher up than Natalia?"

Terrence shook his head. "I'm afraid not. There are other S.H.O.T. headquarters and members in other parts of the world, but nobody as high up on the scale as Natalia. Nor is there any headquarters bigger than ours. There's a reason we decided to set up shop in a town as small as this. Who would think to look for some underground organization here?"

Terrence patted Jack on the back. He then pointed to the ensuing chaos happening outside. "Sorry to tell you this, man, but it looks like this mess is now yours."

Jack closed his eyes and put his head down. He mumbled and groaned. Why him? He already had so many things to do. The question that seemed to stick out the most was why Natalia decided to appoint him, rather than anybody else. From what he understood, Jack felt as though Natalia hated his guts. Before Tarrence left, Jack asked him a question.

"Do you know why Natalia decided to appoint me?"

He quickly looked back.

"From what I've been told, she liked you. She talked about you a lot to other hunters. You kind of have this aura to you here; people gossip about you because Natalia won't shut up about how many balls you have, or how good of a hunter you are. No offense or anything, kid, but you don't look like a badass type to me, nor the type of hunter Natalia describes you as. But hey, I'd be happy if you were to prove me wrong. Now, if you'll excuse me, I need to go and take care of what's happening outside."

With that, Terrence left. Leaving Jack all by himself. Jack took a moment to collect his thoughts and do anything that wasn't too rash. *I'll be damned,* he thought as he took a look at the piece of paper one more time. He couldn't believe that Natalia was the one to set him up as a successor when she passed away. It was supposed to be the person below her, yet here Jack was—not even a year into his hunter job. Jack took a look outside, it really was chaotic. As Jack was about to leave, Dr. Benjamin came into the room and quickly grasped Jack by the shoulders. His face was pale, and he seemed on the brink of a mental collapse.

"Jack, thank goodness you're here. Have you heard the news?"

Jack nodded his head. "Terrence filled me in. It seems like quite a mess indeed."

Dr. Benjamin nodded his head. "Quick, I need all the paperwork and files that you can find on Natalia's desk. And please hurry up; we need to leave here ASAP!"

"W-why? What's wr—"

"What's wrong is that I'm your lawyer and you're going to court, goddammit!"

Dr. Benjamin was grabbing all the pieces of paperwork and files and stuffing them in his suit. He grabbed as many as he could and gave them to Jack. After reviewing everything he needed, he grabbed Jack by the hand and left. They quickly rushed to the elevator and got out of there. Dr. Benjamin took a while to catch his breath and talk to Jack. "S-sorry, Jack, but I'll explain everything.

"In S.H.O.T., there is a legal system. Yes… a legal system. This was created in order to ensure that hunters don't abuse their powers. I don't know if you knew this, but you can practically go inside anybody's mind just by touching them."

"Wait. Anybody? How come whenever I touched someone I—"

"That's because you need to be thinking about entering their mind. If you're just holding someone by the hand and admiring their beauty, you're not going to enter their mind because you're not thinking about it. For example, now that you know this, you can touch me and try to enter my mind. I don't recommend it. I'll probably just be a castle with a bunch of paperwork. Anyway, this legal system was designed so that hunters don't abuse their powers. Also, you're one of the very few hunters to know about this fact. The court was heading to, but almost no hunter had been there. Very few really know what happens there.

"Also, it was specifically made for a situation like this. If somebody like Natalia ever decided to give someone a position as high as hers, to someone as low as you, then legal matters would be taken there. Now, since I like you, I'll be your lawyer. Now, quick, we have to drive to Harrisburg as that is where the court lies."

Jack hurried to Dr. Benjamin's Jaguar, and the two of them headed off. As they were driving, they pulled over to Samantha's house.

"We need a witness. Grab Samantha and let's go!"

Jack quickly hopped out and knocked on Samantha's door. She was asleep. Jack kicked down the door and woke her up.

"What the hell are you doing in my house?"

"No time to explain, we need to leave ASAP! We're going to Allentown."

Samantha's eyes widened as she threw on a pair of comfortable clothes and headed out of her house.

"Dr. Benjamin, nice to finally meet you," said Samantha as she shook Ben's hand.

"You... know him?"

Samantha nodded her head. "He's a good friend of ours. He helps us with anything that we need. And when I say anything... I mean ANYTHING!"

Jack nodded as Dr. Benjamin headed off onto the highway. There were police littered all over, and signs asking and rewarding people for the whereabouts of John. Seeing his picture gave both Samantha and Jack sadness as they remembered their fallen comrade.

Samantha had a vague idea as to how David and John died. She did think that Natalia had something to do with it, but she never expected Natalia to be the one to kill both of them. She didn't know much about Natalia's relationship with David, but she knew that something felt odd and fishy about David's sudden retirement. After doing a little bit of investigation and trying to get answers from John, she was able to deduce that Natalia fired David, and told him to tell everyone it was a retirement. She didn't know why, and to this day, she still didn't know. It didn't matter. David was dead as well as John, and as much as it pained her, she could do nothing about it except honor their memories. She wanted to tell Jack that she felt as though Natalia was responsible for David's and John's deaths, but she decided not to say anything. He was probably going through a lot, and the thought of mentioning David and John brought a tear to her eye.

Dr. Benjamin cleared his throat. "Is anybody hungry? I know it's quite early in the morning, but I am a little bit famished. I'm sure there's some dinner or inn open along the way. Anybody care for some breakfast?"

Jack nodded his head. Samantha as well. They drove a little bit more and soon they stopped at a local small-town dinner. As they walked outside, they realized that they were the only ones there.

Jack asked Dr. Benjamin a question.

"You said we're going to court, and that you're DEFENDING me. I'm guessing someone is trying to… sue me? Is that even the right word?"

Dr. Benjamin nodded his head. "Not sure, but someone is trying to… get in your position. Let's just say that. A man by the name of 'James Donald.' He was supposed to be the next person to succeed Natalia if anything were to happen to her. It seems like he didn't take too kindly to you being chosen. Anyway, let's just forget about that now, and let's chow down on some pancakes."

They were practically the only ones at the diner. There wasn't even a waitress, but just the chefs who placed their meal orders and took their cash. They sat down, and Dr. Benjamin went to the bathroom, leaving only Samantha and Jack.

Jack looked at her. She looked tired, depressed and out of hope. Jack grabbed her hands.

"Is everything OK, Samantha?"

Samantha shook her head. She started to cry.

"N-no. I can't believe it. Jack… everyone is dead, aren't they? They're all dead."

Jack nodded his head. He felt like crying as well.

"Yeah… it looks like it's just us."

"I remember the day we met. I wanted to kill you so badly, and you called me a bitch! I even saved you from that crazed serial killer's mind."

Jack smiled. "Don't forget about the time you tried to kill me too."

She smiled. "What a strange friendship, don't you think?"

"I wouldn't want it any other way. The same with everyone else. I loved them just the way they were. Speaking of friendships, did you and David…"

She nodded her head. "We became a… thing just shortly before he died. The only romantic thing we did was hook up, nothing more. But when we did become a thing, the sex became… better. It felt more… enjoyable. Not only that, but I had a companion with me who I could trust and care for… and now h-hes…"

Samantha couldn't finish her sentence as she cried some more. Jack comforted her, just as Jesus did to him. He hugged her, and she smiled. She wiped the tears away from her eyes and laughed.

"What's with you?"

Jack looked confused. "What do you mean?"

"I mean… you never hugged me. What's the deal, you looking for some action? Because you're not going to get any from me."

"My goodness, of course not. You looked like you were sad, and I just wanted to cheer you up. That's all."

She smiled as their food came. Jack thought about what she said. She was right; he had never hugged her before. Partially because he didn't want anything weird brewing between them, but also because he never really felt the need to comfort her. Now that he was trying to change, he just felt a very strong urge to comfort her. Not in any weird or romantic way, but a kind way to show affection, and to try and cheer the other person up.

Dr. Benjamin came back, and they all finished eating and left. After spending a few hours in the car, they finally arrived.

"Ladies and gentlemen, I present to you Harrisburg. Truly a marvelous dump in the state of Pennsylvania."

They all looked at the entrance to Harrisburg. What a dump indeed. The place was dirty and grimy. It was quite small, and despite it nearly being summer, it looked as if winter had fallen upon the place. Jack had no idea why anybody would want to live in a place like this. As they drove through the streets, Jack saw homeless people and more and more trash as the streets passed on. The houses looked old, like post-WW2 old. There were stray animals plaguing the streets and poor people begging for money on the sidewalk.

"I find it quite fitting for a court to be here," said Dr. Benjamin as he pulled into a driveway just outside a local mall. Jack and Samantha got out and went inside the mall. Even inside, the place looked messy. There was practically nobody there, making the whole place look like a ghost town. Before they entered the store, Dr. Benjamin looked at both of them with very stern and keen eyes. He grabbed something from his pocket and gave it to Jack.

"Here, put this in your pocket."

Jack looked down. It was a pill. Why was he needing a pill? Jack nodded his head in confusion and put it in his back pocket. The doctor leaned in and whispered in Jack's ear, "These men are messy. If things go south, I want you to swallow that pill for me. It's for your own protection. Understand me?"

Jack nodded his head. An eerie feeling arose in him as he looked at the store they were about to enter. It was a pregnancy store. Jack gulped, who exactly were these men that were going to convict him? He had no idea, but he feared as he felt the pill in his back pocket. Whatever happened, whatever went down south, Jack was prepared to do what he needed to do.

Dr. Benjamin also grabbed something from his bag. It was a metal arm. He gave it to Jack.

"Here you go. A nice metal arm for you. It's much better than anything you've ever seen, and 10 times better than what the hospital gave you."

Jack attached the arm. He could move his left arm freely now, and not only that, but the arm felt incredible. He felt so… powerful and so strong. He felt as though he could move swiftly with ease. The arm was all black, and despite it having lots of strength, it was quite thin. Still, that didn't stop Jack from smiling. He finally had an arm, and a much better one than his previous prosthetic arm.

Dr. Benjamin saw Jack's smile. "I see you like it. I'm glad. Courtesy of S.H.O.T. organization. I had one made when I heard the news that you lost your arm."

Jack smiled as Dr. Benjamin leaned into Samantha. He whispered something in her ear and gave her something that she quickly tucked under her shirt and into her pants. Jack only caught a brief glimpse, but if what he saw was what he thought, he knew that this courthouse was not an ordinary courthouse. Dr. Benjamin straightened his tie, and the two of them went inside.

They entered the bathroom and flushed the toilet four times. After one flush, they had to wait 6.5 seconds.

As they were heading down, Jack started to wonder why on earth so many of the S.H.O.T. organizations ended up having bases in bathrooms.

"Why is it that so many of our S.H.O.T. buddies and higher-ups have so many bases underneath bathrooms?"

Dr. Benjamin chuckled. "Well, they're not actually UNDERNEATH a bathroom. In reality, they are in a separate plane of dimension, you can say. Only hunters can enter this dimension. It has the same structure as the dimension when you enter someone's mind. The dimension we are about to enter is called Dimension 2. Dimension 1 is where you enter people's minds."

"Is there a dimension 3?"

"Yes. In fact, you are one of the only living people to have gone there."

Samantha widened her eyes. "Jack? W-where did you go?"

Jack shrugged. He had no idea what Dr. Benjamin was talking about. As he looked up at Dr. Benjamin, the good doctor smiled, and Jack felt a shiver go down his spine. He got goosebumps as Dr. Benjamin knew that Jesus talked to Jack, and they went… somewhere to talk and discuss.

"H-how on earth did you—"

"That's a story for a different time. Come on, we are here."

The elevator stopped, and the doors opened, and all three of them walked into a courtroom. There was something off about this courtroom.

The courtroom was absolutely massive. No, not massive, but humongous. Way bigger than any courtroom on earth. Its walls were thin and sleek, but they continued on forever. There was no end to them. Even until the eyes could see, they kept on going and going. The floor was entirely made of gold. Pure and unsaturated gold. The kind of gold that kings and queens have wet dreams about. The jury box was made completely of diamonds, and there was already a judge sitting there. He didn't look real. It was hard to explain, but he didn't look even the slightest bit human. His hair, his face, his eyes, they were all… so uncanny and perplexing.

Jack saw that James Donald and his lawyer were already there waiting for the boys. James Donald was a very fat man with orange skin. He had a mean face, and he was a little bit taller than Jack. His hands were massive though. Almost as thick as his chubby forearms. Every time he spoke, he spit out saliva, and his voice was ruined because his neck was practically suffocating him with how much fat he had.

"Ah, I see you have arrived. Good!" said James as he waddled over to the three of them. He gave Dr. Benjamin a hug and kissed him on the cheek. He bowed down and kissed Samantha on her hand. She looked like a slug had kissed her. He looked at Jack… and spit on the floor.

"You bastard! Who do you think you are, trying to take my spot away from me?"

Jack smiled as James' face started to get red.

"Easy there, I'm just as confused as you are."

James shook his head and mumbled something inaudible. Not because he was speaking too low, but because he was so fat that nobody could really hear what he had to say. His neck was so thick and filled with fat that grease was coming out of it. He waddled away and sat down. Dr. Benjamin escorted Jack and Samantha to sit down. After a while of gathering their paperwork, the two lawyers were ready. The judge stood up and spoke. When he spoke, he captivated the room. Jack was astonished by his voice. It was… almost something heavenly.

"Now then, I declare that Dr. Benjamin goes first," said the judge. "Please present your argument ahead."

Dr. Benjamin stood up. "Your honor, first and foremost I would—"

Dr. Benjamin was cut short as he was shot in the head. James' lawyer also shot the judge in the head, killing both of them. Jack quickly grabbed the pill from his back pocket and ate it. Samantha grabbed her gun and fired it at the lawyer. It missed, and the lawyer fired his gun at her, hitting her in the shoulder. She fell over, and Jack ducked for cover as the lawyer reloaded his gun. Donald laughed out loud in sheer excitement as he also took cover.

"A-are you alright?" asked Samantha as the blood was trickling down her shirt. Jack nodded his head.

"Don't worry about me, just go and get out of here. Give me the gun and I'll cover you."

She shook her head. "Yeah, no way. You need to leave ASAP! The judge is dead and… wait, Dr. Benjamin. Is… Is the good doctor still alive, or is he dead? I think we can… yes! I have a plan."

Jack looked upward but quickly ducked again as a gun grazed his head. He gritted his teeth and cursed.

"He's dead, dammit!"

Samantha cursed as well. "Well, it's no surprise, he was shot in the head. Anyway, he had something on his tie. Something to help us out in this case."

"And that would be what?"

Before Samantha could speak, a bullet passed through them and hit Samantha in her other shoulder. She yelled as Jack started to feel funny. The pill was kicking in, and holy crap, was it kicking.

Jack's vision heightened. Holy... it was hitting alright. Jack felt himself feeling the molecules on his arm. His pupils dilated so much that they practically disappeared. He smiled as he felt a massive surge of power and energy. He smiled as he jumped up and ran toward the lawyer. He ran at such a fast speed that the lawyer had no time to fire his gun. Jack grabbed the gun and fired it at the lawyer. He then pointed it at James, who pleaded for his life.

"O-oh pwease. I'm so shorry. F-fargive me! I just wanted whet was rightfully meine."

Jack was about to shoot him until he remembered a passage from the Bible. He remembered it stated, "Blessed are those who show mercy, for mercy shall be shown upon them."

Jack gritted his teeth. He threw his gun and yelled at James. He grabbed Dr. Benjamin's tie, and he grabbed Samantha, and he ran toward the elevator. He was so fast, and he felt invincible. What kind of pill did that doctor give him? Jack felt as though he could run across the world, or as if he could beat anybody in a fight. He could smell the colors around him. The color blue smelled like salt and paint. The color green smelled like plastic and Styrofoam. Jack smiled as he never, ever felt so alive in his life. Whatever the good doctor gave him, it sure worked.

They ran out of the mall and quickly went into Dr. Benjamin's car. Samantha screamed.

"Crap. I can't drive... I'm in too much pain. I'm sorry, Jack, I—"

Jack grabbed her and put her on his shoulder. He started running toward the nearest hospital. Jack ran faster than any car on the road. He ran so fast that Samantha even passed out. Jack leaped and jumped over crossroads, railways, railings and sidewalks. He had so much energy. He felt unstoppable. He could feel his muscles moving so fast that he was unable to stop running. He was unable to stop because he had so much energy.

He quickly dropped Samantha off at the hospital and ran away. He wanted to see just how fast he could run. He ran to the train tracks and saw a train coming and approaching him. Jack smiled as he raced alongside the train. The freight train was honking at him to get away, but Jack ignored him as not only was he on par with the train, but he was even FASTER than the freight train. He ran away and practically ran across the whole city in less than 5 minutes.

James got out of the mall. He was REALLY pissed. That damn brat, who did he think he was? He called up some of his friends and yelled at them to come to Harrisburg as fast as they could. He started sweating the grease off his neck. He waited near his car and started to smoke a cigar to calm him down. It didn't work, so he tried the next best thing. He snorted a line of coke. Now that really didn't help. He was so amped up and excited that he went to a brothel nearby to wait and pass the time until his friends arrived.

There was a helicopter approaching the city. Inside the helicopter were 4 different men. One was a skinny-ish and tall man (54 Kilos, 180 centimeters). He was wearing a tight combat shirt with baggy Crye combat pants. He was locked and loaded. He carried two pistols. One was a .50 caliber, and the other one was a .45 revolver. He had a rifle attached to his back and a knife inside his boots. His black emo haircut. His name was Micah.

The other man beside him was even bigger. He was 189 centimeters and 100 kilos of sheer muscle. He had on a beret, a long-sleeved shirt and pants. He had a very thick and horrible scar running down his face. His blonde hair stuck out too much, and he only carried a knife and a small 45. His name was Leon.

The other man was not as tall as the others (176 centimeters), nor was he on the heavier side (70 kilos). However, he was quite gifted in combat. In fact, he was a better combatant than the previous men listed. He knew EVERY SINGLE fighting style on earth and even developed his own fighting style that was unmatched and better than everyone else's. He had a buzz cut and was missing both of his ears. His name was Dutch. He carried no weapons, as his legs, elbows, hands and head were all his weapons.

Finally, the last man on the helicopter. He was… special indeed. Everyone else was kind of scared of him, as they should be. He was an unhinged nightmare who was only part of their squad because he was such a good soldier. His name was Victor, and by all accounts, he was the best of the best. He was a master fighter, a skilled marksman, and despite his somewhat thin frame, he was still quite strong. However, he was insane. He lost his mind in the Iraq war several years ago, and ever since then, he has not been the same. However, thanks to this insanity, he's less likely to be prone to injuries or feel any sort of pain.

All four men got a call on their headsets. It was from the pilot.

"OK, man, listen up. We're heading to the target's last known location. The order is to kill on sight. Should be easy enough. The target's name is Jack. He's just a high schooler, but be careful. Supposedly, this kid is balls to the walls high, so you're gonna have more trouble than normal. But that shouldn't be a worry for a team like you guys. The boss, James Donald, is paying a crap ton of money for this. We don't want to disappoint him. Come back when the target is killed. If you die, then so be it. Best of luck, gentlemen, and prepare yourselves."

The hatch opened, and all four men jumped out and landed on a rooftop below. It was overlooking a series of small shops and restaurants.

Leon spoke up. "OK, men. This kid is thin, has a buzzcut practically, and is dangerous. He's high on something, so we need to be careful."

Micah chuckled. "If he's high, then we don't have to worry about anything. This job is gonna be easier than I thought."

Dutch spit on Micha's hair. "Better watch your tone! James is paying—"

Micha punched Dutch in his mouth. A fight broke out between the two of them. As Leon tried to break it up, Victor looked down. He grabbed his binoculars and saw a kid going way faster than normal. There was. He could tell it was Jack. Nobody was as high as him right now. Victor smiled as he put his binoculars away. He didn't even tell the team. He simply just vanished. He went down and ran toward Jack, knife in hand.

Jack was hyperventilating. That pill that Dr. Benjamin gave him was kicking in HARD! Holy crap, Jack was so far out of this world he didn't even know where he was. It didn't matter; Jack felt invincible. Jack didn't even feel the pain in his shoulder as Victor stabbed a small knife filled with poison. Jack looked at the knife and threw it away. Victor looked surprised. WHAT? Jack was still fine and walking. That knife had enough poison to kill an entire herd of elephants. HOW was he still alive? Jack smiled as he ran away. Victor tried going after him, but it was fruitless. Jack was just too damn fast.

Dutch appeared behind Victor. "You let him get away?"

Victor sneered and growled at Dutch. "No, he's just… he's something else. Stay alert; this man is NOT normal. Also, who are you using that tone with? Because I know it's not me, since you were just fighting instead of doing your damn job, you stupid cunt!"

Dutch was about to punch Victor when Leon grabbed his hand.

"Enough. We're here to do a job, not bicker and argue like some unhappily married couples. We need to come up with a plan. Don't worry, Victor, I saw EVERYTHING from up there. It seems like not even poison can kill this man. Hmmm… yes, I think I have an idea."

"Do tell," said Dutch, leaning in to hear like an eager child. Leon pointed to a rooftop above.

"I have Micah setting up his equipment up top. He should be able to get a clean shot in. Hopefully, that can stop the damn bastard from running everywhere. If that fails, then I'll have you two as backups. If Jack tries to run away, ambush him. There is a park nearby. I'll try to lure him there. Hopefully, this shouldn't take longer than 15 minutes. Everybody understands?"

Both Dutch and Victor nodded their heads. Leon said nothing as he waited for the two to leave and head over to the small park. Leon looked up above and saw that Micah was giving him a thumbs-up. Perfect, the plan was going smoothly. Leon looked at Jack.

Jack was in the middle of the road, just near the park hopping over some cars. Whatever he had taken, it sure as shit was strong. Leon had never seen something so powerful and potent in his time. The closest thing he ever saw was when he was stationed out in India a few years back. He was paid by an oil company in private to take out one of their rival companies. He would never forget as the C.E.O of said rival company took several pills and was balls to the walls high. He was screaming, jumping up and down, stripping naked and talking to himself in the mirror. He got so high that he eventually had a heart attack and collapsed. Leon didn't even need to get his hands dirty.

Leon approached Jack like a predatory animal approached its prey. He had his knife in his right hand, and his eyes were dead focused on Jack. He wanted to get Jack's attention as Jack was out of Micha's range of sight. If only he could draw him out. He wondered if calling Jack's name would startle him. As if he were a timid woodland creature where even the slightest noise would make him run away for miles. Oh well, he had to give it a try. If anything, Jack would run into the park.

"Excuse me," said Leon, just loud enough that it piqued Jack's attention. Jack looked at Leon. Jack's vision was moving at a super high rate. His mind was unbelievably fast, and he was thinking about a bazillion different things all while looking at Leon. Just by looking at Leon, he was able to deduce that the man was out there to kill him. Furthermore, just based on the way he stood and spoke, Jack was able to deduce that there was an ambush waiting to happen. Jack came up with 56 different plans in his mind in less than 5 seconds. The pill made Jack an absolute genius. Wherever the good doctor got it from, it sure as heck worked.

Leon looked at Jack and started to have an internal panic attack. Leon had done this a million times, and he knew that Jack had figured him out. Jack looked at the park and shook his head. He waved his finger at Leon.

"You're trying to lure me out so your sniper can shoot at me, right?"

W-what? Impossible, how did he know? Micah was literally hundreds of meters away from Jack. Not only that, but based on how Jack looked at the park, he knew there was an ambush waiting. How did he know all of this?

Leon kept his cool and started walking forward. "I have no idea what you're talking about. I—"

Jack interrupted him.

"Cut the B.S.! Judging by the way you walk and move, you're here to kill me. You have a small .45 in your back pocket, and you're trying to get close to me since you seem proficient in close-quarters combat."

Leon choked on his own spit. "W-what?" he muttered. Impossible. Jack deduced all of that merely by looking at his stance and by judging how he walked. Leon gritted his teeth. Jack was going to be tougher than he thought. Leon took a deep breath. He was getting nervous. Having a cool head always helped. Leon started to think of a plan. As he was thinking, Jack looked maliciously at him. He gave him a look, a very evil and sly look. A look that screamed, 'I know what you're thinking, and it won't work. Nothing will.'

Leon cursed as he grabbed his gun and fired it at Jack. Micah heard the shot and gasped. Jack was out of his range. He quickly moved to another rooftop to find a better angle.

Jack dodged the bullet and ran toward Leon. Leon grabbed his knife and swung it at Jack. Jack jumped over Leon and backhanded Leon. Leon fell to the floor.

Jack grabbed Leon's knife while he was down, and threw it at a nearby tree. The knife went through the tree, and down fell Dutch with a massive cut on his left cheek.

Leon tripped Jack and tried putting in an armbar. That failed as Jack slithered away and scrambled upward. Dutch yelled as he ran toward Jack. Leon screamed for him to get back, but Dutch refused.

He threw a barrage of punches, kicks, flurries and anything that he could do. He missed all of his hits. He tried taking Jack down, but Jack snuffed all of his takedown attempts. Jack grabbed the back of Dutch's neck… and ripped it out. Dutch screamed in pain as he fell to the floor. Jack kicked him while he was down and ran away. Unfortunately, he was in Micah's line of fire.

Finally, Micah focused. Jack was moving fast—as fast as a cheetah—and the winds were starting to pick up. Furthermore, there was a series of buildings and windows that were blocking Micha's view of Jack. This was all too easy.

Micah aimed eastward and fired a single bullet through 3 different buildings and 6 different windows. It soon hit Jack in the leg. Jack cursed as his face ate concrete. Micah basked in his accomplishment as he cocked the gun again. This time he had a better shot. Jack looked directly at Micha through his scope. Micah was startled and taken aback. Jack grabbed Leon's gun and fired it through the scope. It went through the air and through the scope and hit Micah in his mouth.

I-Impossible, thought Micah as blood poured out. He wasn't supposed to hit him. A .45 can't travel that far, and even if it did, it would be impossible for him to accurately predict his location. How on earth did he know? Micah was so surprised and shocked he was paralyzed. Even the pain wasn't helping make him move.

Then, a horrific and sinister thought approached Micah. Could Jack have really deduced his location, JUST based on the sound alone? Or just by feeling where the shots came from. Another thought occurred. Could Jack know the location JUST BY SENSING THE CHANGE IN THE AIR? No, that was impossible. Nobody could do that. Even drugged out of his mind, he wasn't able to.

Jack looked down at his leg. The wound was already healing. His white blood cells were moving at such ridiculously high speeds that the wounds soon closed. Furthermore, the blood was so hot that it acted as self-cauterization.

Micah started to lose his mind. This was outlandish. How was this possible? What pill did he take?

Jack quickly got up. He jumped up as Victor swung a piece of metal, trying to break Jack's feet. Jack landed back down and kicked Victor in the face. Jack was so fast, so damn fast. He hit Victor so fast that Victor saw afterimages of Jack moving. Victor fell down to the floor. Jack picked up Victor's head and ground it along the road, leaving a trail of blood. His left metal arm was helping out. Jack could easily crush Victor's skull with just his left arm alone. Even his right arm felt indestructible.

Victor kneed Jack in the balls and did a spinning elbow to his face. He managed to hit Jack. Jack staggered backward. And Victor used this opportunity to shove a live grenade into Jack's mouth. Victor pushed Jack away and he jumped away as far as he could. Jack grabbed it with his metal hand... and it exploded.

Victor smiled. Finally, he was able to get him. Hopefully, this would give him the credit and recognition he so deserved and—

From the smoke, Jack emerged. The right side of his face was bloody and had skin missing, but besides that, it was fine. Jack's metal arm was fine, and no damages were done.

Victor yelled from the bottom of his lungs. He screamed and cursed as he ran toward Jack, blinded by rage. How was this man still alive? He had a grenade in his hand for crying out loud!

Victor swung his knife. Jack caught it with his metal arm and broke it. He sent Victor flying with a sidekick into a series of trash cans. Jack looked around. There was almost nobody there in Harrisburg. How strange, it seemed as if the city had suddenly become a ghost town. It was quite unusual indeed.

Jack flashed Victor before he ran away.

All four men were sitting on a nearby bench. Nobody said a word. They were all disappointed and angry at themselves.

"Who... in the FUCK... is this guy?" Micah stood up. His mouth was feeling a little bit better. His face was red, and his blood boiled. Nobody—and he meant nobody—ever hurt him. Now this guy was able to shoot him in his mouth with a gun that wasn't even able to travel that far. HOW?

Leon bowed his head down. He felt ashamed. As a leader, he was supposed to motivate and support his men. He was supposed to show them how things were done. Instead, he felt embarrassed and dumb. He had no clue, the kid knew everything just by looking at them. They were outclassed.

"W-we could try teaming up on him," said Victor. Dutch shook his head.

"What kind of plan is that? That would be a great chance for him!"

"How so?"

"He could attack us all at the same time. Or if he were to run away, then all four of us would have to chase him!"

"He's not running away," said Leon as he stood up. "He can identify and figure out our plans just by looking at us and the way we walk. If all four of us had the intention of going to him just to kill him, he would know from the instant he took a glance at us. I don't think he would run away just by that."

"How do you know?" responded Dutch. Leon shrugged his shoulders. "Call it a hunch. Anyway, I agree with Victor. I think jumping him would do us good. I was able to place a tracker on him when I was grappling with him. He's somewhere near some train tracks. Micha, I want you to set up a position nearby. The rest of you, let's go!"

They all stood up and walked toward the train tracks. As they were walking, they heard police sirens. *Great,* thought Micah as the police arrived.

"You four, what are you doing?" The police officer grabbed his gun and pointed it at Leon. Leon made a snarky smile as he walked away. The police officer fired, but it was deflected as Micah shot a small round at the bullet, making it ricochet and hit the police officer in the neck. The other police officer was about to fire, but Micah killed him. Just then, a new series of police cars pulled up. These police cars looked much bigger and carried more weapons. Dutch took a step back.

"Great, just our luck."

Victor slapped him in the back of his head. "Can it, we don't need your small talk right now."

Dutch punched Victor in the face, and the two of them got into a brawl. Leon tried breaking it up, and Micah looked at the cops leaving the cars. Yeah, they were definitely better prepared. They had bigger guns and fired without asking questions. Micah fired his pistols before the police could even cock their guns. One officer called for backup, and soon, S.W.A.T and a police helicopter were flying overhead. The 4 of them ran into a store and took cover as the police were unloading magazines of high-caliber bullets.

"Fuck, this is bad," said Victor as he grabbed a grenade and threw it back at the SWAT cars. From the back door, more and more police officers were entering and attacking them. Leon tried his best to hold them off, but more and more of them were attacking and coming in.

Leon grabbed Victor and Dutch.

"You two, I need you to find an exit and go to the train tracks. Jack is still there. We'll meet up with you once we're done here."

Both nodded their heads as they made their escape. There seemed to be no end to the cops. Leon was sweating as he started to lose his cool. This was just supposed to be a regular job. He was supposed to get his paycheck and go home and go out drinking. This was NOT what he had in mind. He was planning on either taking James Donald hostage when he got his money or killing the man for putting him in the situation he was in.

Micah could feel his ammo running dry. There were so many police forces and so little ammo. He had to resort to using dead officers' weapons as he was firing at the attack helicopters above. Leon was trying his best to make homemade bombs. They took refuge inside a convenience store, so thankfully there were supplies he could use. He was able to make a small pipe bomb and threw it at a SWAT truck. He saw the truck go up in flames as it caused other cop cars to explode.

As they were trying their best to hold off the police, Dutch and Victor were able to make their way to the train tracks, where they saw Jack racing trains.

"This guy is nuts. Can... we really do this, Victor?"

Victor nodded his head. "We have to. Our livelihood is on the line."

They approached Jack. Jack had his head turned on them. Dutch was about to attack when Victor stopped him.

"Just because he had his back turned doesn't mean he doesn't know where he is. He probably felt us coming 100 meters away. Be careful."

Dutch scoffed as he grabbed a rock and threw it at Jack. Victor yelled in rage as Jack grabbed the rock and threw it back even harder. It hit Dutch in the stomach, and he had the wind knocked out of him. He fell to the floor and held his stomach.

In a split second, Jack was able to dislocate seven of Victor's bones and break all his fingers. In that same split second, Jack was able to trip and tie Victor to a nearby train track. All in a split second.

Victor moved so fast that he threw up. It was almost as if Jack could stop time. He was so damn fast. Whatever that pill was, he needed it for himself. He tried to escape, but Jack just made the ropes harder, and he broke Victor's nose. Jack felt Dutch standing up. He smiled as he blocked and defended against all of the Dutch's attacks.

Dutch tried to roundhouse-kick Jack. Jack blocked it and kneed Dutch in his jaw, dislocating it. Jack then grabbed Dutch's hair with his metal arm and started pulling it off—just like a farmer pulls the weeds off his soil. Dutch yelled in agony as blood trickled down his face. Jack had a menacing smile. He was enjoying every single second of it. The pill made him bloodthirsty the more it was in his system. Soon, he was beating Dutch to a bloody pulp with just his metal arm.

Victor was horrified by what he was seeing. He wasn't best friends with Dutch, nor did he claim to like the man. But he would be lying if he said that he liked seeing him get beat up. Jack had a ferocious and atrocious smile as he pounded and beat the poor man so hard. Victor yelled at the top of his lungs.

"Stop. You're killing him!"

For a second, Jack looked up, then looked back down. He saw Dutch's face, and what he did to the poor man's face. In a moment of shame and guilt, he put Dutch down. Dutch was crying. So much pain… so much agony… so much shame. He was starting to come down and feel sober.

Poor Dutch crawled over to Victor to let him loose. He couldn't even walk. He was in so much pain. He couldn't speak either. Jack had practically beaten his jaw off. There was just some muscle hanging and some teeth. Victor stood up and charged at Jack. Jack was able to do it, partially because Victor had his hands and fingers broken, and was also in a world of pain. Jack disarmed him and pushed him to the ground.

Victor felt something was off. Jack could have killed him when he disarmed him. Yet, he didn't. Was the pill starting to wear off? Did his cries reach Jack? If so, then he would just need to wait for the other two to come. Until then, he would have to stall.

"Stalling isn't going to work, Victor," said Jack. Victor fell backward as he became so shocked. W-what? He could read his mind? IMPOSSIBLE!

"Oh… the pill isn't wearing off. Don't worry. I definitely calmed down, though, but I'm still gonna be off my rockers for a few more days, I imagine."

Victor started to have a panic attack. This nightmare was getting worse and worse by the second!

Jack sat down on a tree stump. He looked into Victor's eyes as he spoke.

"Don't bother trying to fight me or stall. You can't win, and I've already hurt you and your friends enough. I am sorry."

Victor stepped back. What was Jack talking about? Victor ran at him and tried to attack him. Jack dogged all of his attacks and pushed him away, causing Victor to fall and hit his broken nose on a rock. He gritted his teeth as he also wanted to cry. He couldn't, though. he had to show—

"You can cry, it's human emotion."

IMPOSSIBLE! This man was NOT human. You could not convince Victor otherwise. He spun his head around and looked at Jack with wide eyes and heavy breathing.

He gritted his teeth and wanted to cry. Dammit, this Jack kid, or whoever this guy was, was ruining Victor's day. Victor was an accomplished man, with renowned skills in acrobat, combat and education. He was a doctor from Harvard, he was a decorated soldier who fought in the Iraq war, and a world-class Muay Thai fighter. Despite all of this, he was ridiculed by his peers for being weird and unusual. So what if he liked to do kinky stuff, and so what if he had... unusual fetishes? He was still a human at the end of the day. So why? Why... why did this Jack man kick his ass? Why was he so damn good, so wonderful at fighting? Was it the pill? Was it—

"Don't beat yourself up, doctor. I'm just 10 steps ahead of you. Don't worry, it's not the drugs, nor is it because of anything else."

Victor stood up and shook his head. Jack stared at him, expressionless.

"Don't worry, Vic. I won't kill you. I was about to, but you helped me out. And for that, I am forever grateful."

Victor took another step back. He was shocked. He smiled. He said he was forever grateful. Did that mean that Jack would follow one of his orders if he asked him to? After all, he was grateful. A grateful person would try to show their appreciation and gratitude.

Jack shook his head. "However, I won't let you kill me. I have a lady waiting for me in the hospital, and I have a whole life ahead of me. Not today, Victor, but I will show my kindness to you somehow."

Victor grunted as he threw a rock at Jack. Jack grabbed it with his left hand and crushed it. He looked at Victor, except this time, in Jack's eyes, Victor was able to see love and kindness. Jack smiled. He wouldn't lay a finger on Victor.

Leon got hit in the leg. He was having trouble walking. He and Micah were leaving the restaurant. They had caused such a massive and chaotic bloodbath. It was horrendous. Thousands of dead officers littered the streets of Harrisburg. Even the military was involved, and it was not pretty. The coastguard and the army had to be called in. They too were also killed in a horrific turn of events.

Micah was shot in both of his legs, his right arm, his left shoulder and his stomach. A bullet grazed his head. Leon was shot in his butt, his head, his pelvic area, his right shoulder and his chest. He couldn't even walk. Micah was using sheer force and willpower to move and help Leon walk. They sat down near a bench. More officers were soon to come. They were convinced they killed nearly all in the county they were in.

"H-hold on," said Leon as he spat out some blood. Micah cringed as he sat down next to him. They could hear noises in the far-off distance.

"Do you think Dutch and Victor killed Jack?"

Leon chuckled in pain. "Oh… I doubt they even touched him. I didn't think that he would be this much trouble. Look at what happened to us. Look at this mess… we can't ever live normal lives again."

"It's not like they were normal to begin with."

Leon shook his head. "At least I could go outside without being recognized. Now I'll have to be on the run. Live in some damned third-world foreign country out in the middle of Asia."

Micah sighed. He too was also disappointed. He liked to live a quiet life. He owned a farm where he enjoyed shooting, riding horses, snorting coke and having hardcore sex with hookers. It was the life that he loved, and he wouldn't trade it for anything. Now, he had to leave the country if he wanted to live. He would probably work some blue-collar job in some poor eastern European country as a peasant. He didn't mind, though. As long as he could shoot his guns and get away from society, he would be fine.

Micah wheezed and coughed.

"D-do you think—"

"Sorry, man, but I don't want to be thinking about anything. In fact… were done here. Let's get Victor and Dutch and go home."

Micah looked shocked as Leon struggled to stand up.

"Go home. What do you mean by 'go home'? We have a job to do!"

Leon pointed at the thousands of dead bodies, exploded cars and millions of rounds of bullets on the floor.

"From the way I see it, we don't have a job anymore. Were now wanted criminals. We better get out while we still can. Lay low in some countries for the rest of our lives. I'm heading to Turkmenistan. Ain't nobody going to try to find me there. Feel free to join me if you want. I heard there are some nice farms there."

Micah yelled at Leon, but Leon ignored him as he walked away. Micah limped toward him and pushed him.

"So you're just quitting!"

Leon looked back, his face and body dead serious.

"Yes. It's time we finish up here and go home."

"I won't let you!"

Leon was silent for a moment. His eyebrows furled, and he started to grow infuriated. Great, just great. He didn't need this right now. He just wanted to go home.

"And why won't you let me?"

"Because we have a JOB to do! Do you know how much this James guy paid us, for us to try and kill some teenage kid when we can't even touch him? I refuse to let it end like this."

Leon shook his head. "I'm going to tell you something only once, so you better listen to me before I chop off your ears and feed it to my dogs. We're in deep shit now. We fucked with the police, the government, and killed thousands of people. This event is going to go down in the history books. We're going to be remembered as criminals and fugitives. Even if we do decide to run away, it's only a matter of time before we are caught. Enjoy life while you still can. I quit!"

Micah spit in Leon's face.

"You traitor! You coward. Running away like a scared animal!"

"Jesus, man! Do you hear yourself and your twisted and wicked sense of… obligation and pride? I only had this job because I had nothing else better to do in life. You… your just some sick fuck who actually likes this, don't you? The people that hire us don't give a rat's ass about us. They couldn't care less if you died or not. You don't have a sense of duty to them, just because they gave you a paycheck!"

"YOU'RE WRONG! I've heard my name pop up in contacts more times than I can remember. I always do a job right, no matter what. I never leave; if something happens, I take care of it. Just like I did today. I won't let you leave, I won't let you be a coward."

Micah pulled his gun out and pointed it at Leon. Leon didn't change his facial expression, nor did he cower or shiver. He stood bold as death was staring at him through the barrel of the gun.

"Micah… you don't have to do this. Just calm down and put the gun down. It… It doesn't have to be like this."

Micha started to breathe heavily. His eyes widened and his jaw locked. He was sweating, and he started to lose his focus.

"I don't want to be associated with someone like you next time a job offer comes my way!"

"For all things that are good, do you not understand? We… are… done! There is no future for us anymore. Look at the massacre that has happened. If anything, you should be mad at that James Donald guy. He's the one who hired us to be in this mess. In fact, I wouldn't be surprised if this was all his fault!"

"SHUT UP!"

Micah fired the gun. Leon was fast enough to jerk his head to the left as far as he could. Unfortunately, Micah fired his desert eagle. The round was so powerful that it ripped Leon's ear clean off. Leon screamed as he uppercut Micah and sent him staggering backward. He fell down and hit his nose, breaking it on impact.

"WHAT THE HELL IS WRONG WITH YOU?"

Leon put pressure on the wound. He muffled and choked on his words. He fell to his knees. Ow. Leon felt his eyes grow weak and start to become heavy. He looked back to see Micah slowly getting up. He shook his head. This damn kid. He now had two people to worry about. Today was not going great for Leon as he grabbed the knife from inside his boot.

"Micah… I don't want to fight you. I just want to leave. Let's get out of here while we have the chance."

Micah shook his head. "We have a job to do. I'm not leaving here without my paycheck. I'm not fighting you. You can leave if you want, but don't get in my way."

Micah limped away as Leon slowly put his knife away. *Crazy bastard,* he thought as he started walking away. As he was going to the nearest cop car, he looked up and saw a helicopter flying over. It quickly shone a light on him and Micah, and soon both of them could hear more police cars.

"Oh, dammit," said Leon as he limped away.

19

Jack could hear the sirens go off. He looked back and felt the cars driving this way. He grabbed Victor and Dutch.

"Come on, we have to leave."

Victor pulled his hand away.

"Why should I come with you?"

"You don't, but I have a feeling that things will go south if you don't. There are police cars approaching. Take my word. Come with me, and we can get out of here!"

Victor said nothing and just nodded his head as Jack grabbed him and sprinted as hard as he could. He was going so fast that everything moved like a blur to Jack. He thought about killing him as now would be a perfect opportunity, but Victor realized that killing Jack right now would be impossible. He would have to wait to collect his paycheck.

They ran to a random car. Victor broke in and started hotwiring it. He was puzzled again. Jack knew he could hotwire a car, yet how on earth was he able to figure that out? He only talked to Victor for a few minutes. And it was nothing personal anyway.

Victor got the car running, and soon both Victor and Dutch were in the backseat. They drove off. As they were driving, the car suddenly came to a halt when Micah stepped out in front. Not seeing the car, and being blinded so suddenly, Jack tried to swerve out of the way. Micah was hit and was sent flying into a nearby dumpster, breaking his back. The car swerved and hit a tree.

Jack quickly got out and talked to Victor. "Wait here, I'll go get us another car." Jack ran off as fast as he could. Victor got out and saw Micah.

"What the hell were you thinking?"

Micah couldn't talk. He passed out. Victor cursed as he waited for Jack. He could hear police sirens and the military coming. There were dogs barking and people yelling. He could hear them getting closer and closer. Was this how it ended? Victor always imagined he would die in some explosion or by something else. Not by some random cops killing him. He looked back at Dutch, who was barely hanging on by less than a thread.

Leon was limping away. He could hear the dogs barking and the police getting closer to him. Damn, he was NOT getting out of this one. He thought about staying still and waiting for his inevitable fate, but he was better than that. He had to keep on pushing. He would try to find a car and steal it. Then he would drive away and try not to raise any suspicion. Then he would—

Leon stopped. Not because he wanted to, but because he was grabbed. Jack grabbed him. In a blur, they went over to Dr. Benjamin's car.

Leon looked at Jack starting the car. He puked. Why was this man, who they were trying to kill mere seconds ago, now saving their lives?

Jack smiled. "It seems like you don't want to kill me anymore. Plus, your friend Victor helped me calm down. Sorry for earlier. I know you were only trying to do your jobs."

Victor's jaw dropped. W-what? He could read his mind? Impossible, there was no such thing. He was either—

"Get in," said Jack as he was backing up. Leon popped the trunk and hid in there. Jack quickly sped down the road, seeing tanks and helicopters flying above. SWAT cars and police vehicles were driving through the road at crazy speed. Thankfully, Jack was able to blend in with the other civilian vehicles that were driving fast. Jack swerved to the right and cut through the park and was soon at the scene of the massacre. Although this time, he was too late.

The police, military and many more had already arrived. Dogs were running around the area, trying to chase and find out where Victor and the rest of the crew were. Civilians and news reporters were being escorted away.

Jack came up with a million different plans in his head. He only chose three that he thought were a good idea. He got out of the car and quickly ran over to a nearby restaurant that had been evacuated. He set it on fire and made sure to cause quite an explosion.

The explosion and fire garnered enough attention from the cops and military that their attention was diverted for a few seconds. Most of them went to G and checked it out. A few stayed behind. *Crap,* thought Jack as he was analyzing what to do. He could have easily killed the cops, but that's not how he rolled anymore. Instead, he decided to knock them all out.

Jack sensed where everyone was. They were hiding inside the dumpster. One by one, he gathered each and every single one of them and put them in the car. He quickly drove off without arousing any suspicion.

Micah was waking up, his head was hurting like crazy, and ringing like a church bell. Next to him were Victor and Dutch. Leon was in the front seat. Jack was inside the hospital trying to sneak Samantha out.

Micah grumbled. "W-where are we?"

Victor turned to him.

"Relax. We're OK for now."

Micah thought for a moment, and then he panicked. The police, the military, where was he? Did… was he found and were they on their way to prison? If they were, this car didn't look like any prison car.

Jack came outside empty-handed. He entered the car, and Micah lost his shit. He leaned in to go and strangle Jack. Jack grabbed both of his hands and crushed them, causing Micah to wince as he went backward. Leon yelled at him.

"YOU CRAZY BASTARD! This man is saving our lives!"

Jack backed away and started driving to Wilmhelm.

Leon spoke up. "They won't give you her?"

Jack shook his head. "She's still not ready to leave just yet. I would get you guys to a hospital, but unfortunately, you and Micah are now America's most wanted. Good luck trying to go to the grocery store."

Leon scoffed. He looked outside. Hundreds of police cars were all making their way toward Harrisburg.

"You can stay at my place for as long as you like. I can't guarantee anything, but you should be safe for a while. Trust me, the town is quite small indeed."

Leon smiled.

"Thank you… really."

There was a silence, and Micah had his eyes fixated on Jack. He would get his contract and get his money's worth. He had a job to do!

Leon decided to speak up.

"Why are you saving us? We were trying to kill you just a moment ago, and now you're healing us and taking us to safety. Why? We don't deserve it, especially after everything we have done to you."

Jack looked in the rearview mirror directly at Micah and spoke, "Don't worry, you guys have done nothing to me just yet. You were only trying to kill me because that was your job. You have to put food on the table, I understand. Also… I'm in debt to your friend Victor."

Leon looked surprised as he looked back. Victor… the weird one. THAT Victor? Whatever he did, Leon was sure as shit thankful that he was on his side. He would make sure that Victor would be shown gratitude and thanks when this was all over.

Jack smiled. "Are you a religious man, Leon?"

"How do you—"

"Be glad that I am who I am now, and not the person I was so many moons ago. I would have left you all to rot and would have killed you all months ago."

Leon looked at Jack, what a puzzling man.

"N-no. I never really was one for religion."

"Well… there's a quote in the Bible, and it states: 'Those who are merciful shall be shown mercy,' as well as: 'Do not thieves love thieves? Do not sinners love sinners? Therefore, I say, love your enemy as yourself, and pray for those that persecute you, so that you may be sons of your Father who is in heaven."

Leon nodded his head. He started to wonder, could… the powers that he had, could that pill that he had taken… could it be from God himself? Leon scoffed, that sounded stupid, God wasn't real. Yet, the more he looked at Jack, and saw what Jack had done… he started to doubt his own thinking.

A few hours passed by, and the car was dead silent. Everyone was in pain and either mumbled or tried to sleep to ease the pain. The adrenaline had worn off, and the pain really started to settle in. It was NOT fun. Several of the members either cried or complained. Jack sympathized with them and tried to buy medicine. Unfortunately, it didn't help.

It was midnight when they finally reached Jack's house.

"Here we are," said Jack as he got out. The rest of the members limped out and walked over to the garage. Jack gathered a bunch of medical tools and supplies. His mind was moving at such high speeds, just by looking at Dutch, he thought of a few different ways to fix his jaw.

Leon sat down and saw Jack go to work. It was impressive, to say the least. Jack's hands moved so fast at such an incredible speed and pace that Leon couldn't even see with his naked eye. It was almost like a blur.

After a while, Dutch was fixed up. Then, Jack started healing and working on everybody.

As he was working, the garage door opened, and out stepped Rebecca. "Oh crap," muttered Jack as his mind raced. He thought of how he could defuse the situation when she saw all 5 men in her garage.

"J-JACK! What's going on here?"

Jack left Micah, who he was fixing at the time, and went to go and talk to Rebecca.

"Listen, do you mind if they stay here for a while?"

"Excuse me, but have you seen the news as of recently?"

She pointed to all four men and leaned in and whispered in Jack's ear, "I don't know if you know, but there was a massacre in Harrisburg. Two men by the names of Leon and Micah are on the run. What are they doing here in my garage?"

Jack took a deep sigh. "Listen… they were in a bad spot. There's a bigger story here, just trust me. They didn't do any harm to me whatsoever. Can they just stay here for a little bit?"

Rebecca shook her head. "No way. I'm calling the—"

Jack quickly grabbed her hand. He gently squeezed it with his left arm, and Rebecca moaned.

"Ow. Stop that, that hurts. What are you—"

"Just calm down for a second and listen to me. These men are staying here because they have nowhere else to go. If you want to argue and yell with me, that's fine. But they're staying here. End of story. At least until they're good enough and they can find somewhere else to go. Please, Rebecca, I don't want this situation escalating any further."

Rebecca looked at Jack, and then she looked at the four men. She cursed and mumbled, "I want to talk to you later. In private!"

She huffed as she stormed out of the garage. Jack sighed as he went back to fixing Micha's leg.

"Thank you, Jack," said Micah. Jack smiled as he took a bullet out of his calf. Leon was smiling as well. He owed a massive favor and a debt he promised he would pay off, even if Jack didn't want it. Jack showed more kindness to him and his friends than nearly everyone they met in the last 15 years. He was happy he met someone like him.

All four men were passed out. They were healed and were now resting. Jack set up makeshift beds in his room. He tried to make them as comfy as he could, but there was only so little he could do. They were all sleeping nice and soundly. Jack figured that they might as well use his room. Not only was it the quietest room in the whole house, but with the way Jack was, he figured he would be up for a few days.

Downstairs, Rebecca was cooking herself a very early snack when she saw Jack coming downstairs. Without skipping a beat, she yelled and cursed at him, "You stupid motherfucker! Do you have any idea what you've just done? You've brought 2 wanted fugitives into our house! The United States government is looking for them!"

Jack put his hands on her shoulder.

"Just calm down, lady. Everything will be alright. We won't be caught."

She slapped his hands away. "Easy for you to say! Anyway, what's with you? You seem... off."

"I... ate a pill earlier. Don't worry, I'm not going to do anything crazy."

"Be careful with those kinds of stuff. It's easy to get addicted. Andrea was for a while."

Jack was surprised. Andrea was many things, but he doubted she would be the type of person to get hooked on pills.

"Wait... really?"

"Oh yeah. When she was in 10th or 11th grade, she couldn't stop popping pills. Quaaludes, Xanax, whatever she could get her hands on. She went to a lot of parties, so that didn't help her out with her addiction. Eventually, I had to put her in a rehab center for a few months. Then... she became addicted to sex.

"Every night I heard noises coming from her bedroom. I thought it was inadequate of her as a lady to be throwing herself around so much as if she were a basketball. Still, I preferred her being addicted to sex than something that could take her life away."

Jack nodded his head. In that sense, he agreed with her. He was so glad that he was able to quit. Finally, he could stay sober.

Jack spoke up. "I've known a lot of people who have had issues with control over the years. Humans, I think, are just naturally addicted to certain stuff. Whether it is porn, drugs, sex, gambling or whatever, humans naturally have an addiction problem. Since we as humans always want more and always want what we can't have."

Rebecca scoffed as he ate a piece of Kiwi.

"That is such bullshit. Anybody that says that has no self-control whatsoever. It's easy to quit; all you need to do is stop."

"HA! Then you really haven't experienced the real world, have you?"

"What do you mean?"

Jack became serious as he leaned in closer. He started to scare Rebecca with the way he was eyeing her up and down.

"You say it's 'easy' to quit, and that all you need is discipline. Yeah, that may be true, but some things are easier said than done. Try quitting cocaine once you get hooked, or heroin. A drug is so powerful that it feels like God is wrapping you in his divine blanket. Why not try to get sober while being addicted? Then… then tell me if it's as easy as that."

"W-well, maybe… maybe you shouldn't do it in the first place!"

Jack chuckled. His tone and voice became sarcastic.

"Oh, silly me, why didn't I think of that? Guess I should have never tried that stuff!"

Jack became serious again.

"Listen… I don't know much about your life, or where you come from, or anything like that, but judging by the way you carry yourself and by everything else, I can deduce that you seem to live a comfortable life. I can even say that you were given a silver spoon when you were young, and probably the hardest thing you've ever had to do was work a 9-5. So you've probably lived in a fairly nice house in Philadelphia where you've never had to worry about anything, and where you have people always praising you and boasting about you. Yet, that's probably because they want to be your friend since you have so much money.

"I can also safely assume that because from a young age, you were in a rich circle, they probably were super anti-drug and since they were influenced by what the media portrayed, they started developing their own sense of ideas about drugs. About people that use and started telling LIES! All lies!"

Jack grabbed Rebecca by both shoulders and tightened his grip.

"How DARE YOU try and tell me to just 'quit' or to just 'have some discipline.' You have an idea of junkies, and let me tell you, they're COMPLETELY WRONG! If you were addicted, you would know how hard it is! If you went through half of what I've been through, you would be begging to feel good for a single second. To escape the cold harsh reality. You...you grew up in a nice house, a nice family, a nice life! Do you have any idea what's it like to have your life in shambles, to have your home life so fucked up that you would rather sleep on the streets than ever go back inside your own house? Do you have any idea?"

Rebecca was quiet.

"That's what I thought, so you better wipe that facade about you being 'holier than thou'. If you understood the struggles that people went through in life, you would see why people used drugs. You would see why people wanted to feel good before they went into a job they hated, and worked hours and hours doing nothing but working their ass off, just so they could buy crappy food because that's all they can afford! Listen to me, and listen well! Addiction is no joke, and nor is belittling somebody when they're already down! Have you ever considered that if someone were to use substances like heroin, meth and anything else, that maybe, just maybe, they're not right in the head! Maybe instead of belittling them and telling them to just 'quit' and 'suck it up,' you should instead try and find a solution to help them, INSTEAD OF BELITTLING THEM LIKE THE WHORE THAT YOU ARE!

"Tell me, Rebecca, answer me this... how disciplined are you?"

Rebecca started to cry. Jack shoved her away and reached into his back pocket. He grabbed an eightball and threw it on the kitchen counter. He looked at Rebecca, his eyes dead set and focused on her bloodshot eyes.

"Put your money where your mouth is. Snort it."

Rebecca looked at it like it was an alien device capable of mass destruction.

"If you're as disciplined and have as much willpower as you say, then this could be easy enough to quit... right?"

Rebecca looked at Jack.

"Y-you're... sick in the head!"

"No, I'm not. In fact, if it's anybody who needs a wake-up call to reality, it's you. Try to understand the struggles and you'll be singing a different tune. Now SNORT!"

Jack grabbed a one-dollar bill and rolled it up. He gave it to Rebecca, who backed away.

"OK... I get it now."

"No, you don't. You're just saying that because you're scared."

Rebecca's eyes widened. Could… he be reading her mind? Impossible, he was—

"I won't ask again."

Rebecca took the one-dollar bill as Jack started cutting up the coke. She was panicking, and her heart was racing. It felt like she was going to die. This… why… was this really happening? She felt like running for her life, and she felt like yelling at the crazy man in front of her. But she realized that Jack was serious. She saw it in his eyes and the way he moved and talked.

The coke was all ready. Jack looked at her. Rebecca sobbed as she put the dollar bill to the white powder… and she snorted.

Holy shit… now she understood why it was called 'nose candy.' Despite the circumstances she was in, she felt a huge rush. Holy crap, that felt good. She felt nice and good, and she sniffed even more without Jack even telling her to snort anymore. In less than 5 minutes, she snorted the entire eightball.

Jack looked at her again; his eyes were dead center on hers. Never once leaving her sight.

"Judging by your pupils, your reaction, and by how much you're sweating, I can safely say you're pretty high right now. Good… now let's put your money where your mouth is. I want you to quit."

Rebecca looked up at him.

"Q-quit. Why… I… this is my first time doing it. You've probably done it a hundred times more than me. Why do I quit now?"

"Because you were talking SO big earlier about being disciplined and about being better, and how it's so easy. Yes, I may have snorted enough coke to fill half of Brazil, but I never claimed to be a saint. Nor did I say anything about my ability to stay sober. You, on the other hand… that's a different story."

Rebecca snarled and growled at him. She tried clawing his eyes out with her nails, but he just stepped back. She hissed at him.

"Look at you, talking to me like you're holier than thou! Who do you think you are?"

"I'm just someone trying to make a point! Look at yourself, you're freaking out now because of the thought of that booger sugar going away. Don't you have any idea how hypocritical you look now? Sorry, lady, but the joke is on you. I knew this would happen." Rebecca snarled at him again. Jack grabbed the bag and threw it in the trash.

"Rebecca... now the challenge begins. Are you ready?"

She shook her head. Jack couldn't help but smile.

"Not as easy as it looks, hmm? Hopefully, this teaches you a lesson."

Before Rebecca could scream at him, Jack hugged her. She beat his back and tried biting him, but he still hugged her despite all of this.

"Now... now it gets hard. But don't worry, I'm still here for you. Even if you hate me, I'll still try to help you. I know how hard it can be, and I know how much more difficult it is when nobody is there for us. Trust me, I'll help you."

"Even if I hate you?"

"Especially if you hate me, for that's how I show my love to God and to you. That's how you show love, to those who hate and despise you for everything you do. What good is it for someone to love someone who hates them? True love comes from helping those who despise us. We help them for their good, despite their hatred toward us."

Rebecca stopped attacking and became numb. She embraced Jack. She felt... so much love and so much comfort. She tried reaching for his pants, but he smacked her hand away.

"Sorry, but that's not happening."

"O-oh... I'm sorry..."

"It's alright."

They embraced each other, and soon Rebecca came down from her high and went to bed. Jack went for a walk to clear his mind. He would help her no matter what. He knew what it was like, and he knew how miserable he felt. He smiled as he was prepared for the next day.

Jack got a call on his phone. He picked it up.

"Hello?"

"Hey, Jack, it's me, Terrence. Are you free?"

Jack soon rushed over to S.H.O.T. headquarters, where it was practically in shambles. Everything was ruined and destroyed, and there were very few hunters still there.

"What happened here?" asked Jack as he was walking with Terrence. Terrence was smoking a cigarette, and he looked very tired and stressed.

"Nothing good. Now... Jack, I heard what happened with the good doctor and with everybody else. Heck, I know about everything. Even with what

James Donald did. I'm sorry for your loss. The good doctor was a friend to everyone, and he will be missed."

Jack smiled. "Thank you, Terrence. He was indeed a nice man."

Terrence stopped walking and looked at Jack.

"So… I don't know any other way to tell you this, so I'll do the best that I can. With everything that went down, it's safe to say that James Donald will no longer be the new headmaster of S.H.O.T. In fact, as we speak, some of the Hunters are on their way to kill him. But that's not important right now. What is important is that as of today, and officially, you are now the new head chairman of S.H.O.T. Congratulations."

Jack felt his heart race and beat at the speed of sound. The pills didn't help, but Jack couldn't believe what he was hearing. It felt like yesterday he joined, and now he was the new head chairman. Yet… Jack felt unworthy of this. He felt as though he didn't deserve it, nor did he really even want it. He was happy with just being a regular hunter. He now had a massive responsibility on his shoulders. He didn't even know where to start, or what to do. How would he even run things? Would he be going on missions, would he—

"Now… for some bad news." Terrence lit up another cigarette and spoke.

"A lot of hunters weren't happy with the decision that was made. A lot of hunter's left this base, and from what I've been told, a few bases and headquarters around the world are practically rioting due to this decision. Don't worry, though, it's not anything major or grand scale. However… I fear something. I fear as though there is going to be a civil war breaking out soon."

Jack stood back, and his eyes widened. He lost his speech for a split second.

"W-what? W-w-w-wait a minute… a civil war?"

"You saw how it was when Natalia was declared dead. Imagine how it is now when some nobody was just assigned the highest position. Not even a year in training. Some hunters work their whole lives only to have one single promotion. I don't think you deserve it, but what do I know?"

"Anyway, I got to go. I'll leave you to it."

Jack was about to say something, but nothing could come out of his mouth. He was in shambles and was shocked. How could something like this be happening? A civil war, all because of this? Jack rubbed his face. No way… too many things were happening all at the same time. This… this was bad. Real bad.

Jack rushed to Natalia's office. It was empty. The only things still there were some pieces of paper, a computer and a very comfy chair. Jack sat down on the chair. He couldn't do this, how on earth—

A notification on the computer appeared. Jack quickly investigated it. It was a news report of a crooked politician who was caught taking bribe money from a terrorist organization in central Asia. Jack looked at the article and quickly realized how things worked.

Could it be that Natalia simply kept up to date on the news, and told her hunters who to kill and where to go? It seemed unorthodox for Jack. After all, she was just relying on the news. No inside sources, and no nothing. Plus, the news networks could be biased to be either in favor or against. Also, the news had a particular way of lying. A sudden chill came over Jack. What if some of the people he's killed, alongside Samantha and everyone else, if they were all innocent?

No, he couldn't think that way. He figured that S.H.O.T. was operating this long, so things were surely bound to be good if operations had been going on without any complaints… right? Jack tried to shove the thought out of his head… but he just couldn't. He couldn't live with himself if he knew that he was being tricked into killing innocents, or people who crossed or wronged the wrong person.

Jack looked down at the pieces of paper. He investigated them thoroughly. They all had dates on them, and appeared to be in a sloppy-ish handwriting. They gave off the aura that they had been taken from someone's diary. Jack read the pieces of paper… and he couldn't believe his eyes.

He knew it, his suspicions were right all along. The killings, the politicians, everything… all of it was for a secret agenda. It was pages ripped straight from Natalia's diary.

Jack puked. He couldn't believe what he was seeing. It turned out that several years ago, Natalia ended up joining a secret political underground party in eastern Europe. The underground party was pretty far right-wing, and they had such radical views that even the most conservative governments wanted them gone. They were persecuted, so they went underground. That's when they started to make a name for themselves. They started killing off anybody who didn't agree with them. Then, they started killing off people who were actively against them, and soon it devolved into such disarray and chaos that they were killing off anybody who even looked at them funny.

Then Natalia discovered her powers, and the group ended up disbanding. Not because of any differences or whatnot, but because they soon realized that they could use Natalia to solve all of their problems. They could kill anybody without a trace. So she started doing that, and soon she found other people just like her. She quickly joined S.H.O.T. and rose through the ranks as fast as she could. Killing anybody that stood in her way. Soon, the former headmaster of S.H.O.T. had suddenly 'become ill' and passed away in less than a week. She was given the position and became the new headmaster.

For the past 40 years… ALL of the targets that the hunters were assigned, all over the world, was because Natalia had some sort of secret political agenda. She was so close too. She was so close. It stated in her diary that once all of her competition was killed, she would try and murder all of the hunters on earth… starting with JACK! Then, she and her political party would reappear and try to take over the office, then the majority of Europe, and would soon try to become a regime just like the fascist Nazi. With the same plans of world domination, except this time, it wasn't due to race, but rather some weird political goals that she felt could help empower the earth.

Jack put the piece of paper down. He was sweating. He never once said this out loud, but he thanked God almighty above that she was dead. What… what an evil woman! May god have mercy on her.

On the pieces of paper were the names of everyone involved in her political agenda, and who supported her: 4 men and 7 different women.

Jack bowed his head. Great… just great. It seemed like when one thing ended, 15 different other things were popping up and trying to cling themselves to Jack.

Jack rushed out and found Terrence, who was sitting by himself. He handed the papers to Terrence.

"Read this… can you believe it?"

Terrence barely even scanned the paper, and Jack saw it in his face. Terrence knew. Jack wanted to punch him in the face for not telling him, but soon realized that he probably had a valid reason for not telling Jack.

"You didn't tell me… did you think I already knew?"

Terrence shook his head. "No. Judging by the way you were reacting to the whole situation, I just figured that you didn't know. In fact, if I'm being honest, everybody knew. David, Samantha and even Andrea and everyone else. They all knew what they were doing when they went to go and kill their targets."

Jack suddenly came down from his high, and the pill wore off. He felt sick and wanted to go to bed. Nobody told him a damn thing! Jack was furious. Did they think he was meaningless, is that why they decided not to share any information? Did they think he was worthless or meaningless?

He looked up at Terrence. "If you knew, why didn't you tell me?"

"I didn't really feel like it."

Jack controlled himself as he clenched his hands. That bastard! He was a jerk for not telling Jack.

Terrence saw Jack's figure and he could feel his anger. He chuckled.

"Careful there, don't want to go picking fights."

"Yeah, fights that I know I could win."

Terrence looked down at Jack. Now Terrence was the one whose blood was starting to boil. This cocky brat, whoever he was, would show him. Thankfully, there were no hunters around. So a fight could be ideal in a situation like this. He turned his head toward Jack, and spit out his cigarette.

Even though the effects of the pill had worn off, Jack was certain that he was able to take this clown single-handedly. So what if he was big? Yuri was also huge, and Jack took him out. (Although he did sustain some broken bones.)

"Careful there, kid. You—"

Before Terrence could finish his sentence, Jack socked him square in the jaw with his left hand. Terence's jaw broke, and he fell to the floor. Jack jumped on him and tried putting him in a chokehold. Terrence escaped and slammed Jack hard on the floor. Jack felt his spine crack. Terrence started choking the life out of Jack, but that meant that his body was exposed. Jack kicked him in his ribs, causing Terrance to let go of him. Jack quickly jumped up and shoved his hand inside Terrence's mouth. He ripped out his tongue.

Terrence screamed, and it sounded like a goat. Blood poured out of his mouth, and Jack threw the tongue back at Terrence.

"Be careful there, hotshot. You don't want to go around picking fights you know you can't win," said Jack as he started to feel cocky and had a sly and smirky smile on his face. Terrence's face became red with anger, and he charged at Jack. Unfortunately, he was just too slow, and Jack was able to avoid all the attacks and got out of there as quickly as possible. Before he left, he yanked Terrence's hair out of his head. Dandruff and blood flew onto Terrence's shirt as Jack kicked him to the ground.

Terrence's face planted headfirst into the floor, but he was not out of the count just yet. He stood up and grabbed a weapon. *Crap,* thought Jack, as Terrence started swinging a sword like a madman. Terrence was swinging so hard and so violently that he even cut himself. He didn't care though, as he was just trying to kill Jack.

Jack avoided one of the swings, but the other one cut his shirt into two and made a deep enough slash in his chest to warrant stitches. Jack backflipped away and kicked Terrence while he was moving. Terrence fell, and the sword fell onto his shoulder. Terrence couldn't feel it though, as his rage and hatred were just too strong. He stood back up and charged at Jack once more. And once more, Jack avoided all of the sword swings.

Enough, thought Jack as he disarmed Terrence and grabbed his sword. He sliced one of Terrence's feet off, and his right hand. Terrence finally succumbed to the pain as he fell down and hit his head. He screamed out for mercy… and Jack showed it to him by throwing the sword away. He quickly called for some help, and soon Terrence was escorted away. Jack sighed.

What a day. Now that the pill was weaning off, Jack was starting to feel tired. Before he left though, he headed back to Natalia's office. Hopefully, there was something there that he could use for his information.

He searched around but found nothing useful at all. That is… until he realized something. Near the drawer, there was a small, but visible lever. Jack pulled it, and a secret compartment for the desk revealed itself. Jack pulled it open and found dozens of paperwork. They all contained detailed step-by-step plans for her secret political organization. Apparently, it even had a name. They were called "the masters of disguise." Their logo was even a chameleon.

Jack examined the papers. Supposedly, when the group disbanded, some of the members started teaching and spreading their beliefs in secret. Soon, people started believing and attending secret meetings. Eventually, from recent messaging, Natalia's… weird cult thing had gained a mass following. There were at least 100 different members in each European city. Some were even going to other continents like Asia and Africa to spread their message and beliefs.

The people hid in disguise. Nobody knew who they were, nor did people really care. They kept it a secret and attended meetings at night when everybody else was asleep. They blended in so perfectly with the crowd that you would be hard-pressed to point them out at random.

Jack rubbed his head. Perfect, just perfect. He sighed as he bowed his head. He didn't need this right now. He looked at the piece of paper. There was really only one name scribbled on it.

'Darrick Herman' was the person's name. Jack looked them up on the computer. He was a small-time politician located in Latvia. He was operating out of a third party that was quickly gaining popularity and traction. Jack tried finding personal information about the man. Apparently, the man's daughter was missing somewhere, and due to the missing daughter, he and his wife were going through quite a rough patch. (There were other supposed rumors that the man was a white supremacist.) Besides that, Jack found nothing too major.

He turned off the computer and went to the elevator. Terrence was nowhere to be seen. Jack's head hurt. He wondered about 'The masters of disguise' and their plans for 'so-called world domination.' He didn't believe it at first, but the more he thought about it, the more he became paranoid. He wondered what he would be able to do. Was he right in sticking his nose in this business? Was he OK with letting some extremist group in Europe rise? After all, it was a small country in eastern Europe.

Still... Jack knew the risks. Nobody ever thought that the Nazi party would rise the way they did, and nobody ever thought that a failed artist from Austria would lead an army of elite soldiers with plans of world domination. He knew that he had to do something. He didn't want to do anything; in fact, he just wanted to put this whole thing under the rug. Forget about it and move on with life. It didn't affect him, so why should he care?

No, thought Jack as he shook his head. That's not the way he thought. He knew that he could help people, people from these... monsters. He gritted his teeth as he felt a strong conviction in his heart. He would help those people!

Then some more thoughts arose in his mind. Was there really going to be a mini-civil war like Terrence said? Furthermore, from what Terrence said, it seemed like almost all of the hunters' targets had a reason for being killed. Now that Jack was the new headmaster of S.H.O.T., he would be able to send out the target's name. He vowed and swore that he would only send out those who were criminals, and those who needed to be put in jail.

Jack got out and walked home. He was beaten. He thought about sleeping in his nice and comfy bed but soon realized that the room was filled with Leon and his men. Jack sighed; he could always sleep on the couch. But he didn't feel comfortable sleeping that way.

Jack stopped in his tacks on the way home. He was right outside of Audrey's house. He pondered for a moment. He could say he got kicked out, and hopefully, she could give him a place to crash. He smiled—hopefully, she was still awake at this time.

Jack knocked on the door... no answer. He knocked again... no answer. His confidence started to wear thin. He remembered what Audrey said to him last time about him showing his face. He ESPECIALLY didn't need any troubles with the cops right about now. There was no response for a while. Jack left.

Audrey opened the door, and Jack quickly spun around. She had bedhead, her face looked pale, and she looked like she had been rudely interrupted by someone. She looked up at Jack.

There was a moment of silence—a horrible silence. It could only be felt as the two of them looked at each other. One was happy that they were seeing the other. The other person wanted to kill him!

After a while, Jack broke the ice.

"Hi, Audrey. It's so n-nice to... you look good for someone that just woke up."

Audrey said nothing. She coldly looked at him. Jack cleared his throat.

"Right... um, sorry for coming here so late. I locked myself out of the house. Do you think that... I could crash here?"

Audrey looked at him and laughed. It wasn't a giggle or a soft laugh. It was a hard laugh—a laugh that you had when something was so hysterical, so funny, so obnoxiously humorous, you couldn't help but laugh from the depths of your gut.

She smiled at him.

"Are you freaking serious? First of all, I'm calling the cops on you. So you better stay put. Second of all, there's no way in hell I'm letting you sleep in my room. Also, my boyfriend is here."

Jack raised his hands.

"Please don't call the cops. I have a lot on my plate right now and I can't have this right now. Please, I'm sorry for everything I did and put you through. You can hate me all you want, but please don't call the cops on me!"

Audrey stood silent for a moment. She pondered and looked at Jack. Her mind boggled by looking at him.

Damn bastard! Who does he think he is trying to come here and sleep in my room after the stunt he pulled? Oh, HELL no, he can kiss my ass goodbye! She gritted her teeth and spit on the floor.

"Fine... I won't call the cops, but consider yourself lucky. Also, my boyfriend probably wouldn't want you sleeping here anyway. He gets jealous easily."

"What boyfriend?"

Audrey made a sickening face.

"W-what do you mean? The one I got after—"

"I know you're lying to me. You're not the type of girl to brag or boast about a boyfriend, even if you are trying to make your ex feel miserable. Also, knowing the type of guy you like, I doubt you would date anybody nearby. Furthermore, both your parents are home, and they despise the thought of us sleeping in the same bedroom. And we were together for quite some time. So I can only imagine how they would feel if you 'hypothetically' asked them to have a new boyfriend sleep over in less than the span of a week."

Audrey bit down her lip. Dammit, he knew her too well. Jack smiled, and Audrey frowned. Just because he won this battle didn't mean anything. He would lose this as he was trying to start with her. He would see. She would find a new boyfriend fast, even if she didn't like him, just to spite Jack. Just to put him through half the pain he brought her!

Her frown turned upside down. Jack loved her still, she knew it. She would love to see his heart break as she kissed her new boyfriend, went out on dates with him, and constantly bragged about him at school. She loved the idea of Jack feeling miserable and horrible. Him crying in his room. Just to feel what she felt for so long.

Jack spoke up as his smile grew even bigger.

"Oh, and don't think that getting a new boyfriend is going to do anything. I have other women at my disposal. You're not going to make me jealous or upset, since judging by your facial expression I can see that's what you're thinking. I have this beautiful and hot 50-year-old milf at home just waiting for me to take off my pants. Sorry, Audrey, but you're not winning anything."

Audrey yelled at him. Enraged, Jack could see the veins popping out from her forehead and her throat. Her face turned red, and she furled her eyebrows. When she yelled, she snarled at Jack.

"YOU BASTARD! I should have never dated someone as low and miserable as you! I don't know why I ever got the idea of loving you, you sick piece of shit! I... I hope you die! I hope you rot in hell, you miserable and stupid son of a bitch!"

She slammed the door and ran to him. She started hitting him as hard as she could.

"Do you hear me? I HATE YOU! I HATE YOU, JACK! I HOPE YOU DIE! I WISH YOU NEVER ENTERED MY LIFE, YOU MISERABLE SICK JUNKIE! JUST..."

Audrey fell down to the floor. The tears rolled from her eyes as she stopped hitting Jack. Jack picked her up and hugged her. She sobbed and yelled in his chest. He closed his eyes as he let her cry and hit him. Damn... damn this man forever giving me the love and care he did. She wished she never met him... but she would also be wrong in saying that even after what happened... she didn't still love him. His flaws and all. That was true love.

She looked up at Jack. Her face is in complete shambles.

"I can't believe you. You're so weird, you know?"

Jack nodded his head. "Aren't we all?"

He leaned in. "Listen, Audrey... I quit. No longer am I a slave to drugs. No longer will I act out of line. I've changed. Believe me, and trust me, I've changed for the better. I found Jesus, and I found God. Things... things are going well now. Trust me. There's still time to make amends. And I still love you."

Audrey cried even harder. Hearing those words... it touched her heart. She cried some more as Jack chuckled. Man, this girl was a machine when it came to crying. She never stopped. He wondered if she had any eye problems due to the amount of tears she released. Who knew?

"I-I-I don't believe you, Jack. I'm... sorry. I just... I—"

"It's OK. I don't blame you. I understand."

Jack smiled as he let her go. He blew her a kiss and walked away. His face was expressionless. Audrey watched as he walked away. Her heart started to speak against her mind.

Maybe... maybe he did change. He didn't freak out, nor did he rebuke her. He stayed calm, accepted her decision and walked away without any hassle. In fact, no that she thought about it, the entire time that she talked to him, Jack didn't do anything wrong. Did... was he telling the truth?

Her mind told her otherwise, but her heart was too powerful. She looked at Jack as he walked away. She felt an indescribable feeling, one that was being given to her by God as he looked down upon her and used his divine power to transfer love and care to her. God looked down on both of them. He smiled, as he approved of their love and relationship. Everything, all the hardships and difficulties, was orchestrated by him. God smiled as Audrey felt a feeling of overwhelming love and care. She wanted to care for Jack… because, dammit, she loved him. More than Jack could imagine.

She ran behind him and jumped up on him, causing him to stumble and hit the concrete. She laughed as God poured rain down upon them. Audrey had a smile and tears running down her face as she grabbed Jack by his head. She looked deep into his soul, and deep into his eyes. Filled with not only love but friendship.

She laughed as she kissed him.

"I love you, Jack!"

Jack smiled as she hugged him. The rain beat down on their heads, causing their clothes to get wet. She smiled as she cried. He did change, and she could feel God's presence in him. She knew that she would never have to go through those hardships ever again. The days were over, and Jack would come back better than ever. It was like a dream come true. There really was a happy ending!

Jack kissed her as the rain beat down.

20

Samantha was sitting in the hospital bed. She would be free by the end of the day. She watched the TV as news of the massacre was pretty much on everyone's channel. The main suspects were Micah and Leon. Samantha grumbled as she ate her stale and horrible bread. The food at the hospital was horrible, and the staff was even worse. They were cold and mean to her. Worst of all, the hospital itself looked like it hadn't been clean in 100 years.

There was a knock on the door, and Terrence walked in. Samantha's eyes widened. Terrence, damn, she hadn't seen him in what felt like ages. He smiled as he sat down on a chair next to her. He was such a large man that even the chair looked like a kid's chair when he was in it.

"How are you doing?"

Samantha smiled.

"Oh… you know. Just living life. I got hit in the shoulder badly when Dr. Benjamin was killed, but it's nothing too severe."

Terrence nodded his head. He was so happy to see her. They were really good friends. He was the first friend she made when she became a hunter. She was impressed by his coldness and calculations. It took her a while, but afterward, she was able to make Terrence warm up to her. Sooner or later, they became best friends. They would go to each other's house, watch movies, play video games and smoke some weed. They loved it. Terrence was also very good friends with David. In fact, he was better friends with David than Samantha was a lover to him. He and David were inseparable. He knew about the blood diamonds but did not belittle David for it. He understood, and he saw that he regretted it.

Terrence smiled as he was so happy to see his best friend again.

"Is Jack picking you up?"

She nodded her head. "Yeah… I called him earlier today. He's on his way here as we speak."

She pointed to his face. "D-did... he does that?"

Terrence nodded. "He also chopped my foot and my hand off."

Samantha rolled her eyes as she gasped. "Oh my, I'm sorry. He's like some sort of feral dog that doesn't know how to properly be tamed."

"It's alright. Some of it was my own fault for being such a jerk. I guess I was upset at him for taking Natalia's spot. Which, speaking of, have you been up to date?"

Samantha shook her head. "I can guess that things haven't been so smooth as of recently?"

"You can say that again. I have a buddy in South Africa I keep in contact with. He told me that there's already been fighting among the hunters. It's only a matter of time before this thing turns out of control and we get the attention of countries. We need to act quickly now. Oh... and Jack found out about Natalia."

She cringed.

"How did he take it?"

"About as well as you can imagine. Be prepared, he's gonna want to talk to you on the car ride home. Are you sure you don't want me to drive you home?"

She shook her head. "I'm happy for the offer, but I need to clear some things up with Jack. I was also a victim of Natalia's lies and deception. Even when I found out, I only chose to keep on doing what I was doing because she offered me a higher position."

Terrence nodded his head. "She bribed me. I feel so ashamed... and dirty. Like I'm coming down from some crack."

"Good God, are you still smoking that? I told you to quit. That stuff is horrible, and you're gonna end up on the streets if you continue to do that!"

Terrence motioned his hand in a peace gesture. "Calm down, I quit years ago. Don't worry about anything."

She smiled as the two of them continued to talk.

"So," said Samantha as she leaned upward. "Who's side are you on?"

Terrence said nothing for a while. Samantha looked at him the way a disappointed mother looks at a child when he knows he's done something bad.

"Terrence, just give Jack a chance."

Terrence exploded as he practically jumped up from the chair. It even startled Samantha a little bit as the chair went flying.

"I can't! I mean… yeah, OK, he's super good and all, but he knows Jack shit. He doesn't understand the scale of what we do, and how we do it. He's a novice, I have no idea why Natalia decided to appoint him in the first place. Only look at how he reacted to finding out about Natalia's secret, and tell me he's fit for stressful situations. Also, he has NO money whatsoever for funding. All of our missions and items were funded by Natalia because she practically wiped her ass with money. Jack isn't even out of high school yet. What does he know? Furthermore, his sense of justice is what gets me really riled up. If he understood the amount of corruption that lay within every S.H.O.T. base around the world, he would drop dead of a heart attack. We are not some clean company.

"Our jobs are to literally kill people because nobody can escape death. And now Jack thinks that our jobs are supposed to be rewarding and fulfilling? I don't understand. He reminds me of that founder, Jared. I read that he was also some super do-gooder because of his friend. There's a reason he died so young, and mark my words, Jack is going to follow down the same path and end up in a horrible fate!"

Samantha said nothing as she let Terrence calm down. He was practically sweating with how much he was yelling and moving.

She smiled. "Are you done?"

He shook his head. "No, but… just say it."

"Listen… I think Jack is great. Everything you just said has a silver lining. There is too much corruption, and I feel as though Jack could change all of that in a heartbeat, THANKS to his pure heart. He's changed, Terrence. You should have seen him when he first became a hunter. Also, as far as funding goes, don't we already have enough weapons? Plus, Natalia should have left a fortune when she died. I'm sure it's somewhere, all we need to do is find it and our problems are solved. His sense of justice, his heart, his motives and his good nature are what's going to improve S.H.O.T. as a whole. With him as our leader, we don't have to be killing people for political reasons. Don't you understand? Finally, there can be purity in this crooked and dirty job that we do."

The two of them remained silent as the tension in the room started to rise. Terrence sighed.

"Look… I understand and I can see where you're coming from. However, you also have to think of the possibilities. Life is not all sunshine and rainbows, and there are no happy endings!"

"You're right. That's not the case because there are people like Natalia who are in charge of everything. People like Jack… fight to make things right. Even if it cost him his life. Did you ever once see Natalia go into the field with us?"

"That's because she was too busy."

"Too busy with what? Finding out who she didn't like so she could have them killed?"

There was silence again. The tension was now at an all-time high. Even Samantha was now starting to sweat as she could feel that something was about to go down. She tried to play her cards right. She was in no shape to fight, nor did she want to. Terrence was her friend… but he was also unpredictable and prone to violent outbursts. (It was due to all the steroids he took.)

Samantha took a deep breath and tried to destabilize the situation.

"Look… as MUCH as I would love to argue back and forth, there are more pressing matters on our hands. A civil war is about to break out and we need to find solutions instead of arguing about issues. So please… can we just put this behind us?"

Terrence looked at her. He took a deep breath. Deep down, he knew that she was right. They had a damn civil war brewing and they needed to resolve this issue quickly. He picked up the chair and sat down again. He would put his differences aside… for now.

"So… what do you plan on doing?" asked Terrence. Samantha pondered for a bit. The big issue was Jack's likability. Some people thought he was fit, and others… not so much. Yet, people didn't really know WHO Jack was. They just knew he was inexperienced and given a very high position.

"Perhaps… what if we gathered all the hunters into one location, and had Jack give a speech?"

Terrence nearly fell out of his chair again. He chuckled, not because it was funny, and his eyes nearly exploded from shock.

"W-what. You can't be serious. The number of things that could go wrong."

"You're thinking too much about the negative. You need to start focusing on the positive. Yes, things could go to shit really fast, but this could also be a good opportunity for people to see who Jack really is. They might like him. If this fails, then it just means we'll have a war on our hands. No big deal, right?"

Terrence ignored that comment. "Any other suggestions?"

She thought about it. She remembered that even when Natalia was in office, people didn't really like her. Yet she was still respected and feared due to how much power she had. Samantha had another idea.

"People feared Natalia, and they respected her because of how much power she had. What if…we host a tournament to showcase Jack's skills? To show how much of a badass he is in battle?"

Terrence actually liked this one. He nodded his head. He was still unsure, but at least it sounded better than her previous ideas.

"OK, then… what exactly are you thinking?"

"A tournament. Anybody who wants to challenge Jack could do it. (And I'm sure there will be a lot of people who would want to.) If someone beats him, then they are allowed to run things from now on. If not, then Jack is the official headmaster of all of S.H.O.T. Conflict settled."

Terrence smiled. "It seems like you're not caught up on your history. Do you know what happens when people try to resolve issues with violence?"

Samantha shook her head. "No… this is different. Trust me on this one. What do you think?!"

Terrence leaned back in his chair. He wasn't a fan of Jack, but he did have to say that Jack was a damn good fighter. Probably one of the best he's ever seen. This fight tournament could go really well… but it could also go horribly wrong if their cards were placed wrong. He nodded his head. Oh well, it was worth a shot. After all, Samantha said he had to work on the positives instead of the negatives. He nodded his head as he smiled.

"OK, I like it. So, what exactly are you planning on doing?"

"Well… since you know more people than me, I was wondering if you could call up everybody you know to go and tell them the news. There will be a tournament held in a month from now. Any hunter can participate. As well, this would be a good chance for people to also meet Jack as a person. We can do it near David's flower shop."

Terrence nodded his head. "Is the place big enough?"

"It depends on how many people show up. If not, then I have another idea, but for now, let's just stick with plan A. I'm counting on you!"

Terrence smiled as he shook Samantha's hand. He soon left and started calling as many hunters as he could to tell them the news.

Leon woke up. His head was pounding. The room was dark, cold and quiet. It was also smelly. (Someone was farting like crazy.)

Leon slowly got out of Jack's bed and waddled his way toward the door. How long had he been out? It must have been some time. He was thirsty and extremely hungry. He limped downstairs. Everything about him hurt. He could hardly even move his legs. He made grunting noises every time he walked, and he looked like a mummy with how many bandages were wrapped around his body.

He headed downstairs, and saw Rebecca watching TV. She slightly gasped as she saw Leon. He smiled and waved at her. She stood up as she turned off the TV.

"Oh… it's you," was all she said as she walked upstairs. Leon wasn't surprised. He would probably act that way if he was being asked and begged to house two wanted fugitives. He looked around, no sign of Jack. Oh well. He opened the fridge, made himself a nice sandwich and sat down to watch some TV. He felt like he had taken an absolutely banger of a nap. He felt so alive, yet so dead at the same time. He could hardly move his body, but he also felt like going for a run or lifting some heavy weights. He turned on the TV to find a picture of him and Micah from when they were in high school. They had a bounty of nearly 100,000,000 dollars. Furthermore, they would most likely be executed on the spot if they were handed over to the authorities. At that moment, Leon became a religious man.

If it weren't for Jack, he would be in deep, deep shit right now. A man by Jack HAD to be sent from God. He saved him and his friends. And for that, Leon was forever grateful. In a way, he was happy this happened. Leon knew that this life was over now. And he knew that he had to change as a person. Despite the circumstances, Leon was happy that all of this was happening. It was as if God loved him despite all of his unique flaws, and was giving him a second chance at life. Leon smiled as he heard someone else coming downstairs.

It was Micah. Micah looked like he had risen from his tombstone and walked 1,000 miles. He was practically mortified. The bandages were falling off, and with his lanky frame, he looked like he had come out of a horror movie. He sat down next to Jack as he huffed. He could hardly even say anything.

Micah pointed to the TV. "Look… we're famous."

Micah coughed some blood as his face became even more pale. Leon didn't say anything as he couldn't talk. His throat hurt really badly. Not because he was dehydrated or anything, but because he didn't have the strength to even speak. Despite having the best sleep of his entire life.

The two sat in silence for a moment until they also heard a noise. They looked to see Victor coming downstairs. His hand was all messed up, but besides that, he looked like he had been in a car crash. He smiled as he grabbed some water and sat down next to Leon. Again, none of them said anything as they watched the news coverage. Dutch was still upstairs. He would be asleep for quite some time.

A few hours passed by, and still nobody said anything. Micah was internally freaking out. He couldn't believe it; he couldn't believe that now he was a wanted criminal. For so many years, he was able to avoid the spotlight and able to avoid the circumstances that plagued so many mercenaries. Now he was seeing a large bounty on his head, and imagining the possibility of a death sentence. He smiled… he was grateful to whoever this Jack person was. Even though Jack was still his target, Micah thought about dropping it all together. It's not like he could go back to his farm now. The military was probably there. Micah would also get charged with possession of illegal narcotics. It didn't matter; either way, he would die if he was ever caught.

Rebecca came downstairs. She menacingly looked at everyone and proceeded to make dinner. The smell of meatballs and pasta went nicely with the cooked vegetables. Leon smiled; he hadn't smelled a meal this good in years. Hopefully, if she wasn't so mean to them, she would give them just a little bit.

Victor spoke up. "That smells nice." His voice was raspy and weak. Rebecca said nothing as she continued to cook. He and Leon gave each other a look and continued to watch the TV.

After a while, she put four bowls on the table and she sat down to eat. The three men on the couch waddled and limped their way toward the table to eat. They never had food so good and so amazing.

Rebecca was eyeing them like a jealous ex eyes their old lover's partner. She examined everyone by looking at them up and down. Just from analysis, she was able to deduce that Leon was the oldest and probably the most experienced. Then Micah, and then Victor. She didn't get a good glimpse of Dutch when Jack was fixing him up.

Rebecca decided to speak up. Her tone and voice were harsh and cruel.

"What are your jobs?"

Leon and Micah couldn't speak, so they looked at Victor to help them out. Victor spoke up.

"Um... we're mercenaries."

Rebecca nodded her head. She bit down on her lips aggressively, and her eyebrows lowered even more.

"I see... so tell me then, do you ever feel remorse for the people you kill?"

Victor said nothing. He was grateful for Rebecca making dinner and for her housing, them in her house when she could easily be set for life with just one phone call away. Still, Victor did not need this talk at the moment. He just wanted to eat his food in peace and quiet. Nevertheless, Rebecca did not stop.

"Do you... do you ever think about your actions? Do you ever think about having another life? Why... why did you decide to do this? Why did you decide that you were the one who was allowed to judge others and take their lives."

"Who allowed you to judge me?"

Rebecca spit out her food and slammed her fork on the table. She practically lunged across the table and pointed a finger at Victor.

"Make no mistake here! You may be here because Jack took pity on you, but you're only allowed to stay here because of him. If it were up to me, I would have turned you in myself. Good riddance! I want you to leave as soon as you're better. Understood?"

Before Victor could say anything, Rebecca walked upstairs, leaving the three of them alone. Finally, the bitch was gone, and they could enjoy some peace and quiet as they finished their food. Upstairs, Rebecca was freaking out. Dammit, dammit, dammit, she didn't want those goons for hire to be here. They were harboring fugitives. What was Jack smoking to ever think that having those 4 around was a good idea? She sat down on her bed. She wouldn't let this slide. Damn that Jack... if she could just get her hands on him.

Downstairs, Leon and Micah were sitting when Victor spoke up.

"What's going to happen to us now?"

Nobody said anything for a while. Leon's head started to spin. He knew a guy that would ship them out to anywhere in the world they wanted. They would start there once they were all healed up. From there, they would all go their separate ways. At least… that's what Leon wanted.

Leon looked at Micah. Micah was a very, very wildcard. Despite him being quiet most of the time, Leon knew that Micah wouldn't leave his side. He would stay with Leon because Micah had nowhere else to go. He didn't know how to do anything besides shoot. He tried leaving the mercenary life to work at a sales firm. That lasted horribly. Leon sighed.

Jack and Samantha were in the car driving when Samantha spoke up. It was pouring rain outside and the two of them could hardly even see.

"So… Jack, how are you feeling?"

From the moment he picked her up, the tension had become super awkward. She tried to make small talk, but Jack shut her down every time. He was just itching for her to say something about Natalia, for her to say something about everything. His jaw was clenched, and he didn't look at her once during any red stop lights.

Jack didn't say a word. Samantha nodded her head. She looked out the window and imagined all of the events that had transpired in their lives up until that point. She closed her eyes and started to cry. Yuri, Andrea, David, John and even though she didn't like her, Natalia too. They were all gone. Why was all of this happening? Why did they all have to go? It should have been her. She should have been the one to die, not them. They were good people; she was just some suck-up who wanted to get promoted and promoted because she wanted respect from everyone else. The same respect that Natalia had. Instead… she was sobbing and grieving over her dead friends. She should have been the one to die in the gas station, not Andrea.

"I know how you feel," said Jack. Samantha turned her head and saw Jack crying. He wiped a tear from his eyes, and for the first time in the entire ride, he looked at her.

"It's hard. It's hard knowing that your friends are dead. It should have been me. I should have died! Look at everything I've done. I SHOULD HAVE DIED! NOT YURI! NOT DAVID! NOT ANYBODY!

"So please, for all things that are holy, tell me and explain to me why you kept Natalia's secret away from me and Yuri? I need to know, or else I'm gonna lose it. I'm already on edge with everything that's going on, so please… just tell me."

Samantha nodded her head. She owed that to Jack. She sighed as she spoke.

"Well, not everybody knows. A lot of people do, but not everybody. I think in our... group, you and Yuri weren't the ones to know. Once we found out, we were either forced to stay silent, bribed or just rewarded with a promotion if we turned our heads. Believe it or not, it was actually David who found out about the secret political agenda that she had, and it was he who did some digging on the targets and found out that we were actually killing people for a hidden purpose."

Samantha was about to bring up the blood diamond incident, but she kept her mouth shut. She didn't want to break David's promise. Jack saw that she was about to say something, but he let her stay quiet. He didn't want to pressure her anymore.

"So... how long did this go on?"

Samantha shrugged. "I'm not sure. Almost 7 years, I think. At least when you showed up, that's how long. I suppose... even more if we are to believe her notes."

Jack sighed.

"Jack, please tell me you're not planning on going over to Latvia to deal with all of this?"

Jack accelerated as his anger rose. How could Samantha just ignore this? Not only was someone kidnapped, most likely due to political reasons, but there was damn near a plot to probably take over the entire world. And Samantha just wanted to sit back and let this all play out?

"Samantha, you do realize that Natalia was not working alone. Sure, she had the power to go inside other people's minds, but her organization is still a thing. Plaguing and infesting countries around Estonia. I am NOT going to sit back as some political terrorist group tries to take over the earth. You know, judging by the way you're reacting to everything, I'm starting to think you were in cahoots with Natalia."

"Oh please, don't be ridiculous."

Jack menacingly looked at her. "I'm not joking."

She rolled her eyes. It was too late for her to be having this argument. She just wanted to go to bed. At least she got the whole Natalia situation out with Jack. He looked disappointed and angry. Hopefully, he would get over it in a few days. Until then, she would need to help Jack with this tournament.

Samantha spoke up.

"So... about the news regarding the decision to have you as the new headmaster. I talked to Terrence. I believe there is a way to settle this whole ordeal and try to gain favor with the hunters who already don't like you."

Jack raised an eyebrow. "And that would be?"

"You see, Natalia wasn't liked. In fact, I think she was just as disliked as you. Yet, she was highly respected and there wasn't any civil war when she was announced as head chairman. Do you know why?"

Jack shook his head.

"It's because they feared her. They knew how capable she was, and they respected her skills as a boss, and as a businesswoman and fighter. We're going to be instilling that same respect into everyone else when you fight in the tournament."

Jack slowly turned his head toward Samantha.

"A... what?"

"There's going to be a tournament that's going to be held in a month. It's going to be you against... anybody who doesn't like you practically. (Which is basically nearly everyone.) However, there is a silver lining. You're going to get nearly a full month's time of training. I know you can do this! Also... I got you a present."

Samantha pulled something from the back of her pocket. She handed it over to Jack. Jack's eyes widened as he realized it was the same pill that Dr. Benjamin had given him before he entered the courthouse.

"W-where on earth did you—"

"Dr. Benjamin gave it to me, along with the gun that I fired. He told me to save it for a 'safe occasion'. You better use it wisely, since it's the last one that I think exists.

"Also, this pill is FAR more potent than the other one. If you think you were invincible with the other one, just wait until you pop this bad boy. You're going to feel like you can kick superman's ass. However, be warned, it only lasts up to 20 minutes. But with your skills... I think that would be plenty of time."

Jack smiled as he put the pill in the back of his pocket. He felt like this was cheating, but as the old saying goes, 'If you ain't cheating, then you ain't trying.' Yet, the person who said that was probably a gambler. Jack shook his head as he grabbed the pill and thew it out the window.

"WHAT in the WORLD do you think you're doing?"

"I don't need it. That's cheating and—"

Samantha jumped out of the car. Jack lost his breath as he swerved the car and put it to a halt. He slightly dented his car when he smashed into a tree off the side of the road. He quickly got out as Samantha was looking on the ground, searching for the pill. The rain poured hard on them.

"What in the world is your problem?"

Samantha ignored him as she tried digging around. She opened her bullet wound again. She clenched her jaw and gritted her teeth. The pain was coming back, but she needed that pill. She grew furious at Jack as she couldn't find it.

"Damn you! Do you know how important that pill is?"

"Winners don't do drugs."

She slapped him in the face.

"Excuse me, but when did you become such a monk? Last time I checked, you were smoking dope and shooting heroin as your life depended on it."

Jack's eyes widened. She knew? How? that was impossible. Only one person knew and that was…

"Did Audrey tell you?"

"Who?"

Jack shook his head.

"It doesn't matter. First of all, I'm not a monk. I'm a devout Christian. Second of all, I have stopped. No more will I do ANY kind of drugs. I'm done with that lifestyle. I'm also done with anything that's sinful!"

Samantha shook her head. "Look, I'm not much of a religious woman, but I know that it's impossible to escape that lifestyle. We're all sinners at the end of the day! Poor and uncontrollable sinners. Yes, good for you. You found God, you found Jesus, and you found peace and happiness. But how long will that last before you get that itchy feeling again? The feeling of wanting to just get a quick fix, just say 'only this time' and then do a line, or smoke a pound of whatever. Then, you'll be begging for more. I know how it goes… it's not easy."

"With Jesus, anything is possible. I will not fail!"

Samantha smirked as she found the pill on the ground. "Whatever you say, but don't come crawling to me when you need a few thousand dollars for who knows what."

Jack looked down at her, with haughty eyes as she walked back to the car. Jack started walking but caught himself. He caught himself looking at her with haughty eyes. Something the Lord DESPISED! Jack sinned… all because he was trying to act just right and holier than thou. He looked down at himself and shook his head. He had sinned. Jack started to wonder if perhaps drugs were the solution. He felt as though with drugs, he wouldn't sin. He wouldn't look down on people with haughty eyes.

He shook his head. What devilish thoughts. He needed to quit, not for himself, but for Audrey. He promised her. He felt ashamed and conflicted as he walked over to the car. Was it… always going to be like this? A battle in his head for what's really good, and what's really right and wrong. He felt like doing the right thing was bad, but doing the bad thing was right. He shook his head. Dammit… this was all so confusing. He reversed the car and proceeded to drive home.

21

Jack got home soaking wet. Samantha told Jack to meet her tomorrow in mid-afternoon. They were going to start their training. Jack couldn't stop thinking about his thoughts. They were so… conflicting.

He stepped inside Rebecca's house only to find her waiting for him by the door. She grabbed him by his right arm and pulled him into the garage. She hissed and yelled at him. She was infuriated.

"What in the world did you think of when you brought those four men here?"

Jack rolled his eyes. Not this again.

"Look, they're harmless, OK? It's not like their—"

"I don't care! They are WANTED criminals! Understand? They are wanted! Do you know what would happen if we got caught harboring fugitives in our house?"

"Just calm down and think rationally about this. They are fugitives, yes, but who on earth would think to look in Wilmhelm for them? Let alone this small neighborhood. Also, last time I checked, they were going to be leaving soon. Plus, wouldn't you want someone to help the nurse and aid you if you were sick and injured?"

"That's different!"

"How so? You know, you act like such a hypocrite sometimes. I mean, do you hear yourself?"

Rebecca was on the verge of slapping Jack. She furled her eyebrows even more, and veins were appearing on her forehead. She had a mean and menacing look on her face. She gritted her teeth at him and nearly pushed him.

"They… are… NOT staying here. Understand? I don't care if you—"

Jack leaned in and kissed Rebecca. He knew that she wanted to bang him. He was taking a HUGE risk here. It said that adultery was a sin in the Bible, and Jack knew that he was sinning. Yet, this was the only way to keep those men here. May god forgive him in his infinite wisdom. Jack wanted to keep those men safe. 'Do unto others as you would do unto yourselves.' The golden rule. Even Jesus knew. Jack was certain he would go to any lengths if it meant keeping him safe. Even if that meant sleeping with Andrea's mom. At least she wasn't ugly. God... may You forgive me, thought Jack as Rebecca pulled down Jack's pants.

They had sex in the garage right then and there. By far, that was the best sex Jack ever had. By the end, he was sweating and huffing. He never had sex so well. Yet, in the end, he felt shame and guilt. By God, was the sex good, and he wished he could do it every single day. Yet... Jack knew that it was wrong. He did this only one time, and it was for his new friends that he made. But damn... was it good.

Jack thought about what Samantha had said earlier... and he cringed as he fell to his knees. She was right. He was now hooked. He gaslighted himself into thinking he had the discipline and commitment to just sleep with Audrey... but the sex was so good. He knew that Rebecca would be willing to do it anyway and anytime. Audrey, on the other hand, even though she and Jack did have sex, it was different. Some days Jack wanted to have sex, but Audrey refused. Some days Audrey was ready, but Jack was busy with something. With Rebecca, though, it was like his guilty pleasure was on speed dial... and living in the same house.

Jack cried himself to sleep that night. He felt guilty and ashamed. He... cheated on his girlfriend. He... sinned. He, as a Christian, sinned. He felt so ashamed and guilty. What Samantha said was right. He really was just a sinner at the end of the day, no matter how hard he tried, Jack was only human. A human with earthly desires. Even if he did try his hardest, sometimes he would fall short... and that was something he couldn't live with.

Jack soon started becoming suicidal. He couldn't live in a world where he disobeyed God.

The following week all happened so fast. Jack spent his days training with Samantha. She put him through rigorous and visceral drills. The training was so intense he would pass out after every session. Good, he was getting better. Jack practically spent no time with Audrey, as he was just so busy training. Although... there was another reason. Jack couldn't bring himself to look at Audrey. He was too ashamed of what he had done. Even though he knew what he was doing was wrong, Jack continued to sleep and have sex with Rebecca.

He couldn't help it, dammit, it was just so good. Great, from one addiction to another. Jack couldn't stop and he couldn't help it. After every session, it ended with him crying to bed. Why... why did he do the things he did? He knew he was disobeying God, and he continued to do it because, dammit... it was just so damn good. His suicidal tendencies increased every day. Samantha said nothing, but she would see new cuts and bruises on his hand. She got him a new and better-left arm to see if that would cheer him up. That was about as helpful as bringing a knife to a gunfight.

Leon and the rest of his men spent the days resting and eating lots and lots of food. Rebecca tried to have them sleep with her, but they refused. They literally were too weak to even thrust. Even when they were starting to gain their strengths back, they still refused. Leon knew the kind of girl Rebecca was. Despite her age, she still acted out of line. Maybe 20 years ago he would say yes, but not anymore. Besides, he saw the way she looked at Jack. Leon was so indebted and grateful to Jack that he dared not even open the box that had been opened so many times by Jack. He felt as if he were being disloyal to Jack, the man who saved his life. Dutch, after being in bed for nearly a week, finally got up. His jaw was healing, and he was starting to speak again. They all thought about what they were going to do once they were all better.

Audrey had become sad as of recently. Her favorite man in the whole wide world wasn't talking to her, or answering her calls. She became worried. Did he... did he fall into the pit of drugs again? She hoped not. She tried going over to his house, but nobody ever answered the door. Where was he going? She became so distraught and sad that her parents nearly burned down Jack's house. Ever since their daughter had met that man, it had been nothing but misery. Sara cursed Jack, as she wished he was never born.

Audrey was sitting in her room one day when, out of nowhere, she decided to miss Jack. She hadn't talked to him in forever. She grabbed her purse and went to his house. Hopefully, he would be there, and she could actually talk to him and hang out with him. As she walked, she started to wonder why Jack didn't talk to her so much. Why was he ignoring her so much? Was it because she wasn't having enough sex with him? She thought that at the beginning of their relationship, they had plenty of sex and that he was satisfied. *Apparently not,* thought Audrey.

She looked down at her body, and for the first time in her relationship, started getting body conscious. Was she becoming too skinny? Or too... ugly for Jack? No, Jack said he loved her no matter what. She pondered. Jack did like to work out, so he had a high libido. Maybe if she started working out, she would be able to have more sex and they would be happy again. She smiled as she started thinking about getting all nice and toned for Jack. Some days she just didn't want to have sex, and she saw the look Jack gave her. The look of disappointment. She couldn't help it. Some days she literally couldn't because she was on her period, and she shivered at the thought of them having sex when she was having her menstrual cycle.

She knocked on the door. No answer. She knocked again, and this time, Rebecca opened.

She looked and examined Audrey. She snarled at Audrey, and Audrey took offense. Who was this woman?

Rebecca smiled. "Why, hello, you must be Audrey!"

Audrey nodded. "Yes. That's me. I'm sorry to interpret, but by any chance is Jack around?"

Rebecca frowned. "Are you his girlfriend?"

She nodded her head. She was a little bit shocked at the frown when she called her 'girlfriend'.

"Um, yes, I am. We have been—"

"Can it, bitch. I don't need to hear it. You just stay away from Jack. He's mine."

Audrey looked surprised. W-what on earth was she talking about? This woman looked like she could be a very young grandma. Audrey's mind started to race. Could Jack—

"What do you mean by that? And don't call me a bitch! You…"

"Can it… whore. Jack didn't tell you? Oh well, I guess I'll have to spill the beans."

Rebecca leaned in and whispered in Audrey's ear. Her voice was sly and sleek, and very slimy. As if she was trying to seduce Audrey herself.

"Me and Jack have been having sex behind your back. And he loves it. Way more than what you give him."

Audrey's eyes widened as she started to cry. No, her Jack would never. He was loyal, and he loved her. He would never do such a thing. He would never ever… he couldn't. She knew he was a Christian, and she knew that he wouldn't sin because he loved God. That's how it worked… right?

"You're lying! I know Jack would never do something like that!"

Rebecca smiled as she pulled out her phone. During one of their sessions, she secretly placed her phone somewhere and recorded the whole ordeal—just in case something like this would happen.

Rebecca grinned as the life practically faded out of Audrey. She saw Jack, butt naked going absolutely wild on Rebecca. He was moaning and groaning the whole time, talking dirty to her and everything. Rebecca put the phone away, and took pleasure in seeing a poor girl in front of her have her whole world ruined.

"Sorry… but it looks like Jack likes me more. Don't be sad. It's just… I'm better at having sex. Whenever and whatever day Jack wants, I'm in bed waiting for him with my legs spread open wide."

Audrey dropped her purse as she ran away. Tears were hitting the streets. She couldn't believe it. No way, not Jack. Nobody but Jack. He was cheating on her with some fucking grandma. She couldn't believe it.

Jack was walking home from Samantha's house when he saw Audrey running up the street. He saw her face, and he lost his soul at that moment.

"Audrey, are you—"

She pushed him out of the way as she continued to cry. Before she made any further progress to her house, she turned around and started beating on Jack.

"W-what's the wrong, babe?"

She kicked him in the balls. Her face was red, and when Jack saw her facial expression, he never knew a human could become this angry. The way she looked, and the way she yelled, it was like God's wrath and fury were taking control of a human. Jack didn't say anything, as he deserved everything that was coming to him.

"YOU BASTARD! YOU LYING SON OF A BITCH! HOW DARE YOU! You fucking bastard! I hate you. You cheated on me, WITH A FUCKING GRANDMA! I've been nothing but good to you, and THIS IS HOW I GET TREATED? MY BOYFRIEND IS FUCKING ANOTHER WOMAN BEHIND MY BACK! I HATE YOU!

"Jack… I thought things were over. I thought that all the bad blood and everything bad was gone and that things were going to be normal and OK… but it turns out I was FUCKING WRONG! You… I hate YOU! I HAVE TRIED MY HARDEST IN THIS RELATIONSHIP, BUT IT'S IMPOSSIBLE

TO LOVE SOMEONE LIKE YOU! I HATE YOU, YOU STUID COCKSUCKER. I… I hope you die! I hope you…"

Audrey started to break down. Jack went in to hug her, but she pushed him away and spit on his face.

"Don't you fucking touch me! Don't you come near me! Don't you ever… ever speak to me again. I… Jack… I tried my hardest to love you. I gave it all I had… but there's something severely wrong with you. I don't know what's going on… but I can't take it anymore. I love you, and I know I would be with you through thick and thin… but this is too much. You cheated on me… and you said you loved me. What do you have to say for yourself?"

Jack couldn't help but shed a tear. He shook his head.

"No… don't you do that. Don't you fucking dare start to cry? Don't pretend like you're not AT FAULT HERE! Don't act like you're feeling sorry and you need pity. DON'T! JACK…you bastard. I… I just can't believe it. I… please… why?"

Jack reached out his hands. He regretted everything. It felt so good, and the sex was so good. But now he understood that love was more important. Jack reached out his hands, but Audrey slapped it away from him.

"Don't… don't come anywhere near me for a while. I need a break. Leave me alone, and don't expect any sex from me now. Go to that whore of a grandma that's in your house! I don't know how many times I've done this with you. Say that I'm breaking up, and then we get back together, and then it's all good and dandy, and then shit hits the fan because of something YOU DID! Did you ever ONCE think about how I feel? How would I act? Have you ever thought about me? DO YOU EVEN LOVE ME?"

Jack nodded his head. He was about to say something when she interrupted.

"Apparently, it seems not, Jack… I'm going home. Don't come near me, and don't follow me. You… no… you're not good enough for me to insult you."

Audrey cried as she ran home, leaving Jack alone on the street as he saw her run away and sob, like he hadn't seen her do a million times over.

Jack walked away, and back to the house, where he saw Audrey's purse on the floor. He picked it up and examined it.

There were about a dozen photos of him and Audrey together. Playing, eating or just enjoying each other's company. Also, there was a notebook where every day, Audrey wrote one thing she loved about Jack. Even on the days he was cheating on her, she still wrote about how wonderful and great he was.

Jack collapsed into tears. He fell down on his knees and looked up to the sky to pray… but turned away. He was too ashamed to even call out for help. He thought to himself. Yes, I am a liar. Yes, I am a cheater. Yes, I am a junkie. Yes, I am a sinner. Please forgive my broken soul, my God. I cannot do this anymore. I must die; I cannot allow myself to continue to sin.

Jack entered the house. He rushed to his room and threw his face on his pillow. He cried for hours and hours. The snot basically recolored the entire pillow. Jack didn't care. He hoped he would suffer, he hoped he would lose, he hoped that when the day of the tournament came, he would get his ass beat. He did not deserve this. He was too much of a poor sinner. He deserved to be out in the streets, dying and suffering. He deserved to die; he deserved to suffer for all of eternity. He was a human, and by God, was he a sinner.

Jack cried as he closed his eyes and thought about Audrey. He hoped that when he died, she would find someone ten times better than him and that she would find someone way more competent and a better human being. Someone that Jack wished he could be. He prayed that whoever that person was, would fall into her life.

He heard a knock on the door. Without saying who it was, Rebecca opened the door. She had on her bra and panties. She smiled.

"Hey, handsome? How are you doing?"

Jack said nothing as she walked over. She licked his ear.

"You seem… lonely, and sad. I know just what will cheer you up."

As she started to take off her bra, Jack grabbed her by the hand with his left arm. He immediately crushed her hand. She screamed as she fell down in pain.

"What the hell is your problem?"

Jack stood up. His eyes were looking down on her, and his face was expressionless.

He pointed his finger at her. "Leave this house," was all he said. He sounded robotic and horrifying, like he was… some kind of terminator.

She chuckled. "Well, if you think—"

"I'm not asking, I'm telling you to."

Rebecca started to get furious and agitated. Who the hell did he think he was? Just because his girlfriend was crying, that gave him some sort of reason to act like this? Not in her house, it didn't.

She stood up. "Touch me one more time, and I'll call the cops. Not only could I get your ass in jail for assault, but remember who's downstairs. Now you better watch your tone with me, or else—"

Jack grabbed the phone and crushed it. Rebecca became engulfed in fear as she backed up to the window.

"H-hey now, just hold on a second."

Jack stood mere centimeters away from her.

"Listen to me and listen to me well. Your grip on my life is done. I want nothing to do with you anymore. Go back to the house you have in Philadelphia or wherever it is. This is my place now whether you like it or not. I will not have someone as satanic and as devilish as you live with me!"

Before she said anything, Jack gave her a look. A nasty and frightening look that made Rebecca immediately put on her clothes. She panicked as Jack was eyeing her the entire time. He scared the living hell out of her. She felt pale as she rushed downstairs. This guy was insane, and she wanted to get away from him. She quickly rushed to her car and drove away as fast as she could. Never once looking back.

Good riddance, thought Jack as he looked outside the window. She left. Hopefully, she would still pay her mortgage, or else Jack would be screwed. Jack sat down in his bed for a little while.

Jack started to cry again. He couldn't believe what he had done. He was such a horrible person. He felt so much guilt and regret, enough to…

Jack quickly ran into Rebecca's room. After one night of lovemaking, she told him that she kept a gun just in case of a home invasion. He turned her room upside down looking for it. He finally found it. It was a .45 caliber standard pistol. Perfect, he would be able to blow his brains out with this. He loaded the gun and put it to his head.

He did not hear God anymore. He closed his eyes. He deserved all that was coming to him, and he did not blame God for abandoning him. As he would have done the same thing if he were God. He smelled Death in the room; it was there with him. Jack cried as he closed his eyes. May the Lord forgive me.

Jack pulled the trigger.

Everyone downstairs heard a noise.

"What was that?" said Dutch as he stood up. They all quickly rushed upstairs. They all ran into Jack's bedroom.

"Holy crap," said Micah as he saw Jack's body on the floor. The wall was splattered with blood, and the barrel of the gun had smoke.

Leon quickly rushed in and grabbed Jack. He put his head to his chest.

"He's still alive. Quickly, get the car!"

Victor and Dutch rushed downstairs as they put Jack's body in the car. An ambulance wasn't going to make it on time, and they lived more or less nearby to the hospital.

Victor and Dutch sped off as Leon and Micah stayed inside. Leon rubbed his head. He was freaking out. He didn't want Jack to die. The boy was amazing, and he had so much life and potential ahead of him. Micah found himself also being a little bit worried. Even though he was contracted to kill Jack, he quickly grew to respect him for his admirable kindness. As the both of them waited with their anxiousness, Micah spoke, "What… if he doesn't make it?"

Leon shook his head. The way he was pacing himself, it looked as if he was on drugs.

"No. He's going to make it. He's not going to die, c'mon, Micah, we have to think positive."

"I'm just listing the possibilities."

"Liest better ones!"

Leon screamed as he felt like hitting something. Dammit, he didn't know Jack felt… so desperate about his life that he was willing to end it. He wondered if that woman Rebecca was the issue. She could be. If that was the case, then Leon could have a pep talk with Jack. He knew a few things about women. Not enough to write a book, but enough to help a kid going through a rough and difficult time.

Micah started getting desperate. He had no idea how Jack's heart was still beating. He practically blew his brains out, and he was still alive. Somehow, he had a bad feeling that he wouldn't make it past dinner time. The two of them became even more anxious as the time passed. Not saying a word, just merely looking at the floor and hoping for the best!

Victor and Dutch were sitting in the lobby. They had been waiting for a while. When they brought Jack in, the doctors quickly rushed and panicked. They had their hands stained with blood. What a tragedy.

Dutch spoke up. "I didn't think he was depressed."

Victor slapped the back of Dutch's head. "C'mon, you don't know that!"

"Um… newsflash, but he had a gun in his mouth. Did a ghost come in and kill him? I highly doubt that."

"I think there's something bigger at play here."

Dutch shrugged. "Like what?"

"I don't know… that woman seemed to run out of the house just mere seconds before Jack was on the floor. Do you think she had anything to do with it?"

"I doubt it. It doesn't seem like her. I always got some 'amateur porn star' vibes from that woman."

"Excuse me?"

Before Dutch could say anything, a nurse came in. Victor and Dutch quickly stood up.

"D-doctor," said Dutch. "How is he?"

The nurse looked up from her folder. "I'm a nurse, actually, and I want to say that he's OK. He suffered some serious brain damage, and part of his left lobe is missing. Besides that, he's going to make a full recovery."

Both Victor and Dutch smiled as they gleefully jumped up and down. Thank goodness. He was going to be alright. If Dutch was being honest, he genuinely thought that Jack had already died in the car. His eyes were almost open, and he heard moaning and strange noises coming from Jack. He heard from a magazine that dead people did that after a while. But dead people also relieved themselves because their muscles relaxed so much, and Dutch didn't smell any piss or shit in the car.

The nurse talked to Victor, and Dutch sat down. He called Leon and told him the good news.

"Oh, thank goodness," said Leon as he finished his call with Dutch. Micah looked up with a smile. "He's going to be alright!"

Micah smiled; everyone was happy. Even the doctors were relieved. They had never treated someone with a bullet injury this serious. The head surgeon was sure to get a serious promotion because of this. The nurses and staff were all so proud of themselves. This was the first real dangerous situation they had been in, and they worked together as a team to save this kid's life. Everyone rejoiced.

Jack woke up and looked around at the hospital room. The doctor was there with him. He quickly smiled as he saw Jack.

"Jack. Thank God. You're alive! How do you feel?"

Jack looked around the room even more. He... cried. He wasn't dead. Dammit... he was supposed to die! He was supposed to leave this world so he wouldn't commit any more sin! He was supposed to die a death fitting for the scum of the earth like him.

Jack grabbed the doctor's neck and started strangling him.

"WHY? Why didn't you kill me? Why did you save me? I'm supposed to be dead. You—"

A nurse quickly tranquilized Jack, and soon Jack passed out. The doctor freed himself from Jack's grip. Must be the brain damage. That would be a problem. He would get a therapist recommended to Jack as soon as possible to help with the recovery process.

All four men were sitting around in the living room. It had been a few days since Jack had shot himself. They were all fueled up and ready to go.

"Where are we heading to now?" asked Victor. Leon stood up.

"Before we go ANYWHERE, we are going to go and make sure Jack is OK. He's been in the hospital for a few days now, but I guarantee that he's feeling better. So, what we're gonna do is wait here while you and Dutch go and get him. Then... then we'll thank him for everything and be on our merry way. After all, it is LITERALLY the least we could do. The man did save our lives after all."

Victor and Dutch nodded their heads as they went to go and get Jack. Once they left, Micah turned to Leon to talk to him.

"Hey listen, I know that we're all feeling better and we're about to leave, but can you really trust this contact of yours?"

Leon nodded his head. "Of course. I've known the man since high school."

"That's not helpful. May I remind you that we have a bounty on our heads that could set someone and their future generations up for life? Also, if anybody gets caught harboring us, they could get life in prison. I don't think you understand the risk involved in taking just to go and meet this guy, and then fly out to some Asian country in the middle of nowhere."

Leon shook his head. "That's nonsense. I trust this man with my life!"

"Well, maybe you shouldn't."

"I trusted Jack with my life. Look at how that turned out."

Micah gritted his teeth. "Yeah, well, Jack's rare. I highly doubt that your pilot buddy is anything like Jack. You said you knew this guy in high school. Where did you even go?"

"I actually used to live here in Pennsylvania. I used to live in a small town a few miles south of here called 'Center Hall.' It's pretty small, and I went to a high school called 'Penns Valley.' It's very cute. You should check it out."

Micah laughed. "I'm not checking out a town that's got around 1,000 people, and who's only famous landmark is... I don't know... a freaking cave from who knows how many years ago?"

"Well, I never claimed to like the place, but it does have a very nice and cozy small-town charm to it. If you're ever looking to escape, maybe we should just head there."

"That would be nice. Unfortunately, they watch the news, and I'm sure they know all about the massacre by now. Who wouldn't? It's been on damn near every single radio station and news channel on the face of the earth. That's why I'm so hesitant to go to Asia. Instead, let's go to someplace like Africa!"

Leon shot him a disappointed look.

"Do you think Africa is going to be any better?"

Micah shrugged. "I heard Kenya actually has a pretty good economy, and that Botswana has the lowest rate of political corruption out of any country in the world. Who knows?"

"Well, since you like your cocaine so much, you should head on over to Albania. I'm sure the mafia would love to make you a mule. Or some kind of security for a pimp."

Micah scoffed at the idea. He was too 'high class' to be working for something like that. If one thing's for certain, he knew that his days as a mercenary were over. He didn't mind.

Leon chuckled. "That was QUITE some battle that we had."

Micah smiled. "Oh yeah. We killed more than a thousand people and the military. We also couldn't even function as human beings for nearly a week."

The two laughed, and then the room became serious when Leon spoke up.

"Micah... do you ever feel guilty or regret with the life you've lived?"

Micah took a moment to think about it. He purposely decided not to grow conscious so he could be better at his job. Now that things had calmed down, he thought about it. Perhaps… perhaps he did feel guilty. No, he definitely did. Despite him being a sharpshooter, he never felt as though he was a murder— Just a man trying to live in a cruel and harsh world. But now that he was thinking about it… some of those police officers had family and lives ahead of them. The same with the military. He was also purposely never a religious man, but he wondered if one day God would strike him and forsake him for all that he did. It wasn't his fault that he chose this life. He was born into it.

Ever since he was little, his dad was teaching him how to shoot guns. Then he helped his dad kill deer, and later, in high school, he got a passion for shooting things that were shooting back, and soon, before he knew it, he was doing it for a living. He was never smart, nor did he try to be. He liked this life just the way it was. The hookers, the cocaine and the job were all in his pay grade. He was happy living on a farm being a simpleton. But now that he thought about it, he started to feel regret. He had to change for the better.

"Do you, Leon?"

Leon nodded.

"Now I do. Before, I didn't, but then I met Jack. Never have I met someone like Jack. He made me open my eyes to the good of this world. I was in this job only because I could kill people without any thought. I would go to bed at night thinking that it was OK—it was just my job. I didn't need to worry since I was making money. Then I met Jack, and now I'm wondering how many people like him I had to murder to order a bottle of whiskey. I can't do this anymore. I'm glad that was our last job. I'm planning on being a farmer in the middle of nowhere. I might even try to find a wife."

Micah smiled. That was another thing about this job: he couldn't have a wife. He wanted one but did not want to go out in the field worried if he would come home or not, if he would have to leave the burden of raising a child to a single mother. He couldn't live with himself if he did that. That's why he preferred one-night stands, where he was either too drunk or too high to remember anything. But now that he was leaving, he might as well settle down. He liked the idea of raising a son. He would make sure he would do a damn better job at being a father than his own father. Micah never remembered a time when his father wasn't geeked out on crystal meth.

"I think I might also find myself a wife. If we do decide to go and find one, then we better go to a country where they're pretty!"

"You know, women aren't all looks."

"Then go and marry a pig and tell me how long that lasts."

Leon scoffed as Micah chuckled.

"Then… in that case, we might need to go to Indonesia."

"Ewww, you like Asian women."

"There is nothing wrong with Asian women! They have been known to make better housewives and make good traditional meals!"

"Yeah, count me out. I'm going to Mexico or the Bahamas or some place in central America. I don't know if I'll be disciplined enough to keep a wife, if you catch my drift?"

Leon said nothing as the two men waited for Victor and Dutch.

Jack said nothing on the car ride home. He was too depressed to even stand up. He just wanted to die. Why was God keeping him alive?

Dutch tried to make small talk with Jack, but Jack said nothing. Dutch thought that there was something wrong with his brain, so he let Jack be. Victor didn't bother to say anything; he knew that Jack was going through it. He tried to cheer Jack up by asking him what he wanted to listen to. Jack only responded with "The Meadow, by Hed P.E."

Listening to them made Jack upset. He always thought of Yuri when he listened to them. He missed Yuri. He could really use his smile and his friendship right about now. Jack was a horrible friend to him, and still, Yuri stayed with him thick and through. Jack prayed to God that Yuri was enjoying all the wonders of God's kingdom. Even Victor felt a little down in the car. The song was mellow and nice, but there was a certain feel about it that just made the car ride home depressed. It didn't help with the lack of conversation either.

They finally pulled up, and Leon and Micah stepped outside. They were incognito. Their clothes were average and regular, and they didn't stick out.

Leon gave Jack a firm handshake and hugged him.

"Jack… I owe my life to you, and I am forever in your debt. Thank you for everything that you have done. One day, and trust me, that day will come, I will repay my favor to you. Thank you again for everything. If you ever need anything or want to talk, here is my number."

Leon handed him a piece of paper. Jack smiled as he walked away. As he was going nearer to the car, Jack remembered what Leon said about being 'forever in debt,' and then a thought bubble appeared in Jack's mind.

"Wait," said Jack as he grabbed Leon and pulled him aside. The rest of the crew looked shocked that Jack was even saying anything.

Leon listened keenly as Jack spoke.

"You said you were in debt to me. Do you... do you think you could repay me right now?"

Leon looked surprised. He looked at his friend and then looked back at Jack.

"Um... sure. What is it?"

Jack rushed inside and grabbed some pieces of paper. He quickly walked back out and handed it to Leon. It was the same piece of paper that he took from Natalia's desk.

"In Estonia right now, there's a new political party making waves. As you can see from the papers, I think they have plans for world domination. Also, they already have influence in nearly the entire eastern hemisphere. There's a man named 'Derrick Herman' who runs this whole... thing, basically. If you could get in there, take him out, and take out this new political party (which is secretly a cult), I would be extremely happy. Also, from what I've searched, it seems like Derrick's daughter is missing. Most likely kidnapped due to some political reasons. Do you think you could try to find her as well?"

Leon examined the pieces of paper. He started to get excited. A plot to save the world. That sounded... quite interesting. He smiled. He looked at Jack and nodded his head. He was in debt to the man, and from what Leon understood, he would be helping not only Jack but other people. It was about time Leon started to change his life for the better. Finally, a mission where he would do good instead of harm. Furthermore, he wouldn't be getting paid but fulfilling a request by a good man that saved his life. How could Leon refuse?

Jack smiled. "Thank you, Leon. Once again, I am in your debt."

Leon nodded his head. "Please, the pleasure is all mine. I'll call you so we can keep in touch. Sounds like a plan?"

Jack nodded his head. "I have some more papers I could send you once you're on your way. They should help you with the search that's about to happen. Also... be careful. I did some more research on this Derrick guy, and it seems like he's quite paranoid. He'll definitely know if you four are after him, but I don't doubt that you'll succeed. After all, you boys nearly had me."

Leon chuckled. "Well, definitely not, but I appreciate the boost of confidence. Jack… once again, I thank you for everything. Leave this to me. I'll do the best that I can!"

Jack smiled as Leon told the news to his men. They all agreed in unison and gave Jack their word that they would finish the job (free of charge).

Micah spoke up as he got in the car.

"Well, it's settled then. I declare operation 'save the world' officially a go! Let's go, men!"

As they backed the car out, they all waved goodbye to Jack. They would be calling him when they arrived in Estonia. He smiled as he waved goodbye to them. Even though he didn't talk to them very much, he was confident in their abilities. If he wasn't on that pill when he fought them, he would have been dead.

Jack, for the first time in a while, gave a genuine smile as he headed inside.

22

Jack knocked on Samantha's door. The big day was only 3 days away. Jack felt... nervous. (That was putting it mildly.) He had lost some weight in the hospital, and now was weighing in at 70 kilos. He did feel a little bit faster. He hoped that he still had some of his strength, and enough durability to fight whoever wanted to fight him. Jack saw people eyeing him on the street as he was downtown. There was probably a massive surge of new hunters who had been 'visiting' Wilmhelm. Jack noticed that the streets became more crowded and that the hotels and motels were all being booked out. Terrence was nowhere to be seen, although Jack didn't mind. Right now, he needed to talk to Samantha.

Samantha quickly opened the door. She took a sigh of relief when she saw Jack and hugged him. Then she slapped him.

"Damn you! I go to your house and hear that you're in the hospital, and now three days before the tournament, you're here. Is everything alright?"

Jack nodded his head. He held out a very big smile. "Yep, just perfect!"

"OK... good. Can I ask what happened?"

"I went to the hospital because I fell down the stairs. I hit my head pretty hard and had some internal bleeding."

Samantha made a sad face. "Oh no, that's horrible."

Jack hated lying. He didn't want to tell more lies, and he didn't want to sin anymore. However, he also didn't want to tell her the truth. If he really did say what happened, she would probably go and tell Jack to go and see a therapist. Jack didn't want a therapist, nor did he want sympathy. He just wanted to die.

"Well then, sorry to ask so early, but do you still think you'll be OK for the tournament?"

Jack nodded his head. "In fact, we can begin training now if you want."

Samantha looked surprised. "Um... what about your head?"

"It's fully healed up. Wanna start?"

Jack and Samantha started with some sword training, and then they advanced their way toward doing cardiovascular activities and increasing strength. Jack still had his strength, which was good. His speed was actually better due to his weight loss, as well as his stamina. If anything, he actually improved a decent amount with his sudden shift in weight. Samantha didn't take it easy on him though. Through nearly every session, she would make him do 100 push-ups nonstop, and then make him run laps around the neighborhood. Then, without skipping a beat, they would go back to sword training.

She wondered if she was pushing Jack too hard. Yet, whatever worries she had quickly went away when she looked at how Jack performed. He had grown drastically ever since they started training almost a month ago. He was no slouch and was in amazing and top shape when he started, but now Jack looked like an amateur to the way Jack was now. His speed, his technique, his movement, everything about him was perfect. Samantha smiled; she knew that Jack was ready.

Still... despite all of her training, she had her doubts. She talked to Terrence every night, and Terrence told her the news that there definitely were hunters who were out for blood. Samantha was worried that Jack would perhaps be too weak. Even though she knew that he could still kick ass, she heard stories from Terrence about some hunters who took down waves and waves of monsters without being hit whatsoever.

Samantha grabbed the pill from her pocket and looked at it. The pill was practically a 100 percent guaranteed success rate. If she gave it to Jack, then Jack would certainly beat anybody in his way. Still... knowing Jack, she doubted that he would do such a thing. She sighed as the day was done, and Jack went home to rest.

Samantha sat on her couch, watching TV. Wondering and pondering about the next few days. Today was the last day of training, and tomorrow they would start to analyze some people who she knew for sure would come and try to kill Jack. Hopefully, they could come up with a game plan to get him mentally prepared for whatever situation would happen. She started smoking some weed and let her mind wander.

The day was here. It was 10 o'clock sharp in the morning. Everybody was in S.H.O.T.'s base. There was a massive cage in the middle. Big enough to fit a small family of elephants. There were hunters drinking and arguing with each other. Some were cheering for Jack, others were booing him. A few fights broke out, but nothing too serious.

Jack was with Samantha in the bathroom. He was puking uncontrollably. He was so nervous he forgot to even breathe. She rubbed his back as more and more of his breakfast came out. Once he was done, he started to cry.

"Jack... is everything OK?"

Jack shook his head as he rubbed his eyes.

"N-no. Nothing is OK. Nothing was ever OK. None of this is OK! Don't you see? I'm about to go on and fight for my life right now."

"You've done that before when you went on that mission we sent you, with the killer in the trench coat."

Jack shook his head. "I-that's different. You wouldn't understand."

Jack sat down on the toilet. Samantha examined him carefully. She looked at his wrist and then looked at him up and down. She started to wonder something. Did Jack really fall down the stairs? Never once did she ever think about Jack being so clumsy that he could fall down a set of stairs, or that he would fall down so hard he would end up in the hospital for a few days. No... something else was at play.

Whatever it was, she would have to ask him later. She could hear people growing restlessly outside. There were enough hunters here to fill up and create a small town. She cringed as Jack got up and was about to head outside. He opened the door, but Samantha slammed it shut and used her body to block the path. She handed Jack the pill.

"Here... take this."

Jack rolled his eyes. "Please, not this again. I already—"

Samantha grabbed Jack's right arm and squeezed it tightly. The grip was so tight, in fact, that Jack even felt a little bit scared. He had never seen Samantha like this before. Her eyes were low, and she looked concentrated and focused on Jack.

"Listen to me, and listen to me well. I understand that you have some kind of code, some kind of honor, and some kind of... Christian duty you have to fulfill. But that has to go out the window now. Right now, you have to think about other people. Think about me, and everyone else who is supporting you. If you lose this battle, if you fail, then not only will you lose the respect you have, but there could very well be a civil war here. Some people will still defend you, and the people who already hate you will hate you even more. There will be bloodshed, and it won't be pretty, nor will it be good.

"All of that can be avoided… if you just take this pill. Understand that people's lives are at stake because of you. Please try to comprehend that right now, all your ideals need to be thrown out the window because there are people counting on you too much for you to have some sort of duty. There will be a war if you lose. I understand you are skilled and you're good, but some of these men and women are leagues above you and me. Please, Jack, take this pill. Not because I'm telling you to, but because you have people depending on you. You need to throw whatever sense of justice… or whatever you have that may be holding you back out the window. This isn't about you, this is about the entire damn organization. Things will change if you lose, and it won't be pretty. Please, Jack… just take the pill."

Jack looked down and grabbed the pill. He looked at Samantha.

"Winners don't do—"

"GOD FUCKING DAMMIT! Did you not hear a single word I just said? You need to get it together, kid, or else this whole thing is going to collapse on us! This isn't about being just and righteous; this is about other people. You need to suck up your own self-pity, your own rules and philosophy for the greater good! Can you do that?"

Jack looked at the pill one more time. He was confident in his abilities, and he didn't want to do any more drugs. Even if they were good for him. Yet, he couldn't ignore what Samantha said. This wasn't about him, but about people who cared and believed in him. About an organization that would have a war if Jack didn't win. This pill… this thing was the key to preventing something bad, and to help other people. Even though it went against what Jack wanted, he swallowed it.

Samantha smiled. "Thank you, Jack. Trust me, after this, you don't have to do anything anymore. Thank you, Jack!"

She hugged him and kissed him on the cheek. Jack frowned. He didn't deserve a kiss on the cheek. He deserves to die. He would have to think about that later as he walked out of the bathroom and made his way toward the center of the cage. People looked at him, and mummers and gossip were being spread around. Jack could already see the people that were out to get him. He and Samantha went over the possible candidates. Also, judging by the way they looked at him, he was certain they weren't too big of fans.

As Jack made his way, Samantha cleared her throat and started to speak.

"Good morning, everyone, and thank you all for coming!"

As Samantha was speaking, Jack was looking at the audience. He knew nobody, and he realized that if he were to win this fight—no, WHEN he won the fight—he would need to make new friends. Nobody wanted a boss they didn't like. Still, seeing all the unfamiliar faces made Jack upset. He could have really used some motivation by seeing Yuri, Andrea, John and David in the crowd cheering him on. Still, he knew they were watching. Hopefully from above. He smiled as he prepared himself. The pill hadn't kicked in yet.

Jack was wearing the same clothes and the same outfit he wore when he was a hunter: the white robes with the sharp sword.

Samantha continued to speak.

"Anybody who wishes to challenge Jack may step forth and do so. However, be advised that it can only be one on one. Any more than one on one will be permitted."

One hunter screamed from the crowd.

"Who decided you could make the rules, you bitch?"

Samantha smiled. He was going to be the first one Jack would face off. She pointed at him.

"Since you like to talk so much, why don't you see if you're capable of beating your new boss?"

That comment riled up the hunters. There were boos and murmurs, and a small shoving match occurred. The man who yelled at Samantha stepped up to the cage and pulled out his sword.

The man pointed at Jack. "You look pathetic. What's with those clothes? You look like some 12th-century monk, or a scholar, or anything else besides a hunter. I can't believe Natalia decided to have you—"

Jack rushed him. He swung his sword as fast as he could. The other hunter didn't see and react to it on time, and he lost his left arm. He screamed in pain as he was quickly escorted to the hospital. There were nurses and staff all over the place. Samantha smiled as she heard the man scream for mercy and apologized to Jack.

Soon, another hunter decided to step up. He was a big and burly man. He looked like Terrence, but even stronger. He was holding an axe. He spent absolutely no time trying to make conversation or get to know Jack. He immediately rushed him and swung his axe at Jack. Jack quickly dogged it and tried to swing his sword. The man, despite his size, was as agile as a cat. He backflipped away and uppercut Jack. Jack felt his head ringing as the man swung his axe. Jack dodged it, but not before it cut his right leg. He gritted his teeth and avoided another blow. One that would have been fatal.

Samantha grew nervous as Jack was doing his best to block, parry and dodge a series of what would have been fatal blows. Jack rolled out of the way and swung his sword at the man's foot, chopping it off. The massive man yelled and backhanded Jack, breaking his jaw. Jack didn't let this deteriorate him, though, and stood up as fast as he could and ran over and stabbed the man in his lower back. It was so painful that the large man dropped his axe. With his last remaining strength, he back-kicked Jack, breaking one of Jack's ribs. Still, the man couldn't stand up and had to be escorted. Jack won… but barely.

Samantha grew even more weary as she saw who stepped into the cage next. It was one of the hunters they went over. His name was "William."

William was like Jack. They had the same build and the same height. However, William was way more of a crazy person than Jack could ever be. He was a neo-Nazi operating out of central Germany. Despite his reputation as being a good hunter, William had trouble separating his personal life from his job. He constantly killed people in his spare time, usually either because they disagreed with him, or because they annoyed him. Furthermore, he was the president of the German branch of hunters. He was no joke. He once took out 14 different high-ranking politicians, who knew he was coming, in less than a month.

He wore a very old and antique SS officer uniform, and he liked to use a sword as well. He grinned and showed his golden teeth. His blonde hair was much prettier than Jack's, and his eyes were bluer.

He said nothing as he stared at Jack. Jack picked up his sword and prepared himself. The both of them looked at each other meaningly. William did not approve of Jack as the new headmaster. He thought that it should be someone manly, someone better than everyone else, someone with idealistic goals and who worshipped and valued being manly over anything else. He was disgusted when he learned that Natalia had become headmaster, and he cried because she was the one who was appointed, not him. Some dumb female monkey. Now… now was his turn to prove to everyone just what he was capable of.

Jack became nervous as he gripped his sword. He could sense the bloodlust coming out from this guy. He was fast and quick. Jack hardly had any time to react when William slashed his sword. Jack blocked it with his left arm and backflipped away. William did not let Jack out of his sight, and he kneed Jack and stabbed him in his spine. Jack fell to the floor, and William put his sword on Jack's nape. He cackled and laughed as he looked at everyone. He spoke in a very thick and heavy German accent.

"Look at this puny man. He can't even last for a minute, so how do you people expect him to win? I never could imagine why a phony and small man like you would be considered fit to lead such a large organization. No matter, once I am done with you, I shall start having new policies. Every female has to show up to work naked, and they have to do as I say. Mmm, yes. I can already imagine…"

He drifted off as Jack felt his entire body change. The pill started to kick in, and oh… my… goodness, was this pill strong. It made Chump change the last pill that he had. Jack's pupils enlarged so much that his entire eye was just black. He could not help but smile, and his hair raised. Jack quickly moved out of the way.

As Jack was moving, he looked around. Everyone… seemed so slow. They all seemed… like they were a few seconds behind. Jack easily moved out of the way and stood still for a few seconds. Then, William recognized that Jack was gone, and he slowly screamed. It was… almost like slow motion in a way. It was like their brains were fried, and it took them a while to process what was going on. They spoke… so slowly, and Jack actually started to grow bored.

In reality, though, Jack moved so fast that nobody saw him. It was as if he teleported. Nobody knew where he went, and then he appeared next to William. William screamed as Jack caught him off guard. William swung his sword, but before he could even move his hand, William had moved across the cage.

"W-what's happening?"

Jack sat down. Everything was going so slow. He had so much energy. He moved over to William and punched him in the stomach. Unfortunately, Jack punched a little too hard, and his hand went right through William's stomach. Jack pushed his hand upward, but then more of William's body was ripped. Jack jumped back.

William looked down. He saw his stomach was exposed, and parts of his torso and chest were ripped open. Yet, it all happened so fast that he couldn't feel any pain. He tried attacking Jack, but he was literally just swinging at the air. It wasn't until a minute later that William felt the pain, and he fell down and cried for God to save him.

Nurses came and picked him up. Samantha looked surprised as she saw Jack jumping up and down uncontrollably. "Holy crap," she said as she smiled. The pill was working like a charm.

Holy crap, thought Jack as he started wandering around the cage, waiting for someone to enter. He never felt so alive. The feeling was great. As more time passed by, the pill really started to settle in. Jack was moving and thinking so fast that to him, everybody was frozen. It took four minutes for him to see any change. In reality, people saw a moving blur. Was... that Jack? His strength was also no joke. He lightly hit William in the stomach, and his entire stomach practically exploded. It was as if Jack was hitting a playdough. Even when he moved his hand upward, it was so easy. He felt as if his hand was buried under sand, and he was moving it upward.

After waiting forever, someone else entered the stage. Before they could enter, Jack kicked them in the face as hard as he could. He wanted to try something.

The person's head exploded on impact, and so too did his entire body. People screamed as blood flew everywhere.

"Oh my God," said Jack as he couldn't help but chuckle. He had no idea where Samantha got this pill, but he wasn't complaining. It was working like a charm.

Samantha saw the blur that was in the cage practically shift in and out of existence. It moved so fast that sometimes it disappeared, and other times (like when Jack went to go and sit down) the blur was more visible. Either way, she never imagined that this... miracle pill would give Jack super speed. He was moving so fast that they couldn't see him. He was so strong, he could kick someone and they would explode. She remembered that Dr. Benjamin told her that he paid nearly all of his money to have this pill made for Jack. He had a feeling this day would come. He said that some scientists over in Japan helped produce this pill. Well, she was thankful for the good doctor as she knew that the victory was in good hands. She smiled as she walked away. She had other things to do.

Jack was feeling good. Too good... and God saw his cocky attitude.

Then, someone else walked into the cage. To Jack, he was moving at his speed. To everyone else, he was also a blur, phasing in and out of existence. Jack's eyes widened. Woah, someone else who was also just like him.

The man was a very small man, around 157 centimeters tall. He had very long and dark hair. His skin was extremely pale. He wasn't a very strong man either. He had a skinnier frame than Jack. His eyes... they were quite menacing to look at.

Jack was in such a good mood that he decided to talk to the man in front of him.

"Hey there. Nice to meet you. I don't know if you know who I am, but I'm your new boss, Jack! I'm so glad you could come. So, what do—"

Before Jack could even speak, he felt something off. He looked down, only to find blood coming out of his hand. He looked up and saw that the man was gone. He was shocked as he looked around. The man was nowhere to be seen.

Then... he was behind Jack. Jack quickly spun around, but it was no use. The man was gone again, and now Jack had a massive slash on his nose. Jack now started to panic. What the heck? This guy wasn't human.

Jack felt an even sharper pain when he fell to the floor. He quickly stood up and realized that the man was gone again. Jack could feel something running down his back. Blood, mostly likely. He chuckled due to his nervousness. Great, he thought he had this all in the bag. Now there was someone who—

Jack spun around. He could feel the man behind him. Jack swung his sword. He was able to hit the man just a little bit. The dark-haired man took a step back and realized that Jack cut off a piece of his finger. Jack smiled.

"What's your name?" said Jack. He didn't see him when he and Samantha were going over potential candidates who wanted him dead.

The man stood up.

"My name is Dawson. You may know my mother."

Jack looked confused. His mother?

Dawson shook his head.

"It doesn't matter anyway. While you were too busy trying to talk to me, I took your left arm. Have fun fighting with one arm now."

Jack looked down and saw that his left arm was gone. Did this guy really steal it... while Jack asked him a question? No, that's—

"It's not impossible, Jack."

WHAT? Could this guy read—

"No, I cannot read minds, Jack. I just look at people's faces. And judging by your face, I can see that you're quite nervous."

WHAT! Th—

"That is not impossible. If you know my mother, and you do because she talked about you, then you would know that nothing is impossible. You would also know that I'm like this because my mom is kind of crazy. Even though I love her to death, I understood that she was a flawed human just like all of us."

Jack took a step back. His heart was racing at a million miles an hour. W-what? There's no way! Who is Dawson's mother? Jack couldn't sweat because his body was moving so fast that the droplets and trickles of sweat evaporated because his body was so hot. If you touched him, it was like a furnace. Still, if he could sweat, Jack would be in a puddle right about now. This man was insane. Who on earth was his mother?

Dawson disappeared again. Jack gripped his sword tightly. He waited… his senses were now sharper than ever. But Dawson was just too fast. Even if he could notice the slightest change in the air, he wouldn't be able to hit him since he was too fast. It… it was almost as though he could teleport. Jack started to believe that he actually could.

Jack quickly spun around and waved his sword. Dawson avoided it and swung his sword right back at Jack. A massive slash appeared on Jack's clothes, and his stomach was losing blood fast. Jack fell down to the floor and saw Dawson appear above him. How in the world? Was he—

"No. I'm not teleporting."

"IMPOSSIBLE!" Jack kicked Dawson's sword up with such speed that even Dawson couldn't react to it. Jack jumped up, and Dawson was gone. Jack grabbed Dawson's sword and put the handle in his mouth. He clenched it with his teeth. Hopefully, this time, if his right hand was too slow, his head would more than make up for it.

Again… there was no change in the air. Jack started to wonder. Obviously, Dawson wasn't teleporting, he was just going extremely fast. So, where was he? Jack looked around and he couldn't find anybody. He was moving so fast that all the hunters watching were frozen. Jack panicked as he heard a whisper.

"Behind you."

Jack spun around, and Dawson was there, although 15 feet away from him. Dawson chuckled.

"Well... it looks like you're confused. Very well then. As I said earlier, I don't teleport. I am fast. Faster than you think. In fact... I'm so fast that the entire time you're panicking trying to find out where I am, I'm literally behind you."

No. That's—

"Not impossible. I'm moving so fast that you can't even sense me. My movements are so fast that your brain, even though you're on the pill, can't comprehend just how fast I'm moving. It doesn't... absorb the knowledge of something going so fast, that the air can't even pick up the changes in movements. Jack... I'm going so damn fast I'm not even here. I'm going through two different planes of existence."

Jack stepped back. "W-what? That—"

"Like I said... It's not impossible. I'm also on the pill, but I also had more training than you. Also, I took around four of those pills. Did you really think that with something as powerful as this, we wouldn't have more?"

Dawson showed the pill. Jack's eyes wandered. How was there more? Samantha—

"My mother was able to spend nearly a fortune creating a small supply of these pills. Their... for special occasions."

"Who is your mother?"

Dawson shook his head. "Really? I dropped a mega hint earlier when I said 'spent a small fortune'. What kind of person do you know that has that kind of money?"

Jack thought about it for a moment, and then his eyes widened. He looked at Dawson, and Dawson smiled.

Jack spoke up. His words nearly not even being able to come out. He ripped the sword to the ground.

"Your mom is Natalia?"

Dawson nodded his head. "Yes. Oh, and don't worry. I know about everything that's happened. I do have to say, I was a little bit disappointed that my mom decided to appoint you as the new head chairman when I am her son and she's had me for who knows how long. Oh well."

Jack took a step back. This was... no, this was possible. Natalia was a woman of many secrets. She never mentioned a child, but she didn't need to. All she did was do her job and stay quiet. Most hunters feared her, and they dared never ask questions about her personal life.

"Did you—"

"I've been living here since I was 10. Before that, she sent me to study and train in Spain with my cousin. Her name is Felicia, and she's the one who has all the money now! Not me, dammit! Oh well... I still have some money saved up, but that's beside the point.

"When I learned that my mother had passed, I was enraged. Not because she was dead. No, she was quite a mean woman, and she deserved what she got. However... she didn't make me the headmaster. After everything I've been through, after all the training that I've done. She didn't even bother to make me a hunter. She just shipped me away and trained me so she could see me suffer. So she could torture me!

"She gave the title to some... limp-dick person like you. So show me, Jack, please show me! Show me, my new headmaster, how badass and skilled of a fighter you are!"

Jack grabbed the sword from the ground, and Dawson disappeared. Great, just what he needed.

Jack started swinging his head and right arm violently. He didn't even know where Dawson was, but he now knew that Dawson was going to kill him. And he popped a few more pills than Jack. How perfect.

But maybe... if Jack could get his hands on Dawson. Dawson may be faster, but Jack felt as though he was stronger. He remembered when he swung his sword at Dawson's hand. It cut off his finger... but Jack's sword never reached Dawson's hand. Jack just swung it so hard that the pressure of the air caused his fingers to be severed from his hands. Maybe... maybe if he landed one good punch on Dawson's face, he would be able to win this whole thing... and it was a big MAYBE.

Jack was ambushed again. This time from in front. Dawson sliced Jack's leg, and Jack screamed. The sword fell out of his mouth, and Dawson picked it up again. Jack tried uppercutting Dawson, but he was too slow. Dawson moved away and vanished. Jack cursed as he held onto his sword tightly.

Again... more pain. Jack looked down and saw his foot was on the other side of the cage. His body needed a moment to render the pain. The worst part about all of this was that Dawson liked to attack randomly. It could be in front, sideways or behind, but it was all random. There was no pattern... Dawson was playing it smart. Just like that damned mother of his.

Jack swung his sword. He felt something change. He turned around, but there was nobody there. What… he feel?

Jack felt his back rip into two. He yelled like he never yelled before and hit his face on the floor. Dawson smiled.

"Did you like that technique I made? I purposely cause a change in wind, slow enough, of course, for you to recognize it. Then, while you're distracted, I come up from behind and slice your back! Nice move, right?"

Jack stood up, but again, Dawson had vanished. Jack felt another shift in the air. He didn't react, as he knew it was a trick. Or at least that's what he thought as his shoulder blades were sliced away from his body. He screamed as he struggled to maintain balance. Damn that Dawson. He said that so—

Jack spun around and swung his sword again. He saw Dawson, and he was able to slice both of his lower shins. Dawson vanished again. Nice, at least he got a hit. Jack started to come up with a few plans in his head.

He thought about outpacing Dawson. All that running and speed must have been making him tired. Perhaps after a while, he would feel fatigued, and then he wouldn't be so fast. If that was the case, then Jack just needed—

"That's not going to work, Jack. I have enough stamina to keep me up for months."

Jack spun around, and Dawson was holding Jack's other foot. Jack yelled as he fell down. Now he had hardly any way of balancing himself. Damn this man! Damn him, and his stupid mother!

Jack started to panic. There was a massive pool of blood where he was lying. He started to crawl toward the exit. Dammit, he was not about to die now. As he was crawling, in a flash, his right arm and sword vanished. He screamed as the right hand suddenly appeared right next to him, and Dawson was laughing.

"Honestly, do you think that you're getting out of here alive? Once I'm done with you, I'll fight anybody who challenges me. Then, I'll take my spot as the headmaster. Then, I'll run this place better than my mother ever wished she could. How do you feel, Jack?"

Jack said nothing as he tried kicking Dawson. Dawson vanished, and Jack started crawling toward the exit. He was in so much pain, and he could see that his high was coming down. People were starting to act and talk normally, and Dawson was now starting to become a blur. Oh man, this was bad. Really bad.

Jack smiled as he turned back. There was a trail of blood and a massive pool of blood next to him. Good.

The trail of blood was so big that Dawson slipped on it, fell and broke his neck. He became paralyzed. His eyes widened as he couldn't feel his legs, or anything else for that matter. He started to stutter.

"w-what—"

Jack smiled as he crawled over to Dawson.

"You see, you fell right into my trap… sort of. I knew that you had to be moving so fast that you were practically a blur to anyone's eyes. Even my own. I also knew that you were running, and simply not just phasing in and out of two planes of dimension. So I thought of a plan. I was planning on tripping you… somehow. I actually originally intended to trip you by sticking my foot out and you fall. Unfortunately, that didn't happen, but this is way better.

"You tripped on my pool and trail of blood. Causing you to lose your balance. The good news for me is that you broke your neck, and now you can't even speak. Your entire body is paralyzed. How does that feel?"

Dawson could only move his eyes. Jack smiled. "That's what I thought."

Jack, with his forearm and his imbalanced legs, was able to stand up. His high was starting to wear off, and soon people saw what had happened.

To everybody, really only a matter of seconds passed since Dawson entered the cage. There were a few movements of a blur, and then all at once there was blood, a paralyzed person, and now Jack who was the victor of the battle.

A few nurses came and took away Dawson. His gaze never left Jack's. Even as he was being escorted on a stretcher, he still looked at Jack menacingly. As if he was saying, 'One day you'll come to regret this. Mark my words!'

Jack smiled. Finally… it was over. Unfortunately, there were still some people yelling and wanting a fight. Jack could hardly stand up. Let alone fight. He cleared his throat and spoke up.

"Excuse me, ladies and gentlemen. I hope that… I…"

Fuck, I'm losing it, thought Jack as he looked down at the floor. The floor was starting to become very far away, and Jack suddenly was having vertigo. He felt his eyes grow tired, and he was feeling very… very weak. He couldn't stand up anymore, he was done. He collapsed on the ground and closed his eyes.

Samantha was sitting on her porch when she got a call from Terrence. She picked it up and answered.

"Samantha, are you there? Are you at your house?"

Samantha took the phone away from her ear. What had happened? It was almost never common for Terrence to lose his cool like this. She became worried as she answered.

"Um... yes, I'm here. Why, what happened? Is Jack OK?"

"Jack is in bad shape. He's in the hospital right now, but... I don't think he's going to make it if I'm being honest. Just... just please come here."

Terrence hung up the phone. Samantha quickly hurried and made her way to her car. She drove as fast as she could, avoiding all the stop signs and red lights. She made her way toward the elevator and headed downstairs. Once she was downstairs, she saw a massive group of hunters talking with each other. She ignored all of them as she made her way to the infirmary. As she was walking, she could overhear tidbits and whispers of conversations. People saying things like: "I saw kick ass, maybe he's not so bad." As well as: "He looked pretty badly injured. He's definitely skilled, don't get me wrong, but is he worthy enough to be the headmaster?"

She ignored everyone as she made her way to the infirmary. She looked around and saw Jack. He had his eyes closed and his mouth open. She quickly rushed to his side. Next to him was Terrence.

"Jack... are you OK?"

Terrence shook his head. He peered over Jack.

"Don't bother... he's in a coma."

She looked at him, shocked and perplexed.

"WHAT? How did this happen? Was the pill too much?"

"No. It's not that."

Terrence pointed over to Dawson. His gaze never left Jack's body. Even in the state he was in, he was still itching to kill and murder Jack for what he had done to him.

"Do you know who that is?"

She nodded her head. "Isn't that Natalia's son?"

Now Terrence was shocked. He took a step back. From what he knew, the only people who knew that Natalia had a son were Natalia, Terrence, John and David. How on earth did Samantha know?

"How did you know?"

"David told me one night. I... he told me that Natalia told him that Dawson was away and that he wasn't living with her due to... legal reasons." They stayed silent as they looked at Dawson. He was so... eerie. His black hair and his pale face, with his horrific eyes staring at Jack, gave Dawson the appearance of some kind of monster.

Terrence spoke up.

"I don't know what happened, but he entered the ring with Jack. It was a complete blur. One moment, both are moving so fast that they literally just became blurs, and then the next second Jack is on the floor passed out and Dawson is paralyzed forever."

Samantha moaned as she sat down. This was not how this was supposed to go. Jack was supposed to win in an easy fashion. A spectacular show to show everyone that he was worthy. Instead, he was in a coma, and a few of his challengers were right next to him.

Terrence patted Samantha on the back and sat down next to her.

"I understand that this is rough. I heard some hunters talking earlier when Jack was escorted. Some think that he did a really good job today, and others still don't see him as a leader. Unfortunately, as that is, he won't get everyone's love and care."

Samantha shook her head and put her hands on her face. She sobbed a little. Why, oh why was this happening? Who knew that Natalia's son would come out of nowhere and just try to take the spot? Worst of all, it looks like he gave quite the ass-whooping on Jack too. This was not going well. Terrence saw Samantha sobbing, and he stayed quiet. He wanted to help her out at this moment, but he knew that the best thing to do was to let her be with her emotions.

He stood up and patted her on the back one more time. Before he left, he relayed a little bit of some good news.

"If anything, Jack did a good job today. He gained some respect, and he gained some people's approval. Maybe not everyone's approval, but I think people know his skill level just now. I don't think a civil war is going to happen, but I also don't think that hunters across the world are going to be happy with the decision."

Terrence left, leaving Samantha alone with Jack as she sobbed next to him. All the while, Dawson looked on with his eyes that never left Jack's gaze.

Samantha wiped the tears away from her face and examined Jack. His body was bruised and cut. She would go and call a few people to try and get some prosthetic feet and a new prosthetic hand—preferably one that was just as strong and made from the same material as his left arm. Besides all of that, she couldn't help but be proud of Jack. He did such an amazing job, and even though he didn't want to take the damn pill, he was able to because he realized that this event was more than just him. Furthermore, it seemed like a civil war was dying down. Sure, some people weren't going to like him, but nobody on this earth had everyone like them. Even Jesus had haters. It was only natural that people would feel skeptical about Jack. She smiled as he now had several new scars to remember this day.

She grabbed his hand as he struggled to breathe. He had been in a coma before, and he was able to make it out fine. She hoped it would be the same way this time.

She got a phone call. It was from an unknown number. She picked it up and answered it.

"Hello."

"Hello," said the other voice. It sounded like a teenage girl. She had almost a European accent. "Is this Samantha?"

Samantha nodded her head as she slowly stood up, and her attention now shifted from Jack to the phone call.

"Yes. Who is this?"

"Pardon my intrusion, but my name is Felicia. I am Dawson's cousin. Is Jack around?"

Samantha was hesitant for a moment. Was this girl serious? She never heard of Natalia having a niece. Was this girl being serious? Then again, she did just mention Dawson. Yet, how did she have Samantha's number? Hmm... Samantha decided to play ball for now, just in case.

"Sorry, but Jack is unavailable at the moment. How did you get this number?"

"I asked Terrence."

She rolled her eyes. What was that bastard keeping secret from her? Samantha calmed down as she took a quick breather.

"OK. Can I ask why you want to speak with Jack?"

"Not at all. Terrence has told me that Jack has beaten Dawson. I am forever grateful for Jack. I hate Dawson. He is a rapist and a jerk. I am happy someone was able to take him down a peg. I would like to personally thank this man named Jack. Furthermore, my aunt left me detailed instructions about giving Jack some of her inheritance when she passed away. It seemed as if this Jack made quite an impression on her. Now I would like to meet this man myself."

Samantha couldn't help but chuckle. She almost felt jealous in a way. How come Jack was getting money, and she got jack shit for helping him out throughout this entire roller coaster of a journey? Oh well, she would at least hopefully have the second-highest position now that nobody knew where James Donald was. Samantha continued.

"Sorry, but Jack is… well he's not feeling well right now. I can take the money, and I can transfer it to him."

For a while, there was a silence on the line, and then Felicia spoke. "How can I trust you?"

"Because Jack trusts me."

Felicia was silent for a while, and then she spoke up. This time, her tone was a little bit more aggressive and confrontational.

"OK then. Meet me at David's flower shop tomorrow. I am heading over to give you the money."

"Wait, how do you—"

Before Samantha could say anymore, the line was cut. She mumbled as she put away her phone. *Wow, Terrence,* she thought as she walked away. Thanks so much for telling me everything.

She went home and blew off some steam by lifting weights in her garage and smoking some weed. She couldn't stop thinking about Natalia. Even in death, that woman's secrets were being revealed. She only could wonder what she did while she was still alive. The mind wandered.

23

Samantha was outside David's flower shop. She stopped going there so much. It made her miss David more than she already did. It was being run by Terrence now, who clearly knew nothing about how to sell flowers. Still, it was doing well so far.

Samantha noticed, in the distance, a girl walking. The girl looked all posh and neat looking. She had very, very, very black hair, and her skin was even more pale than Dawson's. She looked like a female vampire. She had on black high heels, a very fancy black dress and a black business suit. She was holding a golden briefcase in her left hand. A briefcase actually made out of gold.

She smiled as she approached Samantha. She extended her hands. The woman was tiny. Even with high heels, she was no bigger than 152 centimeters. She was also quite lean. She must have weighed 40 kilos.

"You must be Samantha. Nice to meet you. My name is Felicia. We spoke on the phone yesterday."

Samantha nodded as Felicia handed her the briefcase. Samantha felt so… small compared to Felicia. Even though she was quite literally the bigger person, she still felt insignificant. Perhaps it was the clothes, or makeup and perfume she had; either way, Samantha never felt so insignificant. The way Felicia looked at her, it almost appeared as if Felicia was bored and disgusted by even talking with Samantha.

"In there is a small fraction of Natalia's inheritance. Please give me Jack's number once you have the chance. I would like to call him and ask him if he received all his money. I do not trust you."

Samantha gave a clearly fake smile as she nodded her head. That woman! What she would do to her if she had the chance? But Samantha had to calm down. After all, she needed to show who was more of a more mature person.

"Also, if you have the chance, please give my regards to my cousin. Tell him I wish him the worst, and I hope he suffers. Ciao!"

"W-wait," said Samantha as she stopped Felicia. Felicia looked disgusted that someone like Samantha could touch her fancy shirt, and her 100-dollar makeup could get on her makeup that cost most people's yearly salary.

"Can I ask about your family tree?"

Felicia looked annoyed.

"And may I ask why you want to ask?"

"Not at all. You see, your aunt was a good friend of mine and—"

"HAHAHAH! Do not be ridiculous. I know all about you and everyone else. Natalia told me everything. I know you guys didn't like her, and that you were afraid of her. You're only asking me because you're curious. I do not blame you. I am even curious about my family. Unfortunately, I do not know too much, and from what I do know, I do not wish to tell you. Good day now. Please delete my contact from your number."

She walked away, leaving Samantha in shambles. Why that damn brat. I'm gonna KILL HER!

Samantha took a deep breath. Now was not the time for violence. She immediately deleted Felicia's contact from her phone and walked away. She went to the back of the shop and opened up the briefcase. Holy crap.

There was at least 500 million dollars—no, maybe even more—all in cash. Samantha shrieked when she saw all that money. She had never seen it before in her life. Oh my goodness. It was like heaven. She had never seen so many rubber bands, and had never seen so many Benjamin Franklins, and there were even a few 10,000-dollar bills. How on earth did Natalia get her hands on 10,000-dollar bills? The last time they were printed was in World War 2. Samantha gasped as she put the suitcase in her car. Now even more questions arose about Natalia. What a strange lady she was.

A few weeks had passed, and Jack had finally woken up. His eyes were immediately met by bright lights. He looked around the infirmary and was also met by Dawson, who was looking at him. He was leaning on his side, and he was drooling. Yet, despite all of this, those menacing and horrible eyes never left him. Jack shivered as he wished he could go back to sleep.

In that week, a lot of the hunters quit. Some of them quit because they wanted to pursue more fortunate paths, and others quit because they saw the way things were turning out and knew they should quit while things were still good. There was controversy all around the world about Jack being the new head chairman, but no civil wars broke out, and the tension seemed to have gradually died down as the week progressed. Furthermore, no target had been killed. Everyone had kind of been on hiatus. Enjoying life and rethinking their career paths.

Samantha, slowly but surely, had been trying her best to mourn and forget about what had happened in her life the past few months. It had been a roller coaster of emotions, and the more she could forget the better. Still... she did miss her David. She even had a picture of him she slept with every night. She missed him so much. She continued to train and be disciplined. She even gave up smoking weed, as she realized it caused her to become so frequent in her mood swings. She was doing her best to prepare herself as she wanted to impress Jack. Show him that she was worthy of being second in command. She didn't spend a single dollar and sold the golden briefcase for even more money. Now, Jack was a few more million dollars richer.

Terrence was still running the shop. He hadn't been the happiest about Jack's decision, but he was becoming more and more trustworthy of the man. He went and visited him every single day to see how he was doing while he was in his coma. Every time he went, he got weird looks from Dawson. It creeped him out. He would hang out with Samantha every day. He developed feelings for her—something he regretted doing. He told Samantha that he felt a certain way about her. She was very kind to him, and told him in the nicest way possible that they were 'just friends' and that she really loved David... but he was gone now. Terrence took it well, and they still hung out. Yet... he felt strange around her. She didn't, but he couldn't look her in the eyes like he once did.

Jack looked around. He could feel his right hand moving and felt as though his toes were wiggling. Unfortunately, he was just imagining things. Every time he breathed, he felt like a million tiny holes were being carved into his stomach. He felt lightheaded, and he lost a serious amount of weight. He was just as skinny now as when he first came to Wilmhelm.

After a while of waiting, a very nice and pretty nurse checked up on him. She ran some tests, took his blood, and after a while told him that he was all set and ready to go. Jack smiled as he had the nurse call Samantha to come and pick him up.

Jack was outside waiting for Samantha when, from the corner of his eyes, he saw someone walking near the flower shop. Oh crap, it was Audrey. Jack tried to hide himself as best as he could. He peeked around the wall and saw that she was walking by herself. He sighed. He wanted to go and talk to her. He missed her so much. He wanted to say he was sorry… but how many times had he done that before? How many times were they going to play this cat-and-mouse game? Worst of all… it was all his fault. Jack thought and wondered why God would ever introduce a girl as wonderful as Audrey into his life. He was a mess, and she didn't deserve all the chaos that happened. He wished God could kill him so he could stop sinning.

Samantha pulled up. She smiled as she hopped out of the car and gave Jack a big hug.

"Oh, you're OK! How are you feeling?"

Jack shrugged. He wanted to say that he wished he could die, but he smiled and just said he was feeling hungry.

"Well lucky for you, I made us burgers. Come on, I have a surprise for you. Oh, and here you go. Think of this as a gift for your new introduction as headmaster of S.H.O.T."

Jack had a new prosthetic hand and a new arm. They were way stronger, and way cooler looking than the last one that Dr. Benjamin gave him. As well, he removed the fake feet and placed them with the new prosthetic and robotic feet that Samantha gave him. He smiled, as he actually felt happy.

"I hope you like it. I had to pull some strings to get them, but in the end, they look good on you!"

Jack smiled as she drove off to her house. His smile quickly faded away when he saw Audrey again. This time she was heading to a movie theater. Jack sighed.

He looked outside and saw that there were fewer and fewer people now. He spoke up.

"Hey… doesn't it seem like the city feels… smaller. Smaller than it already is?"

Samantha nodded her head. "The news of you being a headmaster made quite the stir. Some hunters left, and some decided to stay. Thankfully no war broke out, but this company is not the same. There's… a certain vibe and feeling in the air every time I walk inside S.H.O.T. headquarters. It feels… wrong somehow. I can't explain it. We've lost our charm."

She patted Jack on the back.

"But with you, I'm positive that we'll do even better. Yes, we're much smaller now, but bigger doesn't always mean better. Plus, hopefully, this time we can kill targets that are ACTUALLY bad. Don't look so down, man. C'mon. You're alive, and well, and you're the new headmaster. Plus, Natalia left you some of her inheritance. You have everything going for you! BE happy! LETS CELEBRATE!"

Samantha smiled as she turned on the radio and wondered what kind of wine she was going to drink. Jack frowned as he wondered how he was going to end his life tonight.

The celebration was tiny. It was just Samantha and Jack. Terrence couldn't come. He said he was busy with the shop, but he would just feel awkward there. So he canceled on them. It didn't matter; both of them had fun.

Samantha drank wine while Jack drank water. She ate an absurd amount of burgers, while Jack only ate one. She danced, laughed and giggled as she enjoyed the music. Jack sat awkwardly on the couch, wondering how he was going to die. He couldn't be alive anymore. He was too much of a poor sinner. He felt ashamed as he knew he was disappointing God. He went to the bathroom and cried. He wanted God to take his life right then and there.

As the day ended, so too did Samantha's excitement. And so, too, did she come down from the wine, and soon she started feeling sleepy. He put her to bed and wrapped her in her blanket. Before he left and turned off the lights, he took one good look at her face. Jack smiled. He didn't deserve a friend like her. He didn't deserve anyone; he was too much of a poor sinner. He leaned in and whispered in her ear, "Thank you, Samantha... for everything."

He turned off the lights and walked out of the house. He made his way over to his dealer's house. If shooting his brains out didn't work, then Jack didn't know what he would do. He had an idea. To overdose. It failed last time, but hopefully, this time he would be able to snort enough cocaine to make his heart explode. Jack spent nearly a million dollars on cocaine, and he walked away from his dealer.

Jack was heading to his house when he heard someone call him.

"Excuse me."

Jack turned around. Before he did, he knew the voice all too well.

It was Audrey. She was standing still. She... had changed. She looked taller and definitely grew more muscle mass. She appeared stronger. Her hair also changed. It was curly now. Was it always curly, or did she get a perm? Her hair changed colors as well. Now, it was red.

The two of them looked at each other. Nobody said anything. Audrey looked down at the floor. She looked embarrassed and shy. Jack looked like he was about ready to end his life.

Audrey looked up from the floor after nobody said anything for an uncomfortable amount of time. She took a deep breath and smiled. A weak smile, but she still smiled as she looked at Jack.

"I miss you, Jack."

Those words hit Jack like a freight train. No, she couldn't be doing this here. Not here, and not now. Please God, why now? Jack had to control himself as he was on the verge of crying. He gripped the cocaine in his pockets that his jacket had. He had to clear his mind. He was doing this for God. To show God that he cared for the almighty more than anything. He was going to die because he loved God so much that he didn't want to sin anymore because he didn't want to disappoint and go away from God.

Jack nodded his head as he looked to the ground. He had no idea what to say; what would he say? She had no right to love him the way that she did. He was horrible, and he felt like a monster. He nodded his head rapidly, and Audrey tilted her head. Something seemed off about him. He looked... sad, and lonely, and he looked like he was going through the emotions.

Jack smiled as he looked at Audrey.

"I see." That was all he could say. He took a deep breath. Thankfully, it was dark out, and she couldn't see the tears falling from his eyes.

She nodded her head.

"I tried calling you a few times. You didn't pick up your cell. I'm... sorry for yelling at you, and saying all those mean and hurtful things. I just want you to know that I still care for you and that, for the entire time we were apart, I didn't date anybody. I was thinking about you too much to do that."

Oh God, thought Jack as he turned his head away. He started to cry uncontrollably now. Even though it was dark, she could see it. Jack couldn't help himself. He closed his eyes, and his lips quivered. He didn't deserve someone like her. He could only imagine how she would feel when she heard the news about him. Even after everything that he did, she still cared for him so much. And loved him so much that she didn't even date anybody, even though she had every single right to reject and ignore him. Jack couldn't help it. He cried.

Audrey tilted her head. "Jack... is everything alright?"

Those words hit harder than anything that has ever hit Jack. That sentence hit Jack harder than any punch or kick that's been thrown at him. Hearing that sentence coming from Audrey, even after everything, hit harder than Dawson ever hoped he could hit. Jack gripped the cocaine in his pocket. Dammit, Audrey... why did you have to do this now?

Jack couldn't help it. He was now crying uncontrollably. Audrey could hear him sob, and break down on the floor. He clutched his heart, and couldn't help himself. He screamed, and sobbed, and everything that he had built up inside of him was now coming out. He cried so much his teeth were chattering. As Audrey watched him, she put her hands over her mouth and cried with him. She hated seeing him suffer. Whenever he suffered, she suffered. She thought to herself that she didn't deserve a man like Jack. That Jack was too wonderful and great for her. If only she knew.

Jack nearly suffocated because he was having trouble breathing; the tears, the snot, the emotions were all on display now. Jack couldn't help himself. He yelled and screamed and cursed. He clutched his chest as he stood up. He cried on the street for what seemed like an eternity. It was all coming out now. The powerful and sad screams were getting to Audrey as well. She started to sob.

Jack frowned as he wiped away the tears that refused to stop. He shook his head when he looked at her.

"No, Audrey... I am not alright. Nothing is alright."

"W-w-w-why? W-what's the... what's wrong, Jack?"

Jack shook his head as the tears kept on coming. There was no stopping them now. May the Lord have mercy on him, as Jack prayed he would make his suicide a slow and painful one. Jack closed his eyes as he thought he deserved to suffer. He was too much of a poor sinner and deserved everything bad coming to him. He wanted to suffer and burn. That was what he deserved. He didn't deserve Audrye, nor anything.

Audrey spoke again. This time her voice was more powerful.

"Jack, tell me what's wrong!"

Jack shook his head as his lips quivered. He frowned and turned his head away from her. He felt too ashamed to even look at her. Audrey frowned. She knew the look that he had. He was planning on doing something horrible, something horrific. Something bad that would ruin his life. She cried as she wouldn't allow it. She spoke up even louder this time as she saw her love break down in front of her.

"Jack… TELL me what is WRONG right NOW!"

Jack shook his head and threw his arms up in the air, revealing the kilos of cocaine he had in his pockets.

He chuckled as the moonlight hit both of their faces.

"Me… I am what's wrong. I am what's wrong in this world. I… I-I don't belong here anymore. I wake up every morning wondering why God hasn't struck me down. I'm a horrible person; I am a sinner. I am too ashamed to even look at you. You don't deserve me. You're so wonderful, so amazing and so great. So fantastic and perfect. And I… I don't understand why you love someone as miserable and as horrible as me. I probably never will. I… don't belong here. I'm too much of a sinner. I have disappointed God for the last time.

"I'm going to kill myself, and there's nothing you can do about it. I love God too much to do this. To keep on sinning when I am still alive. I am shameful to God. I love him too much to continue to bring shame onto him. I… I'm going to die. Audrey… I love you. Thank you for everything. I hope you find someone better than me."

Jack started walking away. Audrey ran after him. Jack turned around and saw that she was heading for him. He started to spring. There was no way on earth that she would be able to catch up to him. Jack ran to his house and locked all the doors. He cried as he heard her pounding at the door, telling him to open it.

Jack sobbed and couldn't control himself as he collapsed on the floor. He was crying too much, he couldn't even move. He heard Audrey yell downstairs for him to open, up and how she would never forgive him if he went through with this.

Jack grabbed the cocaine and cut it up. All he could hear was her voice downstairs. He sobbed as he snorted a line the size of a millipede. Then the line of a caterpillar, and then the size of a butterfly. He could hear her yelling. The cocaine was kicking in hard. Jack felt his nose bleed, and he started to grow angry. Damn it, this was too cut. The dealer fucking lied to him! HOW DARE HIM! AND WHY WON'T THAT BITCH DOWNSTAIRS SHUT UP?

Outside, Audrey was crying and begging. She pounded and hit the door as hard as she could, but no matter what, it just wouldn't budge. She tried the backdoor, but it wasn't working. She sobbed, as she had no strength left to bang on the door anymore. She pleaded out and cried out for him to stop. She begged and cried for him to stop this. She would make everything feel better.

"PLEASE! Jack, just please stop. You're breaking my heart!"

As Jack was about to sniff another line, he heard this. His hands were shaking, and he was already sweating. He was balls high, and he was afraid that if he saw her, he would do something he would regret. But… he was doing this for God. Not her; he didn't care about her. He needed to show how much he cared for God. How important God was in his life.

"Jack, you're hurting me! You're hurting me!"

Jack stopped. He was pale, and his eyes were red. His pupils were dilated to such an extreme it looked like his eyes were just blue. He sniffled his nose. What was she saying? He wasn't even touching her. He quickly rushed downstairs. What on earth was this woman trying to say?

He opened the door, and there was Audrey, waiting for him. Her eyes were even more red than his. She shook her head as she looked at Jack.

"Jack, STOP! You have to stop. I don't know what you're going through, but suicide is never the answer!"

"YOU'RE WRONG!" Jack leaned in closer to her. Audrey wasn't afraid. She knew that this wasn't him. The devil had taken control of him through the coke. Jack was still there somewhere. She just needed to get to him.

Jack hissed at her. "No… you're wrong. This is what I need. I'm a sinner, and I need to suffer!"

"This isn't the way. I'm no Christian, but it says in the Bible that God will forgive your sins as long as you forgive others!"

"I'VE SINNED TOO MUCH!"

"That's not true! Jack, please… just stop it. You're breaking my heart. You love me, don't you? If you do, then please stop… you're hurting me."

"HOW? Dammit, woman, how am I hurting you?"

"By hurting yourself! I hate to see you suffer. You're breaking my heart, Jack. I don't want to see you like this. Look at yourself! THIS ISN'T YOU!"

Jack stopped. He took a step back and ran to the bathroom. He turned on the lights and looked into the mirror. Holy shit, she was right. It wasn't Jack. Jack was looking at… a hideous monster. Something that was sinister and was lurking beneath, waiting to take him. Jack shook his head. He threw up the cocaine as he shoved his finger in his mouth. To try to sober up. It was no use. He had snorted too much. No matter how much he would throw up, or no matter how hard he tried, he could feel his heart racing at a million miles an hour. He thought about Audrey as she stood outside crying.

"Come inside," he said. She closed the door behind him, and the two went upstairs.

Audrey saw the piles of cocaine. Good God, there looked to be around nearly 12 kilos of cocaine. Where did he even get this much stuff from?

She sat down on his bed and pondered at the sheer amount of cocaine that was on his desk. By God, Audrey thought that nobody in her family had done this much coke, let alone in one sitting. Jack sat down next to her. She hugged him.

"Jack…"

She couldn't even say anything. She merely hugged him. Jack embraced her.

"Jack… you don't deserve this. You deserve better. You deserve a better life. I'm sorry it had to be this way."

Jack shook his head. "No… you're right. I don't deserve this. I deserve to be punished and tortured for all of eternity!"

"We're all sinners, and God knows it. Please, just ask for forgiveness, and all will be well."

"I have sinned too much for God to love me. I keep on doing the same thing over and over again. There is no hope. I must die in order to be free."

"Suicide is never the answer!"

"What would you know? Damn you, you bitch! What would you know about this? About any of this?"

Audrey took a deep breath as Jack's jaw clenched and tightened up. She reassured herself that this wasn't Jack. This was someone else. Someone much more terrifying and demonic. This was not Jack.

"I know that God puts us in situations that we can handle. He'll never put us in something we can't. Furthermore, God loves us. He does everything for a reason. All of this… is for a reason."

"What for, then?"

"To make us stronger. Think about it. Diamonds are widely considered to be the most expensive and valuable jewel on earth. Do you know how you make something so pretty? You have to put it through intense heat and pressure. You have to put PRESSURE in order for it to become beautiful. A human is the same way. We must face hardships to grow in life."

Jack shook his head. He lay down on his bed and looked up at the ceiling.

"I've done too many horrible things, Audrey. I've done horrible things to you. I don't deserve you."

Audrey smiled as she kissed him on the lips.

"No. I don't deserve you. You're so wonderful and great. You are..."

Jack didn't listen to what she said. His mind was too focused on Audrey. What a wonderful and amazing woman. Even after everything that Jack did to her, she was still loyal until the end. Even after putting her through all of the misery, she was still dedicated to helping him out. She was one in 8 billion. She was here with him at his darkest, and at his best. She never left his side. And she deserves better. Yet... she was stuck with him for now. Jack smiled as he could see himself with her. She wasn't lying, she truly did love him. And dammit, Jack loved her as well.

"Audrey, will you marry me?"

Audrey stopped in her tracks. W-what did he say? She chuckled as she stood up, and quickly she became nervous. "Um... I-I... I don't—"

Jack put his hands on her shoulders. "It's OK. Just remember that I'm high as fuck right now. So I'm not thinking straight."

Audrey chuckled, but that really didn't help. She gulped as she looked at Jack, and then at the cocaine. She knew that Jack was a man at the end of the day. And men do certain things. Drugs were a part of that. She knew that some men were controlled by certain vices. Her father was controlled by that damn alcohol, and her uncle and her cousins were controlled by meth. She grew up in that lifestyle. Yet... she pondered. If she was going to marry Jack, she didn't want him to be a man in that lifestyle. She would try to find a solution for his control and desire. He seemed to really like sex, and Audrey could see herself stopping Jack, as long as Jack had sex with her. Was it that simple, really?

Aubrey thought about it for too long of a time. Jack frowned. Oh well. At least he tried.

She nodded her head. "Yes. I will marry you, Jack, but only on one condition."

"Say it!"

She pointed at the pile of cocaine.

"I need you to STOP! Look at you, you're a mess. You need to stop. I explained this to you, and I don't want to feel like a mother and explain it to you again. I've seen too many of my family members, men specifically, fall victim to drugs. Too many have died. Jack, I know you promised me months ago, but since then, you've fallen victim again. I need to know that you won't keep secrets from me. I need to know that you won't lie to me. I need to know that you won't say you'll do one thing, and do it behind my back! I love you, Jack, more than you can imagine. Will you promise me?"

"I promise."

She shook her head. "Say it… in front of God. Promise in front of God that you won't do anything like this anymore!"

Jack was hesitant as she grabbed his hands. He smiled, and she let go of his hands.

"I'm sorry, Jack, but until then, I can't be with you forever anymore. Not until I know that you'll stop."

"Please… what if we have sex? If we have sex every day, every waking moment and every night, I'll stop for good. Isn't that what you want?"

Audrey was taken aback by this comment. She nodded her head.

"Well, yes… but, well, I mean if that will make you stop, then…"

"LETS HAVE SEX RIGHT NOW!"

Audrey blushed as she didn't take off her pants.

"Um… I'm on my period."

"Oh… that's a shame."

"Um… Instead, you could maybe masturbate?"

"No, that's sinful and devilish. I will do no such thing!"

"OK. I see how it is then. So cocaine, heroin and meth is OK, but masturbation is where we draw the line?!"

"Yes. What is there not to understand?"

Audrey rolled her eyes. She loved the man with all her soul, but at the end of the day, he was just a man. Audrey spoke up.

"Jack, please don't get this the wrong way. I do love you so much. More than you could ever possibly imagine. Yet, I can't keep on seeing you like this. If this is going to be an everyday occurrence, then you can forget about us getting married!"

"No, it's not. I'll quit, I promise."

"You said that last time, and look at what happened. Now you're saying it again, but who knows? What if you'll go back to smoking dope and blasting heroin into your veins? I can't have that."

Jack shook his head. "Last time was different. This time, this time It will be different. I know that sounds bad, but please just hear me out on this one. I beg and ask of you, just please… give me another chance. Now you understand what I've been going through, and now we even have a way of ensuring that I'll never do something like that again. Please, Audrey… please, baby, just give me one more chance."

He grabbed her by the hands and kissed her. She kissed back. Her mind boggled and raced. Could he really be telling the truth? She smiled as Jack hugged her. Only time will tell.

Audrey smiled as she and Jack grabbed the cocaine and flushed it all down the sink. She felt good. The way he was looking and smiling, maybe he really was going to change. And best of all… he proposed. He told her that he had a massive surge of income because he won the lottery, and that they would be set for life. She smiled and jumped up with joy, up and down. At that moment, she started believing in God. Miracles and dreams did come true. It was like a fairy tale. They could get away, and start all over again. It would be the three of them. Jack, her and God. They would be happy, have a family, and be wonderful to each other. She could see it now.

They would live in a picturesque house, on a picturesque street with picturesque neighbors. Their kids would go to good schools, and they would eat only good food. They would live in a good place, with only good people. All thanks to God. Audrey smiled as she hugged and kissed Jack. This was surreal. Her heart was racing. She was so happy and so glad that this was happening. She was crying with joy. Finally, no more chaos, no more death and no more sadness. That had all ended. Now… now the real joy started. Now the glory of God was about to shine on them.

Audrey slept over at Jack's house, and in the morning, went to go and tell her parents of the good news.

"They probably won't approve," said Audrey as she put on her shoes. Jack waved his hand.

"Well, I'm sure they'll approve once they see how well we will be doing. And so what if they don't approve? We have each other, and we have God. That is all that matters."

She smiled as she kissed him. He was right. They don't need approval from anybody. They knew what was best, and they had the blessings from God. She kissed him as she skipped over to her house, with the sun shining down and her smile shining brightly.

24

Samantha woke up. The sun was shining down on her head. What time was it? She had passed out. Her head hurt. *Dammit,* she thought as she got up from her bed, I shouldn't drink that much again. She went to drink some water and made her bed. She went out for a run to see if that would help. It did, and she was ready to take on the day.

She got herself dressed and went to S.H.O.T. headquarters. Her face lit up in surprise as she saw Jack sitting in Natalia's office. She smiled as she entered.

"Good morning, headmaster," she said sarcastically. Jack didn't smile. He still wanted to die. He felt so much shame and guilt about everything he had done. He hoped he would be able to die tonight. He regretted telling Audrey. He should have just stayed quiet and gone home and overdosed. Now, there was no more cocaine left. He knew he could easily buy some more... but before he died, he didn't want to sin. He was afraid of going to hell. He thought of a better alternative.

"Good morning to you too, Samantha. How are you feeling?"

She nodded her head. "Still a little bit hungover, but besides that, nothing too bad. How about you?"

Jack gave a fake smile. He wanted to say that he was feeling horrible and that his life was shit and it deserved to be.

"Oh... it's going. Anyway, are you up for a new task today?"

She looked surprised as she nodded her head.

"Why... yes, I am. I'm guessing that we already have some work to do?"

"You would be correct. Take a look at this."

Jack handed her a large photo. She took a look at it. It was a photo of an infamous corrupt politician who had recently bribed his way out of a jury meeting due to photos of him doing... unspeakable things surfaced on the internet.

"His name is Ronald Gary. He's a famous politician in the state of Florida. I want you to end him. For too long, he's been avoiding trouble. Not anymore. Find him, and put an end to him. I already prepared a flight for you. The plane leaves in 5 hours in Pittsburgh. Good luck."

Jack gave her the ticket. She smiled as she took it. She saluted him as she walked away. Finally, things were going well. Now she had a clear conscience, knowing that the people she was killing were actually bad and horrible people. Not people who were against Natalia's weird political agenda. Before Samantha left, Jack called her.

"Yes, Jack?"

Jack took a deep breath. He genuinely smiled when he looked into her eyes.

"Thank you for being such a great friend. If anything happens to me, I would like you to be the new headmaster for S.H.O.T. I know this... company, I guess you could say, would flourish under your rule. I've seen you change so much. Keep up the good work!"

Samantha blushed. Where was this coming from? She smiled as Jack got up and hugged her. Now she was really shocked. What was he doing? She chuckled as she pushed Jack away. With a funny and joking tone, she asked him, "Is everything OK?"

Jack smiled as he nodded his head. "Everything is perfect."

They stood in silence for a moment. Samantha became awkward as Jack looked at her. She quickly waved goodbye and walked away. On her elevator ride, she wondered what was up with Jack. He was... acting strange. He was acting like he would never see her again. *How odd,* she thought as she went to her car and drove to Pittsburgh. She regretted ever going away that day, and she cursed herself because she wished things were different. That was the last time she ever saw Jack.

Jack spent hours and hours doing as much research as he could on politicians, criminals and other scum of the earth. He wrote their names down all on a piece of paper. He hoped that this information could last the hunters a few good months. He also prayed and hoped that Samantha would be a good fit. He knew she would, but he knew she also could get emotional and be irrational at times. He didn't really like working at S.H.O.T., but he became accustomed to the other hunters that were there. He knew that at the end of the day, they were still people. Some of them did have a sense of justice, and others were hunters merely because they liked to fight and kill. Either way, Jack knew that this job meant a lot to a lot of people. So he made sure he would do his best to make the missions as fulfilling and as engaging as possible. He smiled as he put the piece of paper away in a small folder in a drawer. He knew that Samantha would find it. He smiled as he stood up and took the elevator out. It was the last time he would ever be in S.H.O.T.'s headquarters.

Jack walked outside and realized that it was nearly dinnertime. So much time had passed, and he had nearly a dozen missed calls from Audrey. He was planning on calling her… but before he did, he needed something else to take care of.

Jack called Leon.

"Leon… this is Jack. How is everything?"

"JACK! Hey, it's good to hear from you. I haven't heard from you in a while. Is everything OK?"

Jack nodded his head. The waterworks had already started.

"Yeah. Everything is dandy. I just wanted to check up and see how everything was going with you, and if you were able to find Derrick's daughter, and if you were able to take down the political party?"

There was silence, and then Leon spoke.

"Well… we got Darrick's daughter, but things haven't been so great. She's now living with a relative in Venice, but besides that, we haven't really had any luck so far. Don't fret though, we have a lead and we're working on it right now. Don't worry, I promised you that I would succeed and I'm not going to let you down just yet, my friend!"

Jack smiled. "Well, I'm glad to hear that. Keep up the good work, and stay safe, alright?"

"You got it. Anyway, we're about to go into a meeting. I'll see you later. Bye-bye!"

Jack smiled as he hung up the phone. At least they were making progress. That was good. Jack smiled as even though he was crying, he felt at peace. At peace knowing that Leon and his crew were doing all they could, and at peace knowing that there was someone to take his place when he left. That was the last time Jack ever talked to Leon.

Jack and Audrey were walking down the street. They had just finished eating a massive dinner filled with meat and veggies, and topped off with a handful of chocolate. They were laughing as they held each other's hands.

Audrey looked into Jack's eyes. He was so beautiful. She smiled as she kissed him on the cheek. She was so blessed to have a man like him in her life. Not only were they set for life, (according to Jack), but they were now happily married. Sure, she didn't have a ring or a proper wedding ceremony, but that didn't matter. All that mattered was that God saw that they were married, and that's all Audrey wanted. She thought about raising kids and starting a family with Jack. She knew that he would be a wonderful and amazing father. She could feel it. Life was perfect right now, and she didn't have to worry about anything anymore.

Jack looked at Audrey; he wanted to cry. The poor women had suffered so much because of him. He didn't deserve her in the slightest. He felt sad, thinking about how much more she was going to suffer when she found his body. Still… this was all for the best. He was doing this because he couldn't continue to disobey God anymore. His mind had been made up. He hoped that the money he had would be able to set her up for life. He was positive it was. She would never have to raise another finger ever again.

Audrey chuckled as they got near her house.

"You know, now that we're married. Don't you think it would be good for us to live together?"

Jack shook his head. "I don't think that would be a good idea."

Audrey stopped smiling. "Oh… I see."

Jack stopped walking. He grabbed Audrey and kissed her. For the last time. He kissed her like he had never kissed her before. She closed her eyes and kissed him back, not knowing that her whole world was about to flip on its head. He kissed her with such love and passion, she would remember it for the rest of her life.

She smiled as he looked at her eyes.

"What's up with you today? You were acting strange and different during dinner, and now this? Is… is something wrong?"

Jack shook his head. He grabbed her by her arms.

"Audrey… I want you to listen to me and listen to me well. Can you do that?"

Audrey nodded her head. Her smile faded, and she started to grow worried as she saw Jack's eye change.

"I love you. I love you more than anything. I don't deserve you at all. I could not have asked for a better woman than you. Thank you for everything that you do. I hope you can find someone better, and I hope you find someone amazing. Please... I don't deserve you. I love you, Audrey. Know this: I love you now and forever. I just ask one thing... I just ask that you don't lose your faith in God, that you love Him more than you love me."

"Jack, you're making less sense than usual. Tell me—"

She stopped as Jack hugged her. He hugged her with such love, with such care, and with such intensity that she was overwhelmed with the sheer amount of love. She cried as she embraced him. "I love you forever too," she whispered.

She smiled as she ran inside her house. She blew a kiss to Jack.

"Let's meet up tomorrow to watch a movie?"

Jack nodded his head. She jumped up and down with joy as she ran to her room, completely oblivious as to what was about to happen. That was the last time she ever talked to Jack.

Jack was walking down the street. His mind was boggling and racing. All of the events that had transpired, everything that had happened in his life... was all going to come to an end. Jack was planning on jumping from the same height that John's motorcycle fell off from. Jack walked up the hill, getting higher and higher with each step. In his mind, there was nothing better than a swan dive into the asphalt.

His friends were dead, and he didn't have anyone else he could talk to. Samantha was nice, but she wasn't Yuri. He still cared for her and considered a wonderful and great friend. He tried to make friends at school, but it never worked. He didn't look the right way, and he didn't say the right things. He couldn't help it; it's just who he was. Even Audrey... she didn't deserve him. He thought about God as he started getting higher and higher. May the Lord forgive him. Jack was too ashamed to even talk to him. Jack took a deep sigh as he felt the end come near. He could see death right beside him, grinning the same big grin he always had. Jack chuckled.

Finally... he was here. Jack looked down. If he jumped off, it would be an instant death. He wanted to suffer, but he didn't have the balls to make him suffer. He wanted a quick death. His life flashed before his eyes as he looked up at the sky and closed his eyes. He pressed his hands together and prayed.

"My Father in heaven... please forgive me, my Lord. I am a sinner. I am just a human. Please forgive me, for I am just a poor, poor, poor sinner. May you bless Audrey and help everyone in the world who is suffering. May you have mercy on my soul, and by your divine knowledge and grace, please allow me to dwell with you in the kingdom of heaven. May your name be exalted, now until the end of the age. I love you so much, my God. I am doing this because I do not want to sin anymore. I know if I keep on being alive, then I will continue to sin. I cannot say that I love you, and then sin. I want to love you. Please, allow me to enter your kingdom so I can sin no more. Allow me to be perfect in your image. I will never get mad at you, my Lord and savior. Please… I love you so much. Now until the end of the age!"

Jack looked back down, took a deep breath and jumped. He died on impact as his body turned into mush. Death looked down as he saw Jack's body.

"My work here is done. Have mercy, my Lord," said Death as he walked away. Except, this time, when he walked away… he wasn't smiling anymore.

The End